# BROOD OF THE WITCH QUEEN

## THE QUEST OF THE SACRED SLIPPER

# SAX ROHMER

### INTRODUCTION BY
### WILLIAM PATRICK MAYNARD

STARK HOUSE

**Stark House Press • Eureka California**

BROOD OF THE WITCH-QUEEN /
THE QUEST OF THE SACRED SLIPPER

Published by Stark House Press
1315 H Street
Eureka, CA 95501, USA
griffinskye3@sbcglobal.net
www.starkhousepress.com



ISBN-13: 978-1-944520-24-3

Book design by Mark Shepard, SHEPGRAPHICS.COM



First Stark House Press Edition: February 2017

FIRST EDITION

## BROOD OF THE WITCH-QUEEN

Dark magic is afoot in London. Robert Cairn suspects that there is something sinister about classmate Antony Ferrera. Egyptologist Dr. Cairn, Robert's father, suspects that Ferrera may be wielding a malignant influence on those around him. The doctor certainly knows more than he is willing to share about the origins of young Ferrera. Soon, the Cairns find themselves under a strange psychic attack from phantoms in the night. Their enemy: Antony Ferrera! Their only hope is that they find a way to fight Ferrera—a man who can summon the powers of ancient Egypt at will and attack them from the shadows… and in their dreams!

## THE QUEST OF THE SACRED SLIPPER

When Cavanagh befriends Professor Deeping on board the *Mandalay*, little does he realize that he has entered into a world of Eastern assassins, the world of the *Hashishîn*. For Deeping has stolen a holy relic, a slipper belonging to Mohammed, and is now being pursued by someone named Hassan of Aleppo, whose duty it is to guard and return the relic. For an infidel to merely touch the box where the relic resides results in the removal of their hand. But Deeping wants to commit the ultimate sacrilege and put the relic on display in a museum. Now Deeping is dead—murdered in his home—and has bequeathed to Cavanaugh the key to his safe… where resides the sacred slipper!

# EGYPT AND THE MIDDLE EAST: SAX ROHMER'S SECRET PASSIONS

by William Patrick Maynard

Arthur Henry Ward, the British author who (under the exotic pseudonym of Sax Rohmer) found fame a little over a century ago chronicling the exploits of the diabolical Dr. Fu-Manchu, the "Yellow Peril" incarnate in one man, knew just how he wished to spend his newfound fortune in 1913: he would finally take his wife on their long-delayed honeymoon to the one location that had captivated his imagination since childhood, the Nile.

A photograph was published at the time showing Rohmer standing aboard a sailing vessel with three grim-faced Egyptian sailors seated in the foreground manning the oars. The Egyptians are dressed in traditional garb while Rohmer, pipe clenched firmly between his teeth, is dressed like a proper colonial gentleman in suit and hat. The text beneath the photo describes the author as "the master of the occult" who had recently visited Egypt to complete his "profound study of sorcery and the black arts."

Rohmer was, of course, about to publish his non-fiction tome, **The Romance of Sorcery** (1914) and the magazine giving this promotion was about to begin serializing his latest thriller, one which broke from the "Yellow Peril" formula for something closer to Bram Stoker's **Jewel of the Seven Stars** (1903), Guy Boothby's **Pharos the Egyptian** (1899) or Robert W. Chambers' **The King in Yellow** (1895).

Rohmer was far from a "master of the occult." True, he did dabble, but the evidence of his fiction suggests he was mainly interested in knowing just enough to convince the less discriminating reader of an earlier and, in some ways, simpler century that he was well-versed in such matters. Actual adepts will quickly realize that Rohmer was more interested in spinning a good yarn than he was in realistically portraying the accomplishments of the men and women he chronicled in his well-researched occult history.

The key to Rohmer's occult knowledge was not the membership he

falsely claimed to hold with the Hermetic Order of the Golden Dawn
or the Rosicrucians; but rather his friendship with the man who brought
him into the world — the Ward family physician, Dr. R. Watson Councell. It was Dr. Councell who introduced him to valuable contacts and
opened his library to Rohmer to lend him the necessary titles to compile
**The Romance of Sorcery** with its detailed biographies of Apollonius of
Tyana, Dr. John Dee, Eliphas Levi, Edward Kelly, Count St. Germain,
Cagliostro, and Madame Blavatsky. While far from exhaustive, Rohmer's
sole work of non-fiction has remained in print for over a century as a
foundational work in bringing occult knowledge to the general public.
Rohmer would eventually pay back Dr. Councell by penning the Fore-
word to Councell's privately-printed **Apologia Alchymiae** (1923).

Rohmer himself, as his exotic pseudonym suggests, was more interested
in putting on appearances than he was in acquiring actual knowledge
or experience. Throughout his long literary career, he was fond of spinning yarns when talking to gullible members of the press. Not only his
knowledge of the occult, but his background in Fleet Street and experience with Chinese tongs in Limehouse (London's Chinatown district)
were greatly exaggerated when not entirely fictitious.

Bram Stoker's alleged membership with the Hermetic Order of the
Golden Dawn is likewise attributed to Rohmer telling tall-tales to the
press. Informing journalists that he and Stoker were members of a
Gnostic society had the effect of associating his fiction with Stoker's and,
in so doing, reinforcing his exotic mystique by presenting both authors
as practitioners of black magic. The press ate it up at the time and his
spurious statements have been repeated endlessly. It would likely amuse
Rohmer greatly to know that over a century later his false claims are being spread as fact and both he and Stoker are incorrectly cited as members of the Golden Dawn to this day. Rohmer was a storyteller and rarely
failed to capture his readers' imagination as he proved time and again
with his fiction as well as his fictionalized accounts of his life.

Sax Rohmer's **The Brood of the Witch-Queen** was originally serialized
in nine installments in *Premier Magazine* from May 1914 through Jan-
uary 1915. The serial was subsequently published in book form in the
UK in 1918 by Arthur Pearson. A US edition from Doubleday was not
published until 1924. It was among six Rohmer titles not featuring Fu
Manchu to be reprinted by Pyramid Books as a paperback in the 1960s.
The title has rarely been out of print in the century that followed. Its in-
clusion by H. P. Lovecraft in his influential survey, "Supernatural Fiction
in Literature" (1927) certainly helped cement its reputation among fans
of horror fiction, though the modern reader not versed in Victorian or

Edwardian horror, may find aspects of the plot risible.

The story concerns young Robert Cairn who suspects his classmate, Anthony Ferrara (the adopted son of a friend of Robert's father) is an occult practitioner. More than merely dabbling with the black arts, Robert soon suspects young Ferrara has graduated to committing murders and other heinous crimes. Cairn's pursuit of justice leads him to follow Ferrara back to Egypt with a climax in the Great Pyramid.

Rohmer's depiction of the Great Pyramid from Cairn's trip on the back of a donkey to his terrifying descent into the King's Chamber was based on the author's real-life visit to the Pyramid at Meidum when he honeymooned in Egypt. Rex Engelbach, the curator of the Cairo Museum, served as a guide to Rohmer and his wife when they explored the pyramids. Engelbach accompanied the Rohmers down the narrow interior shaft where they were forced to wriggle on their bellies to advance into the burial chamber. This harrowing experience was used as inspiration not only for this book, but also for Rohmer's short story, "The Death-Ring of Sneferu" (1917). Engelbach himself appears as a character in the 1987 novel, **The Fires of Fu Manchu** written by Rohmer's former assistant, Cay Van Ash.

The Witch-Queen of the title, though unnamed in the book, is meant to be Taia who was later the subject of Rohmer's short story, "The Treasure of Taia" (1916). The historical Queen Taia, more commonly rendered Tiye today, was the wife of Amenhotep III, the mother of Akhenaten, and grandmother of Tutankhamun. While long reputed to be a practitioner of witchcraft, it is impossible to separate the truth from Western bias against ancient religions that were predominant at the turn of the last century when her remains were discovered.

The companion novel in this collection, **The Quest of the Sacred Slipper** is, fittingly, another early Rohmer book concerned with the mysterious East. It was first printed in eight installments under the title, **Hassan of Aleppo** in *Short Stories* from November 1913 to June 1914. It was published in book form five years later in 1919 by Arthur Pearson in the UK and Doubleday in the US.

The story sees terror threaten London when a determined archaeologist brings a holy relic of the Prophet back from Syria. Hassan of Aleppo and his followers journey to London and visit death and destruction on all who come in contact with the holy relic until it is returned to them. While the idea of a group of half-naked Syrians riding around London wearing only a turban and loincloth murdering innocent British subjects at random and eluding Scotland Yard at every turn may strike modern readers as politically incorrect and highly offensive, it underscores a common theme in many stories of the period dealing with Egypt or Islam – that the Western raiding of treasures of Eastern cultures was morally indefensible and would result in some form of terrible consequences. Most stories exploited the notion of deadly curses invoked centuries earlier to protect a mummy or buried treasure, but Rohmer preferred the notion of a cult of religious fanatics traveling from East to West to visit justice as the ancient world understood it.

Like **The Brood of the Witch-Queen** which was written shortly after it, **The Quest of the Sacred Slipper** was one of a half-dozen non-Fu Manchu titles kept in print by Pyramid Books in the 1960s. Both novels deliver entertaining reads from a master storyteller. Rohmer was inspired by Sir Richard Burton's translation of **One Thousand and One Nights** (1885) and Sir Flinders Petrie's works of Egyptology that were so revered by Theosophists such as R. Watson Councell. Sir Flinders Petrie's surname became Rohmer's alter ego in the early Fu Manchu stories while Sir Richard Burton was fictionalized in the same as Sir Lionel Barton.

Despite the success of his Yellow Peril fiction that readers demanded Rohmer return to again and again; his own desire was to create fiction under the spell of the Nile or the Middle East. Their exotic women and their ancient beliefs and mores stood in sharp contrast to the staid English life the bohemian Rohmer railed against. Ultimately, it was the allure of the East that led this colonial English author to return several times during a career that spanned over fifty years to attempt a work worthy of Theosophical significance. Rohmer's desire to earn the exotic reputation his fanciful pseudonym and highly-embellished biography suggested were rooted in that childhood love of Arabian Nights. His first full-length evocations of that desire may be found in the present collection.

WPM

# BROOD OF THE WITCH QUEEN

## SAX ROHMER

PREFATORY NOTICE

The strange deeds of Antony Ferrara, as herein related, are intended to illustrate certain phases of Sorcery as it was formerly practised (according to numerous records) not only in Ancient Egypt but also in Europe during the Middle Ages. In no case do the powers attributed to him exceed those which are claimed for a fully equipped Adept.

S. R.

# CHAPTER I
## ANTONY FERRARA

Robert Cairn looked out across the quadrangle. The moon had just arisen, and it softened the beauty of the old college buildings, mellowed the harshness of time, casting shadow pools beneath the cloisteresque arches to the west and setting out the ivy in stronger relief upon the ancient walls. The barred shadow on the lichened stones beyond the elm was cast by the hidden gate; and straight ahead, where, between a quaint chimney-stack and a bartizan, a triangular patch of blue showed like spangled velvet, lay the Thames. It was from there the cooling breeze came.

But Cairn's gaze was set upon a window almost directly ahead and west below the chimneys. Within the room to which it belonged a lambent light played.

Cairn turned to his companion, a ruddy and athletic looking man, somewhat bovine in type, who at the moment was busily tracing out sections on a human skull and checking his calculations from Ross's "Diseases of the Nervous System."

"Sime," he said, "what does Ferrara always have a fire in his rooms for at this time of the year?"

Sime glanced up irritably at the speaker. Cairn was a tall, thin Scotsman, clean-shaven, square jawed, and with the crisp light hair and gray eyes which often bespeak unusual virility.

"Aren't you going to do any work?" he inquired pathetically. "I thought you'd come to give me a hand with my *basal ganglia*. I shall go down on that; and there you've been stuck staring out of the window!"

"Wilson, in the end house, has got a most unusual brain," said Cairn, with apparent irrelevance.

"Has he!" snapped Sime.

"Yes, in a bottle. His governor is at Bart's; he sent it up yesterday. You ought to see it."

"Nobody will ever want to put *your* brain in a bottle," predicted the scowling Sime, and resumed his studies.

Cairn relighted his pipe, staring across the quadrangle again. Then—

"You've never been in Ferrara's rooms, have you?" he inquired.

Followed a muffled curse, a crash, and the skull went rolling across the floor.

"Look here, Cairn," cried Sime, "I've only got a week or so now, and my nervous system is frantically rocky; I shall go all to pieces on my nervous system. If you want to talk, go ahead. When you're finished, I can begin work."

"Right-oh," said Cairn calmly, and tossed his pouch across. "I want to talk to you about Ferrara."

"Go ahead, then. What is the matter with Ferrara?"

"Well," replied Cairn, "he's queer."

"That's no news," said Sime, filling his pipe; "we all know he's a queer chap. But he's popular with women. He'd make a fortune as a nerve specialist."

"He doesn't have to; he inherits a fortune when Sir Michael dies."

"There's a pretty cousin, too, isn't there?" inquired Sime slyly.

"There is," replied Cairn. "Of course," he continued, "my governor and Sir Michael are bosom friends and although I've never seen much of young Ferrara, at the same time I've got nothing against him. But—" he hesitated.

"Spit it out," urged Sime, watching him oddly.

"Well, it's silly, I suppose, but what does he want with a fire on a blazing night like this?"

Sime stared.

"Perhaps he's a throw-back," he suggested lightly. "The Ferraras, although they're counted Scotch—aren't they?—must have been Italian originally."

"Spanish," corrected Cairn. "They date from the son of Andrea Ferrara, the sword-maker, who was a Spaniard. Caesar Ferrara came with the Armada in 1588 as armourer. His ship was wrecked up in the Bay of Tobermory and he got ashore—and stopped."

"Married a Scotch lassie?"

"Exactly. But the genealogy of the family doesn't account for Antony's habits."

"What habits?"

"Well, look." Cairn waved in the direction of the open window. "What does he do in the dark all night, with a fire going?"

"Influenza?"

"Nonsense! You've never been in his rooms, have you?"

"No. Very few men have. But as I said before, he's popular with the women."

"What do you mean?"

"I mean there have been complaints. Any other man would have been sent down."

"You think he has influence—"

"Influence of some sort, undoubtedly."

"Well, I can see you have serious doubts about the man, as I have myself, so I can unburden my mind. You recall that sudden thunderstorm on Thursday?"

"Rather; quite upset me for work."

"I was out in it. I was lying in a punt in the backwater—you know, *our* backwater."

"Lazy dog."

"To tell you the truth, I was trying to make up my mind whether I should abandon bones and take the post on the *Planet* which had been offered me."

"Pills for the pen—Harley for Fleet? Did you decide?"

"Not then; something happened which quite changed my line of reflection."

The room was becoming cloudy with tobacco smoke.

"It was delightfully still," Cairn resumed. "A water rat rose within a foot of me and a kingfisher was busy on a twig almost at my elbow. Twilight was just creeping along, and I could hear nothing but faint creakings of sculls from the river and sometimes the drip of a punt-pole. I thought the river seemed to become suddenly deserted; it grew quite abnormally quiet—and abnormally dark. But I was so deep in reflection that it never occurred to me to move.

"Then the flotilla of swans came round the bend, with Apollo—you know Apollo, the king-swan?—at their head. By this time it had grown tremendously dark, but it never occurred to me to ask myself why. The swans, gliding along so noiselessly, might have been phantoms. A hush, a perfect hush, settled down. Sime, that hush was the prelude to a strange thing—an unholy thing!"

Cairn rose excitedly and strode across to the table, kicking the skull out of his way.

"It was the storm gathering," snapped Sime.

"It was something else gathering! Listen! It got yet darker, but for some inexplicable reason, although I must have heard the thunder muttering, I couldn't take my eyes off the swans. Then it happened—the thing I came here to tell you about; I must tell somebody—the thing that I am not going to forget in a hurry."

He began to knock out the ash from his pipe. "Go on," directed Sime tersely.

"The big swan—Apollo—was within ten feet of me; he swam in open water, clear of the others; no living thing touched him. Suddenly, uttering a cry that chilled my very blood, a cry that I never heard from a swan in my life, he rose in the air, his huge wings extended—like a tortured phantom, Sime; I can never forget it—six feet clear of the water. The uncanny wail became a stifled hiss, and sending up a perfect fountain of water—I was deluged—the poor old king-swan fell, beat the surface with his wings—and was still."

"Well?"

"The other swans glided off like ghosts. Several heavy raindrops pattered on the leaves above. I admit I was scared. Apollo lay with one wing right in the punt. I was standing up; I had jumped to my feet when the thing occurred. I stooped and touched the wing. The bird was quite dead! Sime, I pulled the swan's head out of the water, and—his neck was broken: no fewer than three vertebrae fractured!"

A cloud of tobacco smoke was wafted toward the open window.

"It isn't one in a million who could wring the neck of a bird like Apollo, Sime; but it was done before my eyes without the visible agency of God or man! As I dropped him and took to the pole, the storm burst. A clap of thunder spoke with the voice of a thousand cannon, and I poled for bare life from that haunted backwater. I was drenched to the skin when I got in, and I ran up all the way from the stage."

"Well?" rapped the other again, as Cairn paused to refill his pipe.

"It was seeing the flickering at Ferrara's window that led me to do it. I don't often call on him; but I thought that a rub down before the fire and a glass of toddy would put me right. The storm had abated as I got to the foot of the stair—only a distant rolling of thunder.

"Then, out of the shadows—it was quite dark—into the flickering light of the lamp came somebody all muffled up. I started horribly. It was a girl, quite a pretty girl, too, but very pale, and with over-bright eyes. She gave one quick glance up into my face, muttered something, an apology, I think, and drew back again into her hiding-place."

"He's been warned," growled Sime. "It will be notice to quit next time."

"I ran upstairs and banged on Ferrara's door. He didn't open at first, but shouted out to know who was knocking. When I told him, he let me in, and closed the door very quickly. As I went in, a pungent cloud met me—incense."

"Incense?"

"His rooms smelt like a joss-house; I told him so. He said he was experimenting with *Kyphi*—the ancient Egyptian stuff used in the temples. It was all dark and hot; phew! like a furnace. Ferrara's rooms always were odd, but since the long vacation I hadn't been in. Good lord, they're disgusting!"

"How? Ferrara spent vacation in Egypt; I suppose he's brought things back?"

"Things—yes! Unholy things! But that brings me to something, too. I ought to know more about the chap than anybody; Sir Michael Ferrara and the governor have been friends for thirty years; but my father is oddly reticent—quite singularly reticent—regarding Antony. Anyway, have you heard about him in Egypt?"

"I've heard he got into trouble. For his age, he has a devil of a queer reputation; there's no disguising it."

"What sort of trouble?"

"I've no idea. Nobody seems to know. But I heard from young Ashby that Ferrara was asked to leave."

"There's some tale about the Commander-in-Chief—"

"*By* the Commander-in-Chief, Ashby says; but I don't believe it."

"Well—Ferrara lighted a lamp, an elaborate silver thing, and I found myself in a kind of nightmare museum. There was an unwrapped mummy there, the mummy of a woman—I can't possibly describe it. He had pictures, too—photographs. I shan't try to tell you what they represented. I'm not thin-skinned; but there are some subjects that no man is anxious to come in contact with. On the table by the lamp stood a number of objects such as I had never seen in my life before, evidently of great age. He swept them into a cupboard before I had time to look long. Then he went off to get a bath towel, slippers, and so forth. As he passed the fire he threw something in. A hissing tongue of flame leapt up—and died down again."

"What did he throw in?"

"I am not absolutely certain; so I won't say what I think it was, at the moment. Then he began to help me shed my saturated flannels, and he set a kettle on the fire, and so forth. You know the personal charm of the man? But there was an unpleasant sense of something—what shall I say?—sinister. Ferrara's ivory face was more pale than usual, and he conveyed the idea that he was chewed up—exhausted. Beads of perspiration were on his forehead."

"Heat of his rooms?"

"No," said Cairn shortly. "It wasn't that. I had a rub down and borrowed some slacks. Ferrara brewed grog and pretended to make me welcome. Now I come to something which I can't forget; it may be a mere coincidence, but—He has a number of photographs in his rooms, good ones, which he has taken himself. I'm not speaking now of the monstrosities, the outrages; I mean views, and girls—particularly girls. Well, standing on a queer little easel right under the lamp was a fine picture of Apollo, the swan, lord of the backwater."

Sime stared dully through the smoke haze.

"It gave me a sort of shock," continued Cairn. "It made me think, harder than ever, of the thing he had thrown in the fire. Then, in his photographic zenana, was a picture of a girl whom I am almost sure was the one I had met at the bottom of the stair. Another was of Myra Duquesne."

"His cousin?"

"Yes. I felt like tearing it from the wall. In fact, the moment I saw it, I stood up to go. I wanted to run to my rooms and strip the man's clothes off my back! It was a struggle to be civil any longer. Sime, if you had seen that swan die—"

Sime walked over to the window.

"I have a glimmering of your monstrous suspicions," he said slowly. "The last man to be kicked out of an English varsity for this sort of thing, so far as I know, was Dr. Dee of St. John's, Cambridge, and that's going back to the sixteenth century."

"I know; it's utterly preposterous, of course. But I had to confide in somebody. I'll shift off now, Sime."

Sime nodded, staring from the open window. As Cairn was about to close the outer door:

"Cairn," cried Sime, "since you are now a man of letters and leisure, you might drop in and borrow Wilson's brains for me."

"All right," shouted Cairn.

Down in the quadrangle he stood for a moment, reflecting; then, acting upon a sudden resolution, he strode over toward the gate and ascended Ferrara's stair.

For some time he knocked at the door in vain, but he persisted in his clamouring, arousing the ancient echoes. Finally, the door was opened.

Antony Ferrara faced him. He wore a silver-gray dressing gown trimmed with white swansdown, above which his ivory throat rose statuesque. The almond-shaped eyes, black as night, gleamed strangely beneath the low, smooth brow. The lank black hair appeared lustreless by comparison. His lips were very red. In his whole appearance there was something repellently effeminate.

"Can I come in?" demanded Cairn abruptly.

"Is it—something important?" Ferrara's voice was husky but not unmusical.

"Why, are you busy?"

"Well—er—" Ferrara smiled oddly.

"Oh, a visitor?" snapped Cairn.

"Not at all."

"Accounts for your delay in opening," said Cairn, and turned on his heel. "Mistook me for the proctor, in person, I suppose. Good-night."

Ferrara made no reply. But, although he never once glanced back, Cairn knew that Ferrara, leaning over the rail above, was looking after him; it was as though elemental heat were beating down upon his head.


CHAPTER II
THE PHANTOM HANDS

A week later Robert Cairn quitted Oxford to take up the newspaper appointment offered to him in London. It may have been due to some mysterious design of a hidden providence that Sime 'phoned him early in the week about an unusual case in one of the hospitals.

"Walton is junior-surgeon there," he said, "and he can arrange for you to see the case. She (the patient) undoubtedly died from some rare nervous affection. I have a theory," etc.; the conversation became technical.

Cairn went to the hospital, and by courtesy of Walton, whom he had known at Oxford, was permitted to view the body.

"The symptoms which Sime has got to hear about," explained the surgeon, raising the sheet from the dead woman's face, "are—"

He broke off. Cairn had suddenly exhibited a ghastly pallor; he clutched at Walton for support. "My God!"

Cairn, still holding on to the other, stooped over the discoloured face. It had been a pretty face when warm life had tinted its curves; now it was congested—awful; two heavy discolorations showed, one on either side of the region of the larynx.

"What on earth is wrong with you?" demanded Walton.

"I thought," gasped Cairn, "for a moment, that I knew—"

"Really! I wish you did! We can't find out anything about her. Have a good look."

"No," said Cairn, mastering himself with an effort—"a chance resemblance, that's all." He wiped the beads of perspiration from his forehead.

"You look jolly shaky," commented Walton. "Is she like someone you know very well?"

"No, not at all, now that I come to consider the features; but it was a shock at first. What on earth caused death?"

"Asphyxia," answered Walton shortly. "Can't you see?"

"Someone strangled her, and she was brought here too late?"

"Not at all, my dear chap; nobody strangled her. She was brought here in a critical state four or five days ago by one of the slum priests who keep us so busy. We diagnosed it as exhaustion from lack of food—with other complications. But the case was doing quite well up to last night; she was recovering strength. Then, at about one o'clock, she sprang up in bed, and fell back choking. By the time the nurse got to her it was all over."

"But the marks on her throat?"

Walton shrugged his shoulders.

"There they are! Our men are keenly interested. It's absolutely unique. Young Shaw, who has a mania for the nervous system, sent a long account up to Sime, who suffers from a similar form of aberration."

"Yes; Sime 'phoned me."

"It's nothing to do with nerves," said Walton contemptuously. "Don't ask me to explain it, but it's certainly no nerve case."

"One of the other patients—"

"My dear chap, the other patients were all fast asleep! The nurse was at her table in the corner, and in full view of the bed the whole time. I tell you no one touched her!"

"How long elapsed before the nurse got to her?"

"Possibly half a minute. But there is no means of learning when the paroxysm commenced. The leaping up in bed probably marked the end and not the beginning of the attack."

Cairn experienced a longing for the fresh air; it was as though some evil cloud hovered around and about the poor unknown. Strange ideas, horrible ideas, conjectures based upon imaginings all but insane, flooded his mind darkly.

Leaving the hospital, which harboured a grim secret, he stood at the gate for a moment, undecided what to do. His father, Dr. Cairn, was out of London, or he would certainly have sought him in this hour of sore perplexity.

"What in Heaven's name is behind it all!" he asked himself.

For he knew beyond doubt that the girl who lay in the hospital was the same that he had seen one night at Oxford, was the girl whose photograph he had found in Antony Ferrara's rooms!

He formed a sudden resolution. A taxicab was passing at that moment, and he hailed it, giving Sir Michael Ferrara's address. He could scarcely trust himself to think, but frightful possibilities presented themselves to him, repel them how he might. London seemed to grow dark, over-shadowed, as once he had seen a Thames backwater grow. He shuddered, as though from a physical chill.

The house of the famous Egyptian scholar, dull white behind its rampart of trees, presented no unusual appearances to his anxious scrutiny. What he feared he scarcely knew; what he suspected he could not have defined.

Sir Michael, said the servant, was unwell and could see no one. That did not surprise Cairn; Sir Michael had not enjoyed good health since malaria had laid him low in Syria. But Miss Duquesne was at home.

Cairn was shown into the long, low-ceiled room which contained so many priceless relics of a past civilization. Upon the bookcase stood the stately ranks of volumes which had carried the fame of Europe's foremost Egyptologist to every corner of the civilized world. This queerly furnished room held many memories for Robert Cairn, who had known it from childhood, but latterly it had always appeared to him in his daydreams as the setting for a dainty figure. It was here that he had first met Myra Duquesne, Sir Michael's niece, when, fresh from a Norman convent, she had come to shed light and gladness upon the somewhat sombre household of the scholar. He often thought of that day; he could recall every detail of the meeting—

Myra Duquesne came in, pulling aside the heavy curtains that hung in the arched entrance. With a granite Osiris flanking her slim figure on one side and a gilded sarcophagus on the other, she burst upon the visitor, a radiant vision in white. The light gleamed through her soft brown hair forming a halo for a face that Robert Cairn knew for the sweetest in the world.

"Why, Mr. Cairn," she said, and blushed entrancingly—"we thought you had forgotten us."

"That's not a little bit likely," he replied, taking her proffered hand, and there was that in his voice and in his look which made her lower her frank gray eyes. "I have only been in London a few days, and I find that press work is more exacting than I had anticipated!"

"Did you want to see my uncle very particularly?" asked Myra.

"In a way, yes. I suppose he could not manage to see me—"

Myra shook her head. Now that the flush of excitement had left her face, Cairn was concerned to see how pale she was and what dark shadows lurked beneath her eyes.

"Sir Michael is not seriously ill?" he asked quickly. "Only one of the usual attacks—"

"Yes—at least it began with one."

She hesitated, and Cairn saw to his consternation that her eyes became filled with tears. The real loneliness of her position, now that her guardian was ill, the absence of a friend in whom she could confide her fears, suddenly grew apparent to the man who sat watching her.

"You are tired out," he said gently. "You have been nursing him?"

She nodded and tried to smile.

"Who is attending?"

"Sir Elwin Groves, but—"

"Shall I wire for my father?"

"We wired for him yesterday!"

"What! to Paris?"

"Yes, at my uncle's wish."

Cairn started.

"Then—he thinks he is seriously ill, himself?"

"I cannot say," answered the girl wearily. "His behaviour is—queer. He will allow no one in his room, and barely consents to see Sir Elwin. Then, twice recently, he has awakened in the night and made a singular request."

"What is that?"

"He has asked me to send for his solicitor in the morning, speaking harshly and almost as though—he hated me…"

"I don't understand. Have you complied?"

"Yes, and on each occasion he has refused to see the solicitor when he has arrived!"

"I gather that you have been acting as night-attendant?"

"I remain in an adjoining room; he is always worse at night. Perhaps it is telling on my nerves, but last night—"

Again she hesitated, as though doubting the wisdom of further speech; but a brief scrutiny of Cairn's face, with deep anxiety to be read in his eyes, determined her to proceed.

"I had been asleep, and I must have been dreaming, for I thought that a voice was chanting, quite near to me."

"Chanting?"

"Yes—it was horrible, in some way. Then a sensation of intense coldness came; it was as though some icily cold creature fanned me with its wings! I cannot describe it, but it was numbing; I think I must have felt as those poor travellers do who succumb to the temptation to sleep in the snow."

Cairn surveyed her anxiously, for in its essentials this might be a symptom of a dreadful ailment.

"I aroused myself, however," she continued, "but experienced an unaccountable dread of entering my uncle's room. I could hear him muttering strangely, and—I forced myself to enter! I saw—oh, how can I tell you! You will think me mad!"

She raised her hands to her face; she was trembling. Robert Cairn took them in his own, forcing her to look up.

"Tell me," he said quietly.

"The curtains were drawn back; I distinctly remembered having closed them, but they were drawn back; and the moonlight was shining on to the bed."

"He was dreaming."

"But was *I* dreaming? Mr. Cairn, two hands were stretched out over my uncle, two hands that swayed slowly up and down in the moonlight!"

Cairn leapt to his feet, passing his hand over his forehead.

"Go on," he said.

"I—I cried out, but not loudly—I think I was very near to swooning. The hands were withdrawn into the shadow, and my uncle awoke and sat up. He asked, in a low voice, if I were there, and I ran to him."

"Yes."

"He ordered me, very coldly, to 'phone for his solicitor at nine o'clock this morning, and then fell back, and was asleep again almost immediately. The solicitor came, and was with him for nearly an hour. He sent for one of his clerks, and they both went away at half-past ten. Uncle has been in a sort of dazed condition ever since; in fact, he has only once aroused himself, to ask for Dr. Cairn. I had a telegram sent immediately."

"The governor will be here to-night," said Cairn confidently. "Tell me, the hands which you thought you saw: was there anything peculiar about them?"

"In the moonlight they seemed to be of a dull white colour. There was a ring on one finger—a green ring. Oh!" she shuddered. "I can see it now."

"You would know it again?"

"Anywhere!"

"Actually, there was no one in the room, of course?"

"No one. It was some awful illusion; but I can never forget it."


CHAPTER III

THE RING OF THOTH

Half-Moon Street was very still; midnight had sounded nearly half-an-hour; but still Robert Cairn paced up and down his father's library. He was very pale, and many times he glanced at a book which lay open upon the table. Finally he paused before it and read once again certain passages:

> In the year 1571, the notorious Trois Echelles was executed in the
> Place de Grève. He confessed before the king, Charles IX... that
> he performed marvels... Admiral de Coligny, who also was pres-
> ent, recollected... the death of two gentlemen... He added that they
> were found black and swollen.

He turned over the page with a hand none too steady.

> The famous Maréchal d'Ancre, Concini Concini, was killed by
> a pistol shot on the drawbridge of the Louvre by Vitry, Captain
> of the Bodyguard, on the 24th of April, 1617... It was proved that
> the Maréchal and his wife made use of wax images, which they
> kept in coffins...

Cairn shut the book hastily and began to pace the room again.

"Oh, it is utterly, fantastically incredible!" he groaned. "Yet, with my
own eyes I saw—"

He stepped to a bookshelf and began to look for a book which, so far
as his slight knowledge of the subject bore him, would possibly throw
light upon the darkness. But he failed to find it. Despite the heat of the
weather, the library seemed to have grown chilly. He pressed the bell.

"Marston," he said to the man who presently came, "you must be very
tired, but Dr. Cairn will be here within an hour. Tell him that I have gone
to Sir Michael Ferrara's."

"But it's after twelve o'clock, sir!"

"I know it is; nevertheless I am going."

"Very good, sir. You will wait there for the Doctor?"

"Exactly, Marston. Good-night!"

"Good-night, sir."

Robert Cairn went out into Half-Moon Street. The night was perfect,
and the cloudless sky lavishly gemmed with stars. He walked on heed-
lessly, scarce noting in which direction. An awful conviction was with
him, growing stronger each moment, that some mysterious menace, some
danger unclassifiable, threatened Myra Duquesne. What did he suspect?
He could give it no name. How should he act? He had no idea.

Sir Elwin Groves, whom he had seen that evening, had hinted broadly
at mental trouble as the solution of Sir Michael Ferrara's peculiar symptoms. Although Sir Michael had had certain transactions with his solicitor during the early morning, he had apparently forgotten all about

the matter, according to the celebrated physician.

"Between ourselves, Cairn," Sir Elwin had confided, "I believe he altered his will."

The inquiry of a taxi driver interrupted Cairn's meditations. He entered the vehicle, giving Sir Michael Ferrara's address.

His thoughts persistently turned to Myra Duquesne, who at that moment would be lying listening for the slightest sound from the sick-room; who would be fighting down fear, that she might do her duty to her guardian—fear of the waving phantom hands. The cab sped through the almost empty streets and, at last, rounding a corner, rolled up the tree-lined avenue, past three or four houses lighted only by the glitter of the moon, and came to a stop before that of Sir Michael Ferrara.

Lights shone from the many windows. The front door was open, and light streamed out into the porch.

"My God!" cried Cairn, leaping from the cab. "My God! what has happened ?"

A thousand fears, a thousand reproaches, flooded his brain with frenzy. He went racing up to the steps and almost threw himself upon the man who stood half-dressed in the doorway.

"Felton, Felton!" he whispered hoarsely. "What has happened? Who—"

"Sir Michael, sir," answered the man. "I thought"—his voice broke—"you were the doctor, sir."

"Miss Myra—"

"She fainted away, sir. Mrs. Hume is with her in the library, now."

Cairn thrust past the servant and ran into the library. The housekeeper and a trembling maid were bending over Myra Duquesne, who lay fully dressed, white and still, upon a Chesterfield. Cairn unceremoniously grasped her wrist, dropped upon his knees and placed his ear to the still breast.

"Thank God!" he said. "It is only a swoon. Look after her, Mrs. Hume."

The housekeeper, with set face, lowered her head, but did not trust herself to speak. Cairn went out into the hall and tapped Felton on the shoulder. The man turned with a great start.

"What happened ?" he demanded. "Is Sir Michael—?"

Felton nodded.

"Five minutes before you came, sir." His voice was hoarse with emotion. "Miss Myra came out of her room. She thought someone called her. She rapped on Mrs. Hume's door, and Mrs. Hume, who was just retiring, opened it. She also thought she had someone calling Miss Myra out on the stairhead."

"Well?"

"There was no one there, sir. Everyone was in bed; I was just undressing, myself. But there was a sort of faint perfume—something like a church, only disgusting, sir—"

"How—disgusting! Did you smell it?"

"No, sir, never. Mrs. Hume and Miss Myra have noticed it in the house on other nights, and one of the maids, too. It was very strong, I'm told, last night. Well, sir, as they stood by the door they heard a horrid kind of choking scream. They both rushed to Michael's room, and—"

"Yes, yes?"

"He was lying half out of bed, sir—"

"Dead?"

"Seemed like he'd been strangled, they told me, and—"

"Who is with him now?"

The man grew even paler.

"No one, Mr. Cairn, sir. Miss Myra screamed out that there were two hands just unfastening from his throat as she and Mrs. Hume got to the door, and there was no living soul in the room, sir. I might as well out with it! We're all afraid to go in!"

Cairn turned and ran up the stairs. The upper landing was in darkness and the door of the room which he knew to be Sir Michael's stood wide open. As he entered, a faint scent came to his nostrils. It brought him up short at the threshold, with a chill of supernatural dread.

The bed was placed between the windows, and one curtain had been pulled aside, admitting a flood of moonlight. Cairn remembered that Myra had mentioned this circumstance in connection with the disturbance of the previous night.

"Who, in God's name, opened that curtain!" he muttered.

Fully in the cold white light lay Sir Michael Ferrara, his silver hair gleaming and his strong, angular face upturned to the intruding rays. His glazed eyes were starting from their sockets; his face was nearly black; and his fingers were clutching the sheets in a death grip. Cairn had need of all his courage to touch him.

He was quite dead.

Someone was running up the stairs. Cairn turned, half dazed, anticipating the entrance of a local medical man. Into the room ran his father, switching on the light as he did so. A grayish tinge showed through his ruddy complexion. He scarcely noticed his son.

"Ferrara!" he cried, coming up to the bed. "Ferrara!"

He dropped on his knees beside the dead man.

"Ferrara, old fellow—"

His cry ended in something like a sob. Robert Cairn turned, choking, and went downstairs.

In the hall stood Felton and some other servants.

"Miss Duquesne?"

"She has recovered, sir. Mrs. Hume has taken her to another bed-room."

Cairn hesitated, then walked up into the deserted library, where a light was burning. He began to pace up and down, clenching and unclench-ing his fists. Presently Felton knocked and entered. Clearly the man was glad of the chance to talk to someone.

"Mr. Antony has been 'phoned at Oxford, sir. I thought you might like to know. He is motoring down, sir, and will be here at four o'clock."

"Thank you," said Cairn shortly.

Ten minutes later his father joined him. He was a slim, well-preserved man, alert-eyed and active, yet he had aged five years in his son's eyes. His face was unusually pale, but he exhibited no other signs of emotion.

"Well, Rob," he said tersely. "I can see you have something to tell me. I am listening."

Robert Cairn leant back against a bookshelf.

"I have something to tell you, sir, and something to ask you."

"Tell your story first; then ask your question."

"My story begins in a Thames backwater—"

Dr. Cairn stared, squaring his jaw, but his son proceeded to relate, with some detail, the circumstances attendant upon the death of the king-swan. He went on to recount what had taken place in Antony Ferrara's rooms, and at the point where something had been taken from the table and thrown in the fire.

"Stop!" said Dr. Cairn. "What did he throw in the fire?"

The doctor's nostrils quivered, and his eyes were ablaze with some hardly repressed emotion.

"I cannot swear to it, sir—"

"Never mind. What do you *think* he threw in the fire?"

"A little image, of wax or something similar—an image of—a swan."

At that, despite his self-control, Dr. Cairn became so pale that his son leapt forward.

"All right, Rob," his father waved him away, and turning, walked slowly down the room.

"Go on," he said, rather huskily.

Robert Cairn continued his story up to the time that he visited the hos-pital where the dead girl lay.

"You can swear that she was the original of the photograph in Antony's rooms and the same who was waiting at the foot of the stair?"

"I can, sir."

"Go on."

Again the younger man resumed his story, relating what he had learnt from Myra Duquesne; what she had told him about the phantom hands; what Felton had told him about the strange perfume perceptible in the house.

"The ring," interrupted Dr. Cairn—"she would recognize it again?"

"She says so."

"Anything else?"

"Only that if some of your books are to be believed, sir, Trois Echelle, D'Ancre, and others have gone to the stake for such things in a less enlightened age!"

"Less enlightened, boy!" Dr. Cairn turned his blazing eyes upon him. "*More* enlightened where the powers of hell were concerned!"

"Then you think—"

"*Think!* Have I spent half my life in such studies in vain? Did I labour with poor Michael Ferrara in Egypt and learn *nothing?* Just God! what an end to his labour! What a reward for mine!"

He buried his face in quivering hands.

"I cannot tell exactly what you mean by that, sir," said Robert Cairn; "but it brings me to my question."

Dr. Cairn did not speak, did not move.

"*Who is Antony Ferrara?*"

The doctor looked up at that; and it was a haggard face he raised from his hands.

"You have tried to ask me that before."

"I ask now, sir, with better prospect of receiving an answer."

"Yet I can give you none, Rob."

"Why, sir? Are you bound to secrecy?"

"In a degree, yes. But the real reason is this—don't know."

"You don't know!"

"I have said so."

"Good God, sir, you amaze me! I have always felt certain that he was really no Ferrara, but an adopted son; yet it had never entered my mind that you were ignorant of his origin."

"You have not studied the subjects which I have studied; nor do I wish that you should; therefore it is impossible, at any rate now, to pursue that matter further. But I may perhaps supplement your researches into the history of Trois Eschelles and Concino Concini. I believe you told me that you were looking in my library for some work which you failed to find?"

"I was looking for M. Chabas's translation of the 'Papyrus Harris.'"
"What do you know of it?"

"I once saw a copy in Antony Ferrara's rooms."
Dr. Cairn started slightly.
"Indeed. It happens that my copy is here; I lent it quite recently to—Sir Michael. It is probably somewhere on the shelves."
He turned on more lights and began to scan the rows of books. Presently:
"Here it is," he said, and took down and opened the book on the table. "This passage may interest you."
He laid his finger upon it.
His son bent over the book and read the following:

Hai, the evil man, was a shepherd. He had said: "O, that I might have a book of spells that would give me resistless power!" He obtained a book of the Formulas... By the divine powers of these he enchanted men. He obtained a deep vault furnished with implements. He made waxen images of men, and love-charms. And then he perpetrated all the horrors that his heart conceived.

"Flinders Petrie," said Dr. Cairn, "mentions the Book of Thoth as another magical work conferring similar powers."
"But surely, sir—after all, it's the twentieth century—this is mere superstition!"
"I thought so—*once!*" replied Dr. Cairn. "But I have lived to know that Egyptian magic was a real and a potent force. A great part of it was no more than a kind of hypnotism, but there were other branches. Our most learned modern works are as children's nursery rhymes beside such a writing as the Egyptian 'Ritual of the Dead!' God forgive me! What have I done!"
"You cannot reproach yourself in any way, sir!"
"Can I not?" said Dr. Cairn hoarsely. "Ah, Rob, you don't know!"
There came a rap on the door, and a local practitioner entered.
"This is a singular case, Dr. Cairn," he began diffidently. "An autopsy—"
"Nonsense!" cried Dr. Cairn. "Sir Elwin Groves had foreseen it—so had I!"
"But there are distinct marks of pressure on either side of the windpipe—"
"Certainly. These marks are not uncommon in such cases. Sir Michael

had resided in the East and had contracted a form of plague. Virtually he died from it. The thing is highly contagious, and it is almost impossible to rid the system of it. A girl died in one of the hospitals this week, having identical marks on the throat." He turned to his son. "You saw her, Rob?"

Robert Cairn nodded, and finally the local man withdrew, highly mystified, but unable to contradict so celebrated a physician as Dr. Bruce Cairn.

The latter seated himself in an armchair, and rested his chin in the palm of his left hand. Robert Cairn paced restlessly about the library. Both were waiting, expectantly. At half-past two Felton brought in a tray of refreshments, but neither of the men attempted to avail themselves of the hospitality.

"Miss Duquesne?" asked the younger.

"She has just gone to sleep, sir."

"Good," muttered Dr. Cairn. "Blessed is youth."

Silence fell again, upon the man's departure, to be broken but rarely, despite the tumultuous thoughts of those two minds, until, at about a quarter to three, the faint sound of a throbbing motor brought Dr. Cairn sharply to his feet. He looked toward the window. Dawn was breaking. The car came roaring along the avenue and stopped outside the house.

Dr. Cairn and his son glanced at one another. A brief tumult and hurried exchange of words sounded in the hall; footsteps were heard ascending the stairs, then came silence. The two stood side by side in front of the empty hearth, a haggard pair, fitly set in that desolate room, with the yellowing rays of the lamps shrinking before the first spears of dawn.

Then, without warning, the door opened slowly and deliberately, and Antony Ferrara came in.

His face was expressionless, ivory; his red lips were firm, and he drooped his head. But the long black eyes glinted and gleamed as if they reflected the glow from a furnace. He wore a motor coat lined with leopard skin, and he was pulling off his heavy gloves.

"It is good of you to have waited, Doctor," he said in his huskily musical voice— "you, too, Cairn."

He advanced a few steps into the room. Cairn was conscious of a kind of fear, but uppermost came a desire to pick up some heavy implement and crush this evilly effeminate thing with the serpent eyes. Then he found himself speaking; the words seemed to be forced from his throat.

"Antony Ferrara," he said, "have you read the 'Harris Papyrus?'"

Ferrara dropped his glove, stooped and recovered it, and smiled faintly.

"No," he replied. "Have you?" His eyes were nearly closed, mere luminous slits. "But surely," he continued, "this is no time, Cairn, to discuss books? As my poor father's heir, and therefore your host, I beg of you to partake—"

A faint sound made him turn. Just within the door, where the light from the reddening library windows touched her as if with sanctity, stood Myra Duquesne, in her night robe, her hair unbound and her little bare feet gleaming whitely upon the red carpet. Her eyes were wide open, vacant of expression, but set upon Antony Ferrara's ungloved left hand.

Ferrara turned slowly to face her, until his back was toward the two men in the library. She began to speak, in a toneless, unemotional voice, raising her finger and pointing at a ring which Ferrara wore.

"I know you now," she said; "I know you, son of an evil woman, for you wear her ring, the sacred ring of Thoth. You have stained that ring with blood, as she stained it—with the blood of those who loved and trusted you. I could name you, but my lips are sealed—I could name you, brood of a witch, murderer, for I know you now."

Dispassionately, mechanically, she delivered her strange indictment. Over her shoulder appeared the anxious face of Mrs. Hume, finger to lip.

"My God!" muttered Cairn. "My God! What—"

"S-sh!" his father grasped his arm. "She is asleep!"

Myra Duquesne turned and quitted the room, Mrs. Hume hovering anxiously about her. Antony Ferrara faced around; his mouth was oddly twisted.

"She is troubled with strange dreams," he said, very huskily.

"Clairvoyant dreams!" Dr. Cairn addressed him for the first time. "Do not glare at me in that way for it may be that *I* know you, too! Come, Rob."

"But Myra—"

Dr. Cairn laid his hand upon his son's shoulder, fixing his eyes upon him steadily.

"Nothing in this house can injure Myra," he replied quietly; "for Good is higher than Evil. For the present we can only go."

Antony Ferrara stood aside, as the two walked out of the library.

## CHAPTER IV
## AT FERRARA'S CHAMBERS

Dr. Bruce Cairn swung around in his chair, lifting his heavy eyebrows interrogatively, as his son, Robert, entered the consulting-room. Half-Moon Street was bathed in almost tropical sunlight, but already the celebrated physician had sent those out from his house to whom the sky was overcast, whom the sun would gladden no more, and a group of anxious-eyed sufferers yet awaited his scrutiny in an adjoining room.

"Hullo, Rob! Do you wish to see me professionally?"

Robert Cairn seated himself upon a corner of the big table, shaking his head slowly.

"No, thanks sir; I'm fit enough; but I thought you might like to know about the will—"

"I do know. Since I was largely interested, Jermyn attended on my behalf; an urgent case detained me. He rang up earlier this morning."

"Oh, I see. Then perhaps I'm wasting your time; but it was a surprise—quite a pleasant one—to find that Sir Michael had provided for Myra—Miss Duquesne."

Dr. Cairn stared hard.

"What led you to suppose that he had *not* provided for his niece? She is an orphan, and he was her guardian."

"Of course, he should have done so; but I was not alone in my belief that during the—peculiar state of mind—which preceded his death, he had altered his will—"

"In favour of his adopted son, Antony?"

"Yes. I know *you* were afraid of it, sir! But as it turns out they inherit equal shares, and the house goes to Myra. Mr. Antony Ferrara"—he accentuated the name— "quite failed to conceal his chagrin."

"Indeed!"

"Rather. He was there in person, wearing one of his beastly fur coats—a fur coat, with the thermometer at Africa!—lined with civet-cat, of all abominations!"

Dr. Cairn turned to his table, tapping at the blotting-pad with the tube of a stethoscope.

"I regret your attitude toward young Ferrara, Rob."

His son started.

"Regret it! I don't understand. Why, you, yourself brought about an open rupture on the night of Sir Michael's death."

"Nevertheless, I am sorry. You know, since you were present, that Sir

Michael has left his niece—to my care—"

"Thank God for that!"

"I am glad, too, although there are many difficulties. But, furthermore, he enjoined me to—"

"Keep an eye on Antony! Yes, yes—but, heavens! he didn't know him on for what he is!"

Dr. Cairn turned to him again.

"He did not; by a divine mercy, he never knew—what we know. But"—his clear eyes were raised to his son's—"the charge is none the less sacred, boy!"

The younger man stared perplexedly.

"But he is nothing less than a—"

His father's upraised hand checked the word on his tongue.

"*I* know what he is, Rob, even better than you do. But cannot you see how this ties my hands, seals my lips?"

Robert Cairn was silent, stupefied.

"Give me time to see my way clearly, Rob. At the moment I cannot reconcile my duty and my conscience; I confess it. But give me time. If only as a move—as a matter of policy—keep in touch with Ferrara. You loathe him, I know; but we *must* watch him! There are other interests—"

"Myra!" Robert Cairn flushed hotly. "Yes, I see. I understand. By heavens, it's a hard part to play, but—"

"Be advised by me, Rob. Meet stealth with stealth. My boy, we have seen strange ends come to those who stood in the path of someone. If you had studied the subjects that I have studied you would know that retribution, though slow, is inevitable. But be on your guard. I am taking precautions. We have an enemy; I do not pretend to deny it; and he fights with strange weapons. Perhaps I know something of those weapons, too, and I am adopting—certain measures. But one defense, and the one for you, is guile—stealth!"

Robert Cairn spoke abruptly.

"He is installed in palatial chambers in Piccadilly."

"Have you been there?"

"No."

"Call upon him. Take the first opportunity to do so. Had it not been for your knowledge of certain things which happened in a top set at Oxford we might be groping in the dark now! You never liked Antony Ferrara—no men do; but you used to call upon him in college. Continue to call upon him, in town."

Robert Cairn stood up, and lighted a cigarette.

"Right you are, sir!" he said. "I'm glad I'm not alone in this thing! By the way, about—?"

"Myra? For the present she remains at the house. There is Mrs. Hume, and all the old servants. We shall see what is to be done later. You might run over and give her a look-up, though."

"I will, sir! Good-bye."

"Good-bye," said Dr. Cairn, and pressed the bell which summoned Marston to usher out the caller and usher in the next patient.

In Half-Moon Street Robert Cairn stood irresolute; for he was one of those whose mental moods are physically reflected. He might call upon Myra Duquesne, in which event he would almost certainly be asked to stay to lunch; or he might call upon Antony Ferrara. He determined upon the latter, though less pleasant course.

Turning his steps in the direction of Piccadilly, he reflected that this grim and uncanny secret which he shared with his father was likely to prove prejudicial to his success in journalism. It was eternally uprising, demoniac, between himself and his work. The feeling of fierce resentment toward Antony Ferrara which he cherished grew stronger at every step. *He* was the spider governing the web, the web that clammily touched Dr. Cairn, himself, Robert Cairn, and—Myra Duquesne. Others there had been who had felt its touch, who had been drawn to the heart of the unclean labyrinth—and devoured. In the mind of Cairn, the figure of Antony Ferrara assumed the shape of a monster, a ghoul, an elemental spirit of evil.

And now he was ascending the marble steps. Before the gates of the lift he stood and pressed the bell.

Ferrara's proved to be a first-floor suite, and the doors were opened by an Eastern servant dressed in white.

"His beastly theatrical affectation again!" muttered Cairn. "The man should have been a music-hall illusionist!"

The visitor was salaamed into a small reception room. Of this apartment the walls and ceiling were entirely covered by a fretwork in sandalwood, evidently Oriental in workmanship. In niches, or doorless cupboards, stood curious-looking vases and pots. Heavy curtains of rich fabric draped the doors. The floor was of mosaic, and a small fountain played in the centre. A cushioned divan occupied one side of the place, from which natural light was entirely excluded and which was illuminated only by an ornate lantern swung from the ceiling. This lantern had panes of blue glass, producing a singular effect. A silver *mibkharah*, or incense-burner, stood near to one corner of the divan and emitted a subtle perfume. As the servant withdrew:

"Good heavens!" muttered Cairn, disgustedly; "poor Sir Michael's fortune won't last long at this rate!" He glanced at the smoking *mibkharah*. "Phew! effeminate beast! Ambergris!"

No more singular anomaly could well be pictured than that afforded by the lean, neatly groomed Scotsman, with his fresh, clean-shaven face and typically British air, in this setting of Eastern voluptuousness.

The dusky servitor drew back a curtain and waved him to enter, bowing low as the visitor passed. Cairn found himself in Antony Ferrara's study. A huge fire was blazing in the grate, rendering the heat of the study almost insufferable.

It was, he perceived, an elaborated copy of Ferrara's room at Oxford; infinitely more spacious, of course, and by reason of the rugs, cushions, and carpets with which its floor was strewn, suggestive of great opulence. But the littered table was there, with its nameless instruments and its extraordinary silver lamp; the mummies were there; the antique volumes, rolls of papyrus, preserved snakes and cats and ibises, statuettes of Isis, Osiris, and other Nile deities were there; the many photographs of women, too (Cairn had dubbed it at Oxford "the zenana"); above all, there was Antony Ferrara.

He wore the silver-gray dressing-gown trimmed with white swansdown in which Cairn had seen him before. His statuesque ivory face was set in a smile, which yet was no smile of welcome; the over-red lips smiled alone; the long, glittering dark eyes were joyless; almost, beneath the straightly pencilled brows, sinister. Save for the short, lustreless hair it was the face of a handsome, evil woman.

"My dear Cairn—what a welcome interruption. How good of you!"

There was strange music in his husky tones. He spoke unemotionally, falsely, but Cairn could not deny the charm of that unique voice. It was possible to understand how women—some women—would be as clay in the hands of the man who had such a voice as that.

His visitor nodded shortly. Cairn was a poor actor; already his role was oppressing him. Whilst Ferrara was speaking one found a sort of fascination in listening, but when he was silent he repelled. Ferrara may have been conscious of this, for he spoke much, and well.

"You have made yourself jolly comfortable," said Cairn.

"Why not, my dear Cairn? Every man has within him something of the Sybarite. Why crush a propensity so delightful? The Spartan philosophy is palpably absurd; it is that of one who finds himself in a garden filled with roses and who holds his nostrils; who perceives there shady bowers, but chooses to burn in the sun; who, ignoring the choice fruits which tempt his hand and court his palate, stoops to pluck bitter herbs from the wayside!"

"I see!" snapped Cairn. "Aren't you thinking of doing any more work, then?"

"Work!" Antony Ferrara smiled and sank upon a heap of cushions. "Forgive me, Cairn, but I leave it, gladly and confidently, to more robust characters such as your own."

He proffered a silver box of cigarettes, but Cairn shook his head, balancing himself on a corner of the table.

"No; thanks. I have smoked too much already; my tongue is parched."

"My dear fellow!" Ferrara rose. "I have a wine which, I declare, you will never have tasted but which you will pronounce to be nectar. It is made in Cyprus—"

Cairn raised his hand in a way that might have reminded a nice observer of his father.

"Thank you, nevertheless. Some other time, Ferrara; I am no wine man."

"A whisky and soda, or a burly British B. and S., even a sporty 'Scotch and Polly'?"

There was a suggestion of laughter in the husky voice, now, of a sort of contemptuous banter. But Cairn stolidly shook his head and forced a smile.

"Many thanks; but it's too early."

He stood up and began to walk about the room, inspecting the numberless oddities which it contained. The photographs he examined with supercilious curiosity. Then, passing to a huge cabinet, he began to peer in at the rows of amulets, statuettes, and other, unclassifiable, objects with which it was laden. Ferrara's voice came.

"That head of a priestess on the left, Cairn, is of great interest. The brain had not been removed, and quite a colony of Dermestes beetles had propagated in the cavity. Those creatures never saw the light, Cairn. Yet I assure you that they had eyes. I have nearly forty of them in the small glass case on the table there. You might like to examine them."

Cairn shuddered, but felt impelled to turn and look at these gruesome relics. In a square glass case he saw the creatures. They lay in rows on a bed of moss; one might almost have supposed that unclean life yet survived in the little black insects. They were an unfamiliar species to Cairn, being covered with unusually long black hair except upon the root of the wing-cases where they were of brilliant orange.

"The perfect pupae of this insect are extremely rare," added Ferrara informatively.

"Indeed?" replied Cairn.

He found something physically revolting in that group of beetles whose history had begun and ended in the skull of a mummy.

"Filthy things!" he said. "Why do you keep them?"

Ferrara shrugged his shoulders.

"Who knows?" he answered enigmatically. "They might prove useful some day."

A bell rang; and from Ferrara's attitude it occurred to Cairn that he was expecting a visitor.

"I must be off," he said accordingly.

And indeed he was conscious of a craving for the cool and comparatively clean air of Piccadilly. He knew something of the great evil which dwelt within this man whom he was compelled, by singular circumstances, to tolerate. But the duty began to irk.

"If you must," was the reply. "Of course, your press work no doubt is very exacting."

The note of badinage was discernible again, but Cairn passed out into the *mandarah* without replying, where the fountain plashed coolly and the silver *mibkharah* sent up its pencils of vapour. The outer door was opened by the Oriental servant, and Ferrara stood and bowed to his departing visitor. He did not proffer his hand.

"Until our next meeting, Cairn, *es-selâm aleykûm!*" [peace be with you] he murmured, "as the Moslems say. But indeed I shall be with you in spirit, dear Cairn."

There was something in the tone wherein he spoke those last words that brought Cairn up short. He turned, but the doors closed silently. A faint breath of ambergris was borne to his nostrils.


## CHAPTER V
## THE RUSTLING SHADOWS

Cairn stepped out of the lift, crossed the hall, and was about to walk out on to Piccadilly, when he stopped, staring hard at a taxi-cab which had slowed down upon the opposite side whilst the driver awaited a suitable opportunity to pull across.

The occupant of the cab was invisible now, but a moment before Cairn had had a glimpse of her as she glanced out, apparently toward the very doorway in which he stood. Perhaps his imagination was playing him tricks. He stood and waited, until at last the cab drew up within a few yards of him.

Myra Duquesne got out.

Having paid the cabman, she crossed the pavement and entered the hallway. Cairn stepped forward so that she almost ran into his arms.

"Mr. Cairn!" she cried. "Why! have you been to see Antony?"

"I have," he replied, and paused, at a loss for words.

It had suddenly occurred to him that Antony Ferrara and Myra Duquesne had known one another from childhood; that the girl probably regarded Ferrara in the light of a brother.

"There are so many things I want to talk to him about," she said. "He seems to know everything, and I am afraid I know very little."

Cairn noted with dismay the shadows under her eyes—the gray eyes that he would have wished to see ever full of light and laughter. She was pale, too, or seemed unusually so in her black dress; but the tragic death of her guardian, Sir Michael Ferrara, had been a dreadful blow to this convent-bred girl who had no other kin in the world! A longing swept into Cairn's heart and set it ablaze; a longing to take all her sorrows, all her cares, upon his own broad shoulders, to take her and hold her, shielded from whatever of trouble or menace the future might bring.

"Have you seen his rooms here?" he asked, trying to speak casually; but his soul was up in arms against the bare idea of this girl's entering that perfumed place where abominable and vile things were, and none of them so vile as the man she trusted, whom she counted a brother.

"Not yet," she answered, with a sort of childish glee momentarily lighting her eyes. "Are they *very* splendid?"

"Very," he answered her, grimly.

"Can't you come in with me for awhile? Only just a little while, then you can come home to lunch—you and Antony." Her eyes sparkled now. "Oh, do say yes!"

Knowing what he did know of the man upstairs, he longed to accompany her; yet, contradictorily, knowing what he did he could not face him again, could not submit himself to the test of being civil to Antony Ferrara in the presence of Myra Duquesne.

"Please don't tempt me," he begged, and forced a smile. "I shall find myself enrolled amongst the seekers of soup-tickets if I *completely* ignore the claims of my employer upon my time!"

"Oh, what a shame!" she cried.

Their eyes met, and something—something unspoken but cogent— passed between them; so that for the first time a pretty colour tinted the girl's cheeks. She suddenly grew embarrassed.

"Good-bye, then," she said, holding out her hand. "Will you lunch with us to-morrow?"

"Thanks, awfully," replied Cairn. "Rather—if it's humanly possible. I'll ring you up."

He released her hand, and stood watching her as she entered the lift. When it ascended, he turned and went out to swell the human tide of Piccadilly. He wondered what his father would think of the girl's visiting Ferrara. Would he approve? Decidedly the situation was a delicate one; the wrong kind of interference—the tactless kind—might merely render it worse. It would be extremely difficult, if not impossible, to explain to Myra. If an open rupture were to be avoided (and he had profound faith in his father's acumen), then Myra must remain in ignorance. But was she to be allowed to continue these visits?

Should he have permitted her to enter Ferrara's rooms?

He reflected that he had no right to question her movements. But, at least, he might have accompanied her.

"Oh, heavens!" he muttered—"what a horrible tangle. It will drive me mad!"

There could be no peace for him until he knew her to be safely home again, and his work suffered accordingly; until, at about midday, he rang up Myra Duquesne, on the pretence of accepting her invitation to lunch on the morrow, and heard, with inexpressible relief, her voice replying to him.

In the afternoon he was suddenly called upon to do a big "royal" matinée, and this necessitated a run to his chambers in order to change from Harris tweed into vicuna and cashmere. The usual stream of lawyers' clerks and others poured under the archway leading to the court; but in the far corner shaded by the tall plane tree, where the ascending steps and worn iron railing, the small panes of glass in the solicitor's window on the ground floor and the general air of Dickens-like aloofness prevailed, one entered a sort of backwater. In the narrow hallway quiet reigned—a quiet profound as though motor 'buses were not.

Cairn ran up the stairs to the second landing, and began to fumble for his key. Although he knew it to be impossible, he was aware of a queer impression that someone was waiting for him, inside his chambers. The sufficiently palpable fact—that such a thing was impossible—did not really strike him until he had opened the door and entered. Up to that time, in a sort of subconscious way, he had anticipated finding a visitor there.

"What an ass I am!" he muttered; then, "Phew! there's a disgusting smell!"

He threw open all the windows, and entering his bedroom, also opened both the windows there. The current of air thus established began to disperse the odour—a fusty one as of something decaying—and by the time that he had changed, it was scarcely perceptible. He had little time to waste in speculation, but when, as he ran out to the door, glancing at his watch, the nauseous odour suddenly rose again to his nostrils, he stopped with his hand on the latch.

"What the deuce is it!" he said loudly.

Quite mechanically he turned and looked back. As one might have anticipated, there was nothing visible to account for the odour.

The emotion of fear is a strange and complex one. In this breath of decay rising to his nostrils Cairn found something fearsome. He opened the door, stepped out on to the landing, and closed the door behind him.

At an hour close upon midnight Dr. Bruce Cairn, who was about to retire, received a wholly unexpected visit from his son. Robert Cairn followed his father into the library and sat down in the big, red leathern easy-chair. The doctor tilted the lamp shade, directing the light upon Robert's face. It proved to be slightly pale, and in the clear eyes was an odd expression—almost a hunted look.

"What's the trouble, Rob? Have a whisky and soda."

Robert Cairn helped himself quietly.

"Now take a cigar and tell me what has frightened you."

"Frightened me!" He started, and paused in the act of reaching for a match. "Yes—you're right, sir. I am frightened!"

"Not at the moment. You have been."

"Right again." He lighted his cigar. "I want to begin by saying that— well, how can I put it? When I took up newspaper work, we thought it would be better if I lived in chambers—"

"Certainly."

"Well, at that time"—he examined the lighted end of his cigar— "there was no reason—why I should not live alone. But now—"

"Well?"

"Now I feel, sir, that I have need of more or less constant companionship. Especially I feel that it would be desirable to have a friend handy at—er—at night time!"

Dr. Cairn leant forward in his chair. His face was very stern.

"Hold out your fingers," he said, "extended; left hand."

His son obeyed, smiling slightly. The open hand showed in the lamplight steady as a carven hand.

"Nerves quite in order, sir."

Dr. Cairn inhaled a deep breath.

"Tell me," he said.

"It's a queer tale," his son began, "and if I told it to Craig Fenton, or Madderley round in Harley Street, I know what they would say. But you will understand. It started this afternoon, when the sun was pouring in through the windows. I had to go to my chambers to change; and the rooms were filled with a most disgusting smell."

His father started.

"What kind of smell?" he asked. "Not—incense?"

"No," replied Robert, looking hard at him, "I thought you would ask that. It was a smell of something putrid—something rotten—rotten with the rottenness of ages."

"Did you trace where it came from?"

"I opened all the windows, and that seemed to disperse it for a time. Then, just as I was going out, it returned; it seemed to envelop me like a filthy miasma. You know, sir, it's hard to explain just the way I felt about it—but it all amounts to this: I was glad to get outside!"

Dr. Cairn stood up and began to pace about the room, his hands locked behind him.

"To-night," he rapped suddenly, "what occurred to-night?"

"To-night," continued his son, "I got in at about half-past nine. I had had such a rush, in one way and another, that the incident had quite lost its hold on my imagination; I hadn't forgotten it, of course, but I was not thinking of it when I unlocked the door. In fact, I didn't begin to think of it again until, in slippers and dressing-gown, I had settled down for a comfortable read. There was nothing, absolutely nothing, to influence my imagination—in that way. The book was an old favourite, Mark Twain's 'Up the Mississippi,' and I sat in the armchair with a large bottle of lager beer at my elbow and my pipe going strong."

Becoming restless in turn, the speaker stood up and walking to the fireplace flicked off the long cone of gray ash from his cigar. He leant one elbow upon the mantelpiece, resuming his story:

"St. Paul's had just chimed the half-hour—half-past ten—when my pipe went out. Before I had time to relight it came the damnable smell again. At the moment nothing was farther from my mind, and I jumped up with an exclamation of disgust. It seemed to be growing stronger and stronger. I got my pipe alight quickly. Still I could smell it; the aroma of the tobacco did not lessen its beastly pungency in the smallest degree.

"I tilted the shade of my reading-lamp and looked all about. There was nothing unusual to be seen. Both windows were open and I went to one and thrust my head out, in order to learn if the odour came from outside. It did not. The air outside the window was fresh and clean. Then I remembered that when I had left my chambers in the afternoon the smell had been stronger near the door than anywhere. I ran out to the door. In the passage I could smell nothing; but—"

He paused, glancing at his father.

"Before I had stood there thirty seconds, it was rising all about me like the fumes from a crater. My God, sir! I realized then that it was something... following me!"

Dr. Cairn stood watching him, from the shadows beyond the big table, as he came forward and finished his whisky at a gulp.

"That seemed to work a change in me," he continued rapidly; "I recognized there was something behind this disgusting manifestation, something directing it; and I recognized, too, that the next move was up to me. I went back to my room. The odour was not so pronounced, but as I stood by the table, waiting, it increased, and increased, until it almost choked me. My nerves were playing tricks, but I kept a fast hold on myself. I set to work, very methodically, and fumigated the place. Within myself I knew that it could do no good, but I felt that I had to put up some kind of opposition. You understand, sir?"

"Quite," replied Dr. Cairn quietly. "It was an organized attempt to expel the invader, and though of itself was useless, the mental attitude dictating it was good. Go on."

"The clocks had chimed eleven when I gave up, and I felt physically sick. The air by this time was poisonous, literally poisonous. I dropped into the easy-chair and began to wonder what the end of it would be. Then, in the shadowy parts of the room, outside the circle of light cast by the lamp, I detected—darker patches. For awhile I tried to believe that they were imaginary, but when I saw one move along the bookcase, glide down its side, and come across the carpet, toward me, I knew that they were not. Before heaven, sir"—his voice shook—"either I am mad, or to-night my room was filled with things that *crawled!* They were everywhere: on the floor, on the walls, even on the ceiling above me! Where the light was I couldn't detect them, but the shadows were alive, alive with things—the size of my two hands; and in the growing stillness—"

His voice had become husky. Dr. Cairn stood still, as a man of stone, watching him.

"—in the stillness, very faintly, *they rustled!*"

Silence fell. A car passed outside in Half-Moon Street; its throb died away. A clock was chiming the half-hour after midnight. Dr. Cairn spoke:

"Anything else?"

"One other thing, sir. I was gripping the chair arms; I felt that I had to grip something to prevent myself from slipping into madness. My left hand"—he glanced at it with a sort of repugnance—"something hairy— and indescribably loathsome—touched it; just brushed against it. But it was too much. I'm ashamed to tell you, sir; I screamed, screamed like any hysterical girl, and for the second time, ran! I ran from my own rooms, grabbed a hat and coat; and left my dressing-gown on the floor!"

He turned, leaning both elbows on the mantelpiece, and buried his face in his hands.

"Have another drink," said Dr. Cairn. "You called on Antony Ferrara to-day, didn't you? How did he receive you?"

"That brings me to something else I wanted to tell you," continued Robert, squirting soda-water into his glass. "Myra—goes there."

'Where—to his chambers?"

"Yes."

Dr. Cairn began to pace the room again.

"I am not surprised," he admitted; "she has always been taught to regard him in the light of a brother. But nevertheless we must put a stop to it. How did you learn this?"

Robert Cairn gave him an account of the morning's incidents, describing Ferrara's chambers with a minute exactness which revealed how deep, how indelible an impression their strangeness had made upon his mind.

"There is one thing," he concluded, "against which I am always coming up. I puzzled over it at Oxford, and others did, too; I came against it to-day. Who is Antony Ferrara? Where did Sir Michael find him? What kind of woman bore such a son?"

"Stop, boy!" cried Dr. Cairn.

Robert started, looking at his father across the table.

"You are already in danger, Rob. I won't disguise that fact from you. Myra Duquesne is no relation of Ferrara's; therefore, since she inherits half of Sir Michael's fortune, a certain course must have suggested itself to Antony. You, patently, are an obstacle! That's bad enough, boy; let us deal with it before we look for further trouble."

He took up a blackened briar from the table and began to load it.

"Regarding your next move," he continued slowly, "there can be no question. You must return to your chambers!"

"What!"

"There can be no question, Rob. A kind of attack has been made upon you which only you can repel. If you desert your chambers, it will be repeated here. At present it is evidently localized. There are laws governing these things; laws as immutable as any other laws in Nature. One of them is this: the powers of darkness (to employ a conventional and significant phrase) cannot triumph over the powers of Will. Below the Godhead, Will is the supreme force of the Universe. *Resist!* You *must* resist, or you are lost!"

"What do you mean, sir?"

"I mean that destruction of mind, and of something more than mind, threatens you. If you retreat you are lost. Go back to your rooms. *Seek your foe*; strive to haul him into the light and crush him! The phenomena at your rooms belong to one of two varieties; at present it seems impossible to classify them more closely. Both are dangerous, though in different ways. I suspect, however, that a purely mental effort will be sufficient to disperse these nauseous shadow-things. Probably you will not be troubled again to-night, but whenever the phenomena return, take off your coat to them! You require no better companion than the one you had: Mark Twain! Treat your visitors as one might imagine he would have treated them: as a very poor joke! But whenever it begins again, ring me up. Don't hesitate, whatever the hour. I shall be at the hospital all day, but from seven onward I shall be here and shall make a point of remaining. Give me a call when you return, now, and if there is no earlier occasion, another in the morning. Then rely upon my active cooperation throughout the following night."

"Active, sir?"

"I said active, Rob. The next repetition of these manifestations shall be the last. Good-night. Remember, you have only to lift the receiver to know that you are not alone in your fight."

Robert Cairn took a second cigar, lighted it, finished his whisky, and squared his shoulders.

"Good-night, sir," he said. "I shan't run away a third time!"

When the door had closed upon his exit, Dr. Cairn resumed his restless pacing up and down the library. He had given Roman counsel, for he had sent his son out to face, alone, a real and dreadful danger. Only thus could he hope to save him, but nevertheless it had been hard. The next fight would be a fight to the finish, for Robert had said, "I shan't run away a third time"; and he was a man of his word.

As Dr. Cairn had declared, the manifestations belonged to one of two varieties. According to the most ancient science in the world, the science by which the Egyptians, and perhaps even earlier peoples, ordered their lives, we share this, our plane of existence, with certain other creatures, often called Elementals. Mercifully, these fearsome entities are invisible to our normal sight, just as the finer tones of music are inaudible to our normal powers of hearing.

Victims of delirium tremens, opium smokers, and other debauchees, artificially open that finer, latent power of vision; and the horrors which surround them are not imaginary but are Elementals attracted to the victim by his peculiar excesses.

The crawling things, then, which reeked abominably might be Elementals (so Dr. Cairn reasoned) super-imposed upon Robert Cairn's consciousness by a directing, malignant intelligence. On the other hand, they
might be mere glamours—or thought-forms—thrust upon him by the
same wizard mind; emanations from an evil, powerful will.

His reflections were interrupted by the ringing of the 'phone bell. He
took up the receiver.

"Hullo!"

"That you, sir? All's clear here now. I'm turning in."

"Right. Good-night, Rob. Ring me in the morning."

"Good-night, sir."

Dr. Cairn refilled his charred briar, and, taking from a drawer in the
writing table a thick MS., sat down and began to study the closely written pages. The paper was in the cramped handwriting of the late Sir
Michael Ferrara, his travelling companion through many strange adventures; and the sun had been flooding the library with dimmed golden
light for several hours, and a bustle below stairs acclaiming an awakened
household, ere the doctor's studies were interrupted. Again, it was the
'phone bell. He rose, switched off the reading-lamp, and lifted the instrument.

"That you, Rob?"

"Yes, sir. All's well, thank God! Can I breakfast with you?"

"Certainly, my boy!" Dr. Cairn glanced at his watch.

"Why, upon my soul, it's seven o'clock!"


## CHAPTER VI
## THE BEETLES


Sixteen hours had elapsed and London's clocks were booming eleven
that night, when the uncanny drama entered upon its final stage. Once
more Dr. Cairn sat alone with Sir Michael's manuscript, but at frequent
intervals his glance would stray to the telephone at his elbow. He had
given orders to the effect that he was on no account to be disturbed and
that his car should be ready at the door from ten o'clock onward.

As the sound of the final strokes was dying away the expected sum-
mons came. Dr. Cairn's jaw squared and his mouth was very grim when
he recognized his son's voice over the wires.

"Well, boy?"

"They're here, sir—now, while I'm speaking! I have been fighting—
fighting hard—for half an hour. The place smells like a charnel-house and

the—shapes are taking definite, horrible form! They have... *eyes!*" His voice sounded harsh. "Quite black the eyes are, and they shine like beads! It's gradually wearing me down, although I have myself in hand so far. I mean I might crack up—at any moment. Bah!"

His voice ceased.

"Hullo!" cried Dr. Cairn. "Hullo, Rob!"

"It's all right, sir," came, all but inaudibly. "The—things are all around the edge of the light patch; they make a sort of rustling noise. It is a tremendous, conscious *effort* to keep them at bay. While I was speaking, I somehow lost my grip of the situation. One—crawled... it fastened on my hand ... a hairy, many-limbed horror... Oh, my God! another is touching..."

"Rob! Rob! Keep your nerve, boy! Do you hear?"

"Yes—yes—" faintly.

"*Pray*, my boy—pray for strength, and it will come to you! You *must* hold out for another ten minutes. Ten minutes—do you understand?"

"Yes! yes!—Merciful God!—if you can help me, do it, sir, or—"

"Hold out, boy. In *ten minutes* you'll have won."

Dr. Cairn hung up the receiver, raced from the library, and grabbing a cap from the rack in the hall, ran down the steps and bounded into the waiting car, shouting an address to the man.

Piccadilly was gay with supper-bound theatre crowds when he leapt out and ran into the hallway which had been the scene of Robert's meeting with Myra Duquesne. Dr. Cairn ran past the lift doors and went up the stairs three steps at a time. He pressed his finger to the bell-push beside Antony Ferrara's door and held it there until the door opened and a dusky face appeared in the opening.

The visitor thrust his way in, past the white-clad man holding out his arms to detain him.

"Not at home, *effendim*—"

Dr. Cairn shot out a sinewy hand, grabbed the man—he was a tall *fellahin*—by the shoulder, and sent him spinning across the mosaic floor of the *mandarah*. The air was heavy with the perfume of ambergris.

Wasting no word upon the reeling man, Dr. Cairn stepped to the doorway. He jerked the drapery aside and found himself in a dark corridor. From his son's description of the chambers he had no difficulty in recognizing the door of the study.

He turned the handle—the door proved to be unlocked—and entered the darkened room.

In the grate a huge fire glowed redly; the temperature of the place was almost unbearable. On the table the light from the silver lamp shed a patch of radiance, but the rest of the study was veiled in shadow.

A black-robed figure was seated in a high-backed, carved chair; one corner of the cowl-like garment was thrown across the table. Half rising, the figure turned—and, an evil apparition in the glow from the fire, Antony Ferrara faced the intruder.

Dr. Cairn walked forward, until he stood over the other.

"Uncover what you have on the table," he said succinctly.

Ferrara's strange eyes were uplifted to the speaker's with an expression in their depths which, in the Middle Ages, alone would have sent a man to the stake.

"Dr. Cairn—"

The husky voice had lost something of its suavity. "You heard my order!"

"Your *order!* Surely, Doctor, since I am in my own—"

"Uncover what you have on the table. Or must I do so for you!"

Antony Ferrara placed his hand upon the end of the black robe which lay across the table.

"Be careful, Dr. Cairn," he said evenly. "You—are taking risks."

Dr. Cairn suddenly leapt, seized the shielding hand in a sure grip and twisted Ferrara's arm behind him. Then, with a second rapid movement, he snatched away the robe. A faint smell—a smell of corruption, of ancient rottenness—arose on the super-heated air.

A square of faded linen lay on the table, figured with all but indecipherable Egyptian characters, and upon it, in rows which formed a definite geometrical design, were arranged a great number of little black insects.

Dr. Cairn released the hand which he held, and Ferrara sat quite still, looking straight before him.

"*Dermestes beetles!* from the skull of a mummy! You filthy, obscene beast!"

Ferrara spoke, with a calm suddenly regained:

"Is there anything obscene in the study of beetles?"

"My son saw these things here yesterday; and last night, and again tonight, you cast magnified doubles—glamours—of the horrible creatures into his rooms! By means which you know of, but which *I* know of, too, you sought to bring your thought-things down to the material plane."

"Dr. Cairn, my respect for you is great; but I fear that much study has made you mad."

Ferrara reached out his hand toward an ebony box; he was smiling.

"Don't dare to touch that box!"

He paused, glancing up.

"More orders, doctor?"

"Exactly."

Dr. Cairn grabbed the faded linen, scooping up the beetles within it, and, striding across the room, threw the whole unsavoury bundle into the heart of the fire. A great flame leapt up; there came a series of squeaky explosions, so that, almost, one might have imagined those age-old insects to have had life. Then the doctor turned again.

Ferrara leapt to his feet with a cry that had in it something inhuman, and began rapidly to babble in a tongue that was not European. He was facing Dr. Cairn, a tall, sinister figure, but one hand was groping behind him for the box.

"Stop that!" rapped the doctor imperatively—"and for the last time do not dare to touch that box!"

The flood of strange words was dammed. Ferrara stood quivering, but silent.

"The laws by which such as you were burnt—the wise laws of long ago—are no more," said Dr. Cairn. "English law cannot touch you, but God has provided for your kind!"

"Perhaps," whispered Ferrara, "you would like also to burn this box to which you object so strongly?"

"No power on earth would prevail upon me to touch it! But you—you *have* touched it—and you know the penalty! You raise forces of evil that have lain dormant for ages and dare to wield them. Beware! I know of some whom you have murdered; I cannot know how many you have sent to the madhouse. But I swear that in future your victims shall be few. There is a way to deal with you!"

He turned and walked to the door.

"Beware also, dear Dr. Cairn," came softly. "As you say, I raise forces of evil—"

Dr. Cairn spun about. In three strides he was standing over Antony Ferrara, fists clenched and his sinewy body tense in every fibre. His face was pale, as was apparent even in that vague light, and his eyes gleamed like steel.

"You raise other forces," he said—and his voice, though steady was very low; "evil forces, also."

Antony Ferrara, invoker of nameless horrors, shrank before him—before the primitive Celtic man whom unwittingly he had invoked. Dr. Cairn was spare and lean, but in perfect physical condition. Now he was strong, with the strength of a just cause. Moreover, he was dangerous, and Ferrara knew it well.

"I fear—" began the latter huskily.

"Dare to bandy words with me," said Dr. Cairn, with icy coolness, "answer me back but once again, and before God I'll strike you dead!"

Ferrara sat silent, clutching at the arms of his chair, and not daring to raise his eyes. For ten magnetic seconds they stayed so, then again Dr. Cairn turned, and this time walked out.

The clocks had been chiming the quarter after eleven as he had entered Antony Ferrara's chambers, and some had not finished their chimes when his son, choking, calling wildly upon Heaven to aid him, had fallen in the midst of crowding, obscene things, and, in the instant of his fall, had found the room clear of the waving antennae, the beady eyes, and the beetle shapes. The whole horrible phantasmagoria—together with the odour of ancient rottenness—faded like a fevered dream at the moment that Dr. Cairn had burst in upon the creator of it.

Robert Cairn stood up, weakly, trembling; then dropped upon his knees and sobbed out prayers of thankfulness that came from his frightened soul.


## CHAPTER VII
### SIR ELWIN GROVES'S PATIENT

When a substantial legacy is divided into two shares, one of which falls to a man, young, dissolute, and clever, and the other to a girl, pretty and inexperienced, there is laughter in the hells. But to the girl's legacy add another item—a strong, stern guardian, and the issue becomes one less easy to predict.

In the case at present under consideration, such an arrangement led Dr. Bruce Cairn to pack off Myra Duquesne to a grim Scottish manor in Inverness upon a visit of indefinite duration. It also led to heart burnings on the part of Robert Cairn, and to other things about to be noticed.

Antony Ferrara, the co-legatee, was not slow to recognize that a damaging stroke had been played, but he knew Dr. Cairn too well to put up any protest. In his capacity of fashionable physician, the doctor frequently met Ferrara in society, for a man at once rich, handsome, and bearing a fine name, is not socially ostracized on the mere suspicion that he is a dangerous blackguard. Thus Antony Ferrara was courted by the smartest women in town and tolerated by the men. Dr. Cairn would always acknowledge him, and then turn his back upon the dark-eyed, adopted son of his dearest friend.

There was that between the two of which the world knew nothing. Had the world known what Dr. Cairn knew respecting Antony Ferrara, then, despite his winning manner, his wealth, and his station, every door in London, from those of Mayfair to that of the foulest den in Limehouse, would have been closed to him—closed, and barred with horror and loathing. A tremendous secret was locked up within the heart of Dr. Bruce Cairn.

Sometimes we seem to be granted a glimpse of the guiding Hand that steers men's destinies; then, as comprehension is about to dawn, we lose again our temporal lucidity of vision. The following incident illustrates this.

Sir Elwin Groves, of Harley Street, took Dr. Cairn aside at the club one evening.

"I am passing a patient on to you, Cairn," he said; "Lord Lashmore."

"Ah!" replied Cairn thoughtfully. "I have never met him."

"He has only quite recently returned to England—you may have heard?—and brought a South American Lady Lashmore with him."

"I had heard that, yes."

"Lord Lashmore is close upon fifty-five, and his wife—a passionate Southern type—is probably less than twenty. They are an odd couple. The lady has been doing some extensive entertaining at the town house."

Groves stared hard at Dr. Cairn.

"Your young friend, Antony Ferrara, is a regular visitor."

"No doubt," said Cairn, "he goes everywhere. I don't know how long his funds will last."

"I have wondered, too. His chambers are like a scene from the 'Arabian Nights.'"

"How do you know?" inquired the other curiously. "Have you attended him?"

"Yes," was the reply. "His Eastern servant 'phoned for me one night last week; and I found Ferrara lying unconscious in a room like a pasha's harem. He looked simply ghastly, but the man would give me no account of what had caused the attack. It looked to me like sheer nervous exhaustion. He gave me quite an anxious five minutes. Incidentally, the room was blazing hot, with a fire roaring right up the chimney, and it smelt like a Hindu temple."

"Ah!" muttered Cairn, "between his mode of life and his peculiar studies he will probably crack up. He has a fragile constitution."

"Who the deuce is he, Cairn ?" pursued Sir Elwin. "You must know all the circumstances of his adoption; you were with the late Sir Michael in Egypt at the time. The fellow is a mystery to me; he repels, in some way. I was glad to get away from his rooms."

"You were going to tell me something about Lord Lashmore's case, I think ?" said Cairn.

Sir Elwin Groves screwed up his eyes and readjusted his pince-nez, for the deliberate way in which his companion had changed the conversation was unmistakable. However, Cairn's brusque manners were proverbial, and Sir Elwin accepted the lead.

"Yes, yes, I believe I was," he agreed, rather lamely. "Well, it's very singular. I was called there last Monday, at about two o'clock in the morning. I found the house upside-down, and Lady Lashmore, with a dressing-gown thrown over her nightdress, engaged in bathing a bad wound in her husband's throat."

"What! Attempted suicide?"

"My first idea, naturally. But a glance at the wound set me wondering. It was bleeding profusely, and from its location I was afraid that it might have penetrated the internal jugular; but the external only was wounded. I arrested the flow of blood and made the patient comfortable. Lady Lashmore assisted me coolly and displayed some skill as a nurse. In fact, she had applied a ligature before my arrival."

"Lord Lashmore remained conscious?"

"Quite. He was shaky, of course. I called again at nine o'clock that morning, and found him progressing favourably. When I had dressed the wounds—"

"Wounds?"

"There were two actually; I will tell you in a moment. I asked Lord Lashmore for an explanation. He had given out, for the benefit of the household, that, stumbling out of bed in the dark, he had tripped upon a rug, so that he fell forward almost into the fireplace. There is a rather ornate fender, with an elaborate copper scrollwork design, and his account was that he came down with all his weight upon this, in such a way that part of the copperwork pierced his throat. It was possible, just possible, Cairn; but it didn't satisfy me, and I could see that it didn't satisfy Lady Lashmore. However, when we were alone, Lashmore told me the real facts."

"He had been concealing the truth?"

"Largely for his wife's sake, I fancy. He was anxious to spare her the alarm which, knowing the truth, she must have experienced. His story was this—related in confidence, but he wishes that you should know. He was awakened by a sudden, sharp pain in the throat; not very acute, but accompanied by a feeling of pressure. It was gone again, in a moment, and he was surprised to find blood upon his hands when he felt for the cause of the pain.

"He got out of bed and experienced a great dizziness. The hemorrhage was altogether more severe than he had supposed. Not wishing to arouse his wife, he did not enter his dressing-room, which is situated between his own room and Lady Lashmore's; he staggered as far as the bell-push, and then collapsed. His man found him on the floor—sufficiently near to the fender to lend colour to the story of the accident."

Dr. Cairn coughed drily.

"Do you think it was attempted suicide after all, then?" he asked.

"No—I don't," replied Sir Elwin emphatically. "I think it was something altogether more difficult to explain."

"Not attempted murder?"

"Almost impossible. Excepting Chambers, Lord Lashmore's valet, no one could possibly have gained access to that suite of rooms. They number four. There is a small boudoir, out of which opens Lady Lashmore's bedroom; between this and Lord Lashmore's apartment is the dressing-room. Lord Lashmore's door was locked and so was that of the boudoir. These are the only two means of entrance."

"But you said that Chambers came in and found him."

"Chambers has a key of Lord Lashmore's door. That is why I said 'excepting Chambers.' But Chambers has been with his present master since Lashmore left Cambridge. It's out of the question."

"Windows?"

"First floor, no balcony, and overlook Hyde Park."

"Is there no clue to the mystery?"

"There are three!"

"What are they?"

"First: the nature of the wounds. Second: Lord Lashmore's idea that something was in the room at the moment of his awakening. Third: the fact that an identical attempt was made upon him last night!"

"Last night! Good God! With what result?"

"The former wounds, though deep, are very tiny, and had quite healed over. One of them partially re-opened, but Lord Lashmore awoke altogether more readily and before any damage had been done. He says that some soft body rolled off the bed. He uttered a loud cry, leapt out, and switched on the electric lights. At the same moment he heard a frightful scream from his wife's room. When I arrived—Lashmore himself summoned me on this occasion—I had a new patient."

"Lady Lashmore?"

"Exactly. She had fainted from fright, at hearing her husband's cry, I assume. There had been a slight hemorrhage from the throat, too."

"What! Tuberculous?"

"I fear so. Fright would not produce hemorrhage in the case of a healthy subject, would it?"

Dr. Cairn shook his head. He was obviously perplexed.

"And Lord Lashmore?" he asked.

"The marks were there again," replied Sir Elwin; "rather low on the neck. But they were quite superficial. He had awakened in time and had struck out—hitting something."

"What?"

"Some living thing; apparently covered with long, silky hair. It escaped, however."

"And now," said Dr. Cairn—"these wounds; what are they like ?"

"They are like the marks of fangs," replied Sir Elwin; "of two long, sharp fangs!"


## CHAPTER VIII
## THE SECRET OF DHOON

Lord Lashmore was a big blond man, fresh coloured and having his nearly white hair worn close cut and his moustache trimmed in the neat military fashion. For a fair man, he had eyes of a singular colour. They were of so dark a shade of brown as to appear black: southern eyes; lending to his personality an oddness very striking.

When he was shown into Dr. Cairn's library, the doctor regarded him with that searching scrutiny peculiar to men of his profession, at the same time inviting the visitor to be seated.

Lashmore sat down in the red leathern armchair, resting his large hands upon his knees, with the fingers widely spread. He had a massive dignity, but was not entirely at his ease.

Dr. Cairn opened the conversation, in his direct fashion.

"You come to consult me, Lord Lashmore, in my capacity of occultist rather than in that of physician?"

"In both," replied Lord Lashmore; "distinctly, in both."

"Sir Elwin Groves is attending you for certain throat wounds—"

Lord Lashmore touched the high stock which he was wearing.

"The scars remain," he said. "Do you wish to see them?"

"I am afraid I must trouble you."

The stock was untied; and Dr. Cairn, through a powerful glass, examined the marks. One of them, the lower, was slightly inflamed.

Lord Lashmore retied his stock, standing before the small mirror set in the overmantel.

"You had an impression of some presence in the room at the time of the outrage?" pursued the doctor.

"Distinctly; on both occasions."

"Did you see anything?"

"The room was too dark."

"But you felt something?"

"Hair; my knuckles, as I struck out—I am speaking of the second out-rage—encountered a thick mass of hair."

"The body of some animal?"

"Probably the head."

"But still you saw nothing?"

"I must confess that I had a vague idea of some shape flitting away across the room; a white shape—therefore probably a figment of my imagination."

"Your cry awakened Lady Lashmore?"

"Unfortunately, yes. Her nerves were badly shaken already, and this second shock proved too severe. Sir Elwin fears chest trouble. I am taking her abroad as soon as possible."

"She was found insensible. Where?"

"At the door of the dressing-room—the door communicating with her own room, not that communicating with mine. She had evidently started to come to my assistance when faintness overcame her."

"What is her own account?"

"That is her own account."

"Who discovered her?"

"I did."

Dr. Cairn was drumming his fingers on the table. "You have a theory, Lord Lashmore," he said suddenly. "Let me hear it."

Lord Lashmore started, and glared across at the speaker with a sort of haughty surprise.

"*I* have a theory?"

"I think so. Am I wrong?"

Lashmore stood on the rug before the fireplace, with his hands locked behind him and his head lowered, looking out under his tufted eyebrows at Dr. Cairn. Thus seen, Lord Lashmore's strange eyes had a sinister appearance.

"If I had had a theory—" he began.

"You would have come to me to seek confirmation?" suggested Dr. Cairn.

"Ah! yes, you may be right. Sir Elwin Groves, to whom I hinted something, mentioned your name. I am not quite clear upon one point, Dr. Cairn. Did he send me to you because he thought—in a word, are you a mental specialist?"

"I am not. Sir Elwin has no doubts respecting your brain, Lord Lashmore. He has sent you here because I have made some study of what I may term physical ailments. There is a chapter in your family history"—he fixed his searching gaze upon the other's face—"which latterly has been occupying your mind?"

At that, Lashmore started in good earnest.

"To what do you refer?"

"Lord Lashmore, you have come to me for advice. A rare ailment—happily very rare in England—has assailed you. Circumstances have been in your favour thus far, but a recurrence is to be anticipated at any time. Be good enough to look upon me as a specialist, and give me all your confidence."

Lashmore cleared his throat.

"What do you wish to know, Dr. Cairn?" he asked, with a queer intermingling of respect and hauteur in his tones.

"I wish to know about Mirza, wife of the third Baron Lashmore."

Lord Lashmore took a stride forward. His large hands clenched, and his eyes were blazing.

"What do you know about her?"

Surprise was in his voice, and anger.

"I have seen her portrait in Dhoon Castle; you were not in residence at the time. Mirza, Lady Lashmore, was evidently a very beautiful woman. What was the date of the marriage?"

"1615."

"The third Baron brought her to England from—?"

"Poland."

"She was a Pole?"

"A Polish Jewess."

"There was no issue of the marriage, but the Baron outlived her and married again?"

Lord Lashmore shifted his feet nervously, and gnawed his finger-nails.

"There was issue of the marriage," he snapped. "She was—my ancestress."

"Ah!" Dr. Cairn's gray eyes lighted up momentarily. "We get to the facts! Why was this birth kept secret?"

"Dhoon Castle has kept many secrets!" It was a grim noble of the Middle Ages who was speaking. "For a Lashmore, there was no difficulty in suppressing the facts, arranging a hasty second marriage and representing the boy as the child of the later union. Had the second marriage proved fruitful, this had been unnecessary; but an heir to Dhoon was—

essential."

"I see. Had the second marriage proved fruitful, the child of Mirza would have been—what shall we say? —smothered?"

"Damn it! What do you mean?"

"He was the rightful heir."

"Dr. Cairn," said Lashmore slowly, "you are probing an open wound. The fourth Baron Lashmore represents what the world calls 'The Curse of the House of Dhoon.' At Dhoon Castle there is a secret chamber, which has engaged the pens of many so-called occultists, but which no man, save every heir, has entered for generations. Its very location is a secret. Measurements do not avail to find it. You would appear to know much of my family's black secret; perhaps you know where that room lies at Dhoon?"

"Certainly, I do," replied Dr. Cairn calmly; "it is under the moat, some thirty yards west of the former drawbridge."

Lord Lashmore changed colour. When he spoke again his voice had lost its timbre.

"Perhaps you know—what it contains."

"I do. It contains Paul, fourth Baron Lashmore, son of Mirza, the Polish Jewess!"

Lord Lashmore reseated himself in the big armchair, staring at the speaker, aghast.

"I thought no other in the world knew that!" he said hollowly. "Your studies have been extensive indeed. For three years—three whole years from the night of my twenty-first birthday—the horror hung over me, Dr. Cairn. It ultimately brought my grandfather to the madhouse, but my father was of sterner stuff, and so, it seems, was I. After those three years of horror I threw off the memories of Paul Dhoon, the fourth baron—"

"It was on the night of your twenty-first birthday that you were admitted to the subterranean room?"

"You know so much, Dr. Cairn, that you may as well know all." Lashmore's face was twitching. "But you are about to hear what no man has ever heard from the lips of one of my family before."

He stood up again, restlessly.

"Nearly thirty-five years have elapsed," he resumed, "since that December night; but my very soul trembles now, when I recall it! There was a big house-party at Dhoon, but I had been prepared, for some weeks, by my father, for the ordeal that awaited me. Our family mystery is historical, and there were many fearful glances bestowed upon me, when, at midnight, my father took me aside from the company and led me to the old library. My God! Dr. Cairn—fearful as these reminiscences are, it is a relief to relate them—to *someone!*"

A sort of suppressed excitement was upon Lashmore, but his voice remained low and hollow.

"He asked me," he continued, "the traditional question: if I had prayed for strength. God knows I had! Then, his stern face very pale, he locked the library door, and from a closet concealed beside the ancient fireplace—a closet which, hitherto, I had not known to exist—he took out a bulky key of antique workmanship. Together we set to work to remove all the volumes from one of the bookshelves.

"Even when the shelves were empty, it called for our united efforts to move the heavy piece of furniture; but we accomplished the task ultimately, making visible a considerable expanse of panelling. Nearly forty years had elapsed since that case had been removed, and the carvings which it concealed were coated with all the dust which had accumulated there since the night of my father's coming of age.

"A device upon the top of the centre panel represented the arms of the family; the helm which formed part of the device projected like a knob. My father grasped it, turned it, and threw his weight against the seemingly solid wall. It yielded, swinging inward upon concealed hinges, and a damp, earthy smell came out into the library. Taking up a lamp, which he had in readiness, my father entered the cavity, beckoning me to follow.

"I found myself descending a flight of rough steps, and the roof above me was so low that I was compelled to stoop. A corner was come to, passed, and a further flight of steps appeared beneath. At that time the old moat was still flooded, and even had I not divined as much from the direction of the steps, I should have known, at this point, that we were beneath it. Between the stone blocks roofing us in oozed drops of moisture, and the air was at once damp and icily cold.

"A short passage, commencing at the foot of the steps, terminated before a massive, iron-studded door. My father placed the key in the lock, and holding the lamp above his head, turned and looked at me. He was deathly pale.

"'Summon all your fortitude,' he said.

"He strove to turn the key, but for a long time without success for the lock was rusty. Finally, however—he was a strong man—his efforts were successful. The door opened, and an indescribable smell came out into the passage. Never before had I met with anything like it; I have never met with it since."

Lord Lashmore wiped his brow with his handkerchief.

"The first thing," he resumed, "upon which the lamplight shone, was what appeared to be a blood-stain spreading almost entirely over one wall of the cell which I perceived before me. I have learnt since that this was a species of fungus, not altogether uncommon, but at the time, and in that situation, it shocked me inexpressibly.

"But let me hasten to that which we were come to see—let me finish my story as quickly as may be. My father halted at the entrance to this frightful cell; his hand, with which he held the lamp above his head, was not steady; and over his shoulder I looked into the place and saw... *him.*

"Dr. Cairn, for three years, night and day, that spectacle haunted me; for three years, night and day, I seemed to have before my eyes the dreadful face—the bearded, grinning face of Paul Dhoon. He lay there upon the floor of the dungeon, his fists clenched and his knees drawn up as if in agony. He had laid there for generations; yet, as God is my witness, there was flesh on his bones.

"Yellow and seared it was, and his joints protruded through it, but his features were yet recognizable—horribly, dreadfully recognizable. His black hair was like a mane, long and matted, his eyebrows were incredibly heavy, and his lashes overhung his cheekbones. The nails of his fingers... no! I will spare you! But his teeth, his ivory gleaming teeth— with the two wolf-fangs fully revealed by that death-grin!...

"An aspen stake was driven through his breast, pinning him to the earthen floor, and there he lay in the agonizing attitude of one who had died by such awful means. Yet—that stake was not driven through his unhallowed body until a whole year after his death!

"How I regained the library I do not remember. I was unable to rejoin the guests, unable to face my fellow-men for days afterward. Dr. Cairn, for three years I feared—feared the world—feared sleep—feared myself above all; for I knew that I had in my veins the blood of a *vampire!*"


CHAPTER IX

THE POLISH JEWESS

There was a silence of some minutes' duration. Lord Lashmore sat staring straight before him, his fists clenched upon his knees. Then: "It was after death that the fourth baron developed—certain qualities?" inquired Dr. Cairn.

"There were six cases of death in the district within twelve months," replied Lashmore. "The gruesome cry of 'vampire' ran through the community. The fifth baron—son of Paul Dhoon—turned a deaf ear to these reports, until the mother of a child—a child who had died—traced a man, or the semblance of a man, to the gate of the Dhoon family vault. By night, secretly, the son of Paul Dhoon visited the vault, and found...

"The body, which despite twelve months in the tomb, looked as it had looked in life, was carried to the dungeon—in the Middle Ages a torture-room; no cry uttered there can reach the outer world—and was submitted to the ancient process for slaying a vampire. From that hour no supernatural visitant has troubled the district; but—"

"But," said Dr. Cairn quietly, "the strain came from Mirza, the sorceress. What of her?"

Lord Lashmore's eyes shone feverishly.

"How do you know that she was a sorceress?" he asked, hoarsely. "These are family secrets."

"They will remain so," Dr. Cairn answered. "But my studies have gone far, and I know that Mirza, wife of the third Baron Lashmore, practised the Black Art in life, and became after death a ghoul. Her husband surprised her in certain detestable magical operations and struck her head off. He had suspected her for some considerable time, and had not only kept secret the birth of her son but had secluded the child from the mother. No heir resulting from his second marriage, however, the son of Mirza became Baron Lashmore, and after death became what his mother had been before him.

"Lord Lashmore, the curse of the house of Dhoon will prevail until the Polish Jewess who originated it has been treated as her son was treated!"

"Dr. Cairn, it is not known where her husband had her body concealed. He died without revealing the secret. Do you mean that the taint, the devil's taint, may recur— Oh, my God! do you want to drive me mad?"

"I do not mean that after so many generations which have been free from it, the vampirism will arise again in your blood; but I mean that the spirit, the unclean, awful spirit of that vampire woman, is still earthbound. The son was freed, and with him went the hereditary taint, it seems; but the mother was not freed! Her body was decapitated, but her vampire soul cannot go upon its appointed course until the ancient ceremonial has been performed!"

Lord Lashmore passed his hand across his eyes. "You daze me, Dr. Cairn. In brief, what do you mean?"

"I mean that the spirit of Mirza is to this day loose upon the world, and is forced, by a deathless, unnatural longing, to seek incarnation in a human body. It is such awful pariahs as this, Lord Lashmore, that constitute the danger of so-called spiritualism. Given suitable conditions, such a spirit might gain control of a human being."

"Do you suggest that the spirit of the second lady—"

"It is distinctly possible that she haunts her descendants. I seem to remember a tradition of Dhoon Castle, to the effect that births and deaths are heralded by a woman's mocking laughter?"

"I, myself, heard it on the night—I became Lord Lashmore."

"That is the spirit who was known, in life, as Mirza, Lady Lashmore!"

"But—"

"It is possible to gain control of such a being."

"By what means?"

"By unhallowed means; yet there are those who do not hesitate to employ them. The danger of such an operation is, of course, enormous."

"I perceive, Dr. Cairn, that a theory, covering the facts of my recent experiences, is forming in your mind."

"That is so. In order that I may obtain corroborative evidence, I should like to call at your place this evening. Suppose I come ostensibly to see Lady Lashmore?"

Lord Lashmore was watching the speaker.

"There is someone in my household whose suspicions you do not wish to arouse?" he suggested.

"There is. Shall we make it nine o'clock?"

"Why not come to dinner?"

"Thanks all the same, but I think it would serve my purpose better if I came later."


Dr. Cairn and his son dined alone together in Half-Moon Street that night.

"I saw Antony Ferrara in Regent Street to-day," said Robert Cairn. "I was glad to see him."

Dr. Cairn raised his heavy brows.

"Why?" he asked.

"Well, I was half afraid that he might have left London."

"Paid a visit to Myra Duquesne in Inverness?"

"It would not have surprised me."

"Nor would it have surprised me, Rob, but I think he is stalking other game at present."

Robert Cairn looked up quickly.

"Lady Lashmore—" he began.

"Well?" prompted his father.

"One of the Paul Pry brigade who fatten on scandal sent a veiled paragraph in to us at *The Planet* yesterday, linking Ferrara's name with Lady Lashmore's. Of course we didn't use it; he had come to the wrong market; but—Ferrara was with Lady Lashmore when I met him to-day."

"What of that?"

"It is not necessarily significant, of course: Lord Lashmore in all probability will outlive Ferrara, who looked even more pallid than usual."

"You regard him as an utterly unscrupulous fortune-hunter?"

"Certainly."

"Did Lady Lashmore appear to be in good health?"

"Perfectly."

"Ah!"

A silence fell, of some considerable duration, then:

"Antony Ferrara is a menace to society," said Robert Cairn. "When I meet the reptilian glance of those black eyes of his and reflect upon what the man has attempted—what he has done—my blood boils. It is tragically funny to think that in our new wisdom we have abolished the only laws that could have touched him! He could not have existed in Ancient Chaldea, and would probably have been burnt at the stake even under Charles II; but in this wise twentieth century he dallies in Regent Street with a prominent society beauty and laughs in the face of a man whom he has attempted to destroy!"

"Be very wary," warned Dr. Cairn. "Remember that if you died mysteriously to-morrow, Ferrara would be legally immune. We must wait, and watch. Can you return here to-night, at about ten o'clock?"

"I think I can manage to do so—yes."

"I shall expect you. Have you brought up to date your record of those events which we know of, together with my notes and explanations?"

"Yes, sir, I spent last evening upon the notes."

"There may be something to add. This record, Rob, one day will be a weapon to destroy an unnatural enemy. I will sign two copies to-night and lodge one at my bank."


## CHAPTER X
## THE LAUGHTER


Lady Lashmore proved to be far more beautiful than Dr. Cairn had anticipated. She was a true brunette with a superb figure and eyes like the darkest passion flowers. Her creamy skin had a golden quality, as though it had absorbed within its velvet texture something of the sunshine of the South.

She greeted Dr. Cairn without cordiality.

"I am delighted to find you looking so well, Lady Lashmore," said the doctor. "Your appearance quite confirms my opinion."

"Your opinion of what, Dr. Cairn?"

"Of the nature of your recent seizure. Sir Elwin Groves invited my opinion and I gave it."

Lady Lashmore paled perceptibly.

"Lord Lashmore, I know," she said, "was greatly concerned, but indeed it was nothing serious—"

"I quite agree. It was due to nervous excitement."

Lady Lashmore held a fan before her face.

"There have been recent happenings," she said—"as no doubt you are aware—which must have shaken any one's nerves. Of course, I am familiar with your reputation, Dr. Cairn, as a psychical specialist—"

"Pardon me, but from whom have you learnt of it?"

"From Mr. Ferrara," she answered simply. "He has assured me that you are the greatest living authority upon such matters."

Dr. Cairn turned his head aside.

"Ah!" he said grimly.

"And I want to ask you a question," continued Lady Lashmore. "Have you any idea, any idea at all, respecting the cause of the wounds upon my husband's throat? Do you think them due to—something supernatural?"

Her voice shook, and her slight foreign accent became more marked.

"Nothing is supernatural," replied Dr. Cairn; "but I think they are due to something supernormal. I would suggest that possibly you have suffered from evil dreams recently?"

Lady Lashmore started wildly, and her eyes opened with a sort of sudden horror.

"How can you know?" she whispered. "How can you know! Oh, Dr. Cairn!" She laid her hand upon his arm—"if you can prevent those dreams; if you can assure me that I shall never dream them again—!"

It was a plea and a confession. This was what had lain behind her coldness—this horror which she had not dared to confide in another.

"Tell me," he said gently. "You have dreamt these dreams twice?"

She nodded, wide-eyed with wonder for his knowledge.

"On the occasions of your husband's illnesses?"

"Yes, yes!"

"What did you dream?"

"Oh! can I, dare I tell you!"

"You must."

There was pity in his voice.

"I dreamt that I lay in some very dark cavern. I could hear the sea booming, apparently over my head. But above all the noise a voice was audible, calling to me—not by name; I cannot explain in what way; but calling, calling imperatively. I seemed to be clothed but scantily, in some kind of ragged garments; and upon my knees I crawled toward the voice, through a place where there were other living things that crawled also— things with many legs and clammy bodies..."

She shuddered and choked down an hysterical sob that was half a laugh.

"My hair hung dishevelled about me and in some Inexplicable way— oh! am I going mad!—my head seemed to be detached from my living body! I was ailed with a kind of unholy anger which I cannot describe. Also, I was consumed with thirst, and this thirst—"

"I think I understand," said Dr. Cairn quietly. "What followed?"

"An interval—quite blank—after which I dreamt again. Dr. Cairn, I *cannot* tell you of the dreadful, the blasphemous and foul thoughts that then possessed me! I found myself resisting—resisting— something, some Power that was dragging me back to that foul cavern with my thirst unslaked! I was frenzied; I dare not name, I tremble to think, of the ideas which filled my mind. Then, again came a blank, and I awoke."

She sat trembling. Dr. Cairn noted that she avoided his gaze.

"You awoke," he said, "on the first occasion, to find that your husband had met with a strange and dangerous accident?"

"There was—something else."

Lady Lashmore's voice had become a tremulous whisper.

"Tell me; don't be afraid."

She looked up; her magnificent eyes were wild with horror.

"I believe you know!" she breathed. "Do you?"

Dr. Cairn nodded.

"And on the second occasion," he said, "you awoke earlier?"

Lady Lashmore slightly moved her head.

"The dream was identical?"

"Yes."

"Excepting these two occasions, you never dreamt it before?"

"I dreamt part of it on several other occasions; or only remembered part of it on waking."

"Which part?"

"The first; that awful cavern."

"And now, Lady Lashmore—you have recently been present at a spiritualistic *séance*."

She was past wondering at his power of inductive reasoning and merely nodded.

"I suggest—I do not know—that the *séance* was held under the auspices of Mr. Antony Ferrara, ostensibly for amusement."

Another affirmative nod answered him.

"You prove to be mediumistic?"

It was admitted.

"And now, Lady Lashmore"—Dr. Cairn's face was very stern—"I will trouble you no further." He prepared to depart; when—

"Dr. Cairn!" whispered Lady Lashmore, tremulously, "some dreadful thing, something that I cannot comprehend but that I fear and loathe with all my soul, has come to me. Oh—for pity's sake, give me a word of hope! Save for you, I am alone with a horror I cannot name. Tell me—"

At the door he turned.

"Be brave," he said—and went out.

Lady Lashmore sat still as one who had looked upon Gorgon, her beautiful eyes yet widely opened and her face pale as death; for he had not even told her to hope.


Robert Cairn was sitting smoking in the library, a bunch of notes before him, when Dr. Cairn returned to Half-Moon Street. His face, habitually fresh coloured, was so pale that his son leapt up in alarm. But Dr. Cairn waved him away with a characteristic gesture of the hand.

"Sit down, Rob," he said, quietly; "I shall be all right in a moment. But I have just left a woman—a young woman and a beautiful woman— whom a fiend of hell has condemned to that which my mind refuses to contemplate."

Robert Cairn sat down again, watching his father.

"Make out a report of the following facts," continued the latter, beginning to pace up and down the room.

He recounted all that he had learnt of the history of the house of Dhoon and all that he had learnt of recent happenings from Lord and Lady Lashmore. His son wrote rapidly.

"And now," said the doctor, "for our conclusions. Mirza, the Polish Jewess, who became Lady Lashmore in 1615, practised sorcery in life and became, after death, a ghoul—one who sustained an unholy existence by unholy means—a vampire."

"But, sir! Surely that is but a horrible superstition of the Middle Ages!"

"Rob, I could take you to a castle not ten miles from Cracow in Poland where there are—certain relics, which would forever settle your doubts respecting the existence of vampires. Let us proceed. The son of Mirza, Paul Dhoon, inherited the dreadful proclivities of his mother, but his shadowy existence was cut short in the traditional, and effective, manner. Him we may neglect.

"It is Mirza, the sorceress, who must engage our attention. She was decapitated by her husband. This punishment prevented her, in the unhallowed life which, for such as she, begins after ordinary decease, from practising the horrible rites of a vampire. Her headless body could not serve her as a vehicle for nocturnal wanderings, but the evil spirit of the woman might hope to gain control of some body more suitable.

"Nurturing an implacable hatred against all of the house of Dhoon, that spirit, disembodied, would frequently be drawn to the neighbourhood of Mirza's descendants, both by hatred and by affinity. Two horrible desires of the Spirit Mirza would be gratified if a Dhoon could be made her victim—the desire for blood and the desire for vengeance! The fate of Lord Lashmore would be sealed if that spirit could secure incarnation!"

Dr. Cairn paused, glancing at his son, who was writing at furious speed. Then—

"A magician more mighty and more evil than Mirza ever was or could be," he continued, "a master of the Black Art, expelled a woman's spirit from its throne and temporarily installed in its place the blood-lustful spirit of Mirza!"

"My God, sir!" cried Robert Cairn, and threw down his pencil. "I begin to understand!"

"Lady Lashmore," said Dr. Cairn, "since she was weak enough to consent to be present at a certain séance has, from time to time, been possessed; she has been *possessed* by the spirit of a vampire! Obedient to the nameless cravings of that control, she has sought out Lord Lashmore, the last of the house of Dhoon. The horrible attack made, a mighty will which, throughout her temporary incarnation, has held her like a hound in leash, has dragged her from her prey, has forced her to remove, from the garments clothing her borrowed body, all traces of the deed, and has cast her out again to the pit of abomination where her headless trunk was thrown by the third Baron Lashmore!

"Lady Lashmore's brain retains certain memories. They have been received at the moment when possession has taken place and at the moment when the control has been cast out again. They thus are memories of some secret cavern near Dhoon Castle, where that headless but deathless body lies, and memories of the poignant moment when the vampire has been dragged back, her 'thirst unslaked,' by the ruling Will."

"Merciful God!" muttered Robert Cairn, "Merciful God, can such things be!"

"They can be—they are! Two ways have occurred to me of dealing with the matter," continued Dr. Cairn quietly. "One is to find that cavern and to kill, in the occult sense, by means of a stake, the vampire who lies there; the other which, I confess, might only result in the permanent 'possession' of Lady Lashmore—is to get at the power which controls this disembodied spirit—kill Antony Ferrara!"

Robert Cairn went to the sideboard, and poured out brandy with a shaking hand.

"What's his object?" he whispered.

Dr. Cairn shrugged his shoulders.

"Lady Lashmore would be the wealthiest widow in society," he replied.

"*He* will know now," continued the younger man unsteadily, "that you are up against him. Have you—"

"I have told Lord Lashmore to lock, at night, not only his outer door but also that of his dressing-room. For the rest"—he dropped into an easy-chair—"I cannot face the facts, I—"

The telephone bell rang.

Dr. Cairn came to his feet as though he had been electrified; and as he raised the receiver to his ear, his son knew, by the expression on his face, from where the message came and something of its purport.

"Come with me," was all that he said when he had replaced the instrument on the table.

They went out together. It was already past midnight, but a cab was found at the corner of Half-Moon Street, and within the space of five minutes they were at Lord Lashmore's house.

Excepting Chambers, Lord Lashmore's valet, no servants were to be seen.

"They ran away, sir, out of the house," explained the man, huskily, "when it happened."

Dr. Cairn delayed for no further questions, but raced upstairs, his son close behind him. Together they burst into Lord Lashmore's bedroom. But just within the door they both stopped, aghast.

Sitting bolt upright in bed was Lord Lashmore, his face a dingy gray and his open eyes, though filming over, yet faintly alight with a stark horror... dead. An electric torch was still gripped in his left hand.

Bending over someone who lay upon the carpet near the bedside they perceived Sir Elwin Groves. He looked up. Some little of his usual self-possession had fled.

"Ah, Cairn!" he jerked. "We've both come too late."

The prostrate figure was that of Lady Lashmore, a loose kimono worn over her night-robe. She was white and still and the physician had been engaged in bathing a huge bruise upon her temple.

"She'll be all right," said Sir Elwin; "she has sustained a tremendous blow, as you see. But Lord Lashmore—"

Dr. Cairn stepped closer to the dead man. "Heart," he said. "He died of sheer horror."

He turned to Chambers, who stood in the open doorway behind him.

"The dressing-room door is open," he said. "I had advised Lord Lashmore to lock it."

"Yes, sir; his lordship meant to, sir. But we found that the lock had been broken. It was to have been replaced to-morrow."

Dr. Cairn turned to his son.

"You hear?" he said. "No doubt you have some idea respecting which of the visitors to this unhappy house took the trouble to break that lock? It was to have been replaced to-morrow; hence the tragedy of to-night." He addressed Chambers again. "Why did the servants leave the house to-night?"

The man was shaking pitifully.

"It was the laughter, sir! the laughter! I can never forget it! I was sleeping in an adjoining room and I had the key of his lordship's door in case of need. But when I heard his lordship cry out—quick and loud, sir— like a man that's been stabbed—I jumped up to come to him. Then, as I was turning the door-knob—of my room, sir—someone, something, began to *laugh!* It was in here; it was in here, gentlemen! It wasn't—her ladyship; it wasn't like *any* woman. I can't describe it; but it woke up every soul in the house."

"When you came in?"

"I daren't come in, sir! I ran downstairs and called up Sir Elwin Groves. Before he came, all the rest of the household huddled on their clothes and went away—"

"It was I who found him," interrupted Sir Elwin—"as you see him now; with Lady Lashmore where she lies. I have 'phoned for nurses."

"Ah!" said Dr. Cairn; "I shall come back, Groves, but I have a small matter to attend to."

He drew his son from the room. On the stair:

"You understand?" he said. "The spirit of Mirza came to him again, clothed in his wife's body. Lord Lashmore felt the teeth at his throat, awoke instantly and struck out. As he did so, he turned the torch upon her, and recognized—his wife! His heart completed the tragedy, and so— to the laughter of the sorceress—passed the last of the house of Dhoon."

The cab was waiting. Dr. Cairn gave an address in Piccadilly, and the two entered. As the cab moved off, the doctor took a revolver from his pocket, with some loose cartridges, charged the five chambers, and quietly replaced the weapon in his pocket again.

One of the big doors of the block of chambers was found to be ajar, and a porter proved to be yet in attendance.

"Mr. Ferrara?" began Dr. Cairn.

"You are five minutes too late, sir," said the man. "He left by motor at ten past twelve. He's gone abroad, sir."

## CHAPTER XI
## CAIRO

The exact manner in which mental stress will affect a man's physical health is often difficult to predict. Robert Cairn was in the pink of condition at the time that he left Oxford to take up his London appointment; but the tremendous nervous strain wrought upon him by this series of events wholly outside the radius of normal things had broken him up physically, where it might have left unscathed a more highly strung, though less physically vigorous man.

Those who have passed through a nerve storm such as this which had laid him low will know that convalescence seems like a welcome awakening from a dreadful dream. It was indeed in a state between awaking and dreaming that Robert Cairn took counsel with his father—the latter more pale than was his wont and somewhat anxious-eyed—and determined upon an Egyptian rest-cure.

"I have made it all right at the office, Rob," said Dr. Cairn. "In three weeks or so you will receive instructions at Cairo to write up a series of local articles. Until then, my boy, complete rest and—don't worry; above all, don't worry. You and I have passed through a saturnalia of horror, and you, less inured to horrors than I, have gone down. I don't wonder."

"Where is Antony Ferrara?"

Dr. Cairn shook his head and his eyes gleamed with a sudden anger. "For God's sake don't mention his name!" he said. "That topic is taboo, Rob. I may tell you, however, that he has left England."

In this unreal frame of mind, then, and as one but partly belonging to the world of things actual, Cairn found himself an invalid, who but yesterday had been a hale man; found himself shipped for Port Said; found himself entrained for Cairo, and with the awakening to the realities of life, an emerging from an ill-dream to lively interest in the novelties of

Egypt, found himself following the red-jerseyed Shepheard's porter along the corridor of the train and out on the platform.

A short drive through those singular streets where East meets West and mingles, in the sudden, violet dusk of lower Egypt, and he was amid the bustle of the popular hotel.

Sime was there, whom he had last seen at Oxford, Sime the phlegmatic. He apologized for not meeting the train, but explained that his duties had rendered it impossible. Sime was attached temporarily to an archeological expedition as medical man, and his athletic and somewhat bovine appearance contrasted oddly with the unhealthy gauntness of Cairn.

"I only got in from Wasta ten minutes ago, Cairn. You must come out to the camp when I return; the desert air will put you on your feet again in no time."

Sime was unemotional, but there was concern in his voice and in his glance, for the change in Cairn was very startling. Although he knew something, if but very little, of certain happenings in London—gruesome happenings centring around the man called Antony Ferrara—he avoided any reference to them at the moment.

Seated upon the terrace, Robert Cairn studied the busy life in the street below with all the interest of a new arrival in the capital of the Near East. More than ever, now, his illness and the things which had led up to it seemed to belong to a remote dream existence. Through the railings at his feet a hawker was thrusting fly-whisks, and imploring him in complicated English to purchase one. Vendors of beads, of fictitious "antiques," of sweetmeats, of what-not; fortunetellers—and all that chattering horde which some obscure process of gravitation seems to hurl against the terrace of Shepheard's, buzzed about him. Carriages and motor-cars, camels and donkeys mingled, in the Shâria Kâmel Pasha. Voices American, voices Anglo-Saxon, guttural German tones, and softly murmured Arabic merged into one indescribable chord of sound; but to Robert Cairn it was all unspeakably restful. He was quite contented to sit there sipping his whisky and soda, and smoking his pipe. Sheer idleness was good for him and exactly what he wanted, and idling amid that unique throng is idleness *de luxe*.

Sime watched him covertly, and saw that his face had acquired lines— lines which told of the fires through which he had passed. Something, it was evident—something horrible—had seared his mind. Considering the many indications of tremendous nervous disaster in Cairn, Sime wondered how near his companion had come to insanity, and concluded that he had stood upon the frontiers of that grim land of phantoms, and had only been plucked back in the eleventh hour.

Cairn glanced around with a smile, from the group of hawkers who solicited his attention upon the pavement below.

"This is a delightful scene," he said. "I could sit here for hours; but considering that it's some time after sunset it remains unusually hot, doesn't it?"

"Rather!" replied Sime. "They are expecting *Khamsîn*—the hot wind, you know. I was up the river a week ago and we struck it badly in Assouan. It grew as black as night and one couldn't breathe for sand. It's probably working down to Cairo."

"From your description I am not anxious to make the acquaintance of *Khamsîn!*"

Sime shook his head, knocking out his pipe into the ash-tray.

"This is a funny country," he said reflectively. "The most weird ideas prevail here to this day—ideas which properly belong to the Middle Ages. For instance"—he began to recharge the hot bowl—"it is not really time for *Khamsîn*, consequently the natives feel called upon to hunt up some explanation of its unexpected appearance. Their ideas on the subject are interesting, if idiotic. One of our Arabs (we are excavating in the Fayûm, you know) solemnly assured me yesterday that the hot wind had been caused by an Efreet, a sort of Arabian Nights' demon, who has arrived in Egypt!"

He laughed gruffly, but Cairn was staring at him with a curious expression. Sime continued:

"When I got to Cairo this evening I found news of the Efreet had preceded me. Honestly, Cairn, it is all over the town—the native town, I mean. All the shopkeepers in the Mûski are talking about it. If a puff of *Khamsîn* should come, I believe they would permanently shut up shop and hide in their cellars—if they have any! I am rather hazy on modern Egyptian architecture."

Cairn nodded his head absently.

"You laugh," he said, "but the active force of a superstition—what we call a superstition—is sometimes a terrible thing."

Sime stared.

"Eh!" The medical man had suddenly come uppermost; he recollected that this class of discussion was probably taboo.

"You may doubt the existence of Efreets," continued Cairn, "hut neither you nor I can doubt the creative power of thought. If a trained hypnotist, by sheer concentration, can persuade his subject that the latter sits upon the brink of a river fishing when actually he sits upon a platform in a lecture-room, what result should you expect from a concentration of thousands of native minds upon the idea that an Efreet is visiting

Egypt?"

Sime stared in a dull way peculiar to him.

"Rather a poser," he said. "I have a glimmer of a notion what you mean."

"Don't you think—"

"If you mean don't I think the result would be the creation of an Efreet, no, I don't!"

"I hardly mean that, either," replied Cairn, "but this wave of superstition cannot be entirely unproductive; all that thought energy directed to one point—"

Sime stood up.

"We shall get out of our depth," he replied conclusively. He considered the ground of discussion an unhealthy one; this was the territory adjoining that of insanity.

A fortune-teller from India proffered his services incessantly.

"*Imshi! imshi!*" growled Sime.

"Hold on," said Cairn, smiling; "this chap is not an Egyptian; let us ask him if he has heard the rumour respecting the Efreet!"

Sime reseated himself rather unwillingly. The fortune-teller spread his little carpet and knelt down in order to read the palm of his hypothetical client, but Cairn waved him aside.

"I don't want my fortune told!" he said, "but I will give you your fee"—with a smile at Sime—"for a few minutes' conversation."

"Yes, sir, yes, sir!" The Indian was all attention.

"Why"—Cairn pointed forensically at the fortuneteller—"why is *Khamsîn* come so early this year?"

The Indian spread his hands, palms upward.

"How should I know?" he replied in his soft, melodious voice. "I am not of Egypt; I can only say what is told to me by the Egyptians."

"And what is told to you?"

Sime rested his hands upon his knees, bending forward curiously. He was palpably anxious that Cairn should have confirmation of the Efreet story from the Indian.

"They tell me, sir"—the man's voice sank musically low—"that a thing very evil"—he tapped a long brown finger upon his breast—"not as I am"—he tapped Sime upon the knee—"not as he, your friend" —he thrust the long finger at Cairn—"not as you, sir; not a man at all, though something like a man! not having any father and mother—"

"You mean," suggested Sime, "a spirit?"

The fortune-teller shook his head.

"They tell me, sir, not a spirit—a man, but not as other men; a very,

very bad man; one that the great king, long, long ago, the king you call Wise—"

"Solomon?" suggested Cairn.

"Yes, yes, Suleyman!—one that he, when he banish all the tribe of the demons from earth—one that he not found."

"One he overlooked?" jerked Sime.

"Yes, yes, overlook! A very evil man, my gentlemen. They tell me he has come to Egypt. He come not from the sea, but across the great desert—"

"The Libyan Desert?" suggested Sime.

The man shook his head, seeking for words. "The Arabian Desert?"

"No, no! Away beyond, far up in Africa"—he waved his long arms dramatically—"far, far up beyond the Sudan."

"The Sahara Desert?" proposed Sime.

"Yes, yes! it is Sahara Desert!—come across the Sahara Desert, and is come to Khartûm."

"How did he get there?" asked Crain.

The Indian shrugged his shoulders.

"I cannot say, but next he come to Wady Halfa, then he is in Assouan, and from Assouan he come down to Luxor! Yesterday an Egyptian friend told me *Khamsîn* is in the Fayûm. Therefore *he* is there—the man of evil—for he bring the hot wind with him."

The Indian was growing impressive, and two American tourists stopped to listen to his words.

"To-night—to-morrow"—he spoke now almost in a whisper, glancing about him as if apprehensive of being overheard—"he may be here, in Cairo, bringing with him the scorching breath of the desert—the scorpion wind!"

He stood up, casting off the mystery with which he had invested his story, and smiling insinuatingly. His work was done; his fee was due. Sime rewarded him with five piastres, and he departed, bowing.

"You know, Sime"—Cairn began to speak, staring absently the while after the fortune-teller, as he descended the carpeted steps and rejoined the throng on the sidewalk below—"you know if a man—any one, could take advantage of such a wave of thought as this which is now sweeping through Egypt—if he could cause it to concentrate upon him, as it were, don't you think that would enable him to transcend the normal, to do phenomenal things?"

"By what process should you propose to make yourself such a focus?"

"I was speaking impersonally, Sime. It might be possible—"

"It might be possible to dress for dinner," snapped Sime, "if we shut up talking nonsense! There's a carnival here to-night; great fun. Suppose we concentrate our brain-waves on another Scotch and soda?"

## CHAPTER XII
## THE MASK OF SET

Above the palm trees swept the jewelled vault of Egypt's sky, and set amid the clustering leaves gleamed little red electric lamps; fairy lanterns outlined the winding paths and paper Japanese lamps hung dancing in long rows, whilst in the centre of the enchanted garden a fountain spurned diamond spray high in the air, to fall back coolly plashing into the marble home of the golden carp. The rustling of innumerable feet upon the sandy pathway and the ceaseless murmur of voices, with pealing laughter rising above all, could be heard amid the strains of the military band ensconced in a flower-covered arbour.

Into the brightly lighted places and back into the luminous shadows came and went fantastic forms. Sheikhs there were with flowing robes, dragomans who spoke no Arabic, Sultans and priests of Ancient Egypt, going arm-in-arm. Dancing girls of old Thebes, and harem ladies in silken trousers and high-heeled red shoes. Queens of Babylon and Cleopatras, many Geishas and desert Gypsies mingled, specks in a giant kaleidoscope. The thick carpet of confetti rustled to the tread; girls ran screaming before those who pursued them armed with handfuls of the tiny paper disks. Pipers of a Highland regiment marched piping through the throng, their Scottish kilts seeming wildly incongruous amid such a scene. Within the hotel, where the mosque lanterns glowed, one might catch a glimpse of the heads of dancers gliding shadowlike.

"A tremendous crowd," said Sime, "considering it is nearly the end of the season."

Three silken ladies wearing gauzy white yashmaks confronted Cairn and the speaker. A gleaming of jewelled fingers there was and Cairn found himself half-choked with confetti, which filled his eyes, his nose, his ears, and of which quite a liberal amount found access to his mouth. The three ladies of the yashmak ran screaming from their vengeance-seeking victims, Sime pursuing two, and Cairn hard upon the heels of the third. Amid this scene of riotous carnival all else was forgotten, and only the madness, the infectious madness of the night, claimed his mind. In and out of the strangely attired groups darted his agile quarry, all but captured a score of times, but always eluding him.

Sime he had hopelessly lost, as around fountain and flower-bed, arbour and palm trunk he leapt in pursuit of the elusive yashmak.

Then, in a shadowed corner of the garden, he trapped her. Plunging his hand into the bag of confetti, which he carried, he leapt, exulting, to his revenge: when a sudden gust of wind passed sibilantly through the palm tops, and glancing upward, Cairn saw that the blue sky was overcast and the stars gleaming dimly, as through a veil. That moment of hesitancy proved fatal to his project, for with a little excited scream the girl dived under his outstretched arm and fled back toward the fountain. He turned to pursue again, when a second puff of wind, stronger than the first, set waving the palm fronds and showered dry leaves upon the confetti carpet of the garden. The band played loudly, the murmur of conversation rose to something like a roar, but above it whistled the increasing breeze, and there was a sort of grittiness in the air.

Then, proclaimed by a furious lashing of the fronds above, burst the wind in all its fury. It seemed to beat down into the garden in waves of heat. Huge leaves began to fall from the tree tops and the mast-like trunks bent before the fury from the desert. The atmosphere grew hazy with impalpable dust; and the stars were wholly obscured.

Commenced a stampede from the garden. Shrill with fear rose a woman's scream from the heart of the throng:

"A scorpion! A scorpion!"

Panic threatened, but fortunately the doors were wide so that, without disaster, the whole fantastic company passed into the hotel; and even the military band retired.

Cairn perceived that he alone remained in the garden, and glancing along the path in the direction of the fountain, he saw a blotchy drab creature, fully four inches in length, running zigzag toward him. It was a huge scorpion; but, even as he leapt forward to crush it, it turned and crept in amid the tangle of flowers beside the path, where it was lost from view.

The scorching wind grew momentarily fiercer, and Cairn, entering behind a few straggling revellers, found something ominous and dreadful in its sudden fury. At the threshold he turned and looked back upon the gaily lighted garden. The paper lamps were thrashing in the wind, many extinguished; others were in flames; a number of electric globes fell from their fastenings amid the palm tops, and burst bomb-like upon the ground. The pleasure garden was now a battlefield, beset with dangers, and he fully appreciated the anxiety of the company to get within doors. Where chrysanthemum and yashmak, turban and tarboosh, uræus and Indian plume had mingled gaily, no soul remained; but yet—he was in error... someone did remain.

As if embodying the fear that in a few short minutes had emptied the garden, out beneath the waving lanterns, the flying débris, the whirling dust, pacing sombrely from shadow to light, and to shadow again, advancing toward the hotel steps, came the figure of one sandalled, and wearing the short white tunic or Ancient Egypt. His arms were bare, and he carried a long staff; but rising hideously upon his shoulders was a crocodile-mask, which seemed to grin—the Mask of Set, Set the Destroyer, god of the underworld.

Cairn, alone of all the crowd, saw the strange figure, for the reason that Cairn faced toward the garden. The gruesome mask seemed to fascinate him; he could not take his gaze from that weird advancing god; he felt impelled hypnotically to stare at the gleaming eyes set in the saurian head. The mask was at the foot of the steps, and still Cairn stood rigid. When, as the sandalled foot was set upon the first step, a breeze, dust-laden, and hot as from a furnace door, blew fully into the hotel, blinding him. A chorus arose from the crowd at his back; and many voices cried out for doors to be shut. Someone tapped him on the shoulder, and spun him about.

"By God!"—it was Sime who now had him by the arm—"*Khamsîn* has come with a vengeance! They tell me they have never had anything like it!"

The native servants were closing and fastening the doors. The night was now as black as Erebus, and the wind was howling about the building with the voices of a million lost souls. Cairn glanced back across his shoulder. Men were drawing heavy curtains across the doors and windows.

"They have shut him out, Sime!" he said.

Sime stared in his dull fashion.

"You surely saw him?" persisted Cairn irritably; "the man in the Mask of Set—he was coming in just behind me."

Sime strode forward, pulled the curtains aside, and peered out into the deserted garden.

"Not a soul, old man," he declared. "You must have seen the Efreet!"

## CHAPTER XIII
## THE SCORPION WIND

This sudden and appalling change of weather had sadly affected the mood of the gathering. That part of the carnival planned to take place in the garden was perforce abandoned, together with the firework display. A half-hearted attempt was made at dancing, but the howling of the wind and the omnipresent dust perpetually reminded the pleasure-seekers that *Khamsîn* raged without—raged with a violence unparalleled in the experience of the oldest residents. This was a full-fledged sandstorm, a terror of the Sahara descended upon Cairo.

But there were few departures, although many of the visitors who had long distances to go, especially those from Mena House, discussed the advisability of leaving before this unique storm should have grown even worse. The general tendency, though, was markedly gregarious; safety seemed to be with the crowd, amid the gaiety, where music and laughter were, rather than in the sand-swept streets.

"Guess we've outstayed our welcome!" confided an American lady to Sime. "Egypt wants to drive us all home now."

"Possibly," he replied with a smile. "The season has run very late this year, and so this sort of thing is more or less to be expected."

The orchestra struck up a lively one-step, and a few of the more enthusiastic dancers accepted the invitation, but the bulk of the company thronged around the edge of the floor, acting as spectators.

Cairn and Sime wedged a way through the heterogeneous crowd to the American bar.

"I prescribe a 'tango,'" said Sime.

"A 'tango' is—?"

"A 'tango,'" explained Sime, "is a new kind of cocktail sacred to this buffet. Try it. It will either kill you or cure you."

Cairn smiled rather wanly.

"I must confess that I need bucking up a bit," he said; "that confounded sand seems to have got me by the throat."

Sime briskly gave his orders to the bar attendant.

"You know," pursued Cairn, "I cannot get out of my head the idea that there was someone wearing a crocodile mask in the garden a while ago."

"Look here," growled Sime, studying the operations of the cocktail manufacturer, "suppose there were—what about it?"

"Well, it's odd that nobody else saw him."

"I suppose it hasn't occurred to you that the fellow might have removed his mask?"

Cairn shook his head slowly.

"I don't think so," he declared; "I haven't seen him anywhere in the hotel."

"Seen him?" Sime turned his dull gaze upon the speaker. "How should you know him?"

Cairn raised his hand to his forehead in an oddly helpless way.

"No, of course not—it's very extraordinary."

They took their seats at a small table, and in mutual silence loaded and lighted their pipes. Sime, in common with many young and enthusiastic medical men, had theories—theories of that revolutionary sort which only harsh experience can shatter. Secretly he was disposed to ascribe all the ills to which flesh is heir primarily to a disordered nervous system. It was evident that Cairn's mind persistently ran along a particular groove; something lay back of all this erratic talk; he had clearly invested the Mask of Set with a curious individuality.

"I gather that you had a stiff bout of it in London?" Sime said suddenly. Cairn nodded.

"Beastly stiff. There is a lot of sound reason in your nervous theory, Sime. It was touch and go with me for days, I am told; yet, pathologically, I was a hale man. That would seem to show how nerves can kill. Just a series of shocks—horrors—one piled upon another, did as much for me as influenza, pneumonia, and two or three other ailments together could have done."

Sime shook his head wisely; this was in accordance with his ideas.

"You know Antony Ferrara?" continued Cairn. "Well, he has done this for me. His damnable practices are worse than any disease. Sime, the man is a pestilence! Although the law cannot touch him, although no jury can convict him—he is a murderer. He controls—forces—"

Sime was watching him intently.

"It will give you some idea, Sime, of the pitch to which things had come, when I tell you that my father drove to Ferrara's rooms one night, with a loaded revolver in his pocket—"

"For"—Sime hesitated—"for protection?"

"No." Cairn leant forward across the table—"To shoot him, Sime, shoot him on sight, as one shoots a mad dog!"

"Are you serious?"

"As God is my witness, if Antony Ferrara had been in his rooms that night, my father would have killed him!"

"It would have been a shocking scandal."

"It would have been a martyrdom. The man who removes Antony Ferrara from the earth will be doing mankind a service worthy of the highest reward. He is unfit to live. Sometimes I cannot believe that he does live; I expect to wake up and find that he was a figure of a particularly evil dream."

"This incident—the call at his rooms—occurred just before your illness?"

"The thing which he had attempted that night was the last straw, Sime; it broke me down. From the time that he left Oxford, Antony Ferrara has pursued a deliberate course of crime, of crime so cunning, so unusual, and based upon such amazing and unholy knowledge that no breath of suspicion has touched him. Sime, you remember a girl I told you about at Oxford one evening, a girl who came to visit him?"

Sime nodded slowly.

"Well—he killed her! Oh! there is no doubt about it; I saw her body in the hospital."

"*How* had he killed her, then?"

"How? Only he and the God who permits him to exist can answer that, Sime. He killed her without coming anywhere near her—and he killed his foster father, Sir Michael Ferrara, by the same unholy means!"

Sime watched him, but offered no comment.

"It was hushed up, of course; there is no existing law which could be used against him."

"*Existing* law?"

"They are ruled out, Sime, the laws that *could* have reached him; but he would have been burnt at the stake in the Middle Ages!"

"I see." Sime drummed his fingers upon the table. "You had those ideas about him at Oxford; and does Dr. Cairn seriously believe the same?"

"He does. So would you—you could not doubt it, Sime, not for a moment, if you had seen what we have seen!" His eyes blazed into a sudden fury, suggestive of his old, robust self. "He tried night after night, by means of the same accursed sorcery, which everyone thought buried in the ruins of Thebes, to kill *me!* He projected—things—"

"Suggested these—things, to your mind?"

"Something like that. I saw, or thought I saw, and smelt—pah!—I seem to smell them now!—beetles, mummy-beetles, you know, from the skull of a mummy! My rooms were thick with them. It brought me very near to Bedlam, Sime. Oh! it was not merely imaginary. My father and I caught him red-handed." He glanced across at the other. "You read of the death of Lord Lashmore? It was just after you came out."

"Yes—heart."

"It was his heart, yes—but Ferrara was responsible! That was the business which led my father to drive to Ferrara's rooms with a loaded revolver in his pocket."

The wind was shaking the windows and whistling about the building with demoniacal fury as if seeking admission; the band played a popular waltz; and in and out of the open doors came and went groups representative of many ages and many nationalities.

"Ferrara," began Sime slowly, "was always a detestable man, with his sleek black hair and ivory face. Those long eyes of his had an expression which always tempted me to hit him. Sir Michael, if what you say is true—and after all, Cairn, it only goes to show how little we know of the nervous system—literally took a viper to his bosom."

"He did. Antony Ferrara was his adopted son, of course; God knows to what evil brood he really belongs."

Both were silent for a while. Then:

"Gracious heavens!"

Cairn started to his feet so wildly as almost to upset the table.

"Look, Sime! Look!" he cried.

Sime was not the only man in the bar to hear, and to heed his words. Sime, looking in the direction indicated by Cairn's extended finger, received a vague impression that a grotesque, long-headed figure had appeared momentarily in the doorway opening upon the room where the dancers were; then it was gone again, if it had ever been there, and he was supporting Cairn, who swayed dizzily, and had become ghastly pale. Sime imagined that the heated air had grown suddenly even more heated. Curious eyes were turned upon his companion, who now sank back into his chair, muttering:

"The Mask, the Mask!"

"I think I saw the chap who seems to worry you so much," said Sime soothingly. "Wait here; I will tell the waiter to bring you a dose of brandy; and whatever you do, don't get excited."

He made for the door, pausing and giving an order to a waiter on his way, and pushed into the crowd outside. It was long past midnight, and the gaiety, which had been resumed, seemed of a forced and feverish sort. Some of the visitors were leaving, and a breath of hot wind swept in from the open doors.

A pretty girl wearing a yashmak, who, with two similarly attired companions, was making her way to the entrance, attracted his attention; she seemed to be on the point of swooning. He recognized the trio for the same that had pelted Cairn and himself with confetti earlier in the evening.

"The sudden heat has affected your friend," he said, stepping up to them. "My name is Dr. Sime; may I offer you my assistance?"

The offer was accepted, and with the three he passed out on to the terrace, where the dust grated beneath the tread, and helped the fainting girl into an *arabîyeh*. The night was thunderously black, the heat almost insufferable, and the tall palms in front of the hotel bowed before the might of the scorching wind.

As the vehicle drove off, Sime stood for a moment looking after it. His face was very grave, for there was a look in the bright eyes of the girl in the yashmak which, professionally, he did not like. Turning up the steps, he learnt from the manager that several visitors had succumbed to the heat. There was something furtive in the manner of his informant's glance, and Sime looked at him significantly.

"*Khamsîn* brings clouds of septic dust with it," he said. "Let us hope that these attacks are due to nothing more than the unexpected rise in the temperature."

An air of uneasiness prevailed now throughout the hotel. The wind had considerably abated, and crowds were leaving, pouring from the steps into the deserted street, a dreamlike company.

Colonel Royland took Sime aside, as the latter was making his way back to the buffet. The Colonel, whose regiment was stationed at the Citadel, had known Sime almost from childhood.

"You know, my boy," he said, "I should never have allowed Eileen" [his daughter] "to remain in Cairo if I had foreseen this change in the weather. This infernal wind, coming right through the native town, is loaded with infection."

"Has it affected her, then?" asked Sime anxiously.

"She nearly fainted in the ball-room," replied the Colonel. "Her mother took her home half an hour ago. I looked for you everywhere but couldn't find you."

"Quite a number have succumbed," said Sime.

"Eileen seemed to be slightly hysterical," continued the Colonel. "She persisted that someone wearing a crocodile mask had been standing beside her at the moment that she was taken ill."

Sime started; perhaps Cairn's story was not a matter of imagination, after all.

"There is someone here dressed like that, I believe," he replied, with affected carelessness. "He seems to have frightened several people. Any idea who he is?"

"My dear chap!" cried the Colonel, "I have been searching the place for him! But I have never once set eyes upon him. I was about to ask if you knew anything about it!"

Sime returned to the table where Cairn was sitting. The latter seemed to have recovered somewhat; but he looked far from well. Sime stared at him critically.

"I should turn in," he said, "if I were you. *Khamsîn* is playing the deuce with people. I only hope it does not justify its name and blow for fifty days."

"Have you seen the man in the mask?" asked Cairn.

"No," replied Sime, "but he's here alright; others have seen him."

Cairn stood up rather unsteadily, and with Sime made his way through the moving crowd to the stairs. The band was still playing, but the cloud of gloom which had settled upon the place refused to be dissipated.

"Good-night, Cairn," said Sime; "see you in the morning."

Robert Cairn, with aching head and a growing sensation of nausea, paused on the landing, looking down into the court below. He could not disguise from himself that he felt ill, not nervously ill as in London, but physically sick. This superheated air was difficult to breathe; it seemed to rise in waves from below.

Then, from a weary glancing at the figures beneath him, his attitude changed to one of tense watching.

A man, wearing the crocodile mask of Set, stood by a huge urn containing a palm, looking up to the landing!

Cairn's weakness left him, and in its place came an indescribable anger, a longing to drive his fist into that grinning mask. He turned and ran lightly down the stairs, conscious of a sudden glow of energy. Reaching the floor, he saw the mask making across the hall in the direction of the outer door. As rapidly as possible, for he could not run without attracting undesirable attention, Cairn followed. The figure of Set passed out on to the terrace, but when Cairn in turn swung open the door, his quarry had vanished.

Then, in an *arabîyeh* just driving off, he detected the hideous mask. Hatless as he was, he ran down the steps and threw himself into another. The carriage-controller was in attendance, and Cairn rapidly told him to instruct the driver to follow the *arabîyeh* which had just left. The man lashed up his horses, turned the carriage, and went galloping on after the retreating figure. Past the Esbekîya Gardens they went, through several narrow streets, and on to the quarter of the Mûski. Time after time he thought he had lost the carriage ahead, but his own driver's knowledge of the tortuous streets enabled him always to overtake it again. They went rocking along lanes so narrow that with outstretched arms one could almost have touched the walls on either side; past empty shops and unlighted houses. Cairn had not the remotest idea of his whereabouts save that he was evidently in the district of the bazaars. A right-angled corner was abruptly negotiated—and there, ahead of him, stood the pursued vehicle! The driver was turning his horses around, to return; his fare was disappearing from sight into the black shadows of a narrow alley on the left.

Cairn leaped from the *arabîyeh*, shouting to the man to wait, and went dashing down the sloping lane after the retreating figure. A sort of blind fury possessed him, but he never paused to analyze it, never asked himself by what right he pursued this man, what wrong the latter had done him. His action was wholly unreasoning; he knew that he wished to overtake the wearer of the mask and to tear it from his head; upon that he acted!

He discovered that despite the tropical heat of the night he was shuddering with cold, but he disregarded this circumstance, and ran on.

The pursued stopped before an iron-studded door, which was opened instantly; he entered as the runner came up with him. And, before the door could be re-closed, Cairn thrust his way in.

Blackness, utter blackness, was before him. The figure which he had pursued seemed to have been swallowed up. He stumbled on, gropingly, hands outstretched, then fell—fell, as he realized in the moment of falling, down a short flight of stone steps.

Still amid utter blackness, he got upon his feet, shaken but otherwise unhurt by his fall. He turned about, expecting to see some glimmer of light from the stairway, but the blackness was unbroken. Silence and gloom hemmed him in. He stood for a moment, listening intently.

A shaft of light pierced the darkness as a shutter was thrown open. Through an iron-barred window the light shone; and with the light came a breath of stifling perfume. That perfume carried his imagination back instantly to a room at Oxford, and he advanced and looked through into the place beyond. He drew a swift breath, clutched the bars, and was silent—stricken speechless.

He looked into a large and lofty room lighted by several hanging lamps. It had a carpeted divan at one end and was otherwise scantily furnished, in the Eastern manner. A silver incense-burner smoked upon a large praying-carpet, and by it stood the man in the crocodile mask. An Arab girl, fantastically attired, who had evidently just opened the shutters, was now helping him to remove the hideous head-dress.

She presently untied the last of the fastenings and lifted the thing from the man's shoulders, moving away with the gliding step of the Oriental, and leaving him standing there in his short white tunic, bare-legged and sandalled.

The smoke of the incense curled upward and played around the straight, slim figure, drew vaporous lines about the still ivory face—the handsome, sinister face, sometimes partly veiling the long black eyes and sometimes showing them in all their unnatural brightness. So the man stood, looking toward the barred window.

It was Antony Ferrara!

"Ah, dear Cairn"—the husky musical voice smote upon Cairn's ears as the most hated sound in nature—"you have followed me. Not content with driving me from London, you would also render Cairo—my dear Cairo—untenable for me."

Cairn clutched the bars but was silent.

"How wrong of you, Cairn!" the soft voice mocked. "This attention is so harmful—to you. Do you know, Cairn, the Sudanese formed the extraordinary opinion that I was an *efreet*, and this strange reputation has followed me right down the Nile. Your father, my dear friend, has studied these odd matters, and he would tell you that there is no power, in Nature, higher than the human will. Actually, Cairn, they have ascribed to me the direction of the *Khamsîn*, and so many worthy Egyptians have made up their minds that I travel with the storm—or that the storm follows me—that something of the kind has really come to pass! Or is it merely coincidence, Cairn? Who can say?"

Motionless, immobile, save for a slow smile, Antony Ferrara stood, and Cairn kept his eyes upon the evil face, and with trembling hands clutched the bars.

"It is certainly odd, is it not," resumed the taunting voice, "that *Khamsîn*, so violent, too, should thus descend upon the Cairene season? I only arrived from the Fayûm this evening, Cairn, and, do you know, they have the pestilence there! I trust the hot wind does not carry it to Cairo; there are so many distinguished European and American visitors here. It would be a thousand pities!"

Cairn released his grip of the bars, raised his clenched fists above his head, and in a voice and with a maniacal fury that were neither his own, cursed the man who stood there mocking him. Then he reeled, fell, and remembered no more.

"All right, old man—you'll do quite nicely now."

It was Sime speaking.

Cairn struggled upright...and found himself in bed! Sime was seated beside him.

"Don't talk!" said Sime, "you're in a hospital! I'll do the talking; you listen. I saw you bolt out of Shepheard's last night—shut up! I followed but lost you. We got up a search party, and with the aid of the man who had driven you, ran you to earth in a dirty alley behind the mosque of El-Azhar. Four kindly mendicants, who reside upon the steps of the establishment, had been awakened by your blundering in among them. They were holding you—yes, you were raving pretty badly. You are a lucky man, Cairn. You were innoculated before you left home?"

Cairn nodded weakly.

"Saved you. Be all right in a couple of days. That damned *Khamsîn* has brought a whiff of the plague from somewhere! Curiously enough, over fifty per cent of the cases spotted so far are people who were at the carnival! Some of them, Cairn— But we won't discuss that now. I was afraid of it last night. That's why I kept my eye on you. My boy, you were delirious when you bolted out of the hotel!"

"Was I?" said Cairn wearily, and lay back on the pillow. "Perhaps I was."

## CHAPTER XIV
## DR. CAIRN ARRIVES

Dr. Bruce Cairn stepped into the boat which was to take him ashore, and as it swung away from the side of the liner sought to divert his thoughts by a contemplation of the weird scene. Amid the smoky flare of many lights, amid rising clouds of dust, a line of laden toilers was crawling ant-like from the lighters into the bowels of the big ship; and a second line, unladen, was descending by another gangway. Above, the jewelled velvet of the sky swept in a glorious arc; beyond, the lights of Port Said broke through the black curtain of the night, and the moving ray from the lighthouse intermittently swept the harbour waters; whilst amid the indescribable clamour, the grimily picturesque turmoil, so characteristic of the place, the liner took in coal for her run to Rangoon.

Dodging this way and that, rounding the sterns of big ships, and disputing the water-way with lesser craft, the boat made for shore.

The usual delay at the Customs House, the usual soothing of the excited officials in the usual way, and his *arabîyeh* was jolting Dr. Cairn through the noise and the smell of those rambling streets, a noise and a smell entirely peculiar to this clearing house of the Near East.

He accepted the room which was offered to him at the hotel without troubling to inspect it, and having left instructions that he was to be called in time for the early train to Cairo, he swallowed a whisky and soda at the buffet, and wearily ascended the stairs. There were tourists in the hotel, English and American, marked by a gaping wonderment and loud with plans of sightseeing; but Port Said, nay, all Egypt, had nothing of novelty to offer Dr. Cairn. He was there at great inconvenience; a practitioner of his repute may not easily arrange to quit London at a moment's notice. But the business upon which he was come was imperative. For him the charm of the place had not existence, but somewhere in Egypt his son stood in deadly peril, and Dr. Cairn counted the hours that yet divided them. His soul was up in arms against the man whose evil schemes had led to his presence in Port Said at a time when many sufferers required his ministrations in Half-Moon Street. He was haunted by a phantom, a ghoul in human shape; Antony Ferrara, the adopted son of his dear friend, the adopted son who had murdered his adopter, and who, whilst guiltless in the eyes of the law, was blood-guilty in the eyes of God!

Dr. Cairn switched on the light and seated himself upon the side of the bed, knitting his brows and staring straight before him with an expression in his clear gray eyes the significance of which he would have denied hotly had any man charged him with it. He was thinking of Antony Ferrara's record; the victims of this fiendish youth (for Antony Ferrara was barely of age) seemed to stand before him with hands stretched out appealingly.

"You alone," they seemed to cry, "know who and what he is! You alone know of our awful wrongs; you alone can avenge them!"

And yet he had hesitated! It had remained for his own flesh and blood to be threatened ere he had taken decisive action. The viper had lain within his reach and he had neglected to set his heel upon it. Men and women had suffered and had died of its venom; and he had not crushed it. Then Robert, his son, had felt the poison fang, and Dr. Cairn, who had hesitated to act upon the behalf of all humanity, had leapt to arms. He charged himself with a parent's selfishness, and his conscience would hear no defence.

Dimly the turmoil from the harbour reached him where he sat. He listened dully to the hooting of a siren—that of some vessel coming out of the canal.

His thoughts were evil company, and, with a deep sigh, he rose, crossed the room, and threw open the double windows giving access to the balcony.

Port Said, a panorama of twinkling lights, lay beneath him. The beam from the lighthouse swept the town searchingly like the eye of some pagan god lustful for sacrifice. He imagined that he could hear the shouting of the gangs coaling the liner in the harbour; but the night was full of the remote murmuring inseparable from that gateway of the East. The streets below, white under the moon, looked empty and deserted, and the hotel beneath him gave up no sound to tell of the many birds of passage who sheltered within it. A stunning sense of his loneliness came to him; his physical loneliness was symbolic of that which characterized his place in the world. He, alone, had the knowledge and the power to crush Antony Ferrara. He, alone, could rid the world of the unnatural menace embodied in the person bearing that name.

The town lay beneath his eyes, but now he saw nothing of it; before his mental vision loomed—exclusively—the figure of a slim and strangely handsome young man having jet-black hair, lustreless, a face of uniform ivory hue, long dark eyes wherein lurked lambent fires, and a womanish grace expressed in his whole bearing, and emphasized by his long white hands. Upon a finger of the left hand gleamed a strange green stone.

Antony Ferrara! In the eyes of this solitary traveller who stood looking down upon Port Said that figure filled the entire landscape of Egypt!

With a weary sigh Dr. Cairn turned and began to undress. Leaving the windows open, he switched off the light and got into bed. He was very weary, with a weariness rather of the spirit than of the flesh, but it was of that sort which renders sleep all but impossible. Around and about one fixed point his thoughts circled; in vain he endeavoured to forget, for a while, Antony Ferrara and the things connected with him. Sleep was imperative if he would be in fit condition to cope with the matters which demanded his attention in Cairo.

Yet sleep defied him. Every trifling sound from the harbour and the canal seemed to rise upon the still air to his room. Through a sort of mist created by the mosquito curtains he could see the open windows and look out upon the stars. He found himself studying the heavens with sleepless eyes, and idly working out the constellations visible. Then one very bright star attracted the whole of his attention, and, with the dogged persistency of insomnia, he sought to place it but could not determine to which group it belonged.

So he lay with his eyes upon the stars until the other veiled lamps of heaven became invisible and the patch of sky no more than a setting for that one white orb.

In this contemplation he grew restful; his thoughts ceased feverishly to race along that one hateful groove; the bright star seemed to soothe him. As a result of his fixed gazing, it now appeared to have increased in size. This was a common optical illusion upon which he scarcely speculated at all. He recognized the welcome approach of sleep, and deliberately concentrated his mind upon the globe of light.

Yes, a globe of light indeed—for now it had assumed the dimensions of a lesser moon; and it seemed to rest in the space between the open windows. Then he thought that it crept still nearer. The realities—the bed, the mosquito curtain, the room—were fading, and grateful slumber approached and weighted upon his eyes in the form of that dazzling globe. The feeling of contentment was the last impression which he had, ere, with the bright star seemingly suspended just beyond the netting, he slept.

## CHAPTER XV
## THE WITCH-QUEEN

A man mentally over-tired sleeps either dreamlessly or dreams with a vividness greater than that characterizing the dreams of normal slumber. Dr. Cairn dreamt a vivid dream.

He dreamt that he was awakened by the sound of gentle rapping. Opening his eyes, he peered through the cloudy netting. He started up, and wrenched back the curtain. The rapping was repeated; and peering again across the room, he very distinctly perceived a figure upon the balcony by the open window. It was that of a woman who wore the black silk dress and the white yashmak of the Moslem, and who was bending forward looking into the room.

"Who is there?" he called. "What do you want?"

"S—*sh!*"

The woman raised her hand to her veiled lips, and looked right and left as if fearing to disturb the occupants of the adjacent rooms.

Dr. Cairn reached out for his dressing-gown which lay upon the chair beside the bed, threw it over his shoulders, and stepped out upon the floor. He stooped and put on his slippers, never taking his eyes from the figure at the window. The room was flooded with moonlight.

He began to walk toward the balcony when the mysterious visitor spoke.

"You are Dr. Cairn?"

The words were spoken in the language of dreams; that is to say, although he understood them perfectly, he knew that they had not been uttered in the English language, nor in any language known to him; yet, as is the way with one who dreams, he had understood.

"I am he," he said. "Who are you?"

"Make no noise, but follow me quickly. Someone is very ill."

There was sincerity in the appeal, spoken in the softest, most silvern tone which he had ever heard. He stood beside the veiled woman, and met the glance of her dark eyes with a consciousness of some magnetic force in the glance which seemed to set his nerves quivering.

"Why do you come to the window? How do you know—"

The visitor raised her hand again to her lips. It was of a gleaming ivory colour, and the long tapered fingers were laden with singular jewellery—exquisite enamelwork which he knew to be Ancient Egyptian, but which did not seem out of place in this dream adventure.

"I was afraid to make any unnecessary disturbance," she replied. "Please do not delay, but come at once." Dr. Cairn adjusted his dressing-gown, and followed the veiled messenger along the balcony. For a dream city, Port Said appeared remarkably substantial, as it spread out at his feet, its dingy buildings whitened by the moonlight. But his progress was dreamlike, for he seemed to glide past many windows, around the corner of the building, and, without having consciously exerted any physical effort, found his hands grasped by warm jewelled fingers, found himself guided into some darkened room, and then, possessed by that doubting which sometimes comes in dreams, found himself hesitating. The moonlight did not penetrate to the apartment in which he stood, and the darkness about him was impenetrable. He allowed his unseen guide to lead him forward.

Stairs were descended in phantom silence—many stairs. The coolness of the air suggested that they were outside the hotel. But the darkness remained complete. Along what seemed to be a stone-paved passage they advanced mysteriously, and by this time Dr. Cairn was wholly resigned to the strangeness of his dream adventure.

Then, although the place lay in blackest shadows, he saw that they were in the open air, for the starry sky swept above them.

It was a narrow street—at points the buildings almost met above—wherein he now found himself. In reality, had he been in possession of his usual faculties, awake, he would have asked himself how this veiled woman had gained admittance to the hotel, and why she had secretly led him out from it. But the dreamer's mental lethargy possessed him, and, with the blind faith of a child, he followed on, until he now began vaguely to consider the personality of his guide.

She seemed to be of no more than average height, but she carried herself with unusual grace, and her progress was marked by a certain hauteur. At the point where a narrow lane crossed that which they were traversing the veiled figure was silhouetted for a moment against the light of the moon, and through the gauze-like fabric he perceived the outlines of a perfect shape. His vague wonderment concerned itself now with the ivory, jewel-laden hands. His condition differed from the normal dream state in that he was not entirely resigned to the anomalous.

Misty doubts were forming when his dream guide paused before a heavy door of a typical native house which once had been of some consequence, and which faced the entrance to a mosque, indeed lay in the shadow of the minaret. It was opened from within, although she gave no perceptible signal, and its darkness, to Dr. Cairn's dulled perceptions, seemed to swallow them both. He had an impression of a trap raised, of stone steps descended, of a new darkness almost palpable.

The gloom of the place affected him as a mental blank, and, when a bright light shone out, it seemed to mark the opening of a second dream phase. From where the light came, he knew not, cared not, but it illuminated a perfectly bare room, with a floor of native mud bricks, a plastered wall, and wood-beamed ceiling. A tall sarcophagus stood upright against the wall before him; its lid leant close beside it... and his black-robed guide, her luminous eyes looking straightly over the yashmak, stood rigidly upright within it!

She raised the jewelled hands, and with a swift movement discarded robe and yashmak, and stood before him in the clinging draperies of an ancient queen, wearing the leopard skin and the uræus, and carrying the flail of royal Egypt!

Her pale face formed a perfect oval; the long almond eyes had an evil beauty which seemed to chill; and the brilliantly red mouth was curved in a smile which must have made any man forget the evil in the eyes. But when we move in a dream world, our emotions become dreamlike, too. She placed a sandalled foot upon the mud floor and stepped out of the sarcophagus, advancing toward Dr. Cairn, a vision of such sinful loveliness as he could never have conceived in his waking moments. In that strange dream language, in a tongue not of East nor West, she spoke; and her silvern voice had something of the tone of those Egyptian pipes whose dree fills the nights upon the Upper Nile—the seductive music of remote and splendid wickedness.

"You know me *now?*" she whispered.

And in his dream she seemed to be a familiar figure, at once dreadful and worshipful.

A fitful light played through the darkness, and seemed to dance upon a curtain draped behind the sarcophagus, picking out diamond points. The dreamer groped in the mental chaos of his mind, and found a clue to the meaning of this. The diamond points were the eyes of thousands of tarantula spiders with which the curtain was embroidered.

The sign of the spider! What did he know of it? Yes! of course; it was the secret mark of Egypt's witch-queen—of the beautiful woman whose name, after her mysterious death, had been erased from all her monuments. A sweet whisper stole to his ears:

"You will befriend him, befriend my son—for *my* sake."

And in his dream state he found himself prepared to forswear all that he held holy—for her sake. She grasped both his hands, and her burning eyes looked closely into his.

"Your reward shall be a great one," she whispered, even more softly.

Came a sudden blank, and Dr. Cairn found himself walking again through the narrow street, led by the veiled woman. His impressions were growing dim; and now she seemed less real than hitherto. The streets were phantom streets, built of shadow stuff, and the stairs which presently he found himself ascending were unsubstantial, and he seemed rather to float upward; until, with the jewelled fingers held fast in his own, he stood in a darkened apartment, and saw before him an open window, knew that he was once more back in the hotel. A dim light dawned in the blackness of the room and the musical voice breathed in his ear:

"Your reward shall be easily earned. I did but test you. Strike—and strike truly!"

The whisper grew sibilant—serpentine. Dr. Cairn felt the hilt of a dagger thrust into his right hand, and in the dimly mysterious light looked down at one who lay in a bed close beside him.

At sight of the face of the sleeper—the perfectly chiselled face, with the long black lashes resting on the ivory cheeks—he forgot all else, forgot the place wherein he stood, forgot his beautiful guide, and only remembered that he held a dagger in his hand, and that Antony Ferrara lay there, sleeping!

"Strike!" came the whisper again.

Dr. Cairn felt a mad exultation boiling up within him. He raised his hand, glanced once more on the face of the sleeper, and nerved himself to plunge the dagger in the heart of this evil thing.

A second more, and the dagger would have been buried to the hilt in the sleeper's breast—when there ensued a deafening, an appalling explosion. A wild red light illuminated the room, the building seemed to rock. Close upon that frightful sound followed a cry so piercing that it seemed to ice the blood in Dr. Cairn's veins.

"Stop sir, stop! My God! what are you doing!"

A swift blow struck the dagger from his hand and the figure on the bed sprang upright. Swaying dizzily, Dr. Cairn stood there in the darkness, and as the voice of awakened sleepers reached his ears from adjoining rooms, the electric light was switched on, and across the bed, the bed upon which he had thought Antony Ferrara lay, he saw his son, Robert Cairn!

No one else was in the room. But on the carpet at his feet lay an ancient dagger, the hilt covered with beautiful and intricate gold and enamel work.

Rigid with a mutual horror, these two so strangely met stood staring at one another across the room. Everyone in the hotel, it would appear, had been awakened by the explosion, which, as if by the intervention of God, had stayed the hand of Dr. Cairn—had spared him from a deed impossible to contemplate.

There were sounds of running footsteps everywhere; but the origin of the disturbance at that moment had no interest for these two. Robert was the first to break the silence.

"Merciful God, sir!" he whispered huskily, "how did you come to be here? What is the matter? Are you ill?"

Dr. Cairn extended his hands like one groping in darkness.

"Rob, give me a moment to think, to collect myself. Why am I here? By all that is wonderful, why are you here?"

"I am here to meet you."

"To meet me! I had no idea that you were well enough for the journey, and if you came to meet me, why—"

"That's it, sir! Why did you send me that wireless?"

"I sent no wireless, boy!"

Robert Cairn, with a little colour returning to his pale cheeks, advanced and grasped his father's hand.

"But after I arrived here to meet the boat, sir, I received a wireless from the P. and O. due in the morning, to say that you had changed your mind, and come *via* Brindisi."

Dr. Cairn glanced at the dagger upon the carpet, repressed a shudder, and replied in a voice which he struggled to make firm:

"*I* did not send that wireless!"

"Then you actually came by the boat which arrived last night?—and to think that I was asleep in the same hotel! What an amazing—"

"Amazing indeed, Rob, and the result of a cunning and well-planned scheme." He raised his eyes, looking fixedly at his son. "You understand the scheme; the scheme that could only have germinated in one mind— a scheme to cause me, your father, to—"

His voice failed, and again his glance sought the weapon which lay so close to his feet. Partly in order to hide his emotion, he stooped, picked up the dagger, and threw it on the bed.

"For God's sake, sir," groaned Robert, "what were you doing here in my room with—that!"

Dr. Cairn stood straightly upright and replied in an even voice:

"I was here to do murder!"

"*Murder!*"

"I was under a spell—no need to name its weaver; I thought that a poisonous thing at last lay at my mercy, and by cunning means the primitive evil within me was called up, and braving the laws of God and man, I was about to slay that thing. Thank God—"

He dropped upon his knees, silently bowed his head for a moment, and then stood up, self-possessed again, as his son had always known him. It had been a strange and awful awakening for Robert Cairn—to find his room illuminated by a lurid light, and to find his own father standing over him with a knife! But what had moved him even more deeply than the fear of these things, had been the sight of the emotion which had shaken that stern and unemotional man. Now, as he gathered together his scattered wits, he began to perceive that a malignant hand was moving above them, that his father and himself were pawns which had been moved mysteriously to a dreadful end.

A great disturbance had now arisen in the streets below, streams of people, it seemed, were pouring toward the harbour; but Dr. Cairn pointed to an armchair.

"Sit down, Rob," he said. "I will tell my story, and you shall tell yours. By comparing notes, we can arrive at some conclusion. Then we must act. This is a fight to a finish, and I begin to doubt if we are strong enough to win."

He took up the dagger and ran a critical glance over it, from the keen point to the enamelled hilt.

"This is unique," he muttered, whilst his son, spellbound, watched him; "the blade is as keen as if tempered but yesterday; yet it was made full five thousand years ago, as the workmanship of the hilt testifies. Rob, we deal with powers more than human! We have to cope with a force which might have awed the greatest Masters which the world has known. It would have called for all the knowledge and all the power of Apollonius of Tyana to have dealt with—*him!*"

"Antony Ferrara!"

"Undoubtedly, Rob! it was by the agency of Antony Ferrara that the wireless message was sent to you from the P. and O. It was by the agency of Antony Ferrara that I dreamt a dream to-night. In fact, it was no true dream; I was under the influence of—what shall I term it?—hypnotic suggestion. To what extent that malign will was responsible for you and me being placed in rooms communicating by means of a balcony, we probably shall never know; but if this proximity was merely accidental, the enemy did not fail to take advantage of the coincidence. I lay watching the stars before I slept, and one of them seemed to grow larger as I watched." He began to pace about the room in growing excitement. "Rob, I cannot doubt that a mirror, or a crystal, was actually suspended before my eyes by—someone, who had been watching for the opportunity. I yielded myself to the soothing influence, and thus deliberately— deliberately—placed myself in the power of—Antony Ferrara—"

"You think that he is here, in this hotel?"

"I cannot doubt that he is in the neighbourhood. The influence was too strong to have emanated from a mind at a great distance removed. I will tell you exactly what I dreamt."

He dropped into a cane armchair. Comparative quiet reigned again in the streets below, but a distant clamour told of some untoward happening at the harbour.

Dawn would break ere long, and there was a curious rawness in the atmosphere. Robert Cairn seated himself upon the side of the bed, and watched his father whilst the latter related those happenings with which we are already acquainted.

"You think, sir," said Robert, at the conclusion of the strange story, "that no part of your experience was real?"

Dr. Cairn held up the antique dagger, glancing at the speaker significantly.

"On the contrary," he replied, "I *do* know that part of it was dreadfully real. My difficulty is to separate the real from the phantasmal."

Silence fell for a moment. Then:

"It is almost certain," said the younger man, frowning thoughtfully, "that you did not actually leave the hotel, but merely passed from your room to mine by way of the balcony."

Dr. Cairn stood up, walked to the open window, and looked out, then turned and faced his son again.

"I believe I can put that matter to the test," he declared. "In my dream, as I turned into the lane where the house was—the house of the mummy—there was a patch covered with deep mud, where at some time during the evening a quantity of water had been spilt. I stepped upon that patch, or dreamt that I did. We can settle the point."

He sat down on the bed beside his son, and, stooping, pulled off one of his slippers. The night had been full enough of dreadful surprises; but here was yet another which came to them as Dr. Cairn, with the inverted slipper in his hand, sat looking into his son's eyes.

The sole of the slipper was caked with reddish-brown mud.


## CHAPTER XVI
## LAIR OF THE SPIDERS


We must find that house, find the sarcophagus—for I no longer doubt that it exists—drag it out, and destroy it."

"Should you know it again, sir?"

"Beyond any possibility of doubt. It is the sarcophagus of a queen."

"What queen?"

"A queen whose tomb the late Sir Michael Ferrara and I sought for many months but failed to find."

"Is this queen well-known in Egyptian history?"

Dr. Cairn stared at him with an odd expression in his eyes.

"Some histories ignore her existence entirely," he said; and, with an evident desire to change the subject, added, "I shall return to my room to dress now. Do you dress also. We cannot afford to sleep whilst the situation of that house remains unknown to us."

Robert Cairn nodded, and his father stood up, and went out of the room.

Dawn saw the two of them peering from the balcony upon the streets of Port Said, already dotted with moving figures, for the Egyptian is an early riser.

"Have you any clue," asked the younger man, "to the direction in which this place lies?"

"Absolutely none, for the reason that I do not know where my dreaming left off and reality commenced. Did someone really come to my window, and lead me out through another room, downstairs, and into the street, or did I wander out of my own accord and merely imagine the existence of the guide? In either event, I must have been guided in some way to a back entrance; for had I attempted to leave by the front door of the hotel in that trance-like condition I should certainly have been detained by the *bowwab*. Suppose we commence, then, by inquiring if there is such another entrance?"

The hotel staff was already afoot, and their inquiries led to the discovery of an entrance communicating with the native servants' quarters. This could not be reached from the main hall, but there was a narrow staircase to the left of the lift-shaft by which it might be gained. The two stood looking out across the stone-paved courtyard upon which the door opened.

"Beyond doubt," said Dr. Cairn, "I might have come down that staircase and out by this door without arousing a soul, either by passing through my own room, or through any other on that floor."

They crossed the yard, where members of the kitchen staff were busily polishing various cooking utensils, and opened the gate. Dr. Cairn turned to one of the men near by.

"Is this gate bolted at night?" he asked, in Arabic. The man shook his head, and seemed to be much amused by the question, revealing his white teeth as he assured him that it was not.

A narrow lane ran along behind the hotel, communicating with a maze of streets almost exclusively peopled by natives.

"Rob," said Dr. Cairn slowly, "it begins to dawn upon me that this is the way I came."

He stood looking to right and left, and seemed to be undecided. Then:

"We will try right," he determined.

They set off along the narrow way. Once clear of the hotel wall, high buildings rose upon either side, so that at no time during the day could the sun have penetrated to the winding lane. Suddenly Robert Cairn stopped.

"Look!" he said, and pointed. "The mosque! You spoke of a mosque near to the house?"

Dr. Cairn nodded; his eyes were gleaming, now that he felt himself to be upon the track of this great evil which had shattered his peace.

They advanced until they stood before the door of the mosque—and there in the shadow of a low archway was just such an ancient iron-studded door as Dr. Cairn remembered! Latticed windows overhung the street above, but no living creature was in sight.

He very gently pressed upon the door, but as he had anticipated it was fastened from within. In the vague light his face seemed strangely haggard as he turned to his son, raising his eyebrows interrogatively.

"It is just possible that I may be mistaken," he said; "so that I scarcely know what to do."

He stood looking about him in some perplexity.

Adjoining the mosque was a ruinous house which clearly had had no occupants for many years. As Robert Cairn's gaze lighted upon its gaping window-frames and doorless porch, he seized his father by the arm.

"We might hide up there," he suggested, "and watch for any one entering or leaving the place opposite."

"I have little doubt that this was the scene of my experience," replied Dr. Cairn, "therefore I think we will adopt your plan. Perhaps there is some means of egress at the back. It will be useful if we have to remain on the watch for any considerable time."

They entered the ruined building and, by means of a rickety staircase, gained the floor above. It moved beneath them unsafely, but from the divan which occupied one end of the apartment an uninterrupted view of the door below was obtainable.

"Stay here," said Dr. Cairn, "and watch, whilst I reconnoitre."

He descended the stairs again, to return in a minute or so and announce that another street could be reached through the back of the house. There and then they settled the plan of campaign. One at a time they would go to the hotel for their meals, so that the door would never be un-watched throughout the day. Dr. Cairn determined to make no in-quiries respecting the house, as this might put the enemy upon his guard.

"We are in his own country, Rob," he said. "Here we can trust no one."

Thereupon they commenced their singular and self-imposed task. In turn they went back to the hotel for breakfast, and watched fruitlessly throughout the morning. They lunched in the same way, and through-out the great midday heat sat hidden in the ruined building, mounting guard over that iron-studded door. It was a dreary and monotonous day, long to be remembered by both of them, and when the hour of sunset drew nigh, and their vigil remained unrewarded, they began to doubt the wisdom of their tactics. The street was but little frequented; there was not the slightest chance of their presence being discovered.

It was very quiet, too, so that no one could have approached unheard. At the hotel they had learnt the cause of the explosion during the night: an accident in the engine-room of a tramp steamer, which had done con-siderable damage but caused no bodily injury.

"We may hope to win yet," said Dr. Cairn, in speaking of the incident. "It was the hand of God."

Silence had prevailed between them for a long time, and he was about to propose that his son should go back to dinner, when the rare sound of a footstep below checked the words upon his lips. Both craned their necks to obtain a view of the pedestrian.

An old man stooping beneath the burden of years and resting much of his weight upon a staff came tottering into sight. The watchers crouched back, breathless with excitement, as the newcomer paused be-fore the iron-studded door and from beneath his cloak took out a big key.

Inserting it into the lock, he swung open the door; it creaked upon an-cient hinges as it opened inward, revealing a glimpse of a stone floor. As the old man entered, Dr. Cairn grasped his son by the wrist.

"Down!' he whispered. "Now is our chance!" They ran down the rickety stairs, crossed the narrow street, and Robert Cairn cautiously looked in around the door which had been left ajar.

Black against the dim light of another door at the farther end of the large and barn-like apartment showed the stooping figure. Tap, tap, tap! went the stick; and the old man had disappeared around a corner.

"Where can we hide?" whispered Dr. Cairn. "He is evidently making a tour of inspection."

The sound of footsteps mounting to the upper apartments came to their ears. They looked about them right and left, and presently the younger man detected a large wooden cupboard set in one wall. Opening it, be saw that it contained but one shelf only, near the top.

"When he returns," he said, "we can hide in here until he has gone out."

Dr. Cairn nodded; he was peering about the room intently.

"This is the place I came to, Rob!" he said softly; "but there was a stone stair leading down to some room underneath. We must find it."

The old man could be heard passing from room to room above; then his uneven footsteps sounded on the stair again, and glancing at one another the two stepped into the cupboard, and pulled the door gently inward. A few minutes later the old caretaker—since such appeared to be his office—passed out, slamming the door behind him. At that, they emerged from their hiding-place and began to examine the apartment carefully. It was growing very dark now; indeed, with the door shut, it was difficult to detect the outlines of the room. Suddenly, a loud cry broke the perfect stillness, seeming to come from somewhere above. Robert Cairn started violently, grasping his father's arm, but the older man smiled.

"You forget that there is a mosque almost opposite," he said. "That is the *muezzin!*"

His son laughed shortly.

"My nerves are not yet all that they might be," he explained, and bending low began to examine the pavement.

"There must be a trap-door in the floor," he continued. "Don't you think so?"

His father nodded silently, and upon hands and knees also began to inspect the cracks and crannies between the various stones. In the right-hand corner farthest from the entrance their quest was rewarded. A stone some three feet square moved slightly when pressure was applied to it and gave up a sound of hollowness beneath the tread. Dust and litter covered the entire floor, but having cleared the top of this particular stone, a ring was discovered, lying flat in a circular groove cut to receive it. The blade of a penknife served to raise it from its resting-place, and Dr. Cairn, standing astride across the trap, tugged at the ring, and, without great difficulty, raised the stone block from its place.

A square hole was revealed. There were irregular stone steps leading down into the blackness. A piece of candle, stuck in a crude wooden holder, lay upon the topmost. Dr. Cairn, taking a box of matches from his pocket, very quickly lighted the candle, and with it held in his left hand began to descend. His head was not yet below the level of the upper apartment when he paused.

"You have your revolver?" he said.

Robert nodded grimly, and took his revolver from his pocket.

A singular and most disagreeable smell was arising from the trap which they had opened; but ignoring this they descended, and presently stood side by side in a low cellar. Here the odour was almost insupportable; it had in it something menacing, something definitely repellent; and at the foot of the steps they stood hesitating.

Dr. Cairn slowly moved the candle, throwing the light along the floor, where it picked out strips of wood and broken cases, straw packing, and kindred litter—until it impinged upon a brightly painted slab. Further he moved it, and higher, and the end of a sarcophagus came into view. He drew a quick, hissing breath, and bending forward, directed the light into the interior of the ancient coffin. Then he had need of all his iron nerve to choke down the cry that rose to his lips.

"My God! *Look!*" whispered his son.

Swathed in white wrappings, Antony Ferrara lay motionless before them.

The seconds passed one by one, until a whole minute was told, and still the two remained inert and the cold light shone fully upon that ivory face.

"Is he dead?"

Robert Cairn spoke huskily, grasping his father's shoulder.

"I think not," was the equally hoarse reply. "He is in the state of trance mentioned in—certain ancient writings; he is absorbing evil force from the sarcophagus of the Witch-Queen..."*

There was a faint rustling sound in the cellar, which seemed to grow

---

*Note.*—"It seems exceedingly probable that... the mummy-case (sarcophagus), with its painted presentment of the living person, was the material basis for the preservation of the ... *Khu* (magical powers) of a fully equipped Adept." *Collectanea Hermetica.* Vol. VIII.

louder and more insistent, but Dr. Cairn, apparently, did not notice it, for he turned to his son, and albeit the latter could see him but vaguely, he knew that his face was grimly set.

"It seems like butchery," he said evenly, "but, in the interests of the world, we must not hesitate. A shot might attract attention. Give me your knife."

For a moment the other scarcely comprehended the full purport of the words. Mechanically he took out his knife, and opened the big blade.

"Good heavens, sir," he gasped breathlessly, "it is too awful!"

"Awful I grant you," replied Dr. Cairn, "but a duty —a duty, boy, and one that we must not shirk. I, alone among living men, know whom, and *what*, lies there, and my conscience directs me in what I do. His end shall be that which he had planned for you. Give me the knife."

He took the knife from his son's hand. With the light directed upon the still ivory face, he stepped toward the sarcophagus. As he did so, something dropped from the roof, narrowly missed falling upon his outstretched hand, and with a soft, dull thud dropped upon the mud brick floor. Impelled by some intuition, he suddenly directed the light to the roof above.

Then with a shrill cry which he was wholly unable to repress, Robert Cairn seized his father's arm and began to pull him back toward the stair.

"Quick, sir!" he screamed shrilly, almost hysterically. "My God! my God! *be quick!*"

The appearance of the roof above had puzzled him for an instant as the light touched it, then in the next had filled his very soul with loathing and horror. For directly above them was moving a black patch, a foot or so in extent... and it was composed of a dense moving mass of tarantula spiders! A line of the disgusting creatures was mounting the wall and crossing the ceiling, ever swelling the unclean group!

Dr. Cairn did not hesitate to leap for the stair, and as he did so the spiders began to drop. Indeed, they seemed to leap toward the intruders until the floor all about them and the bottom steps of the stair presented a mass of black, moving insects.

A perfect panic fear seized upon them. At every step spiders *crunched* beneath their feet. They seemed to come from nowhere, to be conjured up out of the darkness, until the whole cellar, the stairs, the very fetid air about them, became black and nauseous with spiders.

Halfway to the top Dr. Cairn turned, snatched out a revolver, and began firing down into the cellar in the direct ion of the sarcophagus.

A hairy, clutching thing ran up his arm, and his son, uttering a groan of horror, struck at it and stained the tweed with its poisonous blood.

They staggered to the head of the steps, and there Dr. Cairn turned and hurled the candle at a monstrous spider that suddenly sprang into view. The candle, still attached to its wooden socket, went bounding down steps that now were literally carpeted with insects.

Tarantulas began to run out from the trap as if pursuing the intruders, and a faint light showed from below. Then came a crackling sound, and a wisp of smoke floated up.

Dr. Cairn threw open the outer door, and the two panic-stricken men leapt out in the street and away from the spider army. White to the lips, they stood leaning against the wall.

"Was it really—Ferrara?" whispered Robert.

"I hope so!" was the answer.

Dr. Cairn pointed to the closed door. A fan of smoke was creeping from beneath it.

The fire which ensued destroyed, not only the house in which it had broken out, but the two adjoining; and the neighbouring mosque was saved only with the utmost difficulty.

When, in the dawn of the new day, Dr. Cairn looked down into the smoking pit which once had been the home of the spiders, he shook his head and turned to his son.

"If our eyes did not deceive us, Rob," he said, "a just retribution at last has claimed him!"

Pressing a way through the surrounding crowd of natives, they returned to the hotel. The hall porter stopped them as they entered.

"Excuse me, sir," he said, "but which is Mr. Robert Cairn?"

Robert Cairn stepped forward.

"A young gentleman left this for you, sir, half an hour ago," said the man—"a very pale gentleman with black eyes. He said you'd dropped it."

Robert Cairn unwrapped the little parcel. It contained a penknife, the ivory handle charred as if it had been in a furnace. It was his own—which he had handed to his father in that awful cellar at the moment when the first spider had dropped; and a card was enclosed, bearing the pencilled words, "With Antony Ferrara's Compliments."

## CHAPTER XVII
## THE STORY OF ALI MOHAMMED

Saluting each of the three in turn, the tall Egyptian passed from Dr. Cairn's room. Upon his exit followed a brief but electric silence. Dr. Cairn's face was very stern and Sime, with his hands locked behind him, stood staring out of the window into the palmy garden of the hotel. Robert Cairn looked from one to the other excitedly.

"What did he say, sir?" he cried, addressing his father. "It had something to do with—"

Dr. Cairn turned. Sime did not move.

"It had something to do with the matter which has brought me to Cairo," replied the former—"yes."

"You see," said Robert, "my knowledge of Arabic is *nil*—"

Sime turned in his heavy fashion, and directed a dull gaze upon the last speaker.

"Ali Mohammed," he explained slowly, "who has just left, had come down from the Fayûm to report a singular matter. He was unaware of its real importance, but it was sufficiently unusual to disturb him, and Ali Mohammed es-Suefi is not easily disturbed."

Dr. Cairn dropped into an armchair, nodding toward Sime.

"Tell him all that we have heard," he said. "We stand together in this affair."

"Well," continued Sime, in his deliberate fashion, "when we struck our camp beside the Pyramid of Méydûm, Ali Mohammed remained behind with a gang of workmen to finish off some comparatively unimportant work. He is an unemotional person. Fear is alien to his composition; it has no meaning for him. But last night something occurred at the camp—or what remained of the camp—which seems to have shaken even Ali Mohammed's iron nerve."

Robert Cairn nodded, watching the speaker intently.

"The entrance to the Méydûm Pyramid," continued Sime.

"*One* of the entrances," interrupted Dr. Cairn, smiling slightly.

"There is only one entrance," said Sime dogmatically.

Dr. Cairn waved his hand.

"Go ahead," he said. "We can discuss these archeological details later."

Sime stared dully, but, without further comment, resumed:

"The camp was situated on the slope immediately below the only *known* entrance to the Méydûm Pyramid; one might say that it lay in the shadow of the building. There are tumuli in the neighbourhood—part of a prehistoric cemetery—and it was work in connection with this which had detained Ali Mohammed in that part of the Fayûm. Last night about ten o'clock he was awakened by an unusual sound, or series of sounds, he reports. He came out of the tent into the moonlight, and looked up at the pyramid. The entrance was a good way above his head, of course, and quite fifty or sixty yards from the point where he was standing, but the moonbeams bathed that side of the building in dazzling light so that he was enabled to see a perfect crowd of bats whirling out of the pyramid."

"Bats!" ejaculated Robert Cairn.

"Yes. There is a small colony of bats in this pyramid, of course; but the bat does not hunt in bands, and the sight of these bats flying out from the place was one which Ali Mohammed had never witnessed before. Their concerted squeaking was very clearly audible. He could not believe that it was this which had awakened him, and which had awakened the ten or twelve workmen who also slept in the camp, for these were now clustering around him, and all looking up at the side of the pyramid.

"Fayûm nights are strangely still. Except for the jackals and the village dogs, and some other sounds to which one grows accustomed, there is nothing—absolutely nothing—audible.

"In this stillness, then, the flapping of the bat regiment made quite a disturbance overhead. Some of the men were only half awake, but most of them were badly frightened. And now they began to compare notes, with the result that they determined upon the exact nature of the sound which had aroused them. It seemed almost certain that this had been a dreadful scream—the scream of a woman in the last agony."

He paused, looking from Dr. Cairn to his son, with a singular expression upon his habitually immobile face.

"Go on," said Robert Cairn.

Slowly Sime resumed:

"The bats had begun to disperse in various directions, but the panic which had seized upon the camp does not seem to have dispersed so readily. Ali Mohammed confesses that he himself felt almost afraid—a remarkable admission for a man of his class to make. Picture these fellows, then, standing looking at one another, and very frequently up at the opening in the side of the pyramid. Then the smell began to reach their nostrils—the smell which completed the panic, and which led to the abandonment of the camp—"

"The smell—what kind of smell?" jerked Robert Cairn.

Dr. Cairn turned himself in his chair, looking fully at his son.

"The smell of Hades, boy!" he said grimly, and turned away again.

"Naturally," continued Sime, "I can give you no particulars on the point, but it must have been something very fearful to have affected the Egyptian native! There was no breeze, but it swept down upon them, this poisonous smell, as though borne by a hot wind."

"Was it actually hot?"

"I cannot say. But Ali Mohammed is positive that it came from the opening in the pyramid. It was not apparently in disgust, but in sheer, stark horror that the whole crowd of them turned tail and ran. They never stopped and never looked back until they came to Rekka on the railway."

A short silence followed. Then:

"That was last night?" questioned Cairn.

His father nodded.

"The man came in by the first train from Wasta," he said, "and we have not a moment to spare!"

Sime stared at him.

"I don't understand—"

"I have a mission," said Dr. Cairn quietly. "It is to run to earth, to stamp out, as I would stamp out a pestilence, a certain *thing*—I cannot call it a man—Antony Ferrara. I believe, Sime, that you are at one with me in this matter?"

Sime drummed his fingers upon the table, frowning thoughtfully, and looking from one to the other of his companions under his lowered brows.

"With my own eyes," he said, "I have seen something of this secret drama which has brought you, Dr. Cairn, to Egypt; and, up to a point, I agree with you regarding Antony Ferrara. You have lost all trace of him?"

"Since leaving Port Said," said Dr. Cairn, "I have seen and heard nothing of him; but Lady Lashmore, who was an intimate—and an innocent victim, God help her—of Ferrara in London, after staying at the Semiramis in Cairo for one day, departed. Where did she go?"

"What has Lady Lashmore to do with the matter?" asked Sime.

"If what I fear be true—" replied Dr. Cairn. "But I anticipate. At the moment it is enough for me that, unless my information be at fault, Lady Lashmore yesterday left Cairo by the Luxor train at 8:30."

Robert Cairn looked in a puzzled way at his father.

"What do you suspect, sir?" he said.

"I suspect that she went no farther than Wasta," replied Dr. Cairn.

"Still I do not understand," declared Sime.

"You may understand later," was the answer. "We must not waste a moment. You Egyptologists think that Egypt has little or nothing to teach you; the Pyramid of Méydûm lost interest directly you learnt that apparently it contained no treasure. How little you know what it *really* contained, Sime! Mariette did not suspect; Sir Gaston Maspero does not suspect! The late Sir Michael Ferrara and I once camped by the Pyramid of Méydûm, as you have camped there, and we made a discovery—"

"Well?" said Sime, with growing interest.

"It is a point upon which my lips are sealed, but—do you believe in black magic?"

"I am not altogether sure that I do—"

"Very well; you are entitled to your opinion. But although you appear to be ignorant of the fact, the Pyramid of Méydûm was formerly one of the strongholds—the second greatest in all the land of the Nile—of Ancient Egyptian sorcery! I pray Heaven I may be wrong, but in the disappearance of Lady Lashmore, and in the story of Ali Mohammed, I see a dreadful possibility. Ring for a time-table. We have not a moment to waste!"


## CHAPTER XVIII
## THE BATS

Rekka was a mile behind.

"It will take us fully an hour yet," said Dr, Cairn, "to reach the pyramid, although it appears so near."

Indeed, in the violet dusk, the great mastaba Pyramid of Méydûm seemed already to loom above them, although it was quite four miles away. The narrow path along which they trotted their donkeys ran through the fertile lowlands of the Fayûm. They had just passed a village, amid an angry chorus from the pariah dogs, and were now following the track along the top of the embankment. Where the green carpet merged ahead into the gray ocean of sand the desert began, and out in that desert, resembling some weird work of Nature rather than anything wrought by the hand of man, stood the gloomy and lonely building ascribed by the Egyptologists to the Pharaoh Sneferu.

Dr. Cairn and his son rode ahead, and Sime, with Ali Mohammed, brought up the rear of the little company.

"I am completely in the dark, sir," said Robert Cairn, "respecting the object of our present journey. What leads you to suppose that we shall find Antony Ferrara here?"

"I scarcely hope to *find* him here," was the enigmatical reply, "but I am almost certain that he is here. I might have expected it, and I blame myself for not having provided against—this."

"Against what?"

"It is impossible, Rob, for you to understand this matter. Indeed, if I were to publish what I know—not what I imagine, but what I know—about the Pyramid of Méydûm I should not only call down upon myself the ridicule of every Egyptologist in Europe; I should be accounted mad by the whole world."

His son was silent for a time; then:

"According to the guide books," he said, "it is merely an empty tomb."

"It is empty, certainly," replied Dr. Cairn, grimly, "or that apartment known as the King's Chamber is now empty. But even the so-called King's Chamber was not empty once; and there is another chamber in the pyramid which is not empty *now!*"

"If you know of the existence of such a chamber, sir, why have you kept it secret?"

"Because I cannot *prove* its existence. I do not know how to enter it, but I know it is there; I know what it was formerly used for, and I suspect that last night it was used for that same unholy purpose again—after a lapse of perhaps four thousand years! Even you would doubt me, I believe, if I were to tell you what I know, if I were to hint at what I suspect. But no doubt in your reading you have met with Julian the Apostate?"

"Certainly, I have read of him. He is said to have practised necromancy."

"When he was at Carra, in Mesopotamia, he retired to the Temple of the Moon with a certain sorcerer and some others, and, his nocturnal operations concluded, he left the temple locked, the door sealed, and placed a guard over the gate. He was killed in the war, and never returned to Carra, but when in the reign of Jovian the seal was broken and the temple opened, a body was found hanging by its hair— I will spare you the particulars; it was a case of that most awful form of sorcery—*anthropomancy!*"

An expression of horror had crept over Robert Cairn's face.

"Do you mean, sir, that this pyramid was used for similar purposes?"

"In the past it has been used for many purposes," was the quiet reply. "The exodus of the bats points to the fact that it was again used for one of those purposes last night; the exodus of the bats—and something else."

Sime, who had been listening to this strange conversation, cried out from the rear:

"We cannot reach it before sunset!"

"No," replied Dr. Cairn, turning in his saddle, "but that does not matter. Inside the pyramid, day and night make no difference."

Having crossed a narrow wooden bridge, they turned now fully in the direction of the great ruin, pursuing a path along the opposite bank of the cutting. They rode in silence for some time, Robert Cairn deep in thought.

"I suppose that Antony Ferrara actually visited this place last night," he said suddenly, "although I cannot follow your reasoning. But what leads you to suppose that he is there now?"

"This," answered his father slowly. "The purpose for which I believe him to have come here would detain him at least two days and two nights. I shall say no more about it, because if I am wrong, or if for any reason I am unable to establish my suspicions as facts, you would certainly regard me as a madman if I had confided those suspicions to you."

Mounted upon donkeys, the journey from Rekka to the Pyramid of Méydûm occupies fully an hour and a half, and the glories of the sunset had merged into the violet dusk of Egypt before the party passed the outskirts of the cultivated land and came upon the desert sands. The mountainous pile of granite, its peculiar orange hue a ghastly yellow in the moonlight, now assumed truly monstrous proportions, seeming like a great square tower rising in three stages from its mound of sand to some three hundred and fifty feet above the level of the desert.

There is nothing more awesome in the world than to find one's self at night, far from all fellow-men, in the shadow of one of those edifices raised by unknown hands, by unknown means, to an unknown end; for, despite all the wisdom of our modern inquirers, these stupendous relics remain unsolved riddles set to posterity by a mysterious people.

Neither Sime nor Ali Mohammed were of highly strung temperament, neither subject to those subtle impressions which more delicate organisms receive, as the nostrils receive an exhalation, from such a place as this. But Dr. Cairn and his son, though each in a different way, came now within the aura of this temple of the dead ages.

The great silence of the desert—a silence like no other in the world; the loneliness, which must be experienced to be appreciated, of that dry and tideless ocean; the traditions which had grown up like fungi about this venerable building; lastly, the knowledge that it was associated in some way with the sorcery, the unholy activity, of Antony Ferrara, combined to chill them with a supernatural dread which called for all their courage to combat.

"What now?" said Sime, descending from his mount.

"We must lead the donkeys up the slope," replied Dr. Cairn, "where those blocks of granite are, and tether them there."

In silence, then, the party commenced the tedious ascent of the mound by the narrow path to the top, until at some hundred and twenty feet above the surrounding plain they found themselves actually under the wall of the mighty building. The donkeys were made fast.

"Sime and I," said Dr. Cairn quietly, "will enter the pyramid."

"But—" interrupted his son.

"Apart from the fatigue of the operation," continued the doctor, "the temperature in the lower part of the pyramid is so tremendous, and the air so bad, that in your present state of health it would be absurd for you to attempt it. Apart from which there is a possibly more important task to be undertaken here, outside."

He turned his eyes upon Sime, who was listening intently, then continued:

"Whilst we are penetrating to the interior by means of the sloping passage on the north side, Ali Mohammed and yourself must mount guard on the south side."

"What for?" said Sime rapidly.

"For the reason," replied Dr. Cairn, "that there is an entrance on to the first stage—"

"But the first stage is nearly seventy feet above us. Even assuming that there were an entrance there—which I doubt—escape by that means would be impossible. No one could climb down the face of the pyramid from above; no one has ever succeeded in climbing up. For the purpose of surveying the pyramid a scaffold had to be erected. Its sides are quite unscaleable."

"That may be," agreed Dr. Cairn; "but nevertheless, I have my reasons for placing a guard over the south side. If anything appears upon the stage above, Rob—*anything*—shoot, and shoot straight!"

He repeated the same instructions to Ali Mohammed, to the evident surprise of the latter.

"I don't understand at all," muttered Sime, "but as I presume you have a good reason for what you do, let it be as you propose. Can you give me any idea respecting what we may hope to find inside this place? I only entered once, and I am not anxious to repeat the experiment. The air is unbreathable, the descent to the level passage below is stiff work, and, apart from the inconvenience of navigating the latter passage, which as you probably know is only sixteen inches high, the climb up the vertical shaft into the tomb is not a particularly safe one. I exclude the possibility of snakes," he added ironically.

"You have also omitted the possibility of Antony Ferrara," said Dr. Cairn.

"Pardon my scepticism, Doctor, but I cannot imagine any man voluntarily remaining in that awful place."

"Yet I am greatly mistaken if he is not there!"

"Then he is trapped!" said Sime grimly, examining a Browning pistol which he carried. "Unless—"

He stopped, and an expression, almost of fear, crept over his stoical features.

"That sixteen-inch passage," he muttered—"with Antony Ferrara at the farther end!"

"Exactly!" said Dr. Cairn. "But I consider it my duty to the world to proceed. I warn you that you are about to face the greatest peril, probably, which you will ever be called upon to encounter. I do not ask you to do this. I am quite prepared to go alone."

"That remark was wholly unnecessary, Doctor," said Sime rather truculently. "Suppose the other two proceed to their post."

"But, sir—" began Robert Cairn.

"You know the way," said the doctor, with an air of finality. "There is not a moment to waste, and although I fear that we are too late, it is just possible we may be in time to prevent a dreadful crime."

The tall Egyptian and Robert Cairn went stumbling off amongst the heaps of rubbish and broken masonry, until an angle of the great wall concealed them from view. Then the two who remained continued the climb yet higher, following the narrow, zigzag path leading up to the entrance of the descending passage. Immediately under the square black hole they stood and glanced at one another.

"We may as well leave our outer garments here," said Sime. "I note that you wear rubber-soled shoes, but I shall remove my boots, as otherwise I should be unable to obtain any foothold."

Dr. Cairn nodded, and without more ado proceeded to strip off his coat, an example which was followed by Sime. It was as he stooped and placed his hat upon the little bundle of clothes at his feet that Dr. Cairn detected something which caused him to stoop yet lower and to peer at that dark object on the ground with a strange intentness.

"What is it?" jerked Sime, glancing back at him.

Dr. Cairn, from a hip pocket, took out an electric lamp, and directed the white ray upon something lying on the splintered fragments of granite.

It was a bat, a fairly large one, and a clot of blood marked the place where its head had been. For the bat was decapitated!

As though anticipating what he should find there, Dr. Cairn flashed the ray of the lamp all about the ground in the vicinity of the entrance to the pyramid. Scores of dead bats, headless, lay there.

"For God's sake, what does this mean?" whispered Sime, glancing apprehensively into the black entrance beside him.

"It means," answered Cairn, in a low voice, "that my suspicion, almost incredible though it seems, was well founded. Steel yourself against the task that is before you, Sime; we stand upon the borderland of strange horrors."

Sime hesitated to touch any of the dead bats, surveying them with an ill-concealed repugnance.

"What kind of creature," he whispered, "has done this?"

"One of a kind that the world has not known for many ages! The most evil kind of creature conceivable—a man-devil!"

"But what does he want with bats' heads?"

"The Cynonycteris, or pyramid bat, has a leaf-like appendage beside the nose. A gland in this secretes a rare oil. This oil is one of the ingredients of the incense which is never named in the magical writings."

Sime shuddered.

"Here!" said Dr. Cairn, proffering a flask. "This is only the overture! No nerves."

The other nodded shortly, and poured out a peg of brandy.

"Now," said Dr. Cairn, "shall I go ahead?"

"As you like," replied Sime quietly, and again quite master of himself. "Look out for snakes. I will carry the light and you can keep yours handy in case you may need it."

Dr. Cairn drew himself up into the entrance. The passage was less than four feet high, and generations of sand-storms had polished its sloping granite floor so as to render it impossible to descend except by resting one's hands on the roof above and lowering one's self foot by foot.

A passage of this description, descending at a sharp angle for over two hundred feet, is not particularly easy to negotiate, and progress was slow. Dr. Cairn at every five yards or so would stop, and, with the pocket-lamp which he carried, would examine the sandy floor and the crevices between the huge blocks composing the passage, in quest of those faint tracks which warn the traveller that a serpent has recently passed that way. Then, replacing his lamp, he would proceed. Sime followed in like manner, employing only one hand to support himself, and, with the other, constantly directing the ray of his pocket torch past his companion, and down into the blackness beneath.

Out in the desert the atmosphere had been sufficiently hot, but now with every step it grew hotter and hotter. That indescribable smell, as of a decay begun in remote ages, that rises with the impalpable dust in these mysterious labyrinths of Ancient Egypt which never know the light of day, rose stiflingly; until, at some forty or fifty feet below the level of the sand outside, respiration became difficult, and the two paused, bathed in perspiration and gasping for air.

"Another thirty or forty feet," panted Sime, "and we shall be in the level passage. There is a sort of low, artificial cavern there, you may remember, where, although we cannot stand upright, we can sit and rest for a few moments."

Speech was exhausting, and no further words were exchanged until the bottom of the slope was reached, and the combined lights of the two pocket-lamps showed them that they had reached a tiny chamber irregularly hewn in the living rock. This also was less than four feet high, but its jagged floor being level, they were enabled to pause here for a while.

"Do you notice something unfamiliar in the smell of the place?"

Dr. Cairn was the speaker. Sime nodded, wiping the perspiration from his face the while.

"It was bad enough when I came here before," he said hoarsely. "It is terrible work for a heavy man. But to-night it seems to be reeking. I have smelt nothing like it in my life."

"Correct," replied Dr. Cairn grimly. "I trust that, once clear of this place, you will never smell it again."

"What is it?"

"It is the incense," was the reply. "Come! The worst of our task is before us yet."

The continuation of the passage now showed as an opening no more than fifteen to seventeen inches high. It was necessary, therefore, to lie prone upon the rubbish of the floor, and to proceed serpent fashion; one could not even employ one's knees, so low was the roof, but was compelled to progress by clutching at the irregularities in the wall, and by digging the elbows into the splintered stones one crawled upon!

For three yards or so they proceeded thus. Then Dr. Cairn lay suddenly still.

"What is it?" whispered Sime.

A threat of panic was in his voice. He dared not conjecture what would happen if either should be overcome in that evil-smelling burrow, deep in the bowels of the ancient building. At that moment it seemed to him, absurdly enough, that the weight of the giant pile rested upon his back, was crushing him, pressing the life out from his body as he lay there prone, with his eyes fixed upon the rubber soles of Dr. Cairn's shoes, directly in front of him.

But softly came a reply:

"Do not speak again! Proceed as quietly as possible, and pray Heaven we are not expected!"

Sime understood. With a malignant enemy before them, this hole in the rock through which they crawled was a certain death-trap. He thought of the headless bats and of how he, in crawling out into the shaft ahead, must lay himself open to a similar fate!

Dr. Cairn moved slowly onward. Despite their anxiety to avoid noise, neither he nor his companion could control their heavy breathing. Both were panting for air. The temperature was now deathly. A candle would scarcely have burnt in the vitiated air; and above that odour of ancient rottenness which all explorers of the monuments of Egypt know, rose that other indescribable odour which seemed to stifle one's very soul.

Dr. Cairn stopped again.

Sime knew, having performed this journey before, that his companion must have reached the end of the passage, that he must be lying peering out into the shaft, for which they were making. He extinguished his lamp.

Again Dr. Cairn moved forward. Stretching out his hand, Sime found only emptiness. He wriggled forward, in turn, rapidly, all the time groping with his fingers. Then:

"Take my hand," came a whisper. "Another two feet, and you can stand upright."

He proceeded, grasped the hand which was extended to him in the impenetrable darkness, and panting, temporarily exhausted, rose upright beside Dr. Cairn and stretched his cramped limbs.

Side by side they stood, mantled about in such a darkness as cannot be described; in such a silence as dwellers in the busy world cannot conceive; in such an atmosphere of horror that only a man morally and physically brave could have retained his composure.

Dr. Cairn bent to Sime's ear.

"We *must* have the light for the ascent," he whispered. "Have your pistol ready; I am about to press the button of the lamp."

A shaft of white light shone suddenly up the rocky sides of the pit in which they stood, and lost itself in the gloom of the chamber above.

"On to my shoulders," jerked Sime. "You are lighter than I. Then, as soon as you can reach, place your lamp on the floor above and mount up beside it. I will follow."

Dr. Cairn, taking advantage of the rugged walls, and of the blocks of stone amid which they stood, mounted upon Sime's shoulders.

"Could you carry your revolver in your teeth? asked the latter. "I think you might hold it by the trigger-guard."

"I proposed to do so," replied Dr. Cairn grimly. "Stand fast!"

Gradually he rose upright upon the other's shoulders; then, placing his foot in a cranny of the rock, and with his left hand grasping a protruding fragment above, he mounted yet higher, all the time holding the lighted lamp in his right hand. Upward he extended his arms, and upward, until he could place the lamp upon the ledge above his head, where its white beam shone across the top of the shaft.

"Mind it does not fall!" panted Sime, craning his head upward to watch these operations.

Dr. Cairn, whose strength and agility were wonderful, twisted around sideways, and succeeded in placing his foot on a ledge of stone on the opposite side of the shaft. Resting his weight upon this, he extended his hand to the lip of the opening, and drew himself up to the top, where he crouched fully in the light of the lamp. Then, wedging his foot into a crevice a little below him, he reached out his hand to Sime. The latter, following much the same course as his companion, seized the extended hand, and soon found himself beside Dr. Cairn.

Impetuously he snatched out his own lamp and shone its beams about the weird apartment in which they found themselves—the so-called King's Chamber of the pyramid. Right and left leapt the searching rays, touching the ends of the wooden beams, which, practically fossilized by long contact with the rock, still survive in that sepulchral place. Above and below and all around he directed the light—upon the litter covering the rock floor, upon the blocks of the higher walls, upon the frowning roof.

They were alone in the King's Chamber!


## CHAPTER XIX
## ANTHROPOMANCY


"There is no one here!"

Sime looked about the place excitedly.

"Fortunately for us!" answered Dr. Cairn.

He breathed rather heavily yet with his exertions, and, moreover, the air of the chamber was disgusting. But otherwise he was perfectly calm, although his face was pale and bathed in perspiration.

"Make as little noise as possible."

Sime, who, now that the place proved to be empty, began to cast off that dread which had possessed him in the passage-way, found something ominous in the words.

Dr. Cairn, stepping carefully over the rubbish of the floor, advanced to the east corner of the chamber, waving his companion to follow. Side by side they stood there.

"Do you notice that the abominable smell of the incense is more overpowering here than anywhere?"

Sime nodded.

"You are right. What does that mean?"

Dr. Cairn directed the ray of light down behind a little mound of rubbish into a corner of the wall.

"It means," he said, with a subdued expression excitement, "that we have got to crawl in *there!*"

Sime stifled an exclamation.

One of the blocks of the bottom tier was missing, a fact which he had not detected before by reason of the presence of the mound of rubbish before the opening.

"Silence again!" whispered Dr. Cairn.

He lay down flat, and, without hesitation, crept into the gap. As his feet disappeared, Sime followed. Here it was possible to crawl upon hands and knees. The passage was formed of square stone blocks. It was but three yards or so in length; then it suddenly turned upward at a tremendous angle of about one in four. Square footholds were cut in the lower face. The smell of incense was almost unbearable.

Dr. Cairn bent to Sime's ear.

"Not a word, now," he said. "No light—pistol ready!"

He began to mount. Sime, following, counted the steps. When they had mounted sixty he knew that they must have come close to the top of the original mastaba and close to the first stage of the pyramid. Despite the shaft beneath there was little danger of falling, for one could lean back against the wall while seeking for the foothold above.

Dr. Cairn mounted very slowly, fearful of striking his head upon some obstacle. Then on the seventieth step he found that he could thrust his foot forward and that no obstruction met his knee. They had reached a horizontal passage.

Very softly he whispered back to Sime:

"Take my hand. I have reached the top."

They entered the passage. The heavy, sickly sweet odour almost overpowered them, but, grimly set upon their purpose, they, after one moment of hesitancy, crept on.

A fitful light rose and fell ahead of them. It gleamed upon the polished walls of the corridor in which they now found themselves—that inexplicable light burning in a place which had known no light since the dim ages of the early Pharaohs!

The events of that incredible night had afforded no such emotion as this. This was the crowning wonder, and, in its dreadful mystery, the crowning terror of Méydûm.

When first that lambent light played upon the walls of the passage both stopped, stricken motionless with fear and amazement. Sime, who would have been prepared to swear that the Méydûm Pyramid contained no apartment other than the King's Chamber, now was past mere wonder, past conjecture. But he could still fear. Dr. Cairn, although he had anticipated this, temporarily also fell a victim to the supernatural character of the phenomenon.

They advanced.

They looked into a square chamber of about the same size as the King's Chamber. In fact, although they did not realize it until later, this second apartment no doubt was situated directly above the first.

The only light was that of a fire burning in a tripod, and by means of this illumination, which rose and fell in a strange manner, it was possible to perceive the details of the place. But, indeed, at the moment they were not concerned with these; they had eyes only for the black-robed figure beside the tripod.

It was that of a man, who stood with his back toward them, and he chanted monotonously in a tongue unfamiliar to Sime. At certain points in his chant he would raise his arms in such a way that, clad in the black robe, he assumed the appearance of a gigantic bat. Each time that he acted thus the fire in the tripod, as if fanned into new life, would leap up, casting a hellish glare about the place. Then, as the chanter dropped his arms again, the flame would drop also.

A cloud of reddish vapour floated low in the apartment. There were a number of curiously shaped vessels upon the floor, and against the farther wall, rendered visible only when the flames leapt high, was some motionless white object, apparently hung from the roof.

Cairn drew a hissing breath and grasped Sime's wrist.

"We are too late!" he said strangely.

He spoke at a moment when his companion, peering through the ruddy gloom of the place, had been endeavouring more clearly to perceive that ominous shape which hung, horrible, in the shadow. He spoke, too, at a moment when the man in the black robe raised his arms—when, as if obedient to his will, the flames leapt up fitfully.

Although Sime could not be sure of what he saw, the recollection came to him of words recently spoken by Dr. Cairn. He remembered the story of Julian the Apostate, Julian the Emperor—the Necromancer. He remembered what had been found in the Temple of the Moon after Julian's death. He remembered that Lady Lashmore—

And thereupon he experienced such a nausea that but for the fact that Dr. Cairn gripped him he must have fallen.

Tutored in a materialistic school, he could not even now admit that such monstrous things could be. With a necromantic operation taking place before his eyes; with the unholy perfume of the secret incense all but suffocating him; with the dreadful Oracle dully gleaming in the shadows of that temple of evil—his reason would not accept the evidences. Any man of the ancient world—of the Middle Ages—would have known that he looked upon a professed wizard, upon a magician, who, according to one of the most ancient formulæ known to mankind, was seeking to question the dead respecting the living.

But how many modern men are there capable of realizing such a circumstance? How many who would accept the statement that such operations are still performed, not only in the East, but in Europe? How many who, witnessing this mass of Satan, would accept it for verity, would not deny the evidence of their very senses?

He could not believe such an orgy of wickedness possible. A Pagan emperor might have been capable of these things, but to-day—wondrous is our faith in the virtue of "to-day"!

"Am I mad?" he whispered hoarsely, "or—"

A thinly veiled shape seemed to float out from that still form in the shadows; it assumed definite outlines; it became a woman, beautiful with a beauty that could only be described as awful.

She wore upon her brow the uræus of Ancient Egyptian royalty; her sole garment was a robe of finest gauze. Like a cloud, like a vision, she floated into the light cast by the tripod.

A voice—a voice which seemed to come from a vast distance, from somewhere outside the mighty granite walls of that unholy place—spoke. The language was unknown to Sime, but the fierce hand-grip upon his wrist grew fiercer. That dead tongue, that language unspoken since the dawn of Christianity, was known to the man who had been the companion of Sir Michael Ferrara.

In upon Sime swept a swift conviction—that one could not witness such a scene as this and live and move again amongst one's fellow-men! In a sort of frenzy, then, he wrenched himself free from the detaining hand, and launched a retort of modern science against the challenge of ancient sorcery.

Raising his Browning pistol, he fired—shot after shot—at that bat-like shape which stood between himself and the tripod!

A thousand frightful echoes filled the chamber with a demon mockery, boomed along those subterranean passages beneath, and bore the conflict of sound into the hidden places of the pyramid which had known not sound for untold generations.

"My God!"

Vaguely he became aware that Dr. Cairn was seeking to drag him away. Through a cloud of smoke he saw the black-robed figure turn; dream fashion, he saw the pallid, glistening face of Antony Ferrara; the long, evil eyes, alight like the eyes of a serpent, were fixed upon him. He seemed to stand amid a chaos, in a mad world beyond the borders of reason, beyond the dominions of God. But to his stupefied mind one astounding fact found access.

He had fired at least seven shots at the black-robed figure, and it was not humanly possible that all could have gone wide of their mark.

Yet Antony Ferrara lived!

Utter darkness blotted out the evil vision. Then there was a white light ahead; and feeling that he was struggling for sanity, Sime managed to realize that Dr. Cairn, retreating along the passage, was crying to him, in a voice rising almost to a shriek, to run—run for his life—for his salvation!

"*You should not have fired!*" he seemed to hear.

Unconscious of any contact with the stones—although afterward he found his knees and shins to be bleeding—he was scrambling down that long, sloping shaft.

He had a vague impression that Dr. Cairn, descending beneath him, sometimes grasped his ankles and placed his feet into the footholes. A continuous roaring sound filled his ears, as if a great ocean were casting its storm waves against the structure around him. The place seemed to rock.

"Down flat!"

Some sense of reality was returning to him. Now he perceived that Dr. Cairn was urging him to crawl back along the short passage by which they had entered from the King's Chamber.

Heedless to hurt, he threw himself down and pressed on.

A blank, like the sleep of exhaustion which follows delirium, came. Then Sime found himself standing in the King's Chamber, Dr. Cairn, who held an electric lamp in his hand, beside him, and half supporting him.

The realities suddenly reasserted themselves.

"I have dropped my pistol!" muttered Sime.

He threw off the supporting arm, and turned to that corner behind the heap of debris where was the opening through which they had entered the satanic temple.

No opening was visible!

"He has closed it!" cried Dr. Cairn. "There are six stone doors between here and the place above! If he had succeeded in shutting *one* of them before we—"

"My God!" whispered Sime. "Let us get out! I am nearly at the end of my tether!"

Fear lends wings, and it was with something like the lightness of a bird that Sime descended the shaft. At the bottom—

"On to my shoulders!" he cried, looking up.

Dr. Cairn lowered himself to the foot of the shaft.

"You go first," he said.

He was gasping, as if nearly suffocated, but retained a wonderful self-control. Once over into the Borderland, and bravery assumes a new guise; the courage which can face physical danger undaunted melts in the fires of the unknown.

Sime, his breath whistling sibilantly between his clenched teeth, hauled himself through the low passage with incredible speed. The two worked their way arduously up the long slope. They saw the blue sky above them.

"Something like a huge bat," said Robert Cairn, "crawled out upon the first stage. We both fired—"

Dr. Cairn raised his hand. He lay exhausted at the foot of the mound.

"He had lighted the incense," he replied, "and was reciting the secret ritual. I cannot explain. But your shots were wasted. We came too late—"

"Lady Lashmore—"

"Until the Pyramid of Méydûm is pulled down, stone by stone, the world will never know her fate! Sime and I have looked in at the gate of hell! Only the hand of God plucked us back! Look!"

He pointed to Sime. He lay, pallid, with closed eyes—and his hair was abundantly streaked with white!

## CHAPTER XX
## THE INCENSE

To Robert Cairn it seemed that the boat-train would never reach Charing Cross. His restlessness was appalling. He perpetually glanced from his father, with whom he shared the compartment, to the flying landscape with its vistas of hop-poles; and Dr. Cairn, although he exhibited less anxiety, was, nevertheless, strung to highest tension.

That dash from Cairo homeward had been something of a fevered dream to both men. To learn, whilst one is searching for a malign and implacable enemy in Egypt, that that enemy, having secretly returned to London, is weaving his evil spells around "some we loved, the loveliest and the best," is to know the meaning of ordeal.

In pursuit of Antony Ferrara—the incarnation of an awful evil—Dr. Cairn had deserted his practice, had left England for Egypt. Now he was hurrying back again; for whilst he had sought in strange and dark places of that land of mystery for Antony Ferrara, the latter had been darkly active in London!

Again and again Robert Cairn read the letter which, surely as a royal command, had recalled them. It was from Myra Duquesne. One line in it had fallen upon them like a bomb, had altered all their plans, had shattered the one fragment of peace remaining to them.

In the eyes of Robert Cairn, the whole universe centred around Myra Duquesne; she was the one being in the world of whom he could not bear to think in conjunction with Antony Ferrara. Now he knew that Antony Ferrara was beside her, was, doubtless at this very moment, directing those Black Arts of which he was master, to the destruction of her mind and body—perhaps of her very soul.

Again he drew the worn envelope from his pocket and read that ominous sentence, which, when his eyes had first fallen upon it, had blotted out the sunlight of Egypt.

"...And you will be surprised to hear that Antony is back in London... and is a frequent visitor here. It is quite like old times..."

Raising his haggard eyes, Robert Cairn saw that his father was watching him.

"Keep calm, my boy," urged the doctor; "it can profit us nothing, it can profit Myra nothing, for you to shatter your nerves at a time when real trials are before you. You are inviting another breakdown. Oh! I know it is hard; but for everybody's sake try to keep yourself in hand."

"I am trying, sir," replied Robert hollowly.

Dr. Cairn nodded, drumming his fingers upon his knee.

"We must be diplomatic," he continued. "That James Saunderson proposed to return to London, I had no idea. I thought that Myra would be far outside the Black maelstrom in Scotland. Had I suspected that Saunderson would come to London, I should have made other arrangements."

"Of course, sir, I know that. But even so we could never have foreseen this."

Dr. Cairn shook his head.

"To think that whilst we have been scouring Egypt from Port Said to Assouan—*he* has been laughing at us in London!" he said. "Directly after the affair at Méydûm he must have left the country—how, Heaven only knows. That letter is three weeks old, now?"

Robert Cairn nodded. "What may have happened since—what may have happened!"

"You take too gloomy a view. James Saunderson is a Roman guardian. Even Antony Ferrara could make little headway there."

"But Myra says that—Ferrara is—a frequent visitor."

"And Saunderson," replied Dr. Cairn with a grim smile, "is a Scotsman! Rely upon his diplomacy, Rob. Myra will be safe enough."

"God grant that she is!"

At that, silence fell between them, until punctually to time the train slowed into Charing Cross. Inspired by a common anxiety, Dr. Cairn and his son were first among the passengers to pass the barrier. The car was waiting for them; and within five minutes of the arrival of the train they were whirling through London's traffic to the house of James Saunderson.

It lay in that quaint backwater, remote from motorbus highways—Dulwich Common—and was a rambling red-tiled building which at some time had been a farmhouse. As the big car pulled up at the gate, Saunderson, a large-boned Scotsman, tawny-eyed, and with his gray hair worn long and untidily, came out to meet them. Myra Duquesne stood beside him. A quick blush coloured her face momentarily, then left it pale again.

Indeed, her pallor was alarming. As Robert Cairn, leaping from the car, seized both her hands and looked into her eyes, it seemed to him that the girl had almost an ethereal appearance. Something clutched at his heart, iced his blood; for Myra Duquesne seemed a creature scarcely belonging to the world of humanity—seemed already half a spirit. The light in her sweet eyes was good to see; but her fragility and a certain transparency of complexion horrified him.

Yet, he knew that he must hide these fears from her; and turning to Mr. Saunderson, he shook him warmly by the hand, and the party of four passed by the low porch into the house.

In the hallway Miss Saunderson, a typical Scottish housekeeper, stood beaming welcome; but in the very instant of greeting her Robert Cairn stopped suddenly as if transfixed.

Dr. Cairn also pulled up just within the door, his nostrils quivering and his clear gray eyes turning right and left—searching the shadows.

Miss Saunderson detected this sudden restraint.

"Is anything the matter?" she asked anxiously.

Myra, standing beside Mr. Saunderson, began to look frightened. But Dr. Cairn, shaking off the incubus which had descended upon him, forced a laugh, and clapping his hand upon Robert's shoulder, cried:

"Wake up, my boy! I know it is good to be back in England again, but keep your day-dreaming for after lunch!"

Robert Cairn forced a ghostly smile in return, and the odd incident promised soon to be forgotten.

"How good of you," said Myra as the party entered the dining room, "to come right from the station to see us. And you must be expected in Half-Moon Street, Dr. Cairn?"

"Of course we came to see *you* first," replied Robert Cairn significantly.

Myra lowered her face and pursued that subject no further.

No mention was made of Antony Ferrara, and neither Dr. Cairn nor his son cared to broach the subject. The lunch passed off, then, without any reference to the very matter which had brought them there that day.

It was not until nearly an hour later that Dr. Cairn and his son found themselves alone for a moment. Then, with a furtive glance about him, the doctor spoke of that which had occupied his mind, to the exclusion of all else, since first they had entered the house of James Saunderson.

"You noticed it, Rob?" he whispered.

"My God! it nearly choked me!"

Dr. Cairn nodded grimly.

"It is all over the house," he continued, "in every room that I have entered. They are used to it, and evidently do not notice it, but coming in from the clean air, it is—"

"Abominable, unclean—unholy!"

"We know it," continued Dr. Cairn softly, "that smell of unholiness; we have good reason to know it. It heralded the death of Sir Michael Ferrara. It heralded the death of—another."

"With a just God in heaven, can such things be?"

"It is the secret incense of Ancient Egypt," whispered Dr. Cairn, glancing toward the open door; "it is the odour of that Black Magic which, by all natural law, should be buried and lost for ever in the tombs of the ancient wizards. Only two living men within my knowledge know the use and the hidden meaning of that perfume; only one living man has ever dared to make it—to use it..."

"Antony Ferrara—"

"We knew he was here, boy; now we know that he is using his powers here. Something tells me that we come to the end of the fight. May victory be with the just."


## CHAPTER XXI
## THE MAGICIAN


Half-Moon Street was bathed in tropical sunlight. Dr. Cairn, with his hands behind him, stood looking out of the window. He turned to his son, who leant against a corner of the bookcase in the shadows of the big room.

"Hot enough for Egypt, Rob," he said.

Robert Cairn nodded.

"Antony Ferrara," he replied, "seemingly travels his own atmosphere with him. I first became acquainted with his hellish activities during a phenomenal thunderstorm. In Egypt his movements apparently corresponded with those of the *Khamsîn*. Now"—he waved his hand vaguely toward the window—"this is Egypt in London."

"Egypt is in London, indeed," muttered Dr. Cairn. "Jermyn has decided that our fears are well-founded."

"You mean, sir, that the will—"

"Antony Ferrara would have an almost unassailable case in the event of—of Myra—"

"You mean that her share of the legacy would fall to that fiend if she—"

"If she died? Exactly."

Robert Cairn began to stride up and down the room, clenching and unclenching his fists. He was a shadow of his former self, but now his cheeks were flushed and his eyes feverishly bright.

"Before Heaven!" he cried suddenly, "the situation is becoming unbearable. A thing more deadly than the Plague is abroad here in London. Apart from the personal aspect of the matter—of which I dare not think!—what do we know of Ferrara's activities? His record is damnable. To our certain knowledge his vice rims are many. If the murder of his foster father, Sir Michael, was actually the first of his crimes, we know of three other poor souls who beyond any shadow of doubt were launched into eternity by the Black Arts of this ghastly villain

"We do, Rob," replied Dr. Cairn sternly.

"He has made attempts upon you; he has made attempts upon me. We owe our survival"—he pointed to a row of books upon a corner shelf—"to the knowledge which you have accumulated in half a lifetime of research. In the face of science, in the face of modern scepticism, in the face of our belief in a benign God, this creature, Antony Ferrara, has proved himself conclusively to be—"

"He is what the benighted ancients called a magician," interrupted Dr. Cairn quietly. "He is what was known in the Middle Ages as a wizard. What that means, exactly, few modern thinkers know; but I know, and one day others will know. Meanwhile, his shadow lies upon a certain house."

Robert Cairn shook his clenched fists in the air. In some men the gesture had seemed melodramatic; in him it was the expression of a soul's agony.

"But, sir!" he cried—"are we to wait, inert, helpless? Whatever he is, he has a human body and there are bullets, there are knives, there are a hundred drugs in the British Pharmacopoeia!"

"Quite so," answered Dr. Cairn, watching his son closely, and, by his own collected manner, endeavouring to check the other's growing excitement. "I am prepared at any personal risk to crush Antony Ferrara as I would crush a scorpion; but where is he?"

Robert Cairn groaned, dropping into the big red leathern armchair, and burying his face in his hands. "Our position is maddening," continued the elder man. "We know that Antony Ferrara visits Mr. Saunderson's house; we know that he is laughing at our vain attempts to trap him. Crowning comedy of all, Saunderson does not know the truth; he is not the type of man who could ever understand; in fact, we dare not tell him—and we dare not tell Myra. The result is that those whom we would protect, unwittingly are working against us, and against themselves."

"That perfume!" burst out Robert Cairn; "that hell's incense which loads the atmosphere of Saunderson's house! To think that we know what it means—that we know what it means!"

"Perhaps *I* know even better than you do, Rob. The occult uses of perfume are not understood nowadays; but you, from experience, know that certain perfumes have occult uses. At the Pyramid of Méydûm in Egypt, Antony Ferrara dared—and the just God did not strike him dead—to make a certain incense. It was often made in the remote past, and a portion of it, probably in a jar hermetically sealed, had come into possession. I once detected its dreadful odour in his rooms in London. Had you asked me prior to that occasion if any of the hellish stuff had survived to the present day, I should most emphatically have said no; I should have been wrong. Ferrara had some. He used it all—and went to the Méydûm Pyramid to renew his stock."

Robert Cairn was listening intently.

"All this brings me back to a point which I have touched upon before, sir," he said: "To my certain knowledge, the late Sir Michael and yourself have delved into the black mysteries of Egypt more deeply than any men of the present century. Yet Antony Ferrara, little more than a boy, has mastered secrets which you, after years of research, have failed to grasp. What does this mean, sir?"

Dr. Cairn, again locking his hands behind him, stared out of the window.

"He is not an ordinary mortal," continued his son. "He is supernormal—and supernaturally wicked. You have admitted— indeed it was evident—that he is merely the adopted son of the late Sir Michael. Now that we have entered upon the final struggle—for I feel that this is so— I will ask you again: *Who is Antony Ferrara?*"

Dr. Cairn spun around upon the speaker; his gray eyes were very bright.

"There is one little obstacle," he answered, "which has deterred me from telling you what you have asked so often. Although—and you have had dreadful opportunities to peer behind the veil—you will find it hard to believe, I hope very shortly to be able to answer that question, and to tell you who Antony Ferrara really is.

Robert Cairn beat his fist upon the arm of the chair.

"I sometimes wonder," he said, "that either of us has remained sane. Oh! what does it mean? What can we do? What can we do?"

"We must watch, Rob. To enlist the services of Saunderson would be almost impossible; he lives in his orchid-houses; they are his world. In matters of ordinary life I can trust him above most men, but in this—"

He shrugged his shoulders.

"Could we suggest to him a reason—any reason but the real one—why he should refuse to receive Ferrara?"

"It might destroy our last chance."

"But, sir," cried Robert wildly, "it amounts to this: we are using Myra as a lure!"

"In order to save her, Rob—simply in order to save her," retorted Dr. Cairn sternly.

"How ill she looks," groaned the other; "how pale and worn. There are great shadows under her eyes—oh! I cannot bear to think about her!"

"When was *he* last there?"

"Apparently some ten days ago. You may depend upon him to be aware of our return! He will not come there again, sir. But there are other ways in which he might reach her—does he not command a whole shadow army! And Mr. Saunderson is entirely unsuspicious—and Myra thinks of the fiend as a brother! Yet—she has never once spoken of him. I wonder...."

Dr. Cairn sat deep in reflection. Suddenly he took out his watch.

"Go around now," he said—"you will be in time for lunch—and remain there until I come. From to-day onward, although actually your health does not permit of the strain, we must watch, watch night and day."

## CHAPTER XXII
## MYRA

Myra Duquesne came under an arch of roses to the wooden seat where Robert Cairn awaited her. In her plain white linen frock, with the sun in her hair and her eyes looking unnaturally large, owing to the pallor of her beautiful face, she seemed to the man who rose to greet her an ethereal creature, but lightly linked to the flesh-and-blood world.

An impulse, which had possessed him often enough before, but which hitherto he had suppressed, suddenly possessed him anew, set his heart beating, and filled his veins with fire. As a soft blush spread over the girl's pale cheeks, and, with a sort of timidity, she held out her hand, he leapt to his feet, threw his arms around her, and kissed her; kissed her eyes, her hair, her lips!

There was a moment of frightened hesitancy... and then she had resigned herself to this sort of savage tenderness which was better in its very brutality than any caress she had ever known, which thrilled her with a glorious joy such as, she realized now, she had dreamt of and lacked, and wanted; which was a harbourage to which she came, blushing, confused—but glad, conquered, and happy in the thrall of that exquisite slavery.

"Myra," he whispered, "Myra! have I frightened you? Will you forgive me—"

She nodded her head quickly and nestled upon his shoulder.

"I could wait no longer," he murmured in her ear. "Words seemed unnecessary; I just wanted you; you are everything in the world; and," he concluded simply, "I took you."

She whispered his name very softly. What a serenity there is in such a moment, what a glow of secure happiness of immunity from the pains and sorrows of the world!

Robert Cairn, his arms about this girl who, from his early boyhood, had been his ideal of womanhood, of love, and of all that love meant, forgot those things which had shaken his life and brought him to the threshold of death, forgot those evidences of illness which marred the once, glorious beauty of the girl, forgot the black menace of the future, forgot the wizard enemy whose hand was stretched over that house and that garden—and was merely happy.

But this paroxysm of gladness—which Eliphas Lévi, last of the Adepts, has so marvellously analyzed in one of his works—is of short duration, as are all joys. It is needless to recount, here, the broken sentences (punctuated with those first kisses which sweeten the memory of old age) that now passed for conversation, and which lovers have believed to be conversation since the world began.

As dusk creeps over a glorious landscape, so the shadow of Antony Ferrara crept over the happiness of these two. Gradually that shadow fell between them and the sun; the grim thing which loomed big in the lives of them both refused any longer to be ignored. Robert Cairn, his arm about the girl's waist, broached the hated subject.

"When did you last see—Ferrara?"

Myra looked up suddenly.

"Over a week—nearly a fortnight ago—"

"Ah!"

Cairn noted that the girl spoke of Ferrara with an odd sort of restraint for which he was at a loss to account. Myra had always regarded her guardian's adopted son in the light of a brother; therefore her present attitude was all the more singular.

"You did not expect him to return to England so soon?" he asked.

"I had no idea that he was in England," said Myra, "until he walked in here one day. I was glad to see him—then."

"And should you not be glad to see him now?" inquired Cairn eagerly.

Myra, her head lowered, deliberately pressed out a crease in her white skirt.

"One day last week," she replied slowly, "he—came here, and—acted strangely—"

"In what way?" jerked Cairn.

"He pointed out to me that actually we—he and I—were in no way related."

"Well?"

"You know how I have always liked Antony? I have always thought of him as my brother."

Again she hesitated, and a troubled expression crept over her pale face. Cairn raised his arm and clasped it about her shoulders.

"Tell me all about it," he whispered reassuringly.

"Well," continued Myra in evident confusion, "his behaviour be-came—embarrassing; and suddenly—he asked me if I could ever love him, not as a brother, but—"

"I understand!" said Cairn grimly. "And you replied?"

"For some time I could not reply at all: I was so surprised, and so—horrified. I cannot explain how I felt about it, but it seemed horrible—it seemed horrible!—"

"But of course you told him?"

"I told him that I could never be fond of him in any different way—that I could never *think* of it. And although I endeavoured to avoid hurting his feelings, he—took it very badly. He said, in such a queer, choking voice, that he was going away—"

"Away!—from England?"

"Yes; and—he made a strange request."

"What was it?"

"In the circumstances—you see—I felt sorry for him—I did not like to refuse him; it was only a trifling thing. He asked for a lock of my hair!"

"A lock of your hair! And you—"

"I told you that I did not like to refuse—and I let him snip off a tiny piece with a pair of pocket scissors which he had. Are you angry?"

"Of course not! You—were almost brought up together. You—"

"Then—" she paused—"he seemed to change. Suddenly I found myself afraid—dreadfully afraid—"

"Of Ferrara?"

"Not of Antony, exactly. But what is the good of my trying to explain! A most awful dread seized me. His face was no longer the face that I have always known; something—"

Her voice trembled, and she seemed disposed to leave the sentence unfinished; then:

"Something evil—sinister, had come into it."

"And since then," said Cairn, "you have not seen him?"

"He has not been here since then—no."

Cairn, his hands resting upon the girl's shoulders, leant back in the seat, and looked into her troubled eyes with a kind of sad scrutiny.

"You have not been fretting about him?"

Myra shook her head.

"Yet you look as though something were troubling you. This house"—he indicated the low-lying garden with a certain irritation—"is not healthily situated. This place lies in a valley; look at the rank grass—and there are mosquitoes everywhere. You do not look well, Myra."

The girl smiled—a little wistful smile.

"But I was so tired of Scotland," she said. "You do not know how I looked forward to London again. I must admit, though, that I was in better health there; I was quite ashamed of my dairy-maid appearance."

"You have nothing to amuse you here," said Cairn tenderly; "no company, for Mr. Saunderson only lives for his orchids."

"They are very fascinating," said Myra dreamily. "I, too, have felt their glamour. I am the only member of the household whom he allows amongst his orchids—"

"Perhaps you spend too much time there," interrupted Cairn; "that superheated, artificial atmosphere—"

Myra shook her head playfully, patting his arm.

"There is nothing in the world the matter with me," she said, almost in her old bright manner—"now that you are back—"

"I do not approve of orchids," jerked Cairn doggedly. "They are parodies of what a flower should be. Place an Odontoglossum beside a rose, and what a distorted, unholy thing it looks!"

"Unholy?" laughed Myra.

"Unholy—yes!—they are products of feverish swamps and deathly jungles. I hate orchids. The atmosphere of an orchid-house cannot possibly be clear and healthy. One might as well spend one's time in a bacteriological laboratory!"

Myra shook her head with affected seriousness.

"You must not let Mr. Saunderson hear you," she said. "His orchids are his children. Their very mystery enthrals him—and really it is most fascinating. To look at one of those shapeless bulbs, and to speculate upon what kind of bloom it will produce, is almost as thrilling as reading a sensational novel! He has one growing now—it will bloom some time this week—about which he is frantically excited."

"Where did he get it?" asked Cairn without interest.

"He bought it from a man who had almost certainly stolen it! There were six bulbs in the parcel; only two have lived, and one of these is much more advanced than the other; it is *so* high."

She held out her hand, indicating a height of some three feet from the ground.

"It has not flowered yet?"

"No. But the buds—huge, smooth, egg-shaped things—seem on the point of bursting at any moment. We call it the 'Mystery,' and it is my special care. Mr. Saunderson has shown me how to attend to its simple needs, and if it proves to be a new species—which is almost certain— he is going to exhibit it, and name it after me! Shall you be proud of having an orchid named after—"

"After my wife?" Cairn concluded, seizing her hands. "I could never be more proud of you than I am already…"


## CHAPTER XXIII
## THE FACE IN THE ORCHID-HOUSE

Dr. Cairn walked to the window with its old-fashioned leaded panes. A lamp stood by the bedside, and he had tilted the shade so that it shone upon the pale face of the patient—Myra Duquesne.

Two days had wrought a dreadful change in her. She lay with closed eyes and sunken face upon which ominous shadows played. Her respiration was imperceptible. The reputation of Dr. Bruce Cairn was a well-deserved one, but this case puzzled him. He knew that Myra Duquesne was dying before his eyes; he could still see the agonized face of his son, Robert, who at that moment was waiting, filled with intolerable suspense, downstairs in Mr. Saunderson's study; but withal, he was helpless. He looked out from the rose-entwined casement across the shrubbery, to where the moonlight glittered among the trees.

Those were the orchid-houses; and with his back to the bed, Dr. Cairn stood for long, thoughtfully watching the distant gleams of reflected light. Craig Fenton and Sir Elwin Groves, with whom he had been consulting, were but just gone. The nature of Myra Duquesne's illness had utterly puzzled them, and they had left, mystified.

Downstairs, Robert Cairn was pacing the study, wondering if his reason would survive this final blow which threatened. He knew, and his father knew, that a sinister something underlay this strange illness—an illness which had commenced on the day that Antony Ferrara had last visited the house.

The evening was insufferably hot; not a breeze stirred in the leaves; and despite open windows, the air of the room was heavy and lifeless. A faint perfume, having a sort of sweetness, but which yet was unutterably revolting, made itself perceptible to the nostrils. Apparently it had pervaded the house by slow degrees. The occupants were so used to it that they did not notice it at all.

Dr. Cairn had busied himself that evening in the sickroom, burning some pungent preparation, to the amazement of the nurse and of the consultants. Now the biting fumes of his pastilles had all been wafted out of the window and the faint sweet smell was as noticeable as ever.

Not a sound broke the silence of the house; and when the nurse quietly opened the door and entered, Dr. Cairn was still standing staring thoughtfully out of the window in the direction of the orchid-houses. He turned, and walking back to the bedside, bent over the patient.

Her face was like a white mask; she was quite unconscious; and so far as he could see showed no change either for better or worse. But her pulse was slightly more feeble and the doctor suppressed a groan of despair; for this mysterious progressive weakness could only have one end. All his experience told him that unless something could be done—and every expedient thus far attempted had proved futile—Myra Duquesne would die about dawn.

He turned on his heel, and strode from the room, whispering a few words of instruction to the nurse. Descending the stairs, he passed the closed study door, not daring to think of his son who waited within, and entered the dining room. A single lamp burnt there, and the gaunt figure of Mr. Saunderson was outlined dimly where he sat in the window seat. Crombie, the gardener, stood by the table.

"Now, Crombie," said Dr. Cairn, quietly, closing the door behind him, "what is this story about the orchid-houses, and why did you not mention it before?"

The man stared persistently into the shadows of the room, avoiding Dr. Cairn's glance.

"Since he has had the courage to own up," interrupted Mr. Saunderson, "I have overlooked the matter: but he was afraid to speak before, because he had no business to be in the orchid-houses." His voice grew suddenly fierce. "He knows it well enough!"

"I know, sir, that you don't want me to interfere with the orchids," replied the man, "but I only ventured in because I thought I saw a light moving there—"

"Rubbish!" snapped Mr. Saunderson.

"Pardon me, Saunderson," said Dr. Cairn, "but a matter of more importance than the welfare of all the orchids in the world is under consideration now."

Saunderson coughed dryly.

"You are right, Cairn," he said. "I shouldn't have lost my temper for such a trifle at a time like this. Tell your own tale, Crombie; I won't interrupt."

"It was last night, then," continued the man. "I was standing at the door of my cottage smoking a pipe before turning in when I saw a faint light moving over by the orchid-houses—"

"Reflection of the moon," muttered Saunderson. "I am sorry. Go on, Crombie!"

"I knew that some of the orchids were very valuable, and I thought there would not be time to call you; also I did not want to worry you, knowing you had worry enough already. So I knocked out my pipe and put it in my pocket, and went through the shrubbery. I saw the light again—it seemed to be moving from the first house into the second. I couldn't see what it was."

"Was it like a candle, or a pocket-lamp?" queried Dr. Cairn.

"Nothing like that, sir; a softer light, more like a glow-worm, but much brighter. I went around and tried the door, and it was locked. Then I remembered the door at the other end, and I cut round by the path between the houses and the wall, so that I had no chance to see the light again until I got to the other door. I found this unlocked. There was a close kind of smell in there, sir, and the air was very hot—"

"Naturally, it was hot," interrupted Saunderson.

"I mean much hotter than it should have been. It was like an oven, and the smell was stifling—"

"What smell?" asked Dr. Cairn. "Can you describe it?"

"Excuse me, sir, but I seem to notice it here in this room to-night, and I think I noticed it about the place before—never so strong as in the orchid-houses."

"Go on!" said Dr. Cairn.

"I went through the first house, and saw nothing. The shadow of the wall prevented the moonlight from shining in there. But just as I was about to enter the middle house I thought I saw—a face."

"What do you mean you *thought* you saw?" snapped Mr. Saunderson.

"I mean, sir, that it was so horrible and so strange that I could not believe it was real—which is one of the reasons why I did not speak before. It reminded me of the face of a gentleman I have seen here—Mr. Ferrara—"

Dr. Cairn stifled an exclamation.

"But in other ways it was quite unlike the gentleman. In some ways it was more like the face of a woman—a very bad woman. It had a sort of bluish light on it, but where it could have come from I don't know. It seemed to be smiling, and two bright eyes looked straight out at me."

Crombie stopped, raising his hand to his head confusedly.

"I could see nothing but just this face—low down, as if the person it belonged to was crouching on the floor; and there was a tall plant of some kind just beside it—"

"Well," said Dr. Cairn, "go on! What did you do?"

"I turned to run!" confessed the man. "If you had seen that horrible face, you would understand how frightened I was. Then when I got to the door, I looked back."

"I hope you had closed the door behind you," snapped Saunderson.

"Never mind that, never mind that!" interrupted Dr. Cairn.

"I had closed the door behind me—yes, sir—but just as I was going to open it again, I took a quick glance back, and the face had gone! I came out, and I was walking over the lawn, wondering whether I should tell you, when it occurred to me that I hadn't noticed whether the key had been left in or not."

"Did you go back to see?" asked Dr. Cairn.

"I didn't want to," admitted Crombie, "but I did—and—"

"Well?"

"The door was locked, sir!"

"So you concluded that your imagination had been playing you tricks," said Saunderson grimly. "In my opinion you were right."

Dr. Cairn dropped into an armchair.

"All right, Crombie; that will do."

Crombie with a mumbled "Good-night, gentlemen," turned and left the room.

"Why are you worrying about this matter," inquired Saunderson, when the door had closed, "at a time like the present?"

"Never mind," replied Dr. Cairn wearily. "I must return to Half-Moon Street, now, but I shall be back within an hour."

With no other word to Saunderson, he stood up and walked out to the hall. He rapped at the study door; and it was instantly opened by Robert Cairn. No spoken word was necessary; the burning question could be read in his too-bright eyes. Dr. Cairn laid his hand upon his son's shoulder.

"I won't excite false hopes, Rob," he said huskily. "I am going back to the house, and I want you to come with me."

Robert Cairn turned his head aside, groaning aloud, but his father grasped him by the arm, and together they left that house of shadows, entered the car which waited at the gate, and without exchanging a word en route, came to Half-Moon Street.

## CHAPTER XXIV
## FLOWERING OF THE LOTUS

Dr. Cairn led the way into the library, switching on the reading-lamp upon the large table. His son stood just within the doorway, his arms folded and his chin upon his breast.

The doctor sat down at the table, watching the other. Suddenly Robert spoke:

"Is it possible, sir, is it possible"—his voice was barely audible—"that her illness can in any way be due to the orchids?"

Dr. Cairn frowned thoughtfully.

"What do you mean, exactly?" he asked.

"Orchids are mysterious things. They come from places where there are strange and dreadful diseases. Is it not possible that they may convey—"

"Some sort of contagion?" concluded Dr. Cairn. "It is a point that I have seen raised, certainly. But nothing of the sort has ever been established. I have heard something to-night, though, which—"

"What have you heard, sir?" asked his son eagerly, stepping forward to the table.

"Never mind at the moment, Rob; let me think."

He rested his elbow upon the table, and his chin in his hand. His professional instincts had told him that unless something could be done—something which the highest medical skill in London had thus far been unable to devise—Myra Duquesne had but four hours to live. Somewhere in his mind a memory lurked, evasive, taunting him. This wild suggestion of his son's, that the girl's illness might be due in some way to her contact with the orchids, was in part responsible for this confused memory, but it seemed to be associated, too, with the story of Crombie, the gardener—and with Antony Ferrara. He felt that somewhere in the darkness surrounding him there was a speck of light, if he could but turn in the right direction to see it. So, whilst Robert Cairn walked restlessly about the big room, the doctor sat with his chin resting in the palm of his hand, seeking to concentrate his mind upon that vague memory, which defied him, whilst the hand of the library clock crept from twelve toward one; whilst he knew that the faint life in Myra Duquesne was slowly ebbing away in response to some mysterious condition utterly outside his experience.

Distant clocks chimed *One!* Three hours only!

Robert Cairn began to beat his fist into the palm of his left hand convulsively. Yet his father did not stir, but sat there, a black-shadowed wrinkle between his brows...

"My God!"

The doctor sprang to his feet, and with feverish haste began to fumble amongst a bunch of keys. "What is it, sir! What is it?"

The doctor unlocked the drawer of the big table, and drew out a thick manuscript written in small and exquisitely neat characters. He placed it under the lamp, and rapidly began to turn the pages.

"It is hope, Rob!" he said with quiet self-possession.

Robert Cairn came round the table, and leant over his father's shoulder.

"Sir Michael Ferrara's writing!"

"His unpublished book, Rob. We were to have completed it, together, but death claimed him, and in view of the contents, I—perhaps superstitiously—decided to suppress it... Ah!"

He placed the point of his finger upon a carefully drawn sketch, designed to illustrate the text. It was evidently a careful copy from the Ancient Egyptian. It represented a row of priestesses, each having her hair plaited in a thick queue, standing before a priest armed with a pair of scissors. In the centre of the drawing was an altar upon which stood vases of flowers; and upon the right ranked a row of mummies, corresponding in number with the priestesses upon the left.

"My God!" repeated Dr. Cairn, "we were both wrong, we were both wrong!"

"What do you mean, sir? For Heaven's sake, what do you mean?"

"This drawing," replied Dr. Cairn, "was copied from the wall of a certain tomb—now reclosed. Since we knew that the tomb was that of one of the greatest wizards who ever lived in Egypt, we knew also that the inscription had some magical significance. We knew that the flowers represented here were a species of the extinct sacred lotus. All our researches did not avail us to discover for what purpose or by what means these flowers were cultivated. Nor could we determine the meaning of the cutting off"—he ran his fingers over the sketch—"of the priestesses' hair by the high priest of the goddess—"

"What goddess, sir?"

"A goddess, Rob, of which Egyptology knows nothing!—a mystical religion the existence of which has been vaguely suspected by a living French *savant*... but this is no time—"

Dr. Cairn closed the manuscript, replaced it, and re-locked the drawer. He glanced at the clock.

"A quarter past one," he said, "Come, Rob!"

Without hesitation his son followed him from the house. The car was waiting, and shortly they were speeding through the deserted streets, back to the house where death in a strange guise was beckoning to Myra Duquesne. As the car started—

"Do you know," asked Dr. Cairn, "if Saunderson has bought any orchids—*quite* recently, I mean?"

"Yes," replied his son dully; "he bought a small parcel only a fortnight ago."

"A fortnight!" cried Dr. Cairn excitedly—"you are sure of that? You mean that the purchase was made since Ferrara—"

"Ceased to visit the house? Yes. Why!—it must have been the very day after!"

Dr. Cairn clearly was labouring under tremendous excitement.

"Where did he buy these orchids?" he asked evenly. "From someone who came to the house—someone he had never dealt with before."

The doctor, his hands resting upon his knees, was rapidly drumming with his fingers.

"And—did he cultivate them?"

"Two only proved successful. One is on the point of blooming—if it is not blooming already. He calls it the 'Mystery.'"

At that the doctor's excitement overcame him. Suddenly leaning out of the window, he shouted to the chauffeur:

"Quicker! Quicker! Never mind risks. Keep on top speed!"

"What is it, sir?" cried his son. "Heavens! what is it?"

"Did you say that it might have bloomed, Rob?"

"Myra"—Robert Cairn swallowed noisily—"told me three days ago that it was expected to bloom before the end of the week."

"What is it like?"

"A thing four feet high with huge egg-shaped buds."

"Merciful God, grant that we are in time," whispered Dr. Cairn. "I could believe once more in the justice of Heaven if the great knowledge of Sir Michael Ferrara should prove to be the weapon to destroy the fiend whom we raised!—he and I. May we be forgiven!"

Robert Cairn's excitement was dreadful.

"Can you tell me nothing?" he cried. "What do you hope? What do you fear?"

"Don't ask me, Rob," replied his father; "you will know within five minutes."

The car indeed was leaping along the dark suburban roads at a speed little below that of an express train. Corners the chauffeur negotiated in racing fashion, so that at times two wheels thrashed the empty air; and once or twice the big car swung round as upon a pivot only to recover again in response to the skilled tactics of the driver.

They roared down the sloping narrow lane to the gate of Mr. Saunderson's house with a noise like the coming of a great storm, and were nearly hurled from their seats when the brakes were applied, and the car brought to a standstill.

Dr. Cairn leapt out, pushed open the gate and ran up to the house, his son closely following. There was a light in the hall and Miss Saunderson, who had expected them, and had heard their stormy approach, already held the door open. In the hall—

"Wait here one moment," said Dr. Cairn.

Ignoring Saunderson, who had come out from the library, he ran upstairs. A minute later, his face very pale, he came running down again.

"She is worse?" began Saunderson, "but—

"Give me the key of the orchid-house!" said Dr. Cairn tersely.

"Orchid-house!"

"Don't hesitate. Don't waste a second. Give me the key."

Saunderson's expression showed that he thought Dr. Cairn to be mad, but nevertheless he plunged his hand into his pocket and pulled out a key-ring. Dr. Cairn snatched it in a flash.

"Which key?" he snapped.

"The Chubb, but—"

"Follow me, Rob!"

Down the hall he raced, his son beside him, and Mr. Saunderson following more slowly. Out into the garden he went and over the lawn toward the shrubbery.

The orchid-houses lay in dense shadow; but the doctor almost threw himself against the door.

"Strike a match!" he panted. Then—"Never mind —I have it!"

The door flew open with a bang. A sickly perfume swept out to them.

"Matches! matches, Rob! this way!"

They went stumbling in. Robert Cairn took out a box of matches and struck one. His father was farther along, in the centre building.

"Your knife, boy—quick! *quick!*"

As the dim light crept along the aisle between the orchids, Robert Cairn saw his father's horror-stricken face... and saw a vivid green plant growing in a sort of tub before which the doctor stood. Four huge, smooth, egg-shaped buds grew upon the leafless stems; two of them were on the point of opening, and one already showed a delicious rosy flush about its apex.

Dr. Cairn grasped the knife which Robert tremblingly offered him. The match went out. There was a sound of hacking, a soft *swishing*, and a dull thud upon the tiled floor.

As another match fluttered into brief life, the mysterious orchid, severed just above the soil, fell from the tub. Dr. Cairn stamped the swelling buds under his feet. A profusion of colourless sap was pouring out upon the floor.

Above the intoxicating odour of the place a smell like that of blood made itself perceptible.

The second match went out.

"Another—"

Dr. Cairn's voice rose barely above a whisper. With fingers quivering, Robert Cairn managed to light a third match. His father, from a second tub, tore out a smaller plant and ground its soft tentacles beneath his feet. The place smelt like an operating theatre. The doctor swayed dizzily as the third match became extinguished, clutching at his son for support.

"Her life was in it, boy!" he whispered. "She would have died in the hour that it bloomed! The priestesses—were consecrated to this... Let me get into the air—"

Mr. Saunderson, silent with amazement, met them.

"Don't speak," said Dr. Cairn to him. "Look at the dead stems of your 'Mystery.' You will find a thread of bright hair in the heart of each!...

Dr. Cairn opened the door of the sick-room and beckoned to his son, who, haggard, trembling, waited upon the landing.

"Come in, boy," he said softly—"and thank God!"

Robert Cairn, on tiptoe, entered. Myra Duquesne, pathetically pale but with that dreadful, ominous shadow gone from her face, turned her wistful eyes toward the door; and their wistfulness became gladness.

"Rob!" she sighed—and stretched out her arms.


## CHAPTER XXV
## CAIRN MEETS FERRARA

Not the least of the trials which Robert Cairn experienced during the time that he and his father were warring with their supernaturally equipped opponent was that of preserving silence upon this matter which loomed so large in his mind, and which already had changed the course of his life.

Sometimes he met men who knew Ferrara, but who knew him only as a man about town of somewhat evil reputation. Yet even to these he dared not confide what he knew of the true Ferrara; undoubtedly they would have deemed him mad had he spoken of the knowledge and of the deeds of this uncanny, this fiendish being. How would they have listened to him had he sought to tell then of the den of spiders in Port Said; of the bats of Méydûm; of the secret incense and of how it was made; of the numberless murders and atrocities, wrought by means not human, which stood to the account of this adopted son of the late Sir Michael Ferrara?

So, excepting his father, he had no confidant; for above all it was necessary to keep the truth from Myra Duquesne—from Myra around whom his world circled, but who yet thought of the dreadful being who wielded the sorcery of forgotten ages as a brother. Whilst Myra lay ill—not yet recovered from the ghastly attack made upon her life by the man whom she trusted—whilst, having plentiful evidence of his presence in London, Dr. Cairn and himself vainly sought for Antony Ferrara; whilst any night might bring some unholy visitant to his rooms, obedient to the will of this modern wizard; whilst these fears, anxieties, doubts, and surmises danced, impishly, through his brain, it was all but impossible to pursue, with success, his vocation of journalism. Yet for many reasons it was necessary that he should do so, and so he was employed upon a series of articles which were the outcome of his recent visit to Egypt—his editor having given him that work as being less exacting than that which properly falls to the lot of the Fleet Street copy-hunter.

He left his rooms about three o'clock in the afternoon, in order to seek, in the British Museum library, a reference which he lacked. The day was an exceedingly warm one, and he derived some little satisfaction from the fact that, at his present work, he was not called upon to endue the armour of respectability. Pipe in mouth, he made his way across the Strand toward Bloomsbury.

As he walked up the steps, crossed the hall-way, and passed in beneath the dome of the reading room, he wondered if, amid those mountains of erudition surrounding him, there was any wisdom so strange, and so awful, as that of Antony Ferrara.

He soon found the information for which he was looking, and having copied it into his notebook, he left the reading room. Then, as he was recrossing the hall near the foot of the principal staircase, he paused. He found himself possessed by a sudden desire to visit the Egyptian rooms upstairs. He had several times inspected the exhibits in those apartments, but never since his return from the land to whose ancient civilization they bore witness.

Cairn was not pressed for time in these days, therefore he turned and passed slowly up the stairs.

There were but few visitors to the grove of mummies that afternoon. When he entered the first room he found a small group of tourists passing idly from case to case; but on entering the second, he saw that he had the apartment to himself. He remembered that his father had mentioned on one occasion that there was a ring in this room which had belonged to the Witch-Queen. Robert Cairn wondered in which of the cases it was exhibited, and by what means he should be enabled to recognize it.

Bending over a case containing scarabs and other amulets, many set in rings, he began to read the inscriptions upon the little tickets placed beneath some of them; but none answered to the description, neither the ticketed nor the unticketed. A second case he examined with like results. But on passing to a third, in an angle near the door, his gaze immediately lighted upon a gold ring set with a strange green stone, engraved in a peculiar way. It bore no ticket, yet as Robert Cairn eagerly bent over it, he knew, beyond the possibility of doubt, that this was the ring of the Witch-Queen.

Where had he seen it, or its duplicate?

With his eyes fixed upon the gleaming stone, he sought to remember. That he had seen this ring before, or one exactly like it, he knew, but strangely enough he was unable to determine where and upon what occasion. So, his hands resting upon the case, he leant, peering down at the singular gem. And as he stood thus, frowning in the effort of recollection, a dull white hand, having long tapered fingers, glided across the glass until it rested directly beneath his eyes. Upon one of the slim fingers was an exact replica of the ring in the case!

Robert Cairn leapt back with a stifled exclamation. Antony Ferrara stood before him!

"The museum ring is a copy, dear Cairn," came the huskily musical, hateful voice; "the one upon my finger is the real one."

Cairn realized, in his own person, the literal meaning of the overworked phrase, "frozen with amazement." Before him stood the most dangerous man in Europe; a man who had done murder and worse; a man only in name, a demon in nature. His long black eyes half-closed, his perfectly chiselled ivory face expressionless, and his blood-red lips parted in a mirthless smile, Antony Ferrara watched Cairn—Cairn whom he had sought to murder by means of hellish art.

Despite the heat of the day he wore a heavy overcoat lined with white fox fur. In his right hand—for his left still rested upon the case—he held a soft hat. With an easy nonchalance, he stood regarding the man who had sworn to kill him, and the latter made no move, uttered no word.

Stark amazement held him inert.

"I knew that you were in the museum, Cairn," Ferrara continued, still having his basilisk eyes fixed upon the other from beneath the drooping lids, "and I called to you to join me here."

Still Cairn did not move, did not speak.

"You have acted very harshly toward me in the past, dear Cairn; but because my philosophy consists in an admirable blending of that practised in Sybaris with that advocated by the excellent Zeno; because whilst I am prepared to make my home in a Diogenes' tub, I nevertheless can enjoy the fragrance of a rose, the flavour of a peach—"

The husky voice seemed to be hypnotizing Cairn; it was a siren's voice, thralling him.

"Because," continued Ferrara evenly, "in common with all humanity I am compound of man and woman, I can resent the enmity which drives me from shore to shore, but being myself a connoisseur of the red lips and laughing eyes of maidenhood—I am thinking more particularly of Myra—I can forgive you, dear Cairn—"

Then Cairn recovered himself.

"You white-faced cur!" he snarled through clenched teeth; his knuckles whitened as he stepped around the case. "You dare to stand there mocking me—"

Ferrara again placed the case between himself and his enemy. "Pause, my dear Cairn," he said, without emotion. "What would you do? Be discreet, dear Cairn; reflect that I have only to call an attendant in order to have you pitched ignominiously into the street."

"Before God! I will throttle the life from you!" said Cairn, in a voice savagely hoarse.

He sprang again toward Ferrara. Again the latter dodged around the case with an agility which defied the heavier man.

"Your temperament is so painfully Celtic, Cairn," he protested mockingly. "I perceive quite clearly that you will not discuss this matter judicially. Must I then call for the attendant?"

Cairn clenched his fists convulsively. Through all the tumult of his rage, the fact had penetrated—that he was helpless. He could not attack Ferrara in that place; he could not detain him against his will. For Ferrara had only to claim official protection to bring about the complete discomfiture of his assailant. Across the case containing the duplicate ring he glared at this incarnate fiend, whom the law, which he had secretly outraged, now served to protect. Ferrara spoke again in his huskily musical voice.

"I regret that you will not be reasonable, Cairn. There is so much that

I should like to say to you; there are so many things of interest which I could tell you. Do you know in some respects I am peculiarly gifted, Cairn? At times I can recollect, quite distinctly, particulars of former incarnations. Do you see that priestess lying there, just through the doorway? I can quite distinctly remember having met her when she was a girl; she was beautiful, Cairn. And I can even recall how, one night beside the Nile— But I see that you are growing impatient! If you will not avail yourself of this opportunity, I must bid you good-day—"

He turned and walked toward the door. Cairn leapt after him; but Ferrara, suddenly beginning to run, reached the end of the Egyptian room and darted out on to the landing before his pursuer had time to realize what he was about.

At the moment that Ferrara turned the corner ahead of him, Cairn saw something drop. Coming to the end of the room, he stooped and picked up this object, which was a plaited silk cord about three feet in length. He did not pause to examine it more closely, but thrust it into his pocket and raced down the steps after the retreating figure of Ferrara. At the foot, a constable held out his arm, detaining him. Cairn stopped in surprise.

"I must ask you for your name and address," said the constable gruffly.

"For Heaven's sake! what for?"

"A gentleman has complained—"

"My good man!" exclaimed Cairn, and proffered his card—"it is—it is a practical joke on his part. I know him well—"

The constable looked at the card and from the card, suspiciously, back to Cairn. Apparently the appearance of the latter reassured him—or he may have formed a better opinion of Cairn from the fact that half-a-crown had quickly changed hands.

"All right, sir," he said, "it is no affair of mine; he did not charge you with anything—he only asked me to prevent you from following him."

"Quite so," snapped Cairn irritably, and dashed off along the gallery in the hope of overtaking Ferrara.

But, as he had feared, Ferrara had made good use of his ruse to escape. He was nowhere to be seen; and Cairn was left to wonder with what object he had risked the encounter in the Egyptian room—for that it had been deliberate, and not accidental, he quite clearly perceived.

He walked down the steps of the museum, deep in reflection. The thought that he and his father for months had been seeking the fiend Ferrara, that they were sworn to kill him as they would kill a mad dog; and that he, Robert Cairn, had stood face to face with Ferrara, had spoken with him, and had let him go free, unscathed, was maddening. Yet, in the circumstances, how could he have acted otherwise?

With no recollection of having traversed the intervening streets, he found himself walking under the archway leading to the court in which his chambers were situated; in the far corner, shadowed by the tall plane tree, where the worn iron railings of the steps and the small panes of glass in the solicitor's window on the ground floor called up memories of Charles Dickens, he paused, filled with a sort of wonderment. It seemed strange to him that such an air of peace could prevail anywhere whilst Antony Ferrara lived and remained at large.

He ran up the stairs to the second landing, opened the door, and entered his chambers. He was oppressed to-day with a memory, the memory of certain gruesome happenings whereof these rooms had been the scene. Knowing the powers of Antony Ferrara he often doubted the wisdom of living there alone, but he was persuaded that to allow these fears to make headway would be to yield a point to the enemy. Yet there were nights when he found himself sleepless, listening for sounds which had seemed to arouse him; imagining sinister whispers in his room—and imagining that he could detect the dreadful odour of the secret incense.

Seating himself by the open window, he took out from his pocket the silken cord which Ferrara had dropped in the museum, and examined it curiously. His examination of the thing did not serve to enlighten him respecting its character. It was merely a piece of silken cord very closely and curiously plaited. He threw it down on the table, determined to show it to Dr. Cairn at the earliest opportunity. He was conscious of a sort of repugnance; and prompted by this, he carefully washed his hands as though the cord had been some unclean thing. Then he sat down to work, only to realize immediately that work was impossible until he had confided in somebody his encounter with Ferrara.

Lifting the telephone receiver, he called up Dr. Cairn, but his father was not at home.

He replaced the receiver, and sat staring vaguely at his open notebook.


CHAPTER XXVI

THE IVORY HAND

For close upon an hour Robert Cairn sat at his writing-table, endeavouring to puzzle out a solution to the mystery of Ferrara's motive. His reflections served only to confuse his mind.

A tangible clue lay upon the table before him—the silken cord. But it was a clue of such a nature that, whatever deductions an expert detective might have based upon it, Robert Cairn could base none. Dusk was not far off, and he knew that his nerves were not what they had been before those events which had led to his Egyptian journey. He was back in his own chamber—scene of one gruesome outrage in Ferrara's unholy campaign; for darkness is the ally of crime, and it had always been in the darkness that Ferrara's activities had most fearfully manifested themselves.

What was that?

Cairn ran to the window, and, leaning out, looked down into the court below. He could have sworn that a voice—a voice possessing a strange music, a husky music, wholly hateful—had called him by name. But at that moment the court was deserted, for it was already past the hour at which members of the legal fraternity desert their business premises to hasten homeward. Shadows were creeping under the quaint old archways; shadows were draping the ancient walls. And there was something in the aspect of the place which reminded him of a quadrangle at Oxford, across which, upon a certain fateful evening, he and another had watched the red light rising and falling in Antony Ferrara's rooms.

Clearly his imagination was playing him tricks; and against this he knew full well that he must guard himself. The light in his rooms was growing dim, but instinctively his gaze sought out and found the mysterious silken cord amid the litter on the table. He contemplated the telephone, but since he had left a message for his father, he knew that the latter would ring him up directly he returned.

Work, he thought, should be the likeliest antidote to the poisonous thoughts which oppressed his mind, and again he seated himself at the table and opened his notes before him. The silken rope lay close to his left hand, but he did not touch it. He was about to switch on the reading-lamp, for it was now too dark to write, when his mind wandered off along another channel of reflection. He found himself picturing Myra as she had looked the last time that he had seen her.

She was seated in Mr. Saunderson's garden, still pale from her dreadful illness, but beautiful—more beautiful in the eyes of Robert Cairn than any other woman in the world. The breeze was blowing her rebellious curls across her eyes—eyes bright with a happiness which he loved to see.

Her cheeks were paler than they were wont to be, and the sweet lips had lost something of their firmness. She wore a short cloak and a wide-brimmed hat, unfashionable, but becoming. No one but Myra could successfully have worn that hat, he thought.

Wrapt in such lover-like memories, he forgot that he had sat down to write—forgot that he held a pen in his hand—and that this same hand had been outstretched to ignite the lamp.

When he ultimately awoke again to the hard facts of his lonely environment, he also awoke to a singular circumstance; he made the acquaintance of a strange phenomenon.

He had been writing unconsciously!

And this was what he had written:

"Robert Cairn—renounce your pursuit of me, and renounce Myra; or to-night—" The sentence was unfinished.

Momentarily, he stared at the words, endeavouring to persuade himself that he had written them consciously, in idle mood. But some voice within gave him the lie; so that with a suppressed groan he muttered aloud:

"It has begun!"

Almost as he spoke there came a sound from the passage outside that led him to slide his hand across the table—and to seize his revolver.

The visible presence of the little weapon reassured him; and, as a further sedative, he resorted to tobacco, filled and lighted his pipe, and leant back in the chair, blowing smoke rings toward the closed door.

He listened intently—and heard the sound again.

It was a soft *hiss!*

And now he thought he could detect another noise—as of some creature dragging its body along the floor.

"A lizard!" he thought; and a memory of the basilisk eyes of Antony Ferrara came to him.

Both sounds seemed to come slowly nearer and nearer—the dragging thing being evidently responsible for the hissing; until Cairn decided that the creature must be immediately outside the door.

Revolver in hand, he leapt across the room and threw the door open.

The red carpet to the right and left was innocent of reptiles!

Perhaps the creaking of the revolving chair, as he had prepared to quit it, had frightened the thing. With the idea before him, he systematically searched all the rooms into which it might have gone.

His search was unavailing; the mysterious reptile was not to be found.

Returning again to the study he seated himself behind the table, facing the door—which he left ajar.

Ten minutes passed in silence—only broken by the dim murmur of the distant traffic.

He had almost persuaded himself that his imagination—quickened by the atmosphere of mystery and horror wherein he had recently moved—was responsible for the hiss, when a new sound came to confute his reasoning.

The people occupying the chambers below were moving about so that their footsteps were faintly audible; but, above these dim footsteps, a rustling—vague, indefinite—demonstrated itself. As in the case of the hiss, it proceeded from the passage.

A light burnt inside the outer door, and this, as Cairn knew, must cast a shadow before any thing—or person—approaching the room.

*Sssf! ssf!*—came, like the rustle of light draperies. The nervous suspense was almost unbearable. He waited.

*What* was creeping, slowly, cautiously, toward the open door?

Cairn toyed with the trigger of his revolver.

"The arts of the West shall try conclusions with those of the East," he said.

A shadow!...

Inch upon inch it grew—creeping across the door, until it covered all the threshold visible.

Someone was about to appear.

He raised the revolver.

The shadow moved along.

Cairn saw the tail of it creep past the door until no shadow was there!

The shadow had come—and gone ... but there was *no substance!*

"I am going mad!"

The words forced themselves to his lips. He rested his chin upon his hands and clenched his teeth grimly. Did the horrors of insanity stare him in the face?

From that recent illness in London—when his nervous system had collapsed utterly—despite his stay in Egypt he had never fully recovered. "A month will see you fit again," his father had said; but—perhaps he had been wrong—perchance the affection had been deeper than he had suspected; and now this endless carnival of supernatural happenings had strained the weakened cells so that he was become as a man in a delirium!

Where did reality end and phantasy begin? Was it all merely subjective?

He had read of such aberrations.

And now he sat wondering if he were the victim of a like affliction—and while he wondered he stared at the rope of silk. That was real.

Logic came to his rescue. If he had seen and heard strange things, so, too, had Sime in Egypt—so had his father, both in Egypt and in London! Inexplicable things were happening around him; and all could not be mad!

"I'm getting morbid again," he told himself; "the tricks of our damnable Ferrara are getting on my nerves. Just what he desires and intends!"

This latter reflection spurred him to new activity; and, pocketing the revolver, he switched off the light in the study and looked out of the window.

Glancing across the court, he thought that he saw a man standing below, peering upward. With his hands resting upon the window ledge, Cairn looked long and steadily.

There certainly was someone standing in the shadow of the tall plane tree—but whether man or woman he could not determine.

The unknown remaining in the same position, apparently watching, Cairn ran downstairs, and, passing out into the court, walked rapidly across to the tree. There he paused in some surprise; there was no one visible by the tree and the whole court was quite deserted.

"Must have slipped off through the archway," he concluded; and, walking back, he remounted the stair and entered his chambers again.

Feeling a renewed curiosity regarding the silken rope which had so strangely come into his possession, he sat down at the table, and mastering his distaste for the thing, took it in his hands and examined it closely by the light of the lamp.

He was seated with his back to the windows, facing the door, so that no one could possibly have entered the room unseen by him. It was as he bent down to scrutinize the curious plaiting that he felt a sensation stealing over him as though someone were standing very close to his chair.

Grimly determined to resist any hypnotic tricks that might be practised against him, and well assured that there could be no person actually present in the chambers, he sat back, resting his revolver on his knee. Prompted by he knew not what, he slipped the silk cord into the table drawer and turned the key upon it.

As he did so a hand crept over his shoulder—followed by a bare arm of the hue of old ivory—a woman's arm!

Transfixed he sat, his eyes fastened upon the ring of dull metal bearing a green stone inscribed with a complex figure vaguely resembling a spider, which adorned the index finger.

A faint perfume stole to his nostrils—that of the secret incense; and the ring was the ring of the Witch-Queen!

In this incredible moment he relaxed that iron control of his mind, which, alone, had saved him before. Even as he realized it, and strove to recover himself, he knew that it was too late; he knew that he was lost!

Gloom... blackness, unrelieved by any speck of light; murmuring, subdued, all around; the murmuring of a concourse of people. The darkness was odorous with a heavy perfume.

A voice came—followed by complete silence.

Again the voice sounded, chanting sweetly.

A response followed in deep male voices.

The response was taken up all around—what time a tiny speck grew in the gloom—and grew, until it took form; and out of the darkness the shape of a white-robed woman appeared—high up—far away.

Wherever the ray that illumined her figure emanated from, it did not perceptibly dispel the Stygian gloom all about her. She was bathed in dazzling light but framed in impenetrable darkness.

Her dull gold hair was encircled by a band of white metal—like silver, bearing in front a round, burnished disk that shone like a minor sun. Above the disk projected an ornament having the shape of a spider.

The intense light picked out every detail vividly. Neck and shoulders were bare—and the gleaming ivory arms were uplifted—the long slender fingers held aloft a golden casket covered with dim figures, almost undiscernible at that distance.

A glittering zone of the same white metal confined the snowy draperies. Her bare feet peeped out from beneath the flowing robe.

Above, below, and around her was—Memphian darkness!

Silence—the perfume was stifling... A voice, seeming to come from a great distance, cried: "On your knees to the Book of Thoth! on your knees to the Wisdom Queen, who is deathless, being unborn, who is dead though living, whose beauty is for all men—that all men may die..."

The whole invisible concourse took up the chant, and the light faded until only the speck on the disk below the spider was visible.

Then that, too, vanished.

A bell was ringing furiously. Its din grew louder and louder; it became insupportable. Cairn threw out his arms and staggered up like a man intoxicated. He grasped at the table-lamp only just in time to prevent it overturning

The ringing was that of his telephone bell. He had been unconscious, then—under some spell!

He unhooked the receiver—and heard his father's voice.

"That you Rob?" asked the doctor anxiously.

"Yes, sir," replied Cairn eagerly, and he opened the drawer and slid his hand in for the silken cord.

"There is something you have to tell me?"

Cairn, without preamble, plunged excitedly into an account of his meeting with Ferrara. "The silk cord," he concluded, "I have in my hand at the present moment, and—"

"Hold on a moment!" came Dr. Cairn's voice, rather grimly.

Followed a short interval; then—

"Hullo, Rob! Listen to this, from to-night's paper: 'A curious discovery was made by an attendant in one of the rooms of the Indian Section of the British Museum late this evening. A case had been opened in some way, and, although it contained more valuable objects, the only item which the thief had abstracted was a Thug's strangling-cord from Kundélee (district of Nursingpore).'"

"But I don't understand—"

"Ferrara *meant* you to find that cord, boy! Remember, he is unacquainted with your chambers and he requires a *focus* for his damnable forces! He knows well that you will have the thing somewhere near to you, and probably he knows something of its awful history! You are in danger! Keep a fast hold upon yourself. I shall be with you in less than half an hour!"


## CHAPTER XXVII
## THE THUG'S CORD


As Robert Cairn hung up the receiver and found himself cut off again from the outer world, he realized with terror beyond his control how in this quiet backwater, so near to the main stream, he yet was far from human companionship.

He recalled a night when, amid such a silence as this which now prevailed about him, he had been made the subject of an uncanny demonstration; how his sanity, his life, had been attacked; how he had fled from the crowding horrors which had been massed against him by his supernaturally endowed enemy.

There was something very terrifying in the quietude of the court—a quietude which to others might have spelled peace, but which to Robert Cairn, spelled menace. That Ferrara's device was aimed at his freedom, that his design was intended to lead to the detention of his enemy whilst he directed his activities in other directions, seemed plausible, if inadequate. The carefully planned incident at the museum whereby the constable had become possessed of Cairn's card; the distinct possibility that a detective might knock upon his door at any moment—with the inevitable result of his detention pending inquiries—formed a chain which had seemed complete, save that Antony Ferrara was the schemer. For another to have compassed so much would have been a notable victory; for Ferrara, such a victory would be trivial.

What, then, did it mean? His father had told him, and the uncanny events of the evening stood evidence of Dr. Cairn's wisdom. The mysterious and evil force which Antony Ferrara controlled was being focussed upon him!

Slight sounds from time to time disturbed the silence; and to these he listened attentively. He longed for the arrival of his father—for the strong, calm counsel of the one man in England fitted to cope with the Hell Thing which had uprisen in their midst. That he had already been subjected to some kind of hypnotic influence he was unable to doubt; and having once been subjected to this influence, he might at any moment (it was a terrible reflection) fall a victim to it again.

Cairn directed all the energies of his mind to resistance; ill-defined reflection must at all costs be avoided, for the brain vaguely employed he knew to be more susceptible to attack than that directed in a well-ordered channel.

Clocks were chiming the hour—he did not know what hour, nor did he seek to learn. He felt that he was at rapier play with a skilled antagonist, and that to glance aside, however momentarily, was to lay himself open to a fatal thrust.

He had not moved from the table, so that only the reading-lamp upon it was lighted, and much of the room lay in half shadow. The silken cord, coiled snake-like, was close to his left hand; the revolver was close to his right. The muffled roar of traffic—diminished, since the hour grew late—reached his ears as he sat. But nothing disturbed the stillness of the court, and nothing disturbed the stillness of the room.

The notes which he had made in the afternoon at the museum were still spread open before him, and he suddenly closed the book, fearful of anything calculated to distract him from the mood of tense resistance. His life, and more than his life, depended upon his successfully opposing the insidious forces which, beyond doubt, invisibly surrounded that lighted table.

There is a courage which is not physical, nor is it entirely moral; a courage often lacking in the most intrepid soldier. And this was the kind of courage which Robert Cairn now called up to his aid. The occult inquirer can face, unmoved, horrors which would turn the brain of many a man who wears the V. C.; on the other hand, it is questionable if the possessor of this peculiar type of bravery could face a bayonet charge. Pluck of the physical sort Cairn had in plenty; pluck of that more subtle kind he was acquiring from growing intimacy with the terrors of the Borderland.

"Who's there?"

He spoke the words aloud, and the eerie sound of his own voice added a new dread to the enveloping shadows.

His revolver grasped in his hand, he stood up, but slowly and cautiously, in order that his own movements might not prevent him from hearing any repetition of that which had occasioned his alarm. And what had occasioned this alarm?

Either he was become again a victim of the strange trickery which already had borne him, though not physically, from Fleet Street to the secret temple of Méydûm, or with his material senses he had detected a soft rapping upon the door of his room.

He knew that his outer door was closed; he knew that there was no one else in his chambers; yet he had heard a sound as of knuckles beating upon the panels of the door—the closed door of the room in which he sat!

Standing upright, he turned deliberately, and faced in that direction.

The light pouring out from beneath the shade of the table-lamp scarcely touched upon the door at all. Only the edges of the lower panels were clearly perceptible; the upper part of the door was masked in greenish shadow.

Intent, tensely strung, he stood; then advanced in the direction of the switch in order to light the lamp fixed above the mantelpiece and to illuminate the whole of the room. One step forward he took, then... the soft rapping was repeated.

"Who's there?"

This time he cried the words loudly, and acquired some new assurance from the imperative note in his own voice. He ran to the switch and pressed it down. The lamp did not light!

"The filament has burnt out," he muttered.

Terror grew upon him—a terror akin to that which children experience in the darkness. But he yet had a fair mastery of his emotions; when— not suddenly, as is the way of a failing electric lamp—but slowly, uncannily, unnaturally, the table-lamp became extinguished!

Darkness... Cairn turned toward the window. This was a moonless night, and little enough illumination entered the room from the court.

Three resounding raps were struck upon the door.

At that, terror had no darker meaning for Cairn; he had plumbed its ultimate deeps; and now, like a diver, he arose again to the surface.

Heedless of the darkness, of the seemingly supernatural means by which it had been occasioned, he threw open the door and thrust his revolver out into the corridor.

For terrors, he had been prepared—for some gruesome shape such as we read of in *The Magus*. But there was nothing. Instinctively he had looked straight ahead of him, as one looks who expects to encounter a human enemy. But the hallway was empty. A dim light, finding access over the door from the stair, prevailed there, yet it was sufficient to have revealed the presence of any one or any thing, had any one or any thing been present.

Cairn stepped out from the room and was about to walk to the outer door. The idea of flight was strong upon him, for no man can fight the invisible; when, on a level with his eyes—flat against the wall, as though someone crouched there—he saw two white hands!

They were slim hands, like the hands of a woman, and upon one of the tapered fingers there dully gleamed a green stone.

A peal of laughter came chokingly from his lips; he knew that his reason was tottering. For these two white hands which now moved along the wall, as though they were sidling to the room which Cairn had just quitted, were attached to no visible body; just two ivory hands were there... *and nothing more!*

That he was in deadly peril, Cairn realized fully. His complete subjection by the will-force of Ferrara had been interrupted by the ringing of the telephone bell. But now the attack had been renewed!

The hands vanished.

Too well he remembered the ghastly details attendant upon the death of Sir Michael Ferrara to doubt that these slim hands were directed upon murderous business.

A soft swishing sound reached him. Something upon the writing-table had been moved.

The strangling cord!

Whilst speaking to his father he had taken it out from the drawer, and when he quitted the room it had lain upon the blotting-pad.

He stepped back toward the outer door.

Something fluttered past his face, and he turned in a mad panic. The dreadful, bodiless hands groped in the darkness between himself and the exit!

Vaguely it came home to him that the menace might be avoidable. He was bathed in icy perspiration.

He dropped the revolver into his pocket, and placed his hands upon his throat. Then he began to grope his way toward the closed door of his bedroom.

Lowering his left hand, he began to feel for the doorknob. As he did so, he saw—and knew the crowning horror of the night—that he had made a false move. In retiring he had thrown away his last, his only, chance.

The phantom hands, a yard apart and holding the silken cord stretched tightly between them, were approaching him swiftly!

He lowered his head, and charged along the passage with a wild cry.

The cord, stretched taut, struck him under the chin.

Back he reeled.

The cord was about his throat!

"God!" he choked, and thrust up his hands.

Madly he strove to pluck the deadly silken thing from his neck. It was useless. A grip of steel was drawing it tightly—and ever more tightly— about him...

Despair touched him, and almost he resigned himself. Then,

"Rob! Rob! open the door!"

Dr. Cairn was outside.

A new strength came—and he knew that it was the last atom left to him. To remove the rope was humanly impossible. He dropped his cramped hands, bent his body by a mighty physical effort, and hurled himself forward upon the door.

The latch, now, was just above his head.

He stretched up... and was plucked back. But the fingers of his right hand grasped the knob convulsively.

Even as that superhuman force jerked him back, he turned the knob— and fell.

All his weight hung upon the fingers which were locked about that brass disk in a grip which even the powers of Darkness could not relax.

The door swung open, and Cairn swung back with it.

He collapsed, an inert heap, upon the floor. Dr. Cairn leapt in over him.

When he reopened his eyes, he lay in bed, and his father was bathing his inflamed throat.

"All right, boy! There's no damage done, thank God..."

"The hands!—"

"I quite understand. But *I* saw no hands but your own, Rob; and if it had come to an inquest I could not even have raised my voice against a verdict of suicide!"

"But I—opened the door!"

"They would have said that you repented your awful act too late. Al- though it is almost impossible for a man to strangle himself under such conditions there is no jury in England who would have believed that Antony Ferrara had done the deed."

## CHAPTER XXVIII
## THE HIGH PRIEST, HORTOTEF

The breakfast room of Dr. Cairn's house in Half-Moon Street presented a cheery appearance, and this despite the gloom of the morning; for thunderous clouds hung low in the sky, and there were distant mutterings ominous of a brewing storm.

Robert Cairn stood looking out of the window. He was thinking of an afternoon at Oxford when to such an accompaniment as this he had witnessed the first scene in the drama of evil wherein the man called Antony Ferrara sustained the leading role.

That the denoument was at any moment to be anticipated, his reason told him; and some instinct that was not of his reason forewarned him, too, that he and his father, Dr. Cairn, were now upon the eve of that final, decisive struggle which should determine the triumph of good over evil—or of evil over good. Already the doctor's house was invested by the uncanny forces marshalled by Antony Ferrara against them. The distinguished patients, who daily flocked to the consulting room of the celebrated specialist, who witnessed his perfect self-possession and took comfort from his confidence, knowing it for the confidence of strength, little suspected that a greater ill than any flesh is heir to assailed the doctor to whom they came for healing.

A menace, dreadful and unnatural, hung over that home as now the thunder clouds hung over it. This well-ordered household, so modern, so typical of twentieth century culture and refinement, presented none of the appearances of a beleaguered garrison; yet the house of Dr. Cairn in Half-Moon Street was nothing less than an invested fortress.

A peal of distant thunder boomed from the direction of Hyde Park. Robert Cairn looked up at the lowering sky as if seeking a portent. To his eyes it seemed that a livid face, malignant with the malignancy of a devil, looked down out of the clouds.

Myra Duquesne came into the breakfast room.

He turned to greet her, and, in his capacity of accepted lover, was about to kiss the tempting lips, when he hesitated—and contented himself with kissing her hand. A sudden sense of the proprieties had assailed him; he reflected that the presence of the girl beneath the same roof as himself—although dictated by imperative need—might be open to misconstruction by the prudish. Dr. Cairn had decided that for the present Myra Duquesne must dwell beneath his own roof, as, in feudal days, the Baron at first hint of an approaching enemy was accustomed to call within the walls of the castle those whom it was his duty to protect. Unknown to the world, a tremendous battle raged in London, the outer works were in the possession of the enemy—and he was now before their very gates.

Myra, though still pale from her recent illness, already was recovering some of the freshness of her beauty and in her simple morning dress, as she busied herself about the breakfast table, she was a sweet picture enough, and good to look upon. Robert Cairn stood beside her, looking into her eyes, and she smiled up at him with a happy contentment, which filled him with a new longing. But:

"Did you dream again last night?" he asked, in a voice which he strove to make matter-of-fact.

Myra nodded—and her face momentarily clouded over.

"The same dream?"

"Yes," she said in a troubled way; "at least—in some respects—"

Dr. Cairn came in, glancing at his watch.

"Good morning!" he cried cheerily. "I have actually overslept myself."

They took their seats at the table.

"Myra has been dreaming again, sir," said Robert Cairn slowly.

The doctor, serviette in hand, glanced up with an inquiry in his gray eyes.

"We must not overlook any possible weapon," he replied. "Give us particulars of your dream, Myra."

As Marston entered silently with the morning fare, and, having placed the dishes upon the table, as silently withdrew, Myra began:

"I seemed to stand again in the barnlike building which I have described to you before. Through the rafters of the roof I could see the cracks in the tiling, and the moonlight shone through, forming light and irregular patches upon the floor. A sort of door, like that of a stable, with a heavy bar across, was dimly perceptible at the farther end of the place. The only furniture was a large deal table and a wooden chair of a very common kind. Upon the table, stood a lamp—"

"What kind of lamp?" jerked Dr. Cairn.

"A silver lamp"—she hesitated, looking from Robert to his father—"one that I have seen in—Antony's rooms. Its shaded light shone upon a closed iron box. I immediately recognized this box. You know that I described to you a dream which—terrified me on the previous night?"

Dr. Cairn nodded, frowning darkly.

"Repeat your account of the former dream," he said. "I regard it as important.”

“In my former dream,” the girl resumed—and her voice had an odd, far-away quality—“the scene was the same, except that the light of the lamp was shining down upon the leaves of an open book—a very, very old book, written in strange characters. These characters appeared to dance before my eyes—almost as though they lived.”

She shuddered slightly; then:

“The same iron box, but open, stood upon the table, and a number of other, smaller, boxes around it. Each of these boxes was of a different material. Some were wooden; one, I think, was of ivory; one was of silver—and one, of some dull metal, which might have been gold. In the chair, by the table, Antony was sitting. His eyes were fixed upon me with such a strange expression that I awoke, trembling frightfully—”

Dr. Cairn nodded again.

“And last night?” he prompted.

“Last night,” continued Myra, with a note of trouble in her sweet voice—“at four points around this table stood four smaller lamps and upon the floor were rows of characters apparently traced in luminous paint. They flickered up and then grew dim, then flickered up again, in a sort of phosphorescent way. They extended from lamp to lamp, so as entirely to surround the table and the chair.

“In the chair Antony Ferrara was sitting. He held a wand in his right hand—a wand with several copper rings about it; his left hand rested upon the iron box. In my dream, although I could see this all very clearly, I seemed to see it from a distance; yet, at the same time, I stood apparently close by the table—I cannot explain. But I could hear nothing; only by the movements of his lips could I tell that he was speaking—or chanting.”

She looked across at Dr. Cairn as if fearful to proceed, but presently continued:

“Suddenly I saw a frightful shape appear on the far side of the circle; that is to say, the table was between me and this shape. It was just like a gray cloud having the vague outlines of a man, but with two eyes of red fire glaring out from it—horribly—oh! horribly! It extended its shadowy arms as if saluting Antony. He turned and seemed to question it. Then with a look of ferocious anger—oh! it was frightful! he dismissed the shape, and began to walk up and down beside the table, but never beyond the lighted circle, shaking his fists in the air, and, to judge by the movements of his lips, uttering most awful imprecations. He looked gaunt and ill. I dreamt no more, but awoke conscious of a sensation as though some dead weight, which had been pressing upon me, had been suddenly removed."

Dr. Cairn glanced across at his son significantly, but the subject was not renewed throughout breakfast.

Breakfast concluded:

"Come into the library, Rob," said Dr. Cairn, "I have half an hour to spare, and there are some matters to be discussed."

He led the way into the library with its orderly rows of obscure works, its store of forgotten wisdom, and pointed to the red leathern armchair. As Robert Cairn seated himself and looked across at his father, who sat at the big writing-table, that scene reminded him of many dangers met and overcome in the past; for the library at Half-Moon Street was associated in his mind with some of the blackest pages in the history of Antony Ferrara.

"Do you understand the position, Rob?" asked the doctor abruptly.

"I think so, sir. This I take it is his last card; this outrageous, ungodly Thing which he has loosed upon us."

Dr. Cairn nodded grimly.

"The exact frontier," he said, "dividing what we may term hypnotism from what we know as sorcery, has yet to be determined; and to which territory the doctrine of Elemental Spirits belongs, it would be purposeless at the moment to discuss. We may note, however, remembering with whom we are dealing, that the one hundred and eighth chapter of the Ancient Egyptian 'Book of the Dead' is entitled 'The Chapter of Knowing the Spirits of the West.' Forgetting, *pro tem.*, that we dwell in the twentieth century, and looking at the situation from the point of view, say, of Eliphas Lévi, Cornelius Agrippa, or the Abbé de Villars—the man whom we know as Antony Ferrara is directing against this house, and those within it, a type of elemental spirit known as a Salamander!"

Robert Cairn smiled slightly.

"Ah!" said the doctor, with an answering smile in which there was little mirth, "we are accustomed to laugh at this medieval terminology; but by what other can we speak of the activities of Ferrara?"

"Sometimes I think that we are the victims of a common madness," said his son, raising his hand to his head in a manner almost pathetic.

"We are the victims of a common enemy," replied his father sternly. "He employs weapons which, often enough in this enlightened age of ours, have condemned poor souls, as sane as you or I, to the madhouse! Why, in God's name," he cried, with a sudden excitement, "does science persistently ignore all those laws which cannot be examined in the laboratory! Will the day never come when some true man of science shall endeavour to explain the movements of a table upon which a ring of hands has been placed? Will no exact scientist condescend to examine the properties of a *planchette?* Will no one do for the phenomena termed thought forms, what Newton did for that of the falling apple? Ah! Rob, in some respects, this is a darker age than those which bear the stigma of darkness."

Silence fell for a few moments between them; then:

"One thing is certain," said Robert Cairn deliberately, "we are in danger!"

"In the greatest danger!"

"Antony Ferrara, realizing that we are bent upon his destruction, is making a final, stupendous effort to compass ours. I know that you have placed certain seals upon the windows of this house, and that after dusk these windows are never opened. I know that imprints, strangely like the imprints of *fiery hands*, may be seen at this moment upon the casements of Myra's room, your room, my room, and elsewhere. I know that Myra's dreams are not ordinary, meaningless dreams. I have had other evidence. I don't want to analyze these things; I confess that my mind is not capable of the task. I do not even want to know the meaning of it all; at the present moment, I only want to know one thing: *Who is Antony Ferrara?*"

Dr. Cairn stood up, and turning, faced his son.

"The time has come," he said, "when that question, which you have asked me so many times before, shall be answered. I will tell you all I know, and leave you to form your own opinion. For ere we go any further, I assure you that I do not know for certain who he is!"

"You have said so before, sir. Will you explain what you mean?"

"When his foster father, Sir Michael Ferrara," resumed the doctor, beginning to pace up and down the library—"when Sir Michael and I were in Egypt, in the winter of 1893, we conducted certain inquiries in the Fayûm. We camped for over three months beside the Méydûm Pyramid. The object of our inquiries was to discover the tomb of a certain queen. I will not trouble you with the details, which could be of no interest to any one but an Egyptologist. I will merely say that apart from the name and titles by which she is known to the ordinary student, this queen is also known to certain inquirers as the Witch-Queen. She was not an Egyptian, but an Asiatic. In short, she was the last high priestess of a cult which became extinct at her death. Her secret mark—I am not referring to a cartouche or anything of that kind—was a spider; it was the mark of the religion or cult which she practised. The high priest of the principal Temple of Ra, during the reign of the Pharaoh who was this queen's husband, was one Hortotef. This was his official position, but secretly he was also the high priest of the sinister creed to which I have referred. The temple of this religion—a religion allied to Black Magic—was the Pyramid of Méydûm.

"So much we knew—or Ferrara knew, and imparted to me—but for any corroborative evidence of this cult's existence we searched in vain. We explored the interior of the pyramid foot by foot, inch by inch—and found nothing. We knew that there was some other apartment in the pyramid, but in spite of our soundings, measurements, and laborious excavations, we did not come upon the entrance to it. The tomb of the queen we failed to discover, also, and therefore concluded that her mummy was buried in the secret chamber of the pyramid. We had abandoned our quest in despair, when, excavating in one of the neighbouring mounds, we made a discovery."

He opened a box of cigars, selected one, and pushed the box toward his son. Robert shook his head, almost impatiently, but Dr. Cairn lighted the cigar ere resuming:

"Directed, as I now believe, by a malignant will, we blundered upon the tomb of the high priest—"

"You found his mummy?"

"We found his mummy—yes. But owing to the carelessness—and the fear—of the native labourers it was exposed to the sun and crumpled—was lost. I would a similar fate had attended the other one which we found!"

"What, another mummy?"

"We discovered"—Dr. Cairn spoke very deliberately—"a certain papyrus. The translation of this is contained"—he rested the point of his finger upon the writing-table—"in the unpublished book of Sir Michael Ferrara, which lies here. That book, Rob, will never be published now! Furthermore, we discovered the mummy of a child—"

"A child?"

"A boy. Not daring to trust the natives, we removed it secretly at night to our own tent. Before we commenced the task of unwrapping it, Sir Michael—the most brilliant scholar of his age—had proceeded so far in deciphering the papyrus that he determined to complete his reading before we proceeded further. It contained directions for performing a certain process. This process had reference to the mummy of the child."

"Do I understand—?"

"Already you are discrediting the story! Ah! I can see it, but let me finish! Unaided, we performed this process upon the embalmed body of the child. Then, in accordance with the directions of that dead magician—that accursed, malignant being, who thus had sought to secure for himself a new tenure of evil life—we laid the mummy, treated in a certain fashion, in the King's Chamber of the Méydûm Pyramid. It remained there for thirty days; from moon to moon—"

"You guarded the entrance?"

"You may assume what you like, Rob, but I could swear before any jury that no one entered the pyramid throughout that time. Yet since we were only human, we may have been deceived in this. I have only to add that when at the rising of the new moon in the ancient Sothic month at Panoi we again entered the chamber, a living baby, some six months old, perfectly healthy, solemnly blinked up at the lights which we held in our trembling hands!"

Dr. Cairn reseated himself at the table, and turned the chair so that he faced his son. With the smouldering cigar between his teeth, he sat, a slight smile upon his lips.

Now it was Robert's turn to rise and begin feverishly to pace the floor.

"You mean, sir, that this infant—which lay in the pyramid—was—adopted by Sir Michael?"

"Was adopted, yes. Sir Michael engaged nurses for him, reared him here in England, educating him as an Englishman, sent him to a public school, sent him to—"

"To Oxford! Antony Ferrara! What! Do you seriously tell me that this is the history of Antony Ferrara?"

"On my word of honour, boy, that is all I know of Antony Ferrara. Is it not enough?"

"Merciful God! It is incredible!" groaned Robert Cairn.

"From the time that he attained to manhood," said Dr. Cairn evenly, "this adopted son of my poor old friend has passed from crime to crime. By means which are beyond my comprehension, and which alone serve to confirm his supernatural origin, he has acquired—knowledge. According to the Ancient Egyptian beliefs the *Khu* (or magical powers) of a fully equipped Adept, at the death of the body, could enter into anything prepared for its reception. According to these ancient beliefs, then, the *Khu* of the high priest, Hortotef, entered into the body of this infant who was his son, and whose mother was the Witch-Queen; and to-day in this modern London a wizard of Ancient Egypt, armed with the lost lore of that magical land, walks amongst us! What that lore is worth, it would be profitless for us to discuss, but that he possesses it— *all* of it—I know, beyond doubt. The most ancient and most powerful magical book which has ever existed was the 'Book of Thoth.'"

He walked across to a distant shelf, selected a volume, opened it at a particular page, and placed it on his son's knees.

"Read there!" he said, pointing.

The words seemed to dance before the younger man's eyes, and this is what he read:

"To read two pages enables you to enchant the heavens, the earth, the abyss, the mountains, and the sea; you shall know what the birds of the sky and the crawling things are saying... and when the second page is read, if you are in the world of ghosts, you will grow again in the shape you were on earth..."

"Heavens!" whispered Robert Cairn, "is this the writing of a madman, or can such things possibly be?" He read on:

"This book is in the middle of the river at Koptos, in an iron box—"

"An iron box," he muttered—"an iron box."

"So you recognize the iron box?" jerked Dr. Cairn. His son read on:

"In the iron box is a bronze box; in the bronze box is a sycamore box; in the sycamore box is an ivory and ebony box; in the ivory and ebony box is a silver box; in the silver box is a golden box; and in that is the book. It is twisted all round with snakes and scorpions, and all the other crawling things..."

"The man who holds the 'Book of Thoth,'" said Dr. Cairn, breaking the silence, "holds a power which should only belong to God. The creature who is known to the world as Antony Ferrara holds that book—do you doubt it?—therefore, you know now, as I have known long enough, with what manner of enemy we are fighting. You know that, this time, it is a fight to the death—"

He stopped abruptly, staring out of the window.

A man with a large photographic camera, standing upon the opposite pavement, was busily engaged in focussing the house!

"What is this ?" muttered Robert Cairn, also stepping to the window.

"It is a link between sorcery and science!" replied the doctor. "You remember Ferrara's photographic gallery at Oxford?—the Zenana, you used to call it!— You remember having seen in his collection photographs of persons who afterward came to violent ends?"

"I begin to understand!"

"Thus far his endeavours to concentrate the whole of the evil forces at his command upon this house have had but poor results: having merely caused Myra to dream strange dreams—clairvoyant dreams, instructive dreams, more useful to us than to the enemy; and having resulted in certain marks upon the outside of the house adjoining the windows—windows which I have sealed in a particular manner. You understand?"

"By means of photographs he—concentrates, in some way, malignant forces upon certain points—"

"He focusses his will—yes! The man who can really control his will, Rob is supreme, below the Godhead. Ferrara can almost do this now. Before he has become wholly proficient—"

"I understand, sir," snapped his son grimly.

"He is barely of age, boy," Dr. Cairn said, almost in a whisper. "In another year he would menace the world. Where are you going?"

He grasped his son's arm as Robert started for the door.

"That man yonder—"

"Diplomacy, Rob! Guile against guile. Let the man do his work, which he does in all innocence; then follow him. Learn where his studio is situated, and, from that point, proceed to learn—"

"The situation of Ferrara's hiding-place?" cried his son excitedly. "I understand! Of course; you are right, sir."

"I will leave the inquiry in your hands, Rob. Unfortunately other duties call me."

CHAPTER XXIX<br>THE WIZARD'S DEN

Robert Cairn entered a photographer's shop in Baker Street.

"You recently arranged to do views of some houses in the West End for a gentleman?" he said to the girl in charge.

"That is so," she replied, after a moment's hesitation. "We did pictures of the house of some celebrated specialist—for a magazine article they were intended. Do you wish us to do something similar?"

"Not at the moment," replied Robert Cairn, smiling slightly. "I merely want the address of your client."

"I do not know that I can give you that," replied the girl doubtfully, "but he will be here about eleven o'clock for proofs, if you wish to see him."

"I wonder if I can confide in you," said Robert Cairn, looking the girl frankly in the eyes.

She seemed rather confused.

"I hope there is nothing wrong," she murmured.

"You have nothing to fear," he replied, "but unfortunately there *is* something wrong, which, however, I cannot explain. Will you promise me not to tell your client—I do not ask his name—that I have been here, or have been making any inquiries respecting him?"

"I think I can promise that," she replied.

"I am much indebted to you."

Robert Cairn hastily left the shop, and began to look about him for a likely hiding-place whence, unobserved, he might watch the photographer's. An antique furniture dealer's, some little distance along on the opposite side, attracted his attention. He glanced at his watch. It was half-past ten.

If, upon the pretence of examining some of the stock, he could linger in the furniture shop for half an hour, he would be enabled to get upon the track of Ferrara!

His mind made up, he walked along and entered the shop. For the next half hour he passed from item to item of the collection displayed there, surveying each in the leisurely manner of a connoisseur; but always he kept a watch, through the window, upon the photographer's establishment beyond.

Promptly at eleven o'clock a taxi-cab drew up at the door, and from it a slim man alighted. He wore, despite the heat of the morning, an overcoat of some woolly material; and in his gait, as he crossed the pavement to enter the shop, there was something revoltingly effeminate; a sort of cat-like grace which had been noticeable in a woman, but which in a man was unnatural, and for some obscure reason sinister.

It was Antony Ferrara!

Even at that distance and in that brief time Robert Cairn could see the ivory face, the abnormal red lips, and the long black eyes of this arch fiend, this monster masquerading as a man. He had much ado to restrain his rising passion; but, knowing that all depended upon his cool action, he waited until Ferrara had entered the photographer's. With a word of apology to the furniture dealer, he passed quickly into Baker Street. Everything rested, now, upon his securing a cab before Ferrara came out again. Ferrara's cabman, evidently, was waiting for him.

A taxi driver fortunately hailed Cairn at the very moment that he gained the pavement; and Cairn, concealing himself behind the vehicle, gave the man rapid instructions:

"You see that taxi outside the photographer's?" he said.

The man nodded.

"Wait until someone comes out of the shop and is driven off in it; then follow. Do not lose sight of the cab for a moment. When it draws up, and wherever it draws up, drive right past it. Don't attract attention by stopping. You understand?"

"Quite, sir," said the man, smiling slightly. And Cairn entered the cab.

The cabman drew up at a point some little distance beyond, whence he could watch. Two minutes later Ferrara came out and was driven off.

The pursuit commenced.

His cab, ahead, proceeded to Westminster Bridge across to the south side of the river, and by way of that commercial thoroughfare at the back of St. Thomas's Hospital, emerged at Vauxhall. Thence the pursuit led to Stockwell, Herne Hill, and yet onward toward Dulwich.

It suddenly occurred to Robert Cairn that Ferrara was making in the direction of Mr. Saunderson's house at Dulwich Common—the house in which Myra had had her mysterious illness, in which she had remained until it had become evident that her safety depended upon her never being left alone for one moment.

"What can be his object?" muttered Cairn.

He wondered if Ferrara, for some inscrutable reason, was about to call upon Mr. Saunderson. But when the cab ahead, having passed the park, continued on past the lane in which the house was situated, he began to search for some other solution to the problem of Ferrara's destination.

Suddenly he saw that the cab ahead had stopped. The driver of his own cab, without slackening speed, pursued his way. Cairn crouched down upon the floor, fearful of being observed. No house was visible to right nor left, merely open fields; and he knew that it would be impossible for him to delay in such a spot without attracting attention.

"Keep on till I tell you to stop!" cried Cairn.

He dropped the speaking-tube, and, turning, looked out through the little window at the back.

Ferrara had dismissed his cab; he saw him entering a gate and crossing a field on the right of the road. Cairn turned again and took up the tube.

"Stop at the first house we come to!" he directed "Hurry!"

Presently a deserted-looking building was reached, a large straggling house which obviously had no tenant. Here the man pulled up and Cairn leapt out. As he did so, he heard Ferrara's cab driving back by the way it had come.

"Here," he said, and gave the man half a sovereign, "wait for me."

He started back along the road at a run. Even had he suspected that he was followed, Ferrara could not have seen him. But when Cairn came up level with the gate through which Ferrara had gone, he slowed down and crept cautiously forward.

Ferrara, who by this time had reached the other side of the field, was in the act of entering a barn-like building which evidently at some time had formed a portion of a farm. As the distant figure, opening one of the big doors, disappeared within:

"The place of which Myra has been dreaming!" muttered Cairn.

Certainly, viewed from that point, it seemed to answer, externally, to the girl's description. The roof was of moss-grown red tiles, and Cairn could imagine how the moonlight would readily find access through the chinks which beyond doubt existed in the weather-worn structure. He had little doubt that this was the place dreamt of, or seen clairvoyantly, by Myra, that this was the place to which Ferrara had retreated in order to conduct his nefarious operations.

It was eminently suited to the purpose, being entirely surrounded by unoccupied land. For what ostensible purpose Ferrara had leased it, he could not conjecture, nor did he concern himself with the matter. The purpose for which actually he had leased the place was sufficiently evident to the man who had suffered so much at the hands of this modern sorcerer.

To approach closer would have been indiscreet; this he knew; and he was sufficiently diplomatic to resist the temptation to obtain a nearer view of the place. He knew that everything depended upon secrecy. Antony Ferrara must not suspect that his black laboratory was known. Cairn decided to return to Half-Moon Street without delay, fully satisfied with the result of his investigation.

He walked rapidly back to where the cab waited, gave the man his father's address, and in three quarters of an hour was back in Half-Moon Street.

Dr. Cairn had not yet dismissed the last of his patients; Myra, accompanied by Miss Saunderson, was out shopping; and Robert found himself compelled to possess his soul in patience. He paced restlessly up and down the library, sometimes taking a book at random, scanning its pages with unseeing eyes, and replacing it without having formed the slightest impression of its contents. He tried to smoke; but his pipe was constantly going out, and he had littered the hearth untidily with burnt matches-when Dr. Cairn suddenly opened the library door, and entered.

"Well?" he said eagerly.

Robert Cairn leapt forward.

"I have tracked him, sir!" he cried. "My God! while Myra was at Saunderson's, she was almost next door to the beast! His den is in a field no more than a thousand yards from the garden wall—from Saunderson's orchid-houses!"

"He is daring," muttered Dr. Cairn, "but his selection of that site served two purposes: The spot was suitable in many ways; and we were least likely to look for him next door, as it were. It was a move characteristic of the accomplished criminal."

Robert Cairn nodded.

"It is the place of which Myra dreamt, sir. I have not the slightest doubt about that. What we have to find out is at what times of the day and night he goes there—"

"I doubt," interrupted Dr. Cairn, "that he often visits the place during the day. As you know, he has abandoned his rooms in Piccadilly, but I have no doubt, knowing his sybaritic habits, that he has some other palatial place in town. I have been making inquiries in several directions, especially in—certain directions—"

He paused, raising his eyebrows significantly.

"Additions to the Zenana?" inquired Robert.

Dr. Cairn nodded his head grimly.

"Exactly," he replied. "There is not a scrap of evidence upon which, legally, he could be convicted; but since his return from Egypt, Rob, he has added other victims to his list!"

"The fiend!" cried the younger man; "the unnatural fiend!"

"Unnatural is the word; he is literally unnatural; but many women find him irresistible; he is typical of the unholy brood to which he belongs. The evil beauty of the Witch-Queen sent many a soul to perdition; the evil beauty of her son has zealously carried on the work."

"What must we do?"

"I doubt that we can do anything to-day. Obviously the early morning is the most suitable time to visit his den at Dulwich Common."

"But the new photographs of the house? There will be another attempt upon us to-night."

"Yes, there will be another attempt upon us tonight," said the doctor wearily. "This is the year 1914; yet, here in Half-Moon Street, when dusk falls, we shall be submitted to an attack of a kind to which mankind probably has not been submitted for many ages. We shall be called upon to dabble in the despised magical art; we shall be called upon to place certain seals upon our doors and windows; to protect ourselves against an enemy, who, like Eros, laughs at locks and bars."

"Is it possible for him to succeed?"

"Quite possible, Rob, in spite of all our precautions. I feel in my very bones that to-night he will put forth a supreme effort."

A bell rang.

"I think," continued the doctor, "that this is Myra. She must get all the sleep she can, during the afternoon, for to-night I have determined that she, and you, and I, must not think of sleep, but must remain together here in the library. We must not lose sight of one another—you understand?"

"I am glad that you have proposed it!" cried Robert Cairn eagerly, "I, too, feel that we have come to a critical moment in the contest."

"To-night," continued the doctor, "I shall be prepared to take certain steps. My preparations will occupy me throughout the rest of to-day."

## CHAPTER XXX
## THE ELEMENTAL

At dusk that evening Dr. Cairn, his son, and Myra Duquesne met together in the library. The girl looked rather pale.

An odour of incense pervaded the house, coming from the doctor's study, wherein he had locked himself early in the evening, issuing instructions that he was not to be disturbed. The exact nature of the preparations which he had been making Robert Cairn was unable to conjecture; and some instinct warned him that his father would not welcome any inquiry upon the matter. He realized that Dr. Cairn proposed to fight Antony Ferrara with his own weapons, and now, when something in the very air of the house seemed to warn them of a tremendous attack impending, that the doctor much against his will was entering the arena in the character of a practical magician—a character new to him, and obviously abhorrent.

At half-past ten the servants all retired in accordance with Dr. Cairn's orders. From where he stood by the tall mantelpiece Robert Cairn could watch Myra Duquesne, a dainty picture in her simple evening-gown, where she sat reading in a distant corner, her delicate beauty forming a strong contrast to the background of sombre volumes. Dr. Cairn sat by the big table, smoking, and apparently listening. A strange device which he had adopted every evening for the past week he had adopted again to-night—there were little white seals bearing a curious figure, consisting in interlaced triangles, upon the insides of every window in the house, upon the doors, and even upon the fire-grates.

Robert Cairn at another time might have thought his father mad, childish, thus to play at wizardry; but he had had experiences which had taught him to recognize that upon which seemingly trivial matters great issues might turn, that in the strange land over the Border there were stranger laws—laws which he could but dimly understand. There he acknowledged the superior wisdom of Dr. Cairn; and did not question it.

At eleven o'clock a comparative quiet had come upon Half-Moon Street. The sound of the traffic had gradually subsided, until it seemed to him that the house stood, not in the busy West End of London, but isolated, apart from its neighbours; it seemed to him an abode marked out and separated from the other abodes of man, a house enveloped in an impalpable cloud, a cloud of evil, summoned up and directed by the wizard hand of Antony Ferrara, son of the Witch-Queen.

Although Myra pretended to read, and Dr. Cairn, from his fixed expression, might have been supposed to be pre-occupied, in point of fact they were all waiting, with nerves at highest tension, for the opening of the attack. In what form it would come—whether it would be vague moanings and tappings upon the windows, such as they had already experienced, whether it would be a phantasmal storm, a clap of phenomenal thunder—they could not conjecture.

It came, then, suddenly and dramatically.

Dropping her book, Myra uttered a piercing scream, and with eyes glaring madly, fell forward on the carpet, unconscious!

Robert Cairn leapt to his feet with clenched fists. His father stood up so rapidly as to overset his chair, which fell crashingly upon the floor.

Together they turned and looked in the direction in which the girl had been looking. They fixed their eyes upon the drapery of the library window—which was drawn together. The whole window was luminous as though a bright light shone outside, but luminous, as though that light were the light of some unholy fire!

Involuntarily they both stepped back, and Robert Cairn clutched his father's arm convulsively.

The curtains seemed to be rendered transparent, as if some powerful ray were directed upon them; the window appeared through them as a rectangular blue patch. Only two lamps were burning in the library, that in the corner by which Myra had been reading, and the green shaded lamp upon the table. The end of the room by the window, then, was in shadow, against which this unnatural light shone brilliantly.

"My God!" whispered Robert Cairn—"that's Half-Moon Street—outside. There can be no light—"

He broke off, for now he perceived the Thing which had occasioned the girl's scream of horror.

In the middle of the rectangular patch of light a gray shape, but partially opaque, moved—shifting, luminous clouds about it—was taking form, growing momentarily more substantial!

It had some remote semblance of a man; but its unique characteristic was its awful *grayness*. It had the grayness of a rain cloud, yet rather that of a column of smoke. And from the centre of the dimly defined head two eyes—balls of living fire—glared out into the room!

Heat was beating into the library from the window—physical heat, as though a furnace door had been opened... and the shape, ever growing more palpable was moving forward toward them—approaching—the heat every instant growing greater.

It was impossible to look at those two eyes of fire; it was almost impossible to move. Indeed, Robert Cairn was transfixed in such horror as, in all his dealings with the monstrous Ferrara, he had never known before. But his father, shaking off the dread which possessed him also, leapt at one bound to the library table.

Robert Cairn vaguely perceived that a small group of objects, looking like balls of wax, lay there. Dr. Cairn had evidently been preparing them in the locked study. Now he took them all up in his left hand, and confronted the Thing—which seemed to be *growing* into the room—for it did not advance in the ordinary sense of the word.

One by one he threw the white pellets into that vapoury grayness. As they touched the curtain they hissed as if they had been thrown into a fire; they melted; and upon the transparency of the drapings, as upon a sheet of gauze, showed faint streaks, where, melting, they trickled down the tapestry.

As he cast each pellet from his hand, Dr. Cairn took a step forward, and cried out certain words in a loud voice—words which Robert Cairn knew he had never heard uttered before, words in a language which some instinct told him to be Ancient Egyptian.

Their effect was to force that dreadful shape gradually to disperse, as a cloud of smoke might disperse when the fire which occasions it is extinguished slowly. Seven pellets in all he threw toward the window—and the seventh struck the curtains, now once more visible in their proper form.

The Fire Elemental had been vanquished!

Robert Cairn clutched his hair in a sort of frenzy. He glared at the draped window, feeling that he was making a supreme effort to retain his sanity. Had it ever looked otherwise? Had the tapestry ever faded before him, becoming visible in a great light which had shone through it from behind? Had the Thing, a Thing unnameable, indescribable, stood there?

He read his answer upon the tapestry.

Whitening streaks showed where the pellets, melting, had trickled down the curtain!

"Lift Myra on to the settee!"

It was Dr. Cairn speaking, calmly, but in a strained voice.

Robert Cairn, as if emerging from a mist, turned to the recumbent white form upon the carpet. Then, with a great cry, he leapt forward and raised the girl's head.

"Myra!" he groaned. "Myra, speak to me."

"Control yourself, boy," rapped Dr. Cairn sternly; "she cannot speak until you have revived her! She has swooned—nothing worse."

"And—"

"We have conquered!"

CHAPTER XXXI
THE BOOK OF THOTH

The mists of early morning still floated over the fields, when these two, set upon strange business, walked through the damp grass to the door of the barn wherefrom radiated the deathly waves which on the previous night had reached them, or almost reached them, in the library at Half-Moon Street.

The big double doors were padlocked, but for this they had come provided. Ten minutes' work upon the padlock sufficed—and Dr. Cairn swung wide the doors.

A suffocating smell—the smell of that incense with which they had too often come in contact, was wafted out to them. There was a dim light inside the place, and without hesitation both entered.

A deal table and chair constituted the sole furniture of the interior. A part of the floor was roughly boarded, and a brief examination of the boarding sufficed to discover the hiding-place in which Antony Ferrara kept the utensils of his awful art.

Dr. Cairn lifted out two heavy boards; and in a recess below lay a number of singular objects. There were four antique lamps of most peculiar design; there was a larger silver lamp, which both of them had seen before in various apartments occupied by Antony Ferrara. There were a number of other things which Robert Cairn could not have described had he been called upon to do so, for the reason that he had seen nothing like them before, and had no idea of their nature or purpose.

But, conspicuous amongst this curious hoard was a square iron box of workmanship dissimilar from any workmanship known to Robert Cairn. Its lid was covered with a sort of scroll work, and he was about to reach down, in order to lift it out, when:

"Do not touch it!" cried the doctor—"for God's sake, do not touch it!"

Robert Cairn started back as though he had seen a snake. Turning to his father, he saw that the latter was pulling on a pair of white gloves. As he fixed his eyes upon these in astonishment, he perceived that they were smeared all over with some white preparation.

"Stand aside, boy," said the doctor—and for once his voice shook slightly. "Do not look again until I call to you. Turn your head aside!"

Silent with amazement, Robert Cairn obeyed. He heard his father lift out an iron box. He heard him open it, for he had already perceived that it was not locked. Then quite distinctly he heard him close it again, and replace it in the cache.

"Do not turn, boy!" came a hoarse whisper.

He did not turn, but waited, his heart beating painfully, for what should happen next.

"Stand aside from the door," came the order, "and when I have gone out, do not look after me. I will call to you when it is finished."

He obeyed, without demur.

His father passed him, and he heard him walking through the damp grass outside the door of the barn. There followed an intolerable interval. From some place, not very distant, he could hear Dr. Cairn moving, hear the chink of glass upon glass, as though he were pouring out something from a stoppered bottle. Then a faint acrid smell was wafted to his nostrils, perceptible even above the heavy odour of the incense from the barn.

"Relock the door!" came the cry.

Robert Cairn reclosed the door, snapped the padlock fast, and began to fumble with the skeleton keys with which they had come provided. He discovered that to reclose the padlock was quite as difficult as to open it. His hands were trembling, too; he was all anxiety to see what had taken place behind him. So that when at last a sharp click told of the task accomplished, he turned in a flash and saw his father placing tufts of grass upon a charred patch from which a faint haze of smoke still arose. He walked over and joined him.

"What have you done, sir?"

"I have robbed him of his armour," replied the doctor grimly. His face was very pale, his eyes were very bright. "I have destroyed the 'Book of Thoth!'"

"Then he will be unable—"

"He will still be able to summon his dreadful servant, Rob. Having summoned him once, he can summon him again, but—"

"Well, sir?"

"He cannot control him."

"Good God!"

That night brought no repetition of the uncanny attack; and in the gray half light before the dawn Dr. Cairn and his son, themselves like two phantoms, again crept across the field to the barn.

The padlock hung loose in the ring.

"Stay where you are, Rob!" cautioned the doctor.

He gently pushed the door open—wider—wider—and looked in. There was an overpowering odour of burning flesh. He turned to Robert, and spoke in a steady voice.

"The brood of the Witch-Queen is extinct!" he said.

THE END

THE

# THE QUEST OF THE SACRED SLIPPER

## SAX ROHMER

# CHAPTER I
## THE PHANTOM SCIMITAR

I was not the only passenger aboard the S.S. *Mandalay* who perceived the disturbance and wondered what it might portend and from whence proceed. A goodly number of passengers were joining the ship at Port Said. I was lounging against the rail, pipe in mouth, lazily wondering, with a large vagueness.

What a heterogeneous rabble it was!—a brightly coloured rabble, but the colours all were dirty, like the town and the canal. Only the sky was clean; the sky and the hard, merciless sunlight which spared nothing of the uncleanness, and defied one even to think of the term dear to tourists, "picturesque." I was in that kind of mood. All the natives appeared to be pockmarked; all the Europeans greasy with perspiration.

But what was the stir about?

I turned to the dark, bespectacled young man who leaned upon the rail beside me. From the first I had taken to Mr. Ahmad Ahmadeen.

"There is some kind of undercurrent of excitement among the natives," I said, "a sort of subdued Greek chorus is audible. What's it all about?"

Mr. Ahmadeen smiled. After a gaunt fashion, he was a handsome man and had a pleasant smile.

"Probably," he replied, "some local celebrity is joining the ship."

I stared at him curiously.

"Any idea who he is?" (The soul of the copyhunter is a restless soul.)

A group of men dressed in semi-European fashion—that is, in European fashion save for their turbans, which were green—passed close to us along the deck.

Ahmadeen appeared not to have heard the question.

The disturbance, which could only be defined as a subdued uproar, but could be traced to no particular individual or group, grew momentarily louder—and died away. It was only when it had completely ceased that one realized how pronounced it had been—how altogether peculiar, secret; like that incomprehensible murmuring in a bazaar when, unknown to the insular visitor, a reputed saint is present.

Then it happened; the inexplicable incident which, though I knew it not, heralded the coming of strange things, and the dawn of a new power; which should set up its secret standards in England, which should flood Europe and the civilized world with wonder.

A shrill scream marked the overture—a scream of fear and of pain, which dropped to a groan, and moaned out into the silence of which it was the cause.

"My God! what's that?"

I started forward. There was a general crowding rush, and a darkly tanned and bearded man came on board, carrying a brown leather case. Behind him surged those who bore the victim.

"It's one of the lascars!"

"No—an Egyptian!"

"It was a porter—?"

"What is it—?"

"Someone been stabbed!"

"Where's the doctor?"

"Stand away there, if you please!"

That was a ship's officer; and the voice of authority served to quell the disturbance. Through a lane walled with craning heads they bore the insensible man. Ahmadeen was at my elbow.

"A Copt," he said softly. "Poor devil!"

I turned to him. There was a queer expression on his lean, clean-shaven, bronze face.

"Good God!" I said. "*His hand has been cut off!*"

That was the fact of the matter. And no one knew who was responsible for the atrocity. And no one knew what had become of the severed hand! I wasted not a moment in linking up the story. The pressman within me acted automatically.

"The gentleman just come aboard, sir," said a steward, "is Professor Deeping. The poor beggar who was assaulted was carrying some of the Professor's baggage...."

The whole incident struck me as most odd. There was an idea lurking in my mind that something else—something more—lay behind all this. With impatience I awaited the time when the injured man, having received medical attention, was conveyed ashore, and Professor Deeping reappeared. To the celebrated traveller and Oriental scholar I introduced myself.

He was singularly reticent.

"I was unable to see what took place, Mr. Cavanagh," he said. "The poor fellow was behind me, for I had stepped from the boat ahead of him. I had just taken a bag from his hand, but he was carrying another, heavier one. It is a clean cut, like that of a scimitar. I have seen very similar wounds in the cases of men who have suffered the old Moslem penalty for theft."

Nothing further had come to light when the *Mandalay* left, but I found new matter for curiosity in the behaviour of the Moslem party who had come on board at Port Said.

In conversation with Mr. Bell, the chief officer, I learned that the supposed leader of the party was one, Mr. Azraeel. "Obviously," said Bell, "not his real name or not all of it. I don't suppose they'll show themselves on deck; they've got their own servants with them, and seem to be people of consequence."

This conversation was interrupted, but I found my unseen fellow voyagers peculiarly interesting and pursued inquiries in other directions. I saw members of the distinguished travellers' retinue going about their duties, but never obtained a glimpse of Mr. Azraeel nor of any of his green-turbaned companions.

"Who is Mr. Azraeel?" I asked Ahmadeen, once.

"I cannot say," replied the Egyptian, and abruptly changed the subject.

Some curious aroma of mystery floated about the ship. Ahmadeen conveyed to me the idea that he was concealing something. Then, one night, Mr. Bell invited me to step forward with him.

"Listen," he said.

From somewhere in the fo'c'sle proceeded a low chanting.

"Hear it?"

"Yes. What the devil is it?"

"It's the lascars," said Bell. "They have been behaving in a most unusual manner ever since the mysterious Mr. Azraeel joined us. I may be wrong in associating the two things, but I shan't be sorry to see the last of our mysterious passengers."

The next happening on board the *Mandalay* which I have to record was the attempt to break open the door of Professor Deeping's stateroom. Except when he was actually within, the Professor left his room door religiously locked.

He made light of the affair, but later took me aside and told me a curious story of an apparition which had appeared to him.

"It was a crescent of light," he said, "and it glittered through the darkness there to the left as I lay in my berth."

"A reflection from something on the deck?"

Deeping smiled, uneasily.

"Possibly," he replied; "but it was very sharply defined. Like the blade of a scimitar," he added.

I stared at him, my curiosity keenly aroused. "Does any explanation suggest itself to you?" I said.

"Well," he confessed, "I have a theory, I will admit; but it is rather going back to the Middle Ages. You see, I have lived in the East a lot; perhaps I have assimilated some of their superstitions."

He was oddly reticent, as ever. I felt convinced that he was keeping something back. I could not stifle the impression that the clue to these mysteries lay somewhere around the invisible Mohammedan party.

"Do you know," said Bell to me, one morning, "this trip's giving me the creeps. I believe the damned ship's *haunted!* Three bells in the middle watch last night, I'll swear I saw some black animal crawling along the deck, in the direction of the forward companion-way."

"Cat?" I suggested.

"Nothing like it," said Mr. Bell. "Mr. Cavanagh, it was some uncanny thing! I'm afraid I can't explain quite what I mean, but it was something I wanted to shoot!"

"Where did it go?"

The chief officer shrugged his shoulders. "Just vanished," he said. "I hope I don't see it again."

At Tilbury the Mohammedan party went ashore in a body. Among them were veiled women. They contrived so to surround a central figure that I entirely failed to get a glimpse of the mysterious Mr. Azraeel. Ahmadeen was standing close by the companionway, and I had a momentary impression that one of the women slipped something into his hand. Certainly, he started; and his dusky face seemed to pale.

Then a deck steward came out of Deeping's stateroom, carrying the brown bag which the Professor had brought aboard at Port Said. Deeping's voice came:

"Hi, my man! let *me* take that bag!"

The bag changed hands. Five minutes later, as I was preparing to go ashore, arose a horrid scream above the berthing clamour. Those passengers yet aboard made in the direction from which the scream had proceeded.

A steward—the one to whom Professor Deeping had spoken—lay writhing at the foot of the stairs leading to the saloon-deck. His right hand had been severed above the wrist!


## CHAPTER II
### THE GIRL WITH THE VIOLET EYES

During the next day or two my mind constantly reverted to the incidents of the voyage home. I was perfectly convinced that the curtain had been partially raised upon some fantasy in which Professor Deeping figured.

But I had seen no more of Deeping nor had I heard from him, when abruptly I found myself plunged again into the very vortex of his troubled affairs. I was half way through a long article, I remember, upon the mystery of the outrage at the docks. The poor steward whose hand had been severed lay in a precarious condition, but the police had utterly failed to trace the culprit.

I had laid down my pen to relight my pipe (the hour was about ten at night) when a faint sound from the direction of the outside door attracted my attention. Something had been thrust through the letter-box.

"A circular," I thought, when the bell rang loudly, imperatively.

I went to the door. A square envelope lay upon the mat—a curious envelope, pale amethyst in colour. Picking it up, I found it to bear my name—written simply—

"Mr. Cavanagh."

Tearing it open I glanced at the contents. I threw open the door. No one was visible upon the landing, but when I leaned over the banister a white-clad figure was crossing the hall, below.

Without hesitation, hatless, I raced down the stairs. As I crossed the dimly lighted hall and came out into the peaceful twilight of the court, my elusive visitor glided under the archway opposite.

Just where the dark and narrow passage opened on to Fleet Street I overtook her—a girl closely veiled and wrapped in a long coat of white ermine.

"Madam," I said.

She turned affrightedly.

"Please do not detain me!" Her accent was puzzling, but pleasing. She glanced apprehensively about her.

You have seen the moon through a mist?—and known it for what it was in spite of its veiling? So, now, through the cloudy folds of the veil, I saw the stranger's eyes, and knew them for the most beautiful eyes I had ever seen, had ever dreamt of.

"But you must explain the meaning of your note!"

"I cannot! I cannot! Please do not ask me!"

She was breathless from her flight and seemed to be trembling. From behind the cloud her eyes shone brilliantly, mysteriously.

I was sorely puzzled. The whole incident was bizarre—indeed, it had in it something of the uncanny. Yet I could not detain the girl against her will. That she went in apprehension of something, of someone, was evident.

Past the head of the passage surged the noisy realities of Fleet Street. There were men there in quest of news; men who would have given much for such a story as this in which I was becoming entangled. Yet a story more tantalizingly incomplete could not well be imagined.

I knew that I stood upon the margin of an arena wherein strange adversaries warred to a strange end. But a mist was over all. Here, beside me, was one who could disperse the mist—and would not. Her one anxiety seemed to be to escape.

Suddenly she raised her veil; and I looked fully into the only really violet eyes I had ever beheld. Mentally, I started. For the face framed in the snowy fur was the most bewitchingly lovely imaginable. One rebellious lock of wonderful hair swept across the white brow. It was brown hair, with an incomprehensible sheen in the high lights that suggested the heart of a blood-red rose.

"Oh," she cried, "promise me that you will never breathe a word to *any one* about my visit!"

"I promise willingly," I said; "but can you give me no hint—?"

"Honestly, truly, I cannot, dare not, say more! Only promise that you will do as I ask!"

Since I could perceive no alternative—"I will do so," I replied.

"Thank you—oh, thank you!" she said; and dropping her veil again she walked rapidly away from me, whispering, "I rely upon you. Do not fail me. Good-bye!"

Her conspicuous white figure joined the hurrying throngs upon the pavement beyond. My curiosity brooked no restraint. I hurried to the end of the courtway. She was crossing the road. From the shadows where he had lurked, a man came forward to meet her. A vehicle obstructed the view ere I could confirm my impression; and when it had passed, neither my lovely visitor nor her companion were anywhere in sight.

But, unless some accident of light and shade had deceived me, the man who had waited was Ahmad Ahmadeen!

It seemed that some astral sluice-gate was raised; a dreadful sense of foreboding for the first time flooded my mind. Whilst the girl had stood before me it had been different—the mysterious charm of her personality had swamped all else. But now, the messenger gone, it was the purport of her message which assumed supreme significance.

Written in odd, square handwriting upon the pale amethyst paper, this was the message—

Prevail upon Professor Deeping to place what he has in the brown case in the porch of his house *to-night*.

If he fails to do so, no power on earth can save him from the Scimitar of Hassan.

A FRIEND.

## CHAPTER III
## "HASSAN OF ALEPPO"

Professor Deeping's number was in the telephone directory, therefore, on returning to my room, where there still lingered the faint perfume of my late visitor's presence, I asked for his number. He proved to be at home.

"Strange you should ring me up, Cavanagh," he said; "for I was about to ring you up."

"First," I replied, "listen to the contents of an anonymous letter which I have received."

(I remembered, and only just in time, my promise to the veiled messenger.)

"To me," I added, having read him the note, "it seems to mean nothing. I take it that you understand better than I do."

"I understand very well, Cavanagh!" he replied. "You will recall my story of the scimitar which flashed before me in the darkness of my stateroom on the *Mandalay?* Well, I have seen it again! I am not an imaginative man: I had always believed myself to possess the scientific mind; but I can no longer doubt that I am the object of a pursuit which commenced in Mecca! The happenings on the steamer prepared me for this, in a degree. When the man lost his hand at Port Said I doubted. I had supposed the days of such things past. The attempt to break into my stateroom even left me still uncertain. But the outrage upon the steward at the docks removed all further doubt. I perceived that the contents of a certain brown leather case were the objective of the crimes."

I listened in growing wonder.

"It was not necessary in order to further the plan of stealing the bag that the hands were severed," resumed the Professor. "In fact, as was rendered evident by the case of the steward, this was a penalty visited upon any one who *touched* it! You are thinking of my own immunity?"

"I am!"

"This is attributable to two things. Those who sought to recover what I had in the case feared that my death en route might result in its being lost to them for ever. They awaited a suitable opportunity. They had designed to take it at Port Said certainly, I think; but the bag was too large to be readily concealed, and, after the outrage, might have led to the discovery of the culprit. In the second place, they are uncertain of my faith. I have long passed for a true Believer in the East! As a Moslem I visited Mecca—"

"You visited Mecca!"

"I had just returned from the *hadj* when I joined the *Mandalay* at Port Said! My death, however, has been determined upon, whether I be Moslem or Christian!"

"Why?"

"Because," came the Professor's harsh voice over the telephone, "of the contents of the brown leather case! I will not divulge to you now the nature of these contents; to know might endanger you. But the case is locked in my safe here, and the key, together with a full statement of the true facts of the matter, is hidden behind the first edition copy of my book 'Assyrian Mythology,' in the smaller bookcase—"

"Why do you tell me all this?" I interrupted.

He laughed harshly.

"The identity of my pursuer has just dawned upon me," he said. "I know that my life is in real danger. I would give up what is demanded of me, but I believe its possession to be my strongest safeguard."

Mystery upon mystery! I seemed to be getting no nearer to the heart of this maze. What in heaven's name did it all mean? Suddenly an idea struck me.

"Is our late fellow passenger, Mr. Ahmadeen, connected with the matter?" I asked.

"In no way," replied Deeping earnestly. "Mr. Ahmadeen is, I believe, a person of some consequence in the Moslem world; but I have nothing to fear from him."

"What steps have you taken to protect yourself?"

Again the short laugh reached my ears.

"I'm afraid long residence in the East has rendered me something of a fatalist, Cavanagh! Beyond keeping my door locked, I have taken no steps whatever. I fear I am quite accessible!"

A while longer we talked; and with every word the conviction was more strongly borne in upon me that some uncanny menace threatened the peace, perhaps the life, of Professor Deeping.

I had hung up the receiver scarce a moment when, acting upon a sudden determination, I called up New Scotland Yard, and asked for Detective-Inspector Bristol, whom I knew well. A few words were sufficient keenly to arouse his curiosity, and he announced his intention of calling upon me immediately. He was in charge of the case of the severed hand.

I made no attempt to resume work in the interval preceding his arrival. I had not long to wait, however, ere Bristol was ringing my bell; and I hurried to the door, only too glad to confide in one so well equipped to analyze my doubts and fears. For Bristol is no ordinary policeman, but a trained observer, who, when I first made his acquaintance, completely up-set my ideas upon the mental limitations of the official detective force.

In appearance Bristol suggests an Anglo-Indian officer, and at the time of which I write he had recently returned from Jamaica and his face was as bronzed as a sailor's. One would never take Bristol for a detective. As he seated himself in the armchair, without preamble I plunged into my story.

He listened gravely.

"What sort of house is Professor Deeping's?" he asked suddenly.

"I have no idea," I replied, "beyond the fact that it is somewhere in Dulwich."

"May I use your telephone?"

"Certainly."

Very quickly Bristol got into communication with the superintendent of P Division. A brief delay, and the man came to the telephone whose beat included the road wherein Professor Deeping's house was situated.

"Why!" said Bristol, hanging up the receiver after making a number of inquiries, "it's a sort of rambling cottage in extensive grounds. There's only one servant, a manservant, and he sleeps in a detached lodge. If the Professor is really in danger of attack he could not well have chosen a more likely residence for the purpose!"

"What shall you do? What do you make of it all?"

"As I see the case," he said slowly, "it stands something like this: Professor Deeping has..."

The telephone bell began to ring.

I took up the receiver.

"Hullo! Hullo."

"Cavanagh!—is that Cavanagh?"

"Yes! yes! who is that?"

"Deeping! I have rung up the police, and they are sending some one. But I wish..."

His voice trailed off. The sound of a confused and singular uproar came to me. "Hullo!" I cried, "Hullo!"

A shriek—a deathful, horrifying cry—and a distant babbling alone answered me. There was a crash. Clearly, Deeping had dropped the receiver. I suppose my face blanched.

"What is it?" asked Bristol anxiously.

"God knows what it is!" I said. "Deeping has met with some mishap—"

When, over the wires—

"Hassan of Aleppo!" came a dying whisper, "Hassan... of Aleppo...!"

## CHAPTER IV
## THE OBLONG BOX

"You had better wait for us," said Bristol to the taxi-man.

"Very good, sir. But I shan't be able to take you further back than the Brixton Garage. You can get another cab there, though."

A clock chimed out—an old-world chime in keeping with the loneliness, the curiously remote loneliness, of the locality. Less than five miles from St. Paul's are spots whereto, with the persistence of Damascus attar, clings the aroma of former days. This iron gateway fronting the old chapel was such a spot.

Just within stood a plain-clothes man, who saluted my companion respectfully.

"Professor Deeping," I began.

The man, with a simple gesture, conveyed the dreadful news.

"Dead! dead!" I cried incredulously.

He glanced at Bristol.

"The most mysterious case I have ever had anything to do with, sir," he said.

The power of speech seemed to desert me. It was unthinkable that Deeping, with whom I had been speaking less than an hour ago, should now be no more; that some malign agency should thus murderously have thrust him into the great borderland.

In that kind of silence which seems to be peopled with whispering spirits we strode forward along the elm avenue. It was very dark where the moon failed to penetrate. The house, low and rambling, came into view, its facade bathed in silver light. Two of the visible windows were illuminated. A sort of loggia ran along one side.

On our left, as we made for this, lay a black ocean of shrubbery. It intruded, raggedly, upon the weed-grown path, for neglect was the keynote of the place.

We entered the cottage, crossed the tiny lobby, and came to the study. A man, evidently Deeping's servant, was sitting in a chair by the door, his head sunken in his hands. He looked up, haggard-faced.

"My God! my God!" he groaned. "He was locked in, gentlemen! He was locked in; and yet something murdered him!"

"What do you mean?" said Bristol. "Where were you?"

"I was away on an errand, sir. When I returned, the police were knocking the door down. He was locked in!"

We passed him, entering the study.

It was a museum-like room, lighted by a lamp on the littered table. At first glance it looked as though some wild thing had run amok there. The disorder was indescribable.

"Touched nothing, of course?" asked Bristol sharply of the officer on duty.

"Nothing, sir. It's just as we found it when we forced the door."

"Why did you force the door?"

"He rung us up at the station and said that something or somebody had got into the house. It was evident the poor gentleman's nerve had broken down, sir. He said he was locked in his study. When we arrived it was all in darkness—but we thought we heard sounds in here."

"What sort of sounds?"

"Something crawling about!"

Bristol turned.

"Key is in the lock on the inside of the door," he said. "Is that where you found it?"

"Yes, sir!'

He looked across to where the brass knob of a safe gleamed dully.

"Safe locked?"

"Yes, sir."

Professor Deeping lay half under the table, a spectacle so ghastly that I shall not attempt to describe it.

"Merciful heavens!" whispered Bristol. "He's nearly *decapitated!*"

I clutched dizzily at the mantelpiece. It was all so utterly, incredibly horrible. How had Deeping met his death? The windows both were latched and the door had been locked from within!

"You searched for the murderer, of course?" asked Bristol.

"You can see, sir," replied the officer, "that there isn't a spot in the room where a man could hide! And there was nobody in here when we forced the door!"

"Why!" cried my companion suddenly. "The Professor has a chisel in his hand!"

"Yes. I think he must have been trying to prise open that box yonder when he was attacked."

Bristol and I looked, together, at an oblong box which lay upon the floor near the murdered man. It was a kind of small packing-case, addressed to Professor Deeping, and evidently had not been opened.

"When did this arrive?" asked Bristol.

Lester, the Professor's man, who had entered the room, replied shakily

"It came by carrier, sir, just before I went out."

"Was he expecting it?"

"I don't think so."

Inspector Bristol and the officer dragged the box fully into the light. It was some three feet long by one foot square, and solidly constructed.

"It is perfectly evident," remarked Bristol, "that the murderer stayed to search for—"

"The key of the safe!"

"Exactly. If the men really heard sounds here, it would appear that the assassin was still searching at that time."

"I assure you," the officer interrupted, "that there was no living thing in the room when we entered."

Bristol and I looked at one another in horrified wonder.

"It's incomprehensible!" he said.

"See if the key is in the place mentioned by the Professor, Mr. Cavanagh, whilst I break the box."

I went to a great, open bookcase, which the frantic searcher seemed to have overlooked. Removing the bulky "Assyrian Mythology," there, behind the volume, lay an envelope, containing a key, and a short letter.

Not caring to approach more closely to the table and to that which lay beneath it, I was peering at the small writing, in the semi-gloom by the bookcase, when Bristol cried

"This box is unopenable by ordinary means! I shall have to smash it!"

At his words, I joined him where he knelt on the floor. Mysteriously, the chest had defied all his efforts.

"There's a pick-axe in the garden," volunteered Lester. "Shall I bring it?"

"Yes."

The man ran off.

"I see the key is safe," said Bristol. "Possibly the letter may throw some light upon all this."

"Let us hope so," I replied. "You might read it."

He took the letter from my hand, stepped up to the table, and by the light of the lamp read as follows

MY DEAR CAVANAGH,—

It has now become apparent to me that my life is in imminent danger. You know of the inexplicable outrages which marked my homeward journey, and if this letter come to your hand it will be because these have culminated in my death.

The idea of a pursuing scimitar is not new to me. This phenomenon, which I have now witnessed three times, is fairly easy of explanation, but its significance is singular. It is said to be one of the devices whereby the *Hashishîn* warn those whom they have marked down for destruction, and is called, in the East, "The Scimitar of Hassan."

The *Hashishîn* were the members of a Moslem secret society, founded in 1090 by one Hassan of Khorassan. There is a persistent tradition in parts of the Orient that this sect still flourishes in Assyria, under the rule of a certain Hassan of Aleppo, the *Sheikh-al-jebal*, or supreme lord of the *Hashishîn*. My careful inquiries, however, at the time that I was preparing matter for my "Assyrian Mythology," failed to discover any trace of such a person or such a group.

I accordingly assumed Hassan to be a myth—a first cousin to the *ginn*. I was wrong. He exists. And by my supremely rash act I have incurred his vengeance, for Hassan of Aleppo is the self-appointed guardian of the traditions and relics of Mohammed. And I have stolen one of the holy slippers of the Prophet!

He, with some of his servants, has followed me from Mecca to England. My precautions have enabled me to retain the relic, but you have seen what fate befell all those others who even touched the receptacle containing it.

If I fall a victim to the *Hashishîn*, I am uncertain how you, as my confidant, will fare. Therefore I have locked the slipper in my safe and to you entrust the key. I append particulars of the lock combination; but I warn you—*do not open the safe*. If their wrath be visited upon you, your possession of the key may prove a safeguard.

Take the copy of "Assyrian Mythology." You will find in it all that I learned respecting the *Hashishîn*. If I am doomed to be assassinated, it may aid you; if not, in avenging me in saving others from my fate. I fear I shall never see you again. A cloud of horror settles upon me like a pall. Do not touch the slipper, nor the case containing it.

EDWARD DEEPING.

"It is almost incredible!" I said hoarsely.

Bristol returned the letter to me without a word, and turning to Lester, who had reentered carrying a heavy pick-axe, he attacked the oblong box with savage energy.

Through the house of death the sound of the blows echoed and rang with a sort of sacrilegious mockery. The box fell to pieces.

"My God! look, sir!"

Lester was the trembling speaker.

The box, I have said, was but three feet long by one foot square, and had clearly defied poor Deeping's efforts to open it. But a crescent-shaped knife, wet with blood, lay within!


## CHAPTER V
## THE OCCUPANT OF THE BOX

Dimly to my ears came the ceaseless murmur of London. The night now was far advanced, and not a sound disturbed the silence of the court below my windows.

Professor Deeping's "Assyrian Mythology" lay open before me, beside it my notebook. A coal dropped from the fire, and I half started up out of my chair. My nerves were all awry, and I had more than my horrible memories of the murdered man to thank for it. Let me explain what I mean.

When, after assisting, or endeavouring to assist, Bristol at his elaborate inquiries, I had at last returned to my chambers, I had become the victim of a singular delusion—though one common enough in the case of persons whose nerves are overwrought. I had thought myself followed.

During the latter part of my journey I found myself constantly looking from the little window at the rear of the cab. I had an impression that some vehicle was tracking us. Then, when I discharged the man and walked up the narrow passage to the court, it was fear of a skulking form that dodged from shadow to shadow which obsessed me.

Finally, as I entered the hall and mounted the darkened stair, from the first landing I glanced down into the black well beneath.

Blazing yellow eyes, I thought, looked up at me!

I will confess that I leapt up the remaining flight of stairs to my door, and, safely within, found myself trembling as if with a palsy.

When I sat down to write (for sleep was an impossible proposition) I placed my revolver upon the table beside me. I cannot say why. It afforded me some sense of protection, I suppose. My conclusions, thus far, amounted to the following—

The apparition of the phantom scimitar was due to the presence of someone who, by means of the moonlight, or of artificial light, cast a *reflection* of such a weapon as that found in the oblong chest upon the wall of a darkened apartment—as, Deeping's stateroom on the *Mandalay*, his study, etc.

A group of highly efficient assassins, evidently Moslem fanatics, who might or might not be of the ancient order of the *Hashishîn*, had pursued the stolen slipper to England. They had severed any hand, other than that of a Believer, which had touched the case containing it. (The Coptic porter was a Christian.)

Uncertain, possibly, of Deeping's faith, or fearful of endangering the success of their efforts by an outrage upon him en route, they had refrained from this until his arrival at his house. He had been warned of his impending end by Ahmad Ahmadeen.

Who was Ahmadeen? And who was his beautiful associate? I found myself unable, at present, to answer either of those questions.

In order to gain access to Professor Deeping, who so carefully secluded himself, a box had been sent to him by ordinary carrier. (As I sat at my table, Scotland Yard was busy endeavouring to trace the sender.) Respecting this box we had made an extraordinary discovery.

It was of the kind used by Eastern conjurors for what is generally known as "the Box Trick." That is to say, it could only be opened (short of smashing it) *from the inside!* You will remember what we found within it? Consider this with the new fact, above, and to what conclusion do you come?

Something (it is not possible to speak of *someone* in connection with so small a box) had been concealed inside, and had killed Professor Deeping whilst he was actually engaged in endeavouring to force it open. This inconceivable creature had then searched the study for the slipper—or for the key of the safe. Interrupted and trapped by the arrival of the police, the creature had returned to the box, re-closed it, and had actually been there when the study was searched!

For a creature so small as the murderous thing in the box to slip out during the confusion, and at some time prior to Bristol's arrival, was no difficult matter. The inspector and I were certain that these were the facts.

But what *was* this creature?

I turned to the chapter in "Assyrian Mythology"—"The Tradition of the *Hashishîn*." The legends which the late Professor Deeping had collected relative to this sect of religious murderers were truly extraordinary. Of the cult's extinction at the time of writing he was clearly certain, but he referred to the popular belief, or Moslem legend, that, since Hassan of Khorassan, there had always been a *Sheikh-al-jebal*, and that a dreadful being known as Hassan of Aleppo was the present holder of, the title.

He referred to the fact that De Sacy has shown the word Assassin to be derived from *Hashishîn*, and quoted El-Idrîsi to the same end. The *Hashishîn* performed their murderous feats under the influence of *hashish*, or Indian hemp; and during the state of ecstasy so induced, according to Deeping, they acquired powers almost superhuman.

I read how they could scale sheer precipices, pass fearlessly along narrow ledges which would scarce afford foothold for a rat, cast themselves from great heights unscathed, and track one marked for death in such a manner as to remain unseen not only by the victim, but by others about him.

At this point of my studies I started, in a sudden nervous panic, and laid my hand upon my revolver.

I thought of the eyes which had seemed to look up from the black well of the staircase—I thought of the horrible end of this man whose book lay upon the table... and I thought I heard a faint sound outside my study door!

The key of Deeping's safe, and his letter to me, lay close by my hand. I slipped them into a drawer and locked it. With every nerve, it seemed, strung up almost to snapping point, I mechanically pursued my reading.

"At the time of the Crusades," wrote Deeping, "there was a story current of this awful Order which I propose to recount. It is one of the most persistent dealing with the *Hashishîn*, and is related to-day of the apparently mythical Hassan of Aleppo. I am disposed to believe that at one time it had a solid foundation, for a similar practice was common in Ancient Egypt and is mentioned by Georg Ebers."

My door began very slowly to open!

Merciful God! *What* was coming into the room!

So very slowly, so gently, nay, all but imperceptibly, did it move, that had my nerves been less keenly attuned I doubt not I should have remained unaware of the happening. Frozen with horror, I sat and watched. Yet my mental condition was a singular one.

My direct gaze never quitted the door, but in some strange fashion I saw the words of the next paragraph upon the page before me!

"As making peculiarly efficient assassins, when under the influence of the drug, and as being capable of concealing themselves where a normal man could not fail to be detected—"

(At this moment I remembered that my bathroom window was open, and that the waste-pipe passed down the exterior wall.)

"—the Sheikh-al-jebal took young boys of a certain desert tribe, and for eight hours of every day, until their puberty, confined them in a wooden frame."

What looked like a reed was slowly inserted through the opening between door and doorpost! It was brought gradually around… until it pointed directly toward me!

I seemed to put forth a mighty mental effort, shaking off the icy hand of fear which held me inactive in my chair. A saving instinct warned me— and I ducked my head.

Something whirred past me and struck the wall behind.

Revolver in hand, I leapt across the room, dashed the door open, and fired blindly again—and again—and again—down the passage.

And in the brief gleams *I saw it!*

I cannot call it man, but I saw the thing which, I doubt not, had killed poor Deeping with the crescent-knife and had propelled a poison-dart at me.

It was a tiny dwarf! Neither within nor without a freak exhibition had I seen so small a human being! A kind of supernatural dread gripped me by the throat at sight of it. As it turned with animal activity and bounded into my bathroom, I caught a three-quarter view of the creature's swollen, incredible head—which was nearly as large as that of a normal man!

Never while my mind serves me can I forget that yellow, grinning face and those canine fangs—the tigerish, blazing eyes—set in the great, misshapen head upon the tiny, agile body.

Wildly, I fired again. I hurled myself forward and dashed into the room.

Like nothing so much as a cat, the gleaming body (the dwarf was but scantily clothed) streaked through the open window!

Certain death, I thought, must be his lot upon the stones of the court far below. I ran and looked down, shaking in every limb, my mind filled with a loathing terror unlike anything I had ever known.

Brilliant moonlight flooded the pavement beneath; for twenty yards to left and right every stone was visible.

The court was empty!

Human, homely London moved and wrought intimately about me; but there, at sight of the empty court below, a great loneliness swept down like a mantle—a clammy mantle of the fabric of dread. I stood remote from my fellows, in an evil world peopled with the creatures of Hassan of Aleppo.

Moved by some instinct, as that of a frightened child, I dropped to my knees and buried my face in trembling hands.

## CHAPTER VI
## THE RING OF THE PROPHET

"There is no doubt," said Mr. Rawson, "that great personal danger attaches to any contact with this relic. It is the first time I have been concerned with—anything of the kind."

Mr. Bristol, of Scotland Yard, standing stiffly military by the window, looked across at the gray-haired solicitor. We were all silent for a few moments.

"My late client's wishes," continued Mr. Rawson, "are explicit. His last instructions, evidently written but a short time prior to his death, advise me that the holy slipper of the Prophet is contained in the locked safe at his house in Dulwich. He was clearly of opinion that you, Mr. Cavanagh, would incur risk—great risk—from your possession of the key. Since attempts have been made upon you, murderous attempts, the late Professor Deeping, my unfortunate client, evidently was not in error."

"Mysterious outrages," said Bristol, "have marked the progress of the stolen slipper from Mecca almost to London."

"I understand," interrupted the solicitor, "that a fanatic known as Hassan of Aleppo seeks to restore the relic to its former resting-place?"

"That is so."

"Exactly; and it accounts for the Professor's wish that the safe should not be touched by any one but a Believer—and for his instructions that its removal to the Antiquarian Museum and the placing of the slipper within that institution be undertaken by a Moslem or Moslems."

Bristol frowned.

"Any one who has touched the receptacle containing the thing," he said, "has either been mutilated or murdered. I want to apprehend the authors of those outrages, but I fail to see why the slipper should be put on exhibition. Other crimes are sure to follow."

"I can only pursue my instructions," said Mr. Rawson dryly. "They are, that the work be done in such a manner as to expose all concerned to a minimum of risk from these mysterious people; that if possible a Moslem be employed for the purpose; and that Mr. Cavanagh, here, shall always hold the key or keys to the case in the museum containing the slipper. Will you undertake to look for some—Eastern workmen, Mr. Bristol? In the course of your inquiries you may possibly come across such a person."

"I can try," replied Bristol. "Meanwhile, I take it, the safe must remain at Dulwich?"

"Certainly. It should be guarded."

"We are guarding it and shall guard it," Bristol assured him. "I only hope we catch someone trying to get at it!"

Shortly afterward Bristol and I left the office, and, his duties taking him to Scotland Yard, I returned to my chambers to survey the position in which I now found myself. Indeed, it was a strange one enough, showing how great things have small beginnings; for, as a result of a steamer acquaintance I found myself involved in a dark business worthy of the Middle Ages. That Professor Deeping should have stolen one of the holy slippers of Mohammed was no affair of mine, and that an awful being known as Hassan of Aleppo should have pursued it did not properly enter into my concerns; yet now, with a group of Eastern fanatics at large in England, I was become, in a sense, the custodian of the relic. Moreover, I perceived that I had been chosen that I might safeguard myself. What I knew of the matter might imperil me, but whilst I held the key to the reliquary, and held it fast, I might hope to remain immune though I must expect to be subjected to attempts. It would be my affair to come to terms.

Contemplating these things I sat, in a world of dark dreams, unconscious of the comings and goings in the court below, unconscious of the hum which told of busy Fleet Street so near to me. The weather, as is its uncomfortable habit in England, had suddenly grown tropically hot, plunging London into the vapours of an African spring, and the sun was streaming through my open window fully upon the table.

I mopped my clammy forehead, glancing with distaste at the pile of work which lay before me. Then my eyes turned to an open quarto book. It was the late Professor Deeping's "Assyrian Mythology," and embodied the result of his researches into the history of the *Hashishîn*, the religious murderers of whose existence he had been so skeptical. To the Chief of the Order, the terrible Sheikh Hassan of Aleppo, he referred as a "fabled being"; yet it was at the hands of this "fabled being" that he had met his end! How incredible it all seemed. But I knew full well how worthy of credence it was.

Then upon my gloomy musings a sound intruded—the ringing of my door bell. I rose from my chair with a weary sigh, went to the door, and opened it. An aged Oriental stood without. He was tall and straight, had a snow-white beard and clear-cut, handsome features. He wore well-cut European garments and a green turban. As I stood staring he saluted me gravely.

"Mr. Cavanagh?" he asked, speaking in faultless English.

"I am he."

"I learn that the services of a Moslem workman are required."

"Quite correct, sir; but you should apply at the offices of Messrs. Rawson & Rawson, Chancery Lane."

The old man bowed, smiling.

"Many thanks; I understood so much. But, my position being a peculiar one, I wished to speak with you—as a friend of the late Professor."

I hesitated. The old man looked harmless enough, but there was an air of mystery about the matter which put me on my guard.

"You will pardon me," I said, "but the work is scarcely of a kind—"

He raised his thin hand.

"I am not undertaking it myself. I wished to explain to you the conditions under which I could arrange to furnish suitable porters."

His patient explanation disposed me to believe that he was merely some kind of small contractor, and in any event I had nothing to fear from this frail old man.

"Step in, sir," I said, repenting of my *brusquerie*—and stood aside for him.

He entered, with that Oriental meekness in which there is something majestic. I placed a chair for him in the study, and reseated myself at the table. The old man, who from the first had kept his eyes lowered deferentially, turned to me with a gentle gesture, as if to apologize for opening the conversation.

"From the papers, Mr. Cavanagh," he began, "I have learned of the circumstances attending the death of Professor Deeping. Your papers"—he smiled, and I thought I had never seen a smile of such sweetness—"your papers know all! Now I understand why a Moslem is required, and I understand what is required of him. But remembering that the object of his labours would be to place a holy relic on exhibition for the amusement of unbelievers, can you reasonably expect to obtain the services of one?"

His point of view was fair enough.

"Perhaps not," I replied. "For my own part I should wish to see the slipper back in Mecca, or wherever it came from. But Professor Deeping—"

"Professor Deeping was a thorn in the flesh of the Faithful!"

My visitor's voice was gravely reproachful.

"Nevertheless his wishes must be considered," I said, "and the methods adopted by those who seek to recover the relic are such as to alienate all sympathy."

"You speak of the *Hashishîn?*" asked the old man. "Mr. Cavanagh, in your own faith you have had those who spilled the blood of infidels as freely!"

"My good sir, the existence of such an organization cannot be tolerated to-day! This survival of the dark ages must be stamped out. However just a cause may be, secret murder is not permissible, as you, a man of culture, a Believer, and"—I glanced at his unusual turban—"a descendant of the Prophet, must admit."

"I can admit nothing against the Guardian of the Tradition, Mr. Cavanagh! The Prophet taught that we should smite the Infidel. I ask you— have you the courage of your convictions?"

"Perhaps; I trust so."

"Then assist me to rid England of what you have called a survival of the dark ages. I will furnish porters to remove and carry the safe, if you will deliver to me the key!"

I sprang to my feet.

"That is madness!" I cried. "In the first place I should be compromising with my conscience, and in the second place I should be defenceless against those who might—"

"I have with me a written promise from one highly placed—one to whose will Hassan of Aleppo bows!"

My mind greatly disturbed, I watched the venerable speaker. I had determined now that he was some religious leader of Islam in England, who had been deputed to approach me; and, let me add, I was sorely tempted to accede to his proposal, for nothing would be gained by any one if the slipper remained for ever at the museum, whereas by conniving at its recovery by those who, after all, were its rightful owners I should be ridding England of a weird and undesirable visitant.

I think I should have agreed, when I remembered that the *Hashishîn* had murdered Professor Deeping and had mutilated others wholly innocent of offence. I looked across at the old man. He had drawn himself up to his great height, and for the first time fully raising the lids, had fixed upon me the piercing gaze of a pair of eagle eyes. I started, for the aspect of this majestic figure was entirely different from that of the old stranger who had stood suppliant before me a moment ago.

"It is impossible," I said. "I can come to no terms with those who shield murderers."

He regarded me fixedly, but did not move.

"*Es-selâm 'aleykûm!*" I added ("Peace be on you!") closing the interview in the Eastern manner.

The old man lowered his eyes, and saluted me with graceful gravity.

"*Wa-'aleykûm!*" he said ("And on you!").

I conducted him to the door and closed it upon his exit. In his last salute

I had noticed the flashing of a ring which he wore upon his left hand, and he was gone scarce ten seconds ere my heart began to beat furiously. I snatched up "Assyrian Mythology" and with trembling fingers turned to a certain page. There I read—

> ... Each Sheikh of the Assassins is said to be invested with the "Ring of the Prophet." It bears a green stone, shaped in the form of a scimitar or crescent....

My dreadful suspicion was confirmed. I knew who my visitor had been. "God in heaven!" I whispered. "It was *Hassan of Aleppo!*"


## CHAPTER VII
### FIRST ATTEMPT ON THE SAFE

In the following morning I was awakened by the arrival of Bristol. I hastened to admit him.

"Your visitor of yesterday," he began, "has wasted no time!"

"What has happened?"

He tugged irritably at his moustache.

"I don't know!" he replied. "Of course it was no surprise to find that there isn't a Mohammedan who'll lay his little finger on Professor Deeping's safe! There's no doubt in my mind that every lascar at the docks knows Hassan of Aleppo to be in England. Some other arrangement will have to be arrived at, if the thing is ever to be taken to the Antiquarian Museum. Meanwhile we stand to lose it. Last night—"

He accepted a cigarette, and lighted it carefully.

"Last night," he resumed, "a member of P Division was on point duty outside the late Professor's house, and two C.I.D. men were actually in the room where the safe is. Result—someone has put in at least an hour's work on the lock, but it proved too tough a job!"

I stared at him amazedly.

"Someone has been at the lock!" I cried. "But that is impossible, with two men in the room—unless—"

"They were both knocked on the head!"

"Both! But by whom! My God! They are not—"

"Oh, no! It was done artistically. They both came round about four o'clock this morning."

"And who attacked them?"

"They had no idea. Neither of them saw a thing!"

My amazement grew by leaps and bounds.

"But, Bristol, *one* of them must have seen the other succumb!"

"Both did! Their statements tally exactly!"

"I quite fail to follow you."

"That's not surprising. Listen: When I got on the scene about five o'-clock, Marden and West, the two C.I.D. men, had quite recovered their senses, though they were badly shaken, and one had a cracked skull. The constable was conscious again, too."

"What! Was he attacked?"

"In exactly the same way! I'll give you Marden's story, as he gave it to me a few minutes after the surgeon had done with him. He said that they were sitting in the study, smoking, and with both windows wide open. It was a fearfully hot night."

"Did they have lights?"

"No. West sat in an armchair near the writing-table; Marden sat by the window next to the door. I had arranged that every hour one of them should go out to the gate and take the constable's report. It was just after Marden had been out at one o'clock that it happened.

"They were sitting as I tell you when Marden thought he heard a curious sort of noise from the gate. West appeared to have heard nothing; but I have no doubt that it was the sound of the constable's fall. West's pipe had gone out, and he struck a match to relight it. As he did so, Marden saw him drop the match, clench both fists, and with eyes glaring in the moonlight and his teeth coming together with a snap, drop from his chair.

"Marden says that he was half up from his seat when something struck him on the back of the head with fearful force. He remembered nothing more until he awoke, with the dawn creeping into the room, and heard West groaning somewhere beside him. They both had badly damaged skulls with great bruises behind the ear. It is instructive to note that their wounds corresponded almost to a fraction of an inch. They had been stunned by someone who thoroughly understood his business, and with some heavy, blunt weapon. A few minutes later came the man to relieve the constable; and the constable was found to have been treated in exactly the same way!"

"But if Marden's account is true—"

"West, as he lost consciousness, saw Marden go in exactly the same way."

"Marden was seated by the open window, but I cannot conjecture how any one can have got at West, who sat by the table!"

"The case of Marden is little less remarkable; he was some distance from the window. No one could possibly have reached him from out-side."

"And the constable?"

"The constable can give us no clue. He was suddenly struck down, as the others were. I examined the safe, of course, but didn't touch it, according to instructions. Someone had been at work on the lock, but it had defied their efforts. I'm fully expecting though that they'll be back to-night, with different tools!"

"The place is watched during the day, of course?"

"Of course. But it's unlikely that anything will be attempted in daylight. Tonight I am going down myself."

"Could you arrange that I join you?"

"I could, but you can see the danger for yourself?"

"It is extraordinarily mysterious."

"Mr. Cavanagh, it's uncanny!" said Bristol. "I can understand that one of these *Hashishîn* could easily have got up behind the man on duty out in the open. I know, and so do you, that they're past masters of that kind of thing; but unless they possess the power to render themselves invisible, it's not evident how they can have got behind West whilst he sat at the table, with Marden actually watching him!"

"We must lay a trap for them to-night."

"Rely upon me to do so. My only fear is that they may anticipate it, and change their tactics. Hassan of Aleppo apparently knows as much of our plans as we do ourselves."

Inspector Bristol, though a man of considerable culture, clearly was infected with a species of supernatural dread.


## CHAPTER VIII
## THE VIOLET EYES AGAIN


At four o'clock in the afternoon I had heard nothing further from Bristol, but I did not doubt that he would advise me of his arrangements in good time. I sought by hard work to forget for a time the extraordinary business of the stolen slipper; but it persistently intruded upon my mind. Particularly, my thoughts turned to the night of Professor Deeping's murder, and to the bewitchingly pretty woman who had warned me of the impending tragedy. She had bound me to secrecy—a secrecy which had proved irksome, for it had since appeared to me that she must have been an accomplice of Hassan of Aleppo. At the time I had been at a loss to define her peculiar accent, now it seemed evidently enough to have been Oriental.

I threw down my pen in despair, for work was impossible, went downstairs, and walked out under the arch into Fleet Street. Quite mechanically I turned to the left, and, still engaged with idle conjectures, strolled along westward.

Passing the entrance to one of the big hotels, I was abruptly recalled to the realities—by a woman's voice.

"Wait for me here," came musically to my ears.

I stopped, and turned. A woman who had just quitted a taxi-cab was entering the hotel. The day was hot and thunderously oppressive, and this woman with the musical voice wore a delicate costume of flimsiest white. A few steps upward she paused and glanced back. I had a view of a Greek profile, and for one magnetic instant looked into eyes of the deepest and most wonderful violet.

Then, shaking off inaction, I ran up the steps and overtook the lady in white as a porter swung open the door to admit her. We entered together.

"Madame," I said in a low tone, "I must detain you for a moment. There is something I have to ask."

She turned, exhibiting the most perfect composure, lowered her lashes and raised them again, the gaze of the violet eyes sweeping me from head to foot with a sort of frigid scorn.

"I fear you have made a mistake, sir. We have never met before!"

Her voice betrayed no trace of any foreign accent!

"But," I began—and paused.

I felt myself flush; for this encounter in the foyer of an hotel, with many curious onlookers, was like to prove embarrassing if my beautiful acquaintance persisted in her attitude. I fully realized what construction would be put upon my presence there, and foresaw that forcible and ignominious ejection must be my lot if I failed to establish my right to address her.

She turned away, and crossed in the direction of the staircase. A sunbeam sought out a lock of hair that strayed across her brow, and kissed it to a sudden glow like that which lurks in the heart of a blush rose.

That wonderful sheen, which I had never met with elsewhere in nature, but which no artifice could lend, served to remove my last frail doubt which had survived the evidence of the violet eyes. I had been deceived by no strange resemblance; this was indeed the woman who had been the harbinger of Professor Deeping's death. In three strides I was beside her again. Curious glances were set upon me, and I saw a servant evidently contemplating approach; but I ignored all save my own fixed purpose.

"You *must* listen to what I have to say!" I whispered. "If you decline, I shall have no alternative but to call in the detective who holds a warrant for your arrest!"

She stood quite still, watching me coolly.

"I suppose you would wish to avoid a scene?" I added.

"You have already made me the object of much undesirable attention," she replied scornfully. "I do not need your assurance that you would disgrace me utterly! You are talking nonsense, as you must be aware—unless you are insane. But if your object be to force your acquaintance upon me, your methods are novel, and, under the circumstances, effective. Come, sir, you may talk to me for—three minutes!"

The musical voice had lost nothing of its imperiousness, but for one instant the lips parted, affording a fleeting glimpse of pearl beyond the coral.

Her sudden change of front was bewildering. Now, she entered the lift and I followed her. As we ascended side by side I found it impossible to believe that this dainty white figure was that of an associate of the *Hashishîn*, that of a creature of the terrible Hassan of Aleppo. Yet that she was the same girl who, a few days after my return from the East, had shown herself conversant with the plans of the murderous fanatics was beyond doubt. Her accent on that occasion clearly had been assumed, with what object I could not imagine. Then, as we quitted the lift and entered a cosy lounge, my companion seated herself upon a Chesterfield, signing to me to sit beside her.

As I did so she lay back smiling, and regarding me from beneath her black lashes. Thus, half veiled, her great violet eyes were most wonderful.

"Now, sir," she said softly, "explain yourself."

"Then you persist in pretending that we have not met before?"

"There is no occasion for pretence," she replied lightly; and I found myself comparing her voice with her figure, her figure with her face, and vainly endeavouring to compute her age. Frankly, she was bewildering—this lovely girl who seemed so wholly a woman of the world.

"This fencing is useless."

"It is quite useless! Come, I know New York, London, and I know Paris, Vienna, Budapest. Therefore I know mankind! You thought I was pretty, I suppose? I may be; others have thought so. And you thought you would like to make my acquaintance without troubling about the usual formalities? You adopted a singularly brutal method of achieving your object, but I love such insolence in a man. Therefore I forgave you.

What have you to say to me?"

I perceive that I had to deal with a bold adventuress, with a consummate actress, who, finding herself in a dangerous situation, had adopted this daring line of defence, and now by her personal charm sought to lure me from my purpose.

But with the scimitar of Hassan of Aleppo stretched over me, with the dangers of the night before me, I was in no mood for a veiled duel of words, for an interchange of glances in thrust and parry, however delightful such warfare might have been with so pretty an adversary.

For a long time I looked sternly into her eyes; but their violet mystery defied, whilst her red-lipped smile taunted me.

"Unfortunately," I said, with slow emphasis, "you are protected by my promise, made on the occasion of our previous meeting. But murder has been done, so that honour scarcely demands that I respect my promise further—"

She raised her eyebrows slightly.

"Surely that depends upon the quality of the honour!" she said.

"I believe you to be a member of a murderous organization, and unless you can convince me that I am wrong, I shall act accordingly."

At that she leaned toward me, laying her hand on my arm.

"Please do not be so cruel," she whispered, "as to drag me into a matter with which truly I have no concern. Believe me, you are utterly mistaken. Wait one moment, and I will prove it."

She rose, and before I could make move to detain her, quitted the room. But the door scarcely had closed ere I was afoot. The corridor beyond was empty. I ran on. The lift had just descended. A dark man whom I recognized stood near the closed gate.

"Quick!" I said, "I am Cavanagh of the *Report!* Did you see a lady enter the lift?"

"I did, Mr. Cavanagh," answered the hotel detective; for this was he.

In such a giant inn as this I knew full well that one could come and go almost with impunity, though one had no right to the hospitality of the establishment; and it was with a premonition respecting what his answer would be, that I asked the man—

"Is she staying here?"

"She is not. I have never seen her before!"

The girl with the violet eyes had escaped, taking all her secrets with her!

## CHAPTER IX
## SECOND ATTEMPT ON THE SAFE

"You see," said Bristol, "the *Hashishîn* must know that the safe won't remain here unopened much longer. They will therefore probably make another attempt to-night."

"It seems likely," I replied; and was silent.

Outside the open windows whispered the shrubbery, as a soft breeze stole through the bushes. Beyond, the moon made play in the dim avenue. From the old chapel hard by the sweet-toned bell proclaimed midnight. Our vigil was begun. In this room it was that Professor Deeping had met death at the hands of the murderous Easterns; here it was that Marden and West had mysteriously been struck down the night before.

To-night was every whit as hot, and Bristol and I had the windows widely opened. My companion was seated where the detective, Marden, had sat, in a chair near the westerly window, and I lay back in the armchair that had been occupied by West.

I may repeat here that the house of the late Professor Deeping was more properly a cottage, surrounded by a fairly large piece of ground, for the most part run wild. The room used as a study was on the ground floor, and had windows on the west and on the south. Those on the west (French windows) opened on a loggia; those on the south opened right into the dense tangle of a neglected shrubbery. The place possessed an oppressive atmosphere of loneliness, for which in some measure its history may have been responsible.

The silence, seemingly intensified by each whisper that sped through the elms and crept about the shrubbery, grew to such a stillness that I told myself I had experienced nothing like it since crossing with a caravan I had slept in the desert. Yet noisy, whirling London was within gunshot of us; and this, though hard enough to believe, was a reflection oddly comforting. Only one train of thought was possible, and this I pursued at random.

By what means were Marden and West struck down? In thus exposing ourselves, in order that we might trap the author or authors of the outrage, did we act wisely?

"Bristol," I said suddenly, "it was someone who came through the open window."

"No one," he replied, "came through the windows. West saw absolutely nothing. But if any one comes that way to-night, we have him!"

"West may have seen nothing; but how else could any one enter?"

Bristol offered no reply; and I plunged again into a maze of speculation.

Powerful mantraps were set in such a way that any one or anything, ignorant of their positions, coming up to the windows must unavoidably be snared. These had been placed in position with much secrecy after dusk, and the man on duty at the gate stood with his back to the wall. No one could approach him except from the front. My thoughts took a new turn.

Was the girl with the violet eyes an ally of the *Hashishîn?* Thus far, although she so palpably had tricked me, I had found myself unable to speak of her to Bristol; for the idea had entered my mind that she might have learned of the plan to murder Deeping without directly being implicated. Now came yet another explanation. The publicity given to that sensational case might have interested some third party in the fate of the stolen slipper! Could it be that others, in no way connected with the dreadful Hassan of Aleppo, were in quest of the slipper?

Scotland Yard had taken care to ensure that the general public be kept in ignorance of the existence of such an organization as the *Hashishîn,* but I must assume that this hypothetical third party were well aware that they had Hassan, as well as the authorities, to count with. Granting the existence of such a party, my beautiful acquaintance might be classified as one of its members. I spoke again.

"Bristol," I said, "has it occurred to you that there may be others, as well as Hassan of Aleppo, seeking to gain possession of the sacred slipper?"

"It has not," he replied. "In the strictest sense of the expression, they would be out for trouble! What gave you the idea?"

"I hardly know," I returned evasively, for even now I was loath to betray the mysterious girl with the wonderful eyes.

The chapel bell sounding the half-hour, Bristol rose with a sigh that might have been one of relief, and went out to take the report of the man on duty at the gate. As his footsteps died away along the elm avenue, it came to me how, in the darkness about, menace lurked; and I felt myself succumbing to the greatest dread experienced by man—the dread of the unknown.

All that I knew of the weird group of fanatics—survivals of a dim and evil past who must now be watching this cottage as blood-lustful devotees watch a shrine violated, burst upon my mind. I peopled the still blackness with lurking assassins, armed with the murderous knowledge of by-gone centuries, armed with invisible weapons which struck down from afar, supernaturally.

I glanced toward the corner of the room where the safe stood, reliquary of a worthless thing for which much blood had been spilled.

Then sounded footsteps along the avenue, and my fear whispered that they were not those of Bristol but of one who had murdered him, and who came guilefully, to murder *me!*

I snatched the revolver from my pocket and crossed the darkened room. Just to the right of one of the French windows I stood looking out across the loggia to the end of the avenue. The night was a bright one, and the room was flooded with a reflected mystic light, but outside the moon paved the avenue with pearl, and through the trees I saw a figure approaching.

Was it Bristol? It had his build, it had his gait; but my fears remained. Then the figure crossed the patch of shrubbery and stepped on to the loggia.

"Mr. Cavanagh!"

I laughed dryly at my own cowardice, but my heart was still beating abnormally.

"Here I am, Bristol, in a ghastly funk!"

"I don't wonder! They may be on us any time now. All's well at the gate, but Morris says he heard, or thought he heard, something at the side of the chapel opposite, a while ago."

"Wind in the bushes?"

"It may have been; but he says there was no breeze at the time."

We resumed our seats.

"Bristol," I said, "now that the danger grows imminent, doesn't it seem to you foolhardy for us thus to expose ourselves?"

"Perhaps it is," he agreed; "but how otherwise are we likely to learn what happened to Marden and West?"

"The enemy may adopt different measures to-night."

"I think not. Our dispositions are the same, and I credit them with cunning enough to know it. At the same time I credit ourselves with having kept the existence of the steel traps completely secret. They will assume (so I've reasoned) that we intend to rely entirely upon our superior vigilance, therefore they will try the same game as last night."

Silence fell.

The moon rays, creeping around from the right of the avenue, crossing the shrubbery and encroaching upon the low wall of the loggia, now flooded its floor. Against the silvern light, Bristol appeared to me in black silhouette. The breeze, too, seemed now to blow from a slightly different direction. It came through the windows on my right, beyond which lay the unkempt bushes which extended on that side to the wall of the grounds.

So we sat, until the moonlight poured fully in upon Bristol's back. So we sat when the clock chimed the hour of one.

Bristol arose and once more went out to the gate. He had arranged to visit Morris's post every half-hour. Again I experienced the nervous dread that he would be attacked in the avenue; but again he returned un-scathed.

"All's well," he said.

But from his tones I knew that he had not forgotten that it was at this hour Marden and West had suffered mysterious attack.

Neither of us, I think, was disposed to talk. We both were unwilling to break the silence, wherein, with all our ears, we listened for the slightest disturbance.

And now my attention turned anew to the course of the slowly creeping moon rays. In my mind an idea was struggling for definition. There was something significant in the lunar lighting of the room. Why, I asked myself, had the attack been made at one o'clock? Did the time signify anything? If so, what? I looked toward Bristol.

His figure, the chair upon which he sat, were sharply outlined by the cold light. The wall behind me, and to my left, was illuminated brilliantly; but no light fell directly upon me.

The idea was taking shape. From the loggia and the avenue Bristol, I reasoned, must be clearly visible. From the shrubbery on the south, through the other windows... could I be seen? Yes, silhouetted against the moonlight!

A faint sound, quite indescribable, came to my ears from somewhere outside—beyond.

"My God!" whispered Bristol. "Did you hear it?"

"Yes! What—"

"It must have been Morris!—"

Bristol was half standing, one hand upon the arm of the chair, the other concealed, but grasping his revolver as I well knew. I, too, had my revolver in my hand, and as I twisted in my seat, preparatory to rising, in sheer nervousness I dropped the weapon upon the carpet.

With an exclamation of dismay, I stooped quickly to recover it.

As I did so *something* whistled past my ear, so closely as almost to touch it—and struck with a dull thud upon the wall beyond!

"Bristol!" I whispered.

But as I raised my eyes to him he seemed to crumple up, and fell loosely forward into the patch of moonlight spread upon the floor!

"God in heaven!" I said aloud.

In a cold sweat of fear I crouched there, for it had become evident to me that, as I bent, I was entirely in shadow.

There was a rustling in the bushes on the left; but before I could turn in that direction, my attention was claimed elsewhere. Over into the loggia leapt an almost naked brown figure!

It was that of a small but strongly built man, who carried a short, exceedingly thick bamboo rod in his hand. My fear was too great to admit of my accurately observing anything at that time, but I noticed that some kind of leather thong or loop was attached to the end of the squat cane.

The panic fear of the supernatural was strongly upon me, and I was unable to realize that this Eastern apparition was a creature of flesh and blood. With my nerves strung up to snapping point, I crouched watching him. He entered the room, bending over the body of Bristol.

A hot breath fanned my cheek!

At that my overwrought nerves betrayed me. I uttered a stifled cry, looking upward... and into a pair of gleaming eyes which looked down into mine!

A second brown man (who must have entered by one of the windows overlooking the shrubbery) was bending over me!

Scarce knowing what I did, I raised my revolver and blazed straight into the dimly-seen face. Down upon me silently dropped a naked body, and something warm came flowing over my hand. But, knowing my foes to be of flesh and blood, feeling myself at handgrips now with a palpable enemy, I threw off the body, leapt up and fired, though blindly, at the flying shape that flashed across the loggia—and was lost in the shadow pools under the elms.

Upon the din of my shooting fell silence like a cloak. A moment I listened, tense, still; then I turned to the table and lighted the lamp.

In its light I saw Bristol lying like a dead man. Close beside him was a big and heavy lump of clay. It had been shaped as a ball, but now it was flattened out curiously. Bending over my unfortunate companion and learning that, though unconscious, he lived, I learnt, too, how the *Hashishîn* contrived to strike men insensible without approaching them; I learnt that the one whom I had shot, who lay in his blood almost on the spot where Professor Deeping once had lain, was an expert *slinger*.

The contrivance which he carried, as did the other who had escaped, was a sling, of the ancient Persian type. In place of stones, heavy lumps of clay were used, which operated much the same as a sand-bag, whilst enabling the operator to work from a considerable distance.

Hidden, over by the ancient chapel it might be, one of this evil twain had struck down Morris, the constable; from the shelter of the trees, from many yards away, they had shot their singular missiles through the open windows at Bristol and myself. Bristol had succumbed, and now, with a redness showing through his close-cut hair immediately behind the right ear, lay wholly unconscious at my feet.

It had been a divine accident which had caused me to drop my revolver, and, stooping to recover it, unknowingly to frustrate the design of the second slinger upon myself. The light of the lamp fell upon the face of the dead *Hashishîn.* He lay forward upon his hands, crouching almost, but with his face, his dreadful, featureless face, twisted up at me from under his left shoulder.

God knows he deserved his end; but that mutilated face is often grinning, bloodily, in my dreams.

And then as I stood, between that horrid exultation which is born of killing and the panic which threatened me out of the darkness, I saw something advancing... slowly... slowly... from the elmen shades toward the loggia.

It was a shape—it was a shadow. Silent it came—on—and on. Where the dusk lay deepest it paused, undefined; for I could give it no name of man or spirit. But a horror seemed to proceed from it as light from a lamp.

I groped about the table near to me, never taking my eyes from that sinister form outside. As my fingers closed upon the telephone, distant voices and the sound of running footsteps (of those who had heard the shots) came welcome to my ears.

The form stirred, seeming to raise phantom arms in execration, and a stray moonbeam pierced the darkness shrouding it. For a fleeting instant something flashed venomously.

The sounds grew nearer. I could tell that the newcomers had found Morris lying at the gate. Yet still I stood, frozen with uncanny fear, and watching—watching the spot to which that stray beam had pierced; the spot where I had seen the moon gleam upon *the ring of the Prophet!*

# CHAPTER X
## AT THE BRITISH ANTIQUARIAN MUSEUM

A little group of interested spectators stood at the head of the square glass case in the centre of the lofty apartment in the British Antiquarian Museum known as the Burton Room (by reason of the fact that a fine painting of Sir Richard Burton faces you as you enter). A few other people looked on curiously from the lower end of the case. It contained but one exhibit—a dirty and dilapidated *markoob*—or slipper of morocco leather that had once been red.

"Our latest acquisition, gentlemen," said Mr. Mostyn, the curator, speaking in a low tone to the distinguished Oriental scholars around him. "It has been left to the Institution by the late Professor Deeping. He describes it in a document furnished by his solicitor as one of the slippers worn by the Prophet Mohammed, but gives us no further particulars. I myself cannot quite place the relic."

"Nor I," interrupted one of the group. "It is not mentioned by any of the Arabian historians to my knowledge—that is, if it comes from Mecca, as I understand it does."

"I cannot possibly assert that it comes from Mecca, Dr. Nicholson," Mostyn replied. "The Professor may have taken it from Al-Madinah—perhaps from the mysterious inner passage of the *baldaquin* where the treasures of the place lie. But I can assure you that what little we do know of its history is sufficiently unsavoury."

I fancied that the curator's tired cultured voice faltered as he spoke; and now, without apparent reason, he moved a step to the right and glanced oddly along the room. I followed the direction of his glance, and saw a tall man in conventional morning dress, irreproachable in every detail, whose head was instantly bent upon his catalogue. But before his eyes fell I knew that their long almond shape, as well as the peculiar burnt pallor of his countenance, were undoubtedly those of an Oriental.

"There have been mysterious outrages committed, I believe, upon many of those, who have come in contact with the slipper?" asked one of the savants.

"Exactly. Professor Deeping was undoubtedly among the victims. His instructions were explicit that the relic should be brought here by a Moslem, but for a long time we failed to discover any Moslem who would undertake the task; and, as you are aware, while the slipper remained at the Professor's house attempts were made to steal it."

He ceased uneasily, and glanced at the tall Eastern figure. It had edged a little nearer; the head was still bowed and the fine yellow waxen fingers of the hand from which he had removed his glove fumbled with the catalogue's leaves. It may well have been that in those days I read menace in every eye, yet I felt assured that the yellow visitor was eavesdropping—was malignantly attentive to the conversation.

The curator spoke lower than ever now; no one beyond the circle could possibly hear him as he proceeded—

"We discovered an Alexandrian Greek who, for personal reasons, not unconnected with matrimony, had turned Moslem! He carried the slipper here, strongly escorted, and placed it where you now see it. *No other hand has touched it.*" (The speaker's voice was raised ever so slightly.) "You will note that there is a rail around the case, to prevent visitors from touching even the glass."

"Ah," said Dr. Nicholson quizzically. "And has anything untoward happened to our Græco-Moslem friend?"

"Perhaps Inspector Bristol can tell you," replied the curator.

The straight, military figure of the well-known Scotland Yard man was conspicuous among the group of distinguished—and mostly round-shouldered—scholars.

"Sorry, gentlemen," he said, smiling, "but Mr. Acepulos has vanished from his tobacco shop in Soho. I am not apprehensive that he had been kidnapped or anything of that kind. I think rather that the date of his disappearance tallies with that on which he cashed his cheque for service rendered! His present wife is getting most unbeautifully fat, too."

"What precautions," someone asked, "are being taken to guard the slipper?"

"Well," Mostyn answered, "though we have only the bare word of the late Professor Deeping that the slipper was actually worn by Mohammed, it has certainly an enormous value according to Moslem ideas. There can be no doubt that a group of fanatics known as *Hashishîn* are in London engaged in an extraordinary endeavour to recover it."

Mostyn's voice sank to an impressive whisper. My gaze sought again the tall Eastern visitor and was held fascinated by the baffled straining in those velvet eyes. But the lids fell as I looked; and the effect was that of a fire suddenly extinguished. I determined to draw Bristol's attention to the man.

"Accordingly," Mostyn continued, "we have placed it in this room, from which I fancy it would puzzle the most accomplished thief to remove it."

The party, myself included, stared about the place, as he went on to explain—

"We have four large windows here, as you see. The Burton Room occupies the end of a wing; there is only one door; it communicates with the next room, which in turn opens into the main building by another door on the landing. We are on the first floor; these two east windows afford a view of the lawn before the main entrance; those two west ones face Orpington Square; all are heavily barred as you see. During the day there is a man always on duty in these two rooms. At night that communicating door is locked. Short of erecting a ladder in full view either of the Square or of Great Orchard Street, filing through four iron bars and breaking the window and the case, I fail to see how anybody can get at the slipper here."

"If a duplicate key to the safe—" another voice struck in; I knew it afterward for that of Professor Rhys-Jenkyns.

"Impossible to procure one, Professor," cried Mostyn, his eyes sparkling with an almost boyish interest. "Mr. Cavanagh here holds the keys of the case, under the will of the late Professor Deeping. They are of foreign workmanship and more than a little complicated."

The eyes of the savants were turned now in my direction.

"I suppose you have them in a place of safety?" said Dr. Nicholson.

"They are at my bankers," I replied.

"Then I venture to predict," said the celebrated Orientalist, "that the slipper of the Prophet will rest here undisturbed."

He linked his arm into that of a brother scholar and the little group straggled away, Mostyn accompanying them to the main entrance.

But I saw Inspector Bristol scratching his chin; he looked very much as if he doubted the accuracy of the doctor's prediction. He had already had some experience of the implacable devotion of the Moslem group to this treasure of the Faithful.

"The real danger begins," I suggested to him, "when the general public is admitted—after to-day, is it not?"

"Yes. All to-day's people are specially invited, or are using special invitation cards," he replied. "The people who received them often give their tickets away to those who will be likely really to appreciate the opportunity."

I looked around for the tall Oriental. He seemed to have vanished, and for some reason I hesitated to speak of him to Bristol; for my gaze fell upon an excessively thin, keen-faced man whose curiously wide-open eyes met mine smilingly, whose gray suit spoke Stein-Bloch, whose felt was a Boss raw-edge unmistakably of a kind that only Philadelphia can produce. At the height of the season such visitors are not rare, but this one had an odd personality, and moreover his keen gaze was raking the place from ceiling to floor.

Where had I met him before? To the best of my recollection I had never set eyes upon the man prior to that moment; and since he was so palpably an American I had no reason for assuming him to be associated with the *Hashishîn*. But I remembered—indeed, I could never forget—how, in the recent past, I had met with an apparent associate of the Moslems as evidently European as this curiously alert visitor was American. Moreover... there was something tauntingly familiar, yet elusive, about that gaunt face.

Was it not upon the eve of the death of Professor Deeping that the girl with the violet eyes had first intruded her fascinating personality into my tangled affairs? Patently, she had then been seeking the holy slipper, and by craft had endeavoured to bend me to her will. Then had I not encountered her again, meeting the glance of her unforgettable violet eyes outside a Strand hotel? The encounter had presaged a further attempt upon the slipper! Certainly she acted on behalf of someone interested in it; and since neither Bristol nor I could conceive of any one seeking to possess the bloodstained thing except the mysterious leader of the *Hashishîn*—Hassan of Aleppo—as a creature of that awful fanatic being I had written her down.

Why, then, if the mysterious Eastern employed a European girl, should he not also employ an American man? It might well be that the relic, in entering the doors of the impregnable Antiquarian Museum, had passed where the diabolical arts of the *Hashishîn* had no power to reach it—where the beauty of Western women and the craft of Eastern man were equally useless weapons. Perhaps Hassan's campaign was entering upon a new phase.

Was it a shirking of plain duty on my part that wish—that ever-present hope—that the murderous company of fanatics who had pursued the stolen slipper from its ancient resting-place to London, should succeed in recovering it? I leave you to judge.

The crescent of Islâm fades to-day and grows pale, but there are yet fierce Believers, alust for the blood of the infidel. In such as these a faith dies the death of an adder, and is more venomous in its death-throes than in the full pulse of life. The ghastly indiscretion of Professor Deeping, in rifling a Moslem Sacristy, had led to the mutilation of many who, unwittingly, had touched the looted relic, had brought about his own end, had established a league of fantastic assassins in the heart of the metropolis.

Only once had I seen the venerable Hassan of Aleppo—a stately, gentle old man; but I knew that the velvet eyes could blaze into a passionate fury that seemed to scorch whom it fell upon. I knew that the saintly Hassan was Sheikh of the *Hashishîn*. And familiarity with that dreadful organization had by no means bred contempt. I was the holder of the key, and my fear of the fanatics grew like a magic mango, darkened the sunlight of each day, and filled the night with indefinable dread.

You, who have not read poor Deeping's "Assyrian Mythology," cannot picture a creature with a huge, distorted head, and a tiny, dwarfed body—a thing inhuman, yet human—a man stunted and malformed by the cruel arts of brother men—a thing obnoxious to life, with but one passion, the passion to kill. You cannot conceive of the years of agony spent by that creature strapped to a wooden frame—in order to prevent his growth! You cannot conceive of his fierce hatred of all humanity, inflamed to madness by the Eastern drug, *hashish*, and directed against the enemies of Islâm—the holders of the slipper—by the wonderful power of Hassan of Aleppo.

But I had not only read of such beings, I had encountered one!

And he was but one of the many instruments of the *Hashishîn*. Perhaps the girl with the violet eyes was another. What else to be dreaded Hassan might hold in store for us I could not conjecture.

Do you wonder that I feared? Do you wonder that I *hoped* (I confess it), hoped that the slipper might be recovered without further bloodshed?

CHAPTER XI

THE HOLE IN THE BLIND

I stepped over to the door, where a constable stood on duty.

"You observed a tall Eastern gentleman in the room a while ago, officer?"

"I did, sir."

"How long is he gone?"

The man started and began to peer about anxiously.

"That's a funny thing, sir," he said. "I was keeping my eyes specially upon him. I noticed him hovering around while Mr. Mostyn was speaking; but although I could have sworn he hadn't passed out, he's gone!"

"You didn't notice his departure, then?"

"I'm sorry to say I didn't, sir."

The man clearly was perplexed, but I found small matter for wonder in the episode. I had more than suspected the stranger to be a spy of Hassan's, and members of that strange company were elusive as will-o'-the-wisps.

Bristol, at the far end of the room, was signalling to me. I walked back and joined him.

"Come over here," he said, in a low voice, "and pretend to examine these things."

He glanced significantly to his left. Following the glance, my eyes fell upon the lean American; he was peering into the receptacle which held the holy slipper.

Bristol led me across the room, and we both faced the wall and bent over a glass case. Some yellow newspaper cuttings describing its contents hung above it, and these we pretended to read.

"Did you notice that man I glanced at?"

"Yes."

"Well, that's Earl Dexter, the first crook in America! Ssh! Only goes in on very big things. We had word at the Yard he was in town; but we can't touch him—we can only keep our eyes on him. He usually travels openly and in his own name, but this time he seems to have slipped over quietly. He always dresses the same and has just given me 'good day!' They call him The Stetson Man. We heard this morning that he had booked two first-class sailings in the *Oceanic*, leaving for New York three weeks hence. Now, Mr. Cavanagh, what is his game?"

"It has occurred to me before, Bristol," I replied, "and you may remember that I mentioned the idea to you, that there might be a third party interested in the slipper. Why shouldn't Earl Dexter be that third party?"

"Because he isn't a fool," rapped Bristol shortly. "Earl Dexter isn't a man to gather up trouble for himself. More likely if his visit has anything really to do with the slipper he's retained by Hassan and Company. Museum-breaking may be a bit out of the line of *Hashishîn!*"

This latter suggestion dovetailed with my own ideas, and oddly enough there was something positively wholesome in the notion of the straightforward crookedness of a mere swell cracksman.

Then happened a singular thing, and one that effectually concluded our whispered colloquy. From the top end of the room, beyond the case containing the slipper, one of the yellow blinds came down with a run.

Bristol turned in a flash. It was not a remarkable accident, and might portend no more than a loose cord; but when, having walked rapidly up the room, we stood before the lowered blind, it appeared that this was no accident at all.

Some four feet from the bottom of the blind (or five feet from the floor) a piece of linen a foot square had been neatly slashed out!

I glanced around the room. Several fashionably dressed visitors were looking idly in our direction, but I could fasten upon no one of them as a likely perpetrator.

Bristol stared at me in perplexity.

"Who on earth did it," he muttered, "and what the blazes for?"


## CHAPTER XII
## THE HASHISHÎN WATCH


The American gentleman has just gone out, sir," said the sergeant at the door.

I nodded grimly and raced down the steps. Despite my half-formed desire that the slipper should be recovered by those to whom properly it belonged, I experienced at times a curious interest in its welfare. I cannot explain this. Across the hall in front of me I saw Earl Dexter passing out of the Museum. I followed him—through into Kingsway and thence to Fleet Street. He sauntered easily along, a nonchalant gray figure. I had begun to think that he was bound for his hotel and that I was wasting my time when he turned sharply into quiet Salisbury Square; it was almost deserted.

My heart leapt into my mouth with a presentiment of what was coming as I saw an elegant and beautifully dressed woman sauntering along in front of us on the far side.

Was it that I detected something familiar in her carriage, in the poise of her head—something that reminded me of former unforgettable encounters; encounters which without exception had presaged attempts upon the slipper of the Prophet? Or was it that I recollected how Dexter had booked two passages to America? I cannot say, but I felt my heart leap; I knew beyond any possibility of doubt that this meeting in Salisbury Square marked the opening of a new chapter in the history of the slipper.

Dexter slipped his arm within that of the girl in front of him and they paced slowly forward in earnest conversation. I suppose my action was very amateurish and very poor detective work; but regardless of discovery I crossed the road and passed close by the pair.

I am certain that Dexter was speaking as I came up, but, well out of earshot, his voice was suddenly arrested. His companion turned and looked at me.

I was prepared for it, yet was thrilled electrically by the flashing glance of the violet eyes—for it was she—the beautiful harbinger of calamities!

My brain was in a whirl; complication piled itself upon complication; yet in the heart of all this bewilderment I thought I could detect the key of the labyrinth, but at the time my ideas were in disorder, for the violet eyes were not lowered but fixed upon me in cold scorn.

I knew myself helpless, and bending my head with conscious embarrassment I passed on hurriedly.

I had work to do in plenty, but I could not apply my mind to it; and now, although the obvious and sensible thing was to go about my business, I wandered on aimlessly, my brain employed with a hundred idle conjectures and the query, "Where have I seen The Stetson Man?" seeming to beat, like a tattoo, in my brain. There was something magnetic about the accursed slipper, for without knowing by what route I had arrived there, I found myself in Great Orchard Street and close under the walls of the British Antiquarian Museum. Then I was effectually aroused from my reverie.

Two men, both tall, stood in the shadow of a doorway on the opposite side of the street, staring intently up at the Museum windows. It was a tropically hot afternoon and they stood in deepest shadow. No one else was in Orchard Street—that odd little backwater—at the time, and they stood gazing upward intently and gave me not even a passing glance.

But I knew one for the Oriental visitor of the morning, and despite broad noonday and the hum of busy London about me, my blood seemed to turn to water. I stood rooted to the spot, held there by a most surprising horror.

For the gray-bearded figure of the other watcher was one I could never forget; its benignity was associated with the most horrible hours of my life, with deeds so dreadful that recollection to this day sometimes breaks my sleep, arousing me in the still watches, bathed in a cold sweat of fear.

It was Hassan of Aleppo!

If he saw me, if either of them saw me, I cannot say. What I should have done, what I might have done, it is useless to speak of here—for I did nothing. Inert, thralled by the presence of that eerie, dreadful being, I watched them leave the shadow of the doorway and pace slowly on with their dignified Eastern gait.

Then, knowing how I had failed in my plain duty to my fellow-men—how, finding a serpent in my path, I had hesitated to crush it, had weakly succumbed to its uncanny fascination—I made my way round to the door of the Museum.

## CHAPTER XIII
## THE WHITE BEAM

That night the deviltry began. Mr. Mostyn found himself wholly unable to sleep. Many relics have curious histories, and the experienced archæologist becomes callous to that uncanniness which seems to attach to some gruesome curios. But the slipper of the Prophet was different. No mere ghostly menace threatened its holders; an avenging scimitar followed those who came in contact with it; gruesome tragedies, mutilations, murders, had marked its progress throughout.

The night was still—as still as a London night can be; for there is always a vague murmuring in the metropolis as though the sleeping city breathed gently and sometimes stirred in its sleep.

Then, distinct amid these usual nocturnal noises, rose another, unaccountable sound, a muffled crash followed by a musical tinkling.

Mostyn sprang up in bed, drew on a dressing-gown, and took from the small safe at his bed-head the Museum keys and a loaded revolver. A somewhat dishevelled figure, pale and wild-eyed, he made his way through the private door and into the ghostly precincts of the Museum. He did not hesitate, but ascended the stairs and unlocked the door of the Assyrian gallery.

Along its ghostly aisles he passed, and before the door which gave admittance to the Burton Room paused, fumbling a moment for the key.

Inside the room something was moving!

Mostyn was keenly alarmed; he knew that he must enter at once or never. He inserted the key in the lock, swung open the heavy door, stepped through and closed it behind him. He was a man of tremendous moral courage, for now, alone in the apartment which harboured the uncanny relic, alone in the discharge of his duty, he stood with his back to the door trembling slightly, but with the idea of retreat finding no place in his mind.

One side of the room lay in blackest darkness; through the furthermost window of the other a faint yellowed luminance (the moonlight through the blind) spread upon the polished parquet flooring. But that which held the curator spell-bound—that which momentarily quickened into life the latent superstition, common to all mankind, was a beam of cold light which poured its effulgence fully upon the case containing the Prophet's slipper! Where the other exhibits lay either in utter darkness or semi-darkness this one it seemed was supernaturally picked out by this lunar searchlight!

It was ghostly—unnerving; but, the first dread of it passed, Mostyn recalled how during the day a hole inexplicably had been cut in that blind; he recalled that it had not been mended, but that the damaged blind had merely been rolled up again.

And as a dawning perception of the truth came to him, as falteringly he advanced a step toward the mystic beam, he saw that one side of the case had been shattered—he saw the broken glass upon the floor; and in the dense shadow behind and under the beam of light, vaguely he saw a dull red object.

It moved—it seemed to live! It moved away from the case and in the direction of the, eastern windows.

"My God!" whispered Mostyn; "it's the Prophet's slipper!"

And wildly, blindly, he fired down the room. Later he knew that he had fired in panic, for nothing human was or could be in the place; yet his shot was not without effect. In the instant of its flash, something struck sharply against the dimly seen blind of one of the east windows; he heard the crash of broken glass.

He leapt to the switch and flooded the room with light. A fear of what it might hold possessed him, and he turned instantly.

Hard by the fragments of broken glass upon the floor and midway between the case and the first easterly window lay the slipper. A bell was ringing somewhere. His shot probably had aroused the attention of the policeman. Someone was clamouring upon the door of the Museum, too. Mostyn raced forward and raised the blind—that toward which the slipper had seemed to move.

The lower pane of the window was smashed. Blood was trickling down upon the floor from the jagged edges of the glass.

"Hullo there! Open the door! Open the door!"

Bells were going all over the place now; sounds of running footsteps came from below; but Mostyn stood staring at the broken window and at the solid iron bars which protected it without, which were intact, substantial—which showed him that nothing human could possibly have entered.

Yet the case was shattered, the holy slipper lay close beside him upon the floor, and from the broken window-pane blood was falling—drip— drip—drip.

That was the story as I heard it half an hour later. For Inspector Bristol, apprised of the happening, was promptly on the scene; and knowing how keen was my interest in the matter, he rang me up immediately. I arrived soon after Bristol and found a perplexed group surrounding the uncanny slipper of the Prophet. No one had dared to touch it; the dread vengeance of Hassan of Aleppo would visit any unbeliever who ventured to lay hand upon the holy, bloody thing. Well we knew it, and as though it had been a venomous scorpion we, a company of up-to-date, prosaic men of affairs, stood around that dilapidated *markoob*, and kept a respectful distance.

Mostyn, an odd figure in pyjamas and dressing-gown, turned his pale, intellectual face to me as I entered.

"It will have to be put back... secretly," he said.

His voice was very unsteady. Bristol nodded grimly and glanced at the two constables, who, with a plain-clothes man unknown to me, made up that midnight company.

"I'll do it, sir," said one of the constables suddenly.

"One moment"—Mostyn raised his hand.

In the ensuing silence I could hear the heavy breathing of those around me. We were all looking at the slipper, I think.

"Do you understand, fully," the curator continued, "the risk you run?"

"I think so, sir," answered the constable; "but I'm prepared to chance it."

"The hands," resumed Mostyn slowly, "of those who hitherto have ventured to touch it have been"—he hesitated—"cut off."

"Your career in the Force would be finished if it happened to you, my lad," said Bristol shortly.

"I suppose they'd look after me," said the man, with grim humour.

"They would if you met with—an accident, in the discharge of your duty," replied the inspector; "but I haven't ordered you to do it, and I'm not going to."

"All right, sir," said the man, with a sort of studied truculence, "I'll take my chance."

I tried to stop him; Mostyn, too, stepped forward, and Bristol swore frankly. But it was all of no avail.

A sort of chill seemed to claim my very soul when I saw the constable stoop, unconcernedly pick up the slipper, and replace it in the broken case.

It was out of a silence cathedral-like, awesome, that he spoke.

"All you want is a new pane of glass, sir," he said—"and the thing's done."

I anticipate in mentioning it here; but since Constable Hughes has no further place in these records I may perhaps be excused for dismissing him at this point.

He was picked up outside the section house on the following evening with his right hand severed just above the wrist.

## CHAPTER XIV
## A SCREAM IN THE NIGHT

The day that followed was one of the hottest which we experienced during the heat wave. It was a day crowded with happenings. The Burton Room was closed to the public, whilst a glazier worked upon the broken east window and a new blind was fitted to the west. Behind the workmen, guarded by a watchful commissionaire, yawned the shattered case containing the slipper.

I wondered if the visitors to the other rooms of the Museum realized, as I realized, that despite the blazing sunlight of tropical London, the shadow of Hassan of Aleppo lay starkly on that haunted building?

At about eleven o'clock, as I hurried along the Strand, I almost collided with the girl of the violet eyes! She turned and ran like the wind down Arundel Street, whilst I stood at the corner staring after her in blank amazement, as did other passers-by; for a man cannot with dignity race headlong after a pretty woman down a public thoroughfare!

My mystification grew hourly deeper; and Bristol wallowed in perplexities.

"It's the most horrible and confusing case," he said to me when I joined him at the Museum, "that the Yard has ever had to handle. It bristles with outrages and murders. God knows where it will all end. I've had London scoured for a clue to the whereabouts of Hassan and Company and drawn absolutely blank! Then there's Earl Dexter. Where does *he* come in? For once in a way he's living in hiding. I can't find his headquarters. I've been thinking—"

He drew me aside into the small gallery which runs parallel with the Assyrian Room.

"Dexter has booked *two* passages in the *Oceanic*. Who is his companion?"

I wondered, I had wondered more than once, if his companion were my beautiful violet-eyed acquaintance. A scruple—perhaps an absurd scruple—hitherto had kept me silent respecting her, but now I determined to take Bristol fully into my confidence. A conviction was growing upon me that she and Earl Dexter together represented that third party whose existence we had long suspected. Whether they operated separately or on behalf of the Moslems (of which arrangement I could not conceive) remained to be seen. I was about to voice my doubts and suspicions when Bristol went on hurriedly—

"I have thoroughly examined the Burton Room, and considering that the windows are thirty feet from the ground, that there is no sign of a ladder having stood upon the lawn, and that the iron bars are quite intact, it doesn't look humanly possible for *any one* to have been in the room last night prior to Mostyn's arrival!"

"One of the dwarfs—"

"Not even one of the dwarfs," said Bristol, "could have passed between those iron bars!"

"But there was blood on the window!"

"I know there was, and *human* blood. It's been examined!"

He stared at me fixedly. The thing was unspeakably uncanny.

"To-night," he went on, "I am remaining in here"—nodding toward the Assyrian Room—"and I have so arranged it that no mortal being can possibly know I am here. Mostyn is staying, and you can stay, too, if you care to. Owing to Professor Deeping's will you are badly involved in the beastly business, and I have no doubt you are keen to see it through."

"I am," I admitted, "and the end I look for and hope for is the recovery of the slipper by its murderous owners!"

"I am with you," said Bristol. "It's just a point of honour; but I should be glad to make them a present of it. We're ostentatiously placing a constable on duty in the hallway to-night—largely as a blind. It will appear that we're taking no other additional precautions."

He hurried off to make arrangements for my joining him in his watch, and thus again I lost my opportunity of confiding in him regarding the mysterious girl.

I half anticipated, though I cannot imagine why, that Earl Dexter would put in an appearance during the day. He did not do so, however, for Bristol had put a constable on the door who was well acquainted with the appearance of the Stetson Man. The inspector, in the course of his investigations, had come upon what might have been a clue, but what was at best a confusing one. Close by the wall of the curator's house and lying on the gravel path he had found a part of a gold cuff link. It was of American manufacture.

Upon such slender evidence we could not justly assume that it pointed to the presence of Dexter on the night of the attempted robbery, but it served to complicate a matter already sufficiently involved.

In pursuance of Bristol's plan, I concealed myself that evening just before the closing of the Museum doors, in a recess behind a heavy piece of Babylonian sculpture. Bristol was similarly concealed in another part of the room, and Mostyn joined us later.

The Museum was closed; and so far as evidence went the authorities had relied again upon the bolts and bars hitherto considered impregnable, and upon the constable in the hall. The broken window was mended, the cut blind replaced, and within, in its shattered case, reposed the slipper of the Prophet.

All the blinds being lowered, the Assyrian Room was a place of gloom, yellowed on the western side by the moonlight through the blind. The door communicating with the Burton Room was closed but not fastened.

"They operated last night," Bristol whispered to me, "at the exact time when the moonlight shone through the hole in the westerly blind on to the case. If they come to-night, and I am quite expecting them, they will have to dispense with that assistance; but they know by experience where to reach the case."

"Despite our precautions," I said, "they will almost certainly know that a watch is being kept."

"They may or they may not," replied Bristol. "Either way I'm disposed to think there will be another attempt. Their mysterious method is so rapid that they can afford to take chances."

This was not my first night vigil since I had become in a sense the custodian of the relic, but it was quite the most dreary. Amid the tomb-like objects about us we seemed two puny mortals toying with stupendous things. We could not smoke and must converse only in whispers; and so the night wore on until I began to think that our watch would be dully uneventful.

"Our big chance," whispered Mostyn, "is in the fact that any day may change the conditions. They can't afford to wait."

He ceased abruptly, grasping my arm. From somewhere, somewhere outside the building, we all three had heard a soft whistle. A moment of tense listening followed.

"If only we could have had the place surrounded," whispered Bristol— "but it was impossible, of course."

A faint grating noise echoed through the lofty Burton Room. Bristol slipped past me in the semi-gloom, and gently opened the communicating door a few inches.

A-tiptoe, I joined him, and craning across his shoulder saw a strange and wonderful thing.

The newly glazed east window again was shattered with a booming crash! The yellow blind was thrust aside. A long *something* reached out toward the broken case. There was a sort of fumbling sound, and paralyzed with the wonder of it—for the window, remember, was thirty feet from the ground—I stood frozen to my post.

Not so Bristol. As the weird tentacle (or more exactly it reminded me of a gigantic crab's claw) touched the case, the Inspector leapt forward. A white beam from his electric torch cut through to the broken cabinet.

The thing was withdrawn... *and with it went the slipper of the Prophet.*

"Raise the blinds!" cried Bristol. "Mr. Cavanagh! Mr. Mostyn! We must not let them give us the slip!"

I got up the blind of the nearer window as Bristol raised the other. Not a living thing was in sight from either!

Mostyn was beside me, his hand resting on my shoulder. I noted how he trembled. Bristol turned and looked back at us. The light from his pocket torch flashed upon the curator's face; and I have never seen such an expression of horrified amazement as that which it wore. Faintly, I could hear the constable racing up the steps from the hall.

Ideas of the supernatural came to us all, I know; when, with a scuffling sound not unlike that of a rat in a ceiling, something moved above us!

"Damn my thick head!" roared Bristol, furiously. "*He's on the roof!* It's flat as a floor and there's enough ivy alongside the water-spout on your house adjoining, Mr. Mostyn, to afford foothold to an invading army!"

He plunged off toward the open door, and I heard him racing down the Assyrian Room.

"He had a short rope ladder fixed from the gutter!" he cried back at us. "Graham! Graham!" (the constable on duty in the hall)—"Get the front door open! Get..." His voice died away as he leapt down the stairs.

From the direction of Orpington Square came a horrid, choking scream. It rose hideously; it fell, rose again—and died.

The thief escaped. We saw the traces upon the ivy where he had hastened down. Bristol ascended by the same route, and found where the ladder-hooks had twice been attached to the gutterway. Constable Graham, who was first actually to leave the building, declared that he heard the whirr of a re-started motor lower down Great Orchard Street.

Bristol's theory, later to be dreadfully substantiated, was that the thief had broken the glass and reached into the case with an arrangement similar to that employed for pruning trees, having a clutch at the end, worked with a cord.

"Hassan has been too clever for us!" said the inspector. "But—what in God's name did that awful screaming mean?"

I had a theory, but I did not advance it then.

It was not until nearly dawn that my theory, and Bristol's, regarding the clutch arrangement, both were confirmed. For close under the railings which abut on Orpington Square, in a pool of blood we found just such an instrument as Bristol had described.

And still clutching it was a pallid and ghastly shrunken hand that had been severed from above the wrist!

"Merciful God!" whispered the inspector—"look at the opal ring on the finger! Look at the bandage where he cut himself on the broken window-glass that first night, when Mr. Mostyn disturbed him. It wasn't the *Hashishîn* who stole the thing.... *It's Earl Dexter's hand!*"

No one spoke for a moment. Then—

"Which of them has—" began Mostyn huskily.

"The slipper of the Prophet?" interrupted Bristol. "I wonder if we shall ever know?"


CHAPTER XV
A SHRIVELLED HAND

Around a large square table in a room at New Scotland Yard stood a group of men, all of whom looked more or less continuously at something that lay upon the polished deal. One of the party, none other than the Commissioner himself, had just finished speaking, and in silence now we stood about the gruesome object which had furnished him with the text of his very terse address.

I knew myself privileged in being admitted to such a conference at the C.I.D. headquarters and owed my admission partly to Inspector Bristol, and partly to the fact that under the will of the late Professor Deeping I was concerned in the uncanny business we were met to discuss.

Novelty has a charm for every one; and to find oneself immersed in a maelstrom of Eastern devilry, with a group of scientific murderers in pursuit of a holy Moslem relic, and unexpectedly to be made a trustee of that dangerous curiosity, makes a certain appeal to the adventurous. But to read of such things and to participate in them are widely different matters. The slipper of the Prophet and the dreadful crimes connected with it, the mutilations, murders, the uncanny mysteries which made up its history, were filling my world with horror.

Now in silence we stood around that table at New Scotland Yard and watched, as though we expected it to move, the ghastly "clue" which lay there. It was a shrivelled human hand, and about the thumb and forefinger there still dryly hung a fragment of lint which had bandaged a jagged wound. On one of the shrunken fingers was a ring set with a large opal.

Inspector Bristol broke the oppressive silence.

"You see, sir," he said, addressing the Commissioner, "this marks a new complication in the case. Up to this week although, unfortunately, we had made next to no progress, the thing was straightforward enough. A band of Eastern murderers, working along lines quite novel to Europe, were concealed somewhere in London. We knew that much. They murdered Professor Deeping, but failed to recover the slipper. They mutilated everyone who touched it mysteriously. The best men in the department, working night and day, failed to effect a single arrest. In spite of the mysterious activity of Hassan of Aleppo the slipper was safely lodged in the British Antiquarian Museum."

The Commissioner nodded thoughtfully.

"There is no doubt," continued Bristol, "that the *Hashishîn* were watching the Museum. Mr. Cavanagh, here"—he nodded in my direction—"saw Hassan himself lurking in the neighbourhood. We took every precaution, observed the greatest secrecy; but in spite of it all a constable who touched the accursed thing lost his right hand. Then the slipper was taken."

He stopped, and all eyes again were turned to the table.

"The Yard," resumed Bristol slowly, "had information that Earl Dexter, the cleverest crook in America, was in England. He was seen in the Museum, and the night following the slipper was stolen. Then outside the place I found—that!"

He pointed to the severed hand. No one spoke for a moment. Then—

"The new problem," said the Commissioner, "is this: who took the slipper, Dexter or Hassan of Aleppo?"

"That's it, sir," agreed Bristol. "Dexter had two passages booked in the *Oceanic*: but he didn't sail with her, and—that's his hand!"

"You say he has not been traced?" asked the Commissioner.

"No doctor known to the Medical Association," replied Bristol, "is attending him! He's not in any of the hospitals. He has completely vanished. The conclusion is obvious!"

"The evident deduction," I said, "is that Dexter stole the slipper from the Museum—God knows with what purpose—and that Hassan of Aleppo recovered it from him—"

"You think we shall next hear of Earl Dexter from the river police?" suggested Bristol.

"Personally," replied the Commissioner, "I agree with Mr. Cavanagh. I think Dexter is dead, and it is very probable that Hassan and Company are already homeward bound with the slipper of the Prophet."

With all my heart I hoped that he might be right, but an intuition was with me crying that he was wrong, that many bloody deeds would be, ere the sacred slipper should return to the East.

## CHAPTER XVI
## THE DWARF

The manner in which we next heard of the whereabouts of the Prophet's slipper was utterly unforeseen, wildly dramatic. That the *Hashishîn* were aware that I, though its legal trustee, no longer had charge of the relic nor knowledge of its resting-place, was sufficiently evident from the immunity which I enjoyed at this time from that ceaseless haunting by members of the uncanny organization ruled by Hassan. I had begun to feel more secure in my chambers, and no longer worked with a loaded revolver upon the table beside me. But the slightest unusual noise in the night still sufficed to arouse me and set me listening intently, to chili me with dread of what it might portend. In short, my nerves were by no means recovered from the ceaseless strain of the events connected with and arising out of the death of my poor friend, Professor Deeping.

One evening as I sat at work in my chambers, with the throb of busy Fleet Street and its thousand familiar sounds floating in to me through the open windows, my 'phone bell rang.

Even as I turned to take up the receiver a foreboding possessed me that my trusteeship was no longer to be a sinecure. It was Bristol who had rung me up, and upon very strange business.

"A development at last!" he said; "but at present I don't know what to make of it. Can you come down now?"

"Where are you speaking from?"

"From the Waterloo Road—a delightful neighbourhood. I shall be glad if you can meet me at the entrance to Wyatt's Buildings in half an hour."

"What is it? Have you found Dexter?"

"No, unfortunately. But it's murder!"

I knew as I hung up the receiver that my brief period of peace was ended; that the lists of assassination were reopened. I hurried out through the court into Fleet Street, thinking of the key of the now empty case at the Museum which reposed at my bankers, thinking of the devils who pursued the slipper, thinking of the hundred and one things, strange and terrible, which went to make up the history of that gruesome relic.

Wyatt's Buildings, Waterloo Road, are a gloomy and forbidding block of dwellings which seem to frown sullenly upon the high road, from which they are divided by a dark and dirty courtyard. Passing an iron gateway, you enter, by way of an arch, into this sinister place of uncleanness. Male residents in their shirt sleeves lounge against the several entrances. Bedraggled women nurse dirty infants and sit in groups upon the stone steps, rendering them almost impassable. But to-night a thing had happened in Wyatt's 'Buildings which had awakened in the inhabitants, hardened to sordid crime, a sort of torpid interest.

Faces peered from most of the windows which commanded a view of the courtyard, looking like pallid blotches against the darkness; but a number of police confined the loungers within their several doorways, so that the yard itself was comparatively clear.

I had had some difficulty in forcing a way through the crowd which thronged the entrance, but finally I found myself standing beside Inspector Bristol and looking down upon that which had brought us both to Wyatt's Buildings.

There was no moon that night, and only the light of the lamp in the archway, with some faint glimmers from the stairways surrounding the court, reached the dirty paving. Bristol directed the light of a pocket-lamp upon the hunched-up figure which lay in the dust, and I saw it to be that of a dwarfish creature, yellow skinned and wearing only a dark loin cloth. He had a malformed and disproportionate head, a head that had been too large even for a big man. I knew after my first glance that this was one of the horrible dwarfs employed by the *Hashishîn* in their murderous business. It might even be the one who had killed Deeping; but this was impossible to determine by reason of the fact that the hideous, swollen head, together with the features, was completely crushed. I shall not describe the creature's appearance in further detail.

Having given me an opportunity of examining the dead dwarf, Bristol returned the electric lamp to his pocket and stood looking at me in the semi-gloom. A constable stood on duty quite near to us, and others guarded the archway and the doors to the dwellings. The murmur of subdued voices echoed hollowly in the wells of the staircases, and a constant excited murmur proceeded from the crowd at the entrance. No pressmen had yet been admitted, though numbers of them were at the gates.

"It happened less than an hour ago," said Bristol. "The place was much as you see it now, and from what I can gather there came the sound of a shot and several people saw the dwarf fall through the air and drop where he lies!"

The light was insufficient to show the expression upon the speaker's face, but his voice told of a great wonder.

"It is a bit like an Indian conjuring trick," I said, looking up to the sky above us; "who fired the shot?"

"So far," replied Bristol, "I have failed to find out; but there's a bullet in the thing's head. He was dead before he reached the pavement."

"Did no one see the flash of the pistol?"

"No one that I have got hold of yet. Of course this kind of evidence is very unreliable; these people regularly go out of their way to mislead the police."

"You think the body may have been carried here from somewhere else?"

"Oh, no; this is where it fell, right enough. You can see where his head struck the stones."

"He has not been moved at all?"

"No; I shall not move him until I've worked out where in heaven's name he can have fallen from! You and I have seen some mysterious things happen, Mr. Cavanagh, since the slipper of the Prophet came to England and brought these people"—he nodded toward the thing at our feet—"in its train; but this is the most inexplicable incident to date. I don't know what to make of it at all. Quite apart from the question of where the dwarf fell from, who shot at him and why?"

"Have you no theory?" I asked. "The incident to my mind points directly to one thing. We know that this uncanny creature belonged to the organization of Hassan of Aleppo. We know that Hassan implacably pursues one object—the slipper. In pursuit of the slipper, then, the dwarf came here. Bristol"—I laid my hand upon his arm, glancing about me with a very real apprehension—"the slipper must be somewhere near!"

Bristol turned to the constable standing hard by.

"Remain here," he ordered. Then to me: "I should like you to come up on to the roof. From there we can survey the ground and perhaps arrive at some explanation of how the dwarf came to fall upon that spot."

Passing the constable on duty at one of the doorways and making our way through the group of loiterers there, we ascended amid conflicting odours to the topmost floor. A ladder was fixed against the wall communicating with a trap in the ceiling. Several individuals in their shirt sleeves and all smoking clay pipes had followed us up. Bristol turned upon them.

"Get downstairs," he said—"all the lot of you, and stop there!"

With muttered imprecations our audience dispersed, slowly returning by the way they had come. Bristol mounted the ladder and opened the trap. Through the square opening showed a velvet patch spangled with starry points. As he passed up on to the roof and I followed him, the comparative cleanness of the air was most refreshing after the varied fumes of the staircase.

Side by side we leaned upon the parapet looking down into the dirty courtyard which was the theatre of this weird mystery; looking down upon the stage, sordidly Western, where a mystic Eastern tragedy had been enacted.

I could see the constable standing beside the crushed thing upon the stones.

"Now," said Bristol, with a sort of awe in his voice, "where did he fall from?"

And at his words, looking down at the spot where the dwarf lay, and noting that he could not possibly have fallen there from any of the buildings surrounding the courtyard, an eerie sensation crept over me; for I was convinced that the happening was susceptible of no natural explanation.

I had heard—who has not heard?—of the Indian rope trick, where a *fakîr* throws a rope into the air which remains magically suspended whilst a boy climbs upward and upward until he disappears into space. I had never credited accounts of the performance; but now I began seriously to wonder if the arts of Hassan of Aleppo were not as great or greater than the arts of any *fakîr*. But the crowning mystery to my mind was that of the *Hashishîn's* death. It would seem that as he had hung suspended in space he had been shot!

"You say that someone heard the sound of the shot?" I asked suddenly.

"Several people," replied Bristol; "but no one knows, or no one will say, from what direction it came. I shall go on with the inquiry, of course, and cross-examine every soul in Wyatt's Buildings. Meanwhile, I'm open to confess that I am beaten."

In the velvet sky countless points blazed tropically. The hum of the traffic in Waterloo Road reached us only in a muffled way. Sordidness lay beneath us, but up there under the heavens we seemed removed from it as any Babylonian astronomer communing with the stars.

When, some ten minutes later, I passed out into the noise of Waterloo Road, I left behind me an unsolved mystery and took with me a great dread; for I knew that the quest of the sacred slipper was not ended, I knew that another tragedy was added to its history—and I feared to surmise what the future might hold for all of us.

## CHAPTER XVII
## THE WOMAN WITH THE BASKET

Deep in thought respecting the inexplicable nature of this latest mystery, I turned in the direction of the bridge, and leaving behind me an ever-swelling throng at the gate of Wyatt's Buildings, proceeded westward.

The death of the dwarf had lifted the case into the realms of the marvellous, and I noted nothing of the bustle about me, for mentally I was still surveying that hunched-up body which had fallen out of empty space.

Then in upon my preoccupation burst a woman's scream!

I aroused myself from reverie, looking about to right and left. Evidently I had been walking slowly, for I was less than a hundred yards from Wyatt's Buildings, and hard by the entrance to an uninviting alley from which I thought the scream had proceeded.

And as I hesitated, for I had no desire to become involved in a drunken brawl, again came the shrill scream: "Help! help!"

I cannot say if I was the only passer-by who heard the cry; certainly I was the only one who responded to it. I ran down the narrow street, which was practically deserted, and heard windows thrown up as I passed for the cries for help continued.

Just beyond a patch of light cast by a street lamp a scene was being enacted strange enough at any time and in any place, but doubly singular at that hour of the night, or early morning, in a lane off the Waterloo Road.

An old woman, from whose hand a basket of provisions had fallen, was struggling in the grasp of a tall Oriental! He was evidently trying to stifle her screams and at the same time to pinion her arms behind her!

I perceived that there was more in this scene than met the eye. Oriental footpads are rarities in the purlieus of Waterloo Road. So much was evident; and since I carried a short, sharp argument in my pocket, I hastened to advance it.

At the sight of the gleaming revolver barrel the man, who was dressed in dark clothes and wore a turban, turned and ran swiftly off. I had scarce a glimpse of his pallid brown face ere he was gone, nor did the thought of pursuit enter my mind. I turned to the old woman, who was dressed in shabby black and who was rearranging her thick veil in an oddly composed manner, considering the nature of the adventure that had befallen her.

She picked up her basket, and turned away. Needless to say I was rather shocked at her callous ingratitude, for she offered no word of thanks, did not even glance in my direction, but made off hurriedly toward Waterloo Road.

I had been on the point of inquiring if she had sustained any injury, but I checked the words and stood looking after her in blank wonderment. Then my ideas were diverted into a new channel. I perceived, as she passed under an adjacent lamp, that her basket contained provisions such as a woman of her appearance would scarcely be expected to purchase. I noted a bottle of wine, a chicken, and a large melon.

The nationality of the assailant from the first had marked the affair for no ordinary one, and now a hazy notion of what lay behind all this began to come to me.

Keeping well in the shadows on the opposite side of the way, I followed the woman with the basket. The lane was quite deserted; for, the disturbance over, those few residents who had raised their windows had promptly lowered them again. She came out into Waterloo Road, crossed over, and stood waiting by a stopping-place for electric cars. I saw her arranging a cloth over her basket in such a way as effectually to conceal the contents. A strong mental excitement possessed me. The detective fever claims us all at one time or another, I think, and I had good reason for pursuing any inquiry that promised to lead to the elucidation of the slipper mystery. A theory, covering all the facts of the assault incident, now presented itself, and I stood back in the shadow, watchful; in a degree, exultant.

A Greenwich-bound car was hailed by the woman with the basket. I could not be mistaken, I felt sure, in my belief that she cast furtive glances about her as she mounted the steps. But, having seen her actually aboard, my attention became elsewhere engaged. All now depended upon securing a cab before the tramcar had passed from view!

I counted it an act of Providence that a disengaged taxi appeared at that moment, evidently bound for Waterloo Station. I ran out into the road with cane upraised.

As the man drew up—

"Quick!" I cried. "You see that Greenwich car—nearly at the Ophthalmic Hospital? Follow it. Don't get too near. I will give you further instructions through the tube."

I leapt in. We were off!

The rocking car ahead was rounding the bend now toward St. George's Circus. As it passed the clock and entered South London Road it stopped. I raised the tube.

"Pass it slowly!"

We skirted the clock tower, and bore around to the right. Then I drew well back in the corner of the cab.

The woman with the basket was descending!

"Pull up a few yards beyond!" I directed.

As the car re-started, and passed us, the taxi became stationary. I peered out of the little window at the back.

The woman was returning in the direction of Waterloo Road!

"Drive slowly back along Waterloo Road," was my next order. "Pretend you are looking for a fare; I will keep out of sight."

The man nodded. It was unlikely that any one would notice the fact that the cab was engaged.

I was borne back again upon my course. The woman kept to the right, and, once we were entered into the straight road which leads to the bridge, I again raised the speaking-tube.

"Pull up," I said. "On the right-hand side is an old woman carrying a basket, fifty yards ahead. Do you see her? Keep well behind, but don't lose sight of her."

The man drew up again and sat watching the figure with the basket until it was almost lost from sight. Then slowly we resumed our way. I would have continued the pursuit afoot now, but I feared that my quarry might again enter a vehicle. She did not do so, however, but coming abreast of the turning in which the mysterious assault had taken place, she crossed the road and disappeared from view.

I leapt out of the cab, thrust half a crown into the man's hand, and ran on to the corner. The night was now far advanced, and I knew that the chances of detection were thereby increased. But the woman seemed to have abandoned her fears, and I saw her just ahead of me walking resolutely past the lamp beyond which a short time earlier she had met with a dangerous adventure.

Since the opposite side of the street was comparatively in darkness, I slipped across, and in a state of high nervous tension pursued this strange work of espionage. I was convinced that I had forestalled Bristol and that I was hot upon the track of those who could explain the mystery of the dead dwarf.

The woman entered the gate of the block of dwellings even more forbidding in appearance than those which that night had staged a dreadful drama.

As the figure with the basket was lost from view I crept on, and in turn entered the evil-smelling hallway. I stepped cautiously, and standing beneath a gaslight protected by a wire frame, I congratulated myself upon having reached that point of vantage as silently as any Sioux stalker.

Footsteps were receding up the stone stairs. Craning my neck, I peered up the well of the staircase. I could not see the woman, but from the sound of her tread it was possible to count the landings which she passed. When she had reached the fourth, and I heard her step upon yet another flight, I knew that she must be bound for the topmost floor; and observing every precaution, almost holding my breath in a nervous endeavour to make not the slightest sound, rapidly I mounted the stairs.

I was come to the third landing in this secret fashion when quite distinctly I heard the grating of a key in a lock!

Since four doors opened upon each of the landings, at all costs, I thought, I must learn by which door she entered.

Throwing caution to the winds I raced up the remaining flights... and there at the top the woman confronted me, with blazing eyes!—with eyes that thrilled every nerve; for they were violet eyes, the only truly violet eyes I have ever seen! They were the eyes of the woman who like a charming, mocking will-o'-the-wisp had danced through this tragic scene from the time that poor Professor Deeping had brought the Prophet's slipper to London up to this present hour!

There at the head of those stone steps in that common dwelling-house I knew her—and in the violet eyes it was written that she knew, and feared, *me!*

"What do you want? Why are you following me?"

She made no endeavour to disguise her voice. Almost, I think, she spoke the words involuntarily.

I stood beside her. Quickly as she had turned from the door at my ascent, I had noted that it was that numbered forty-eight which she had been about to open.

"You waste words," I said grimly. "Who lives there?"

I nodded in the direction of the doorway.

The violet eyes watched me with an expression in their depths which I find myself wholly unable to describe. Fear predominated, but there was anger, too, and with it a sort of entreaty which almost made me regret that I had taken this task upon myself. From beneath the shabby black hat escaped an errant lock of wavy hair wholly inconsistent with the assumed appearance of the woman. The flickering gaslight on the landing sought out in that wonderful hair shades which seemed to glow with the soft light seen in the heart of a rose. The thick veil was raised now and all attempts at deception abandoned. At bay she faced me, this secret woman whom I knew to hold the key to some of the darkest places which we sought to explore.

"I live there," she said slowly. "What do you want with me?"

"I want to know," I replied, "for whom are those provisions in your basket?"

She watched me fixedly.

"And I want to know," I continued, "something that only you can tell me. We have met before, madam, but you have always eluded me. This time you shall not do so. There's much I have to ask of you, but particularly I want to know who killed the *Hashishîn* who lies dead at no great distance from here!"

"How can I tell you that? Of what are you speaking?"

Her voice was low and musical; that of a cultured woman. She evidently recognized the futility of further subterfuge in this respect.

"You know quite well of what I am speaking! You know that you can tell me if any one can! The fact that you go disguised alone condemns you! Why should I remind you of our previous meetings—of the links which bind you to the history of the Prophet's slipper?" She shuddered and closed her eyes. "Your present attitude is a sufficient admission!"

She stood silent before me, with something pitiful in her pose—a wonderfully pretty woman, whose disarranged hair and dilapidated hat could not mar her beauty; whose clumsy, ill-fitting garments could not conceal her lithe grace.

Our altercation had not thus far served to arouse any of the inhabitants and on that stuffy landing, beneath the flickering gaslight, we stood alone, a group of two which epitomized strange things.

Then, with that quietly dramatic note which marks real life entrances and differentiates them from the loudly acclaimed episodes of the stage, a third actor took up his cue.

"Both hands, Mr. Cavanagh!" directed an American voice.

Nerves atwitch, I started around in its direction.

From behind the slightly opened door of No. 48 protruded a steel barrel, pointed accurately at my head!

I hesitated, glancing from the woman toward the open door.

"Do it quick!" continued the voice incisively. "You are up against a desperate man, Mr. Cavanagh. Raise your hands. Carnéta, relieve Mr. Cavanagh of his gun!"

Instantly the girl, with deft fingers, had obtained possession of my revolver.

"Step inside," said the crisp, strident voice.

Knowing myself helpless and quite convinced that I was indeed in the clutches of desperate people, I entered the doorway, the door being held open from within. She whom I had heard called Carnéta followed. The door was reclosed; and I found myself in a perfectly bare and dim passageway. From behind me came the order—

"Go right ahead!"

Into a practically unfurnished room, lighted by one gas jet, I walked. Some coarse matting hung before the two windows and a fairly large grip stood on the floor against one wall. A gas-ring was in the hearth, together with a few cheap cooking utensils.

I turned and faced the door. First entered Carnéta, carrying the basket; then came a man with a revolver in his left hand and his right arm strapped across his chest and swathed in bandages. One glance revealed the fact that his right hand had been severed—revealed the fact, though I knew it already, that my captor was Earl Dexter.

He looked even leaner than when I had last seen him. I had no doubt that his ghastly wound had occasioned a tremendous loss of blood. His gaunt face was positively emaciated, but the steely gray eyes had lost nothing of their brightness. There was a good deal about Mr. Earl Dexter, the cracksman, that any man must have admired.

"Shut the door, Carnéta," he said quietly.

His companion closed the door and Dexter sat down on the grip, regarding me with his oddly humorous smile.

"You're a visitor I did not expect, Mr. Cavanagh," he said. "I expected someone worse. You've interfered a bit with my plans, but I don't know that I can't rearrange things satisfactorily. I don't think I'll stop for supper, though—" He glanced at the girl, who stood silent by the door.

"Just pack up the provisions," he directed, nodding toward the basket—"in the next room."

She departed without a word.

"That's a noticeable dust coat you're wearing, Mr. Cavanagh," said the American; "it gives me a great notion. I'm afraid I'll have to borrow it."

He glanced, smiling, at the revolver in his left hand and back again to me. There was nothing of the bully about him, nothing melodramatic; but I took off the coat without demur and threw it across to him.

"It will hide this stump," he said grimly; "and any of the *Hashishîn* gentlemen who may be on the look-out—though I rather fancy the road is clear at the moment—will mistake me for you. See the idea? Carnéta will be in a cab and I'll be in after her and away before they've got time to so much as whistle."

Very awkwardly he got into the coat.

"She's a clever girl, Carnéta," he said. "She's doctored me all along since those devils cut my hand off."

As he finished speaking Carnéta returned. She had discarded her rags and wore a large travelling coat and a fashionable hat.

"Ready?" asked Dexter. "We'll make a rush for it. We meant to go to-night anyway. It's getting too hot here!" He turned to me.

"Sorry to say," he drawled, "I'll have to tie you up and gag you. Apologize; but it can't be helped."

Carnéta nodded and went out of the room again, to return almost immediately with a line that looked as though it might have been employed for drying washing.

"Hands behind you," rapped Dexter, toying with the revolver—"and think yourself lucky you've got *two!*"

There was no mistaking the manner of man with whom I had to deal, and I obeyed; but my mind was busy with a hundred projects. Very neatly the girl bound my wrists, and in response to a slight nod from Dexter threw the end of the line up over a beam in the sloping ceiling, for the room was right under the roof, and drew it up in such a way that my wrists being raised behind me, I became utterly helpless. It was an ingenious device indicating considerable experience.

"Just tie his handkerchief around his mouth," directed Dexter: "that will keep him quiet long enough for our purpose. I hope you will be released soon, Mr. Cavanagh," he added. "Greatly regret the necessity."

Carnéta bound the handkerchief over my mouth.

Dexter extinguished the gas.

"Mr. Cavanagh," he said, "I've gone through hell and I've lost the most useful four fingers and a thumb in the United States to get hold of the Prophet's slipper. Any one can have it that's open to pay for it—but I've got to retire on the deal, so I'll drive a hard bargain! Good-night!"

There was a sound of retreating footsteps, and I heard the entrance door close quietly.


## CHAPTER XVIII
### WHAT CAME THROUGH THE WINDOW

I had not been in my unnatural position for many minutes before I began to suffer agonies, agonies not only physical but mental; for standing there like some prisoner of the Inquisition, it came to me how this dismantled apartment must be the focus of the dreadful forces of Hassan of Aleppo!

That Earl Dexter had the slipper of the Prophet I no longer doubted, and that he had sustained, in this dwelling beneath the roof, an uncanny siege during the days which had passed since the theft from the Antiquarian Museum, was equally certain. Helpless, gagged, I pictured those hideous creatures, evil products of the secret East, who might, nay, who must surround that place! I thought of the horrible little yellow man who lay dead in Wyatt's Buildings; and it became evident to me that the house in which I was now imprisoned must overlook the back of those unsavoury tenements. The windows, sack-covered now, no doubt commanded a view of the roofs of the buildings. One of the mysteries that had puzzled us was solved. It was Earl Dexter who had shot the yellow dwarf as he was bound for this very room! But how humanly the *Hashishîn* had proposed to gain his goal, how he had travelled through empty space—for from empty space the shot had brought him down—I could not imagine.

I knew something of the almost supernatural attributes of these people. From Professor Deeping's book I knew of the incredible feats which they could perform when under the influence of the drug *hashish*. From personal experience also I knew that they had powers wholly abnormal.

The pain in my arms and back momentarily increased. An awesome silence ruled. I tortured myself with pictures of murderous yellow men possessed of the power claimed by the Mahatmas, of levitation. Mentally I could see a distorted half-animal creature carrying a great gleaming knife and floating supernaturally toward me through the night!

A soft pattering sound became perceptible on the sloping roof above!

I think I have never known such intense and numbing fear as that which now descended upon me. Perhaps I may be forgiven it. A more dreadful situation it would be hard to devise. Knowing that I was on the fifth story of a house, bound, helpless, I knew, too, that a second mystic guardian of the slipper was come to accomplish the task in which the first had failed!

I began to pray fervently.

Neither of the windows were closed; and now through the intense darkness I heard one of them being raised up—up—up....

The sacking was pulled aside inch by inch.

Silhouetted against the faintly luminous background I saw a hunched, unnatural figure. The real was more dreadful even than the imaginary—for some stray beam of light touched into cold radiance a huge curved knife which the visitant held between his teeth!

My fear became a madness, and I twisted my body violently in a wild endeavour to free myself. A dreadful pain shot through my left shoulder, and the whole nightmare scene—the thing with the knife at the window—the low-ceiled room—began to fade away from me. I seemed to be falling into deep water....

A splintering crash and the sound of shouting formed my last recollections ere unconsciousness came....

I found myself lying in an armchair with Bristol forcing brandy between my lips. My left arm hung limply at my side and the pain in my dislocated shoulder was excruciating.

"Thank God you are all right, Mr. Cavanagh!" said the inspector. "I got the surprise of my life when we smashed the door in and found *you* tied up here!"

"You came none too soon," I said feebly. "God knows how Providence directed you here."

"Providence it was," replied Bristol. "From the roof of Wyatt's Buildings—you know the spot?—I saw the second yellow devil coming. By God! They meant to have it to-night! They don't value their lives a brass farthing against that damned slipper!"

"But how—"

"Along the telegraph-wires, Mr. Cavanagh! They cross Wyatt's Buildings and cross this house. It was a moonless night or we should have seen it at once! I watched him, saw him drop to this roof—and brought the men around to the front."

"Did *he*, that awful thing, escape?"

"He dropped full forty feet into a tree—from the tree to the ground, and went off like a cat!"

"Earl Dexter has escaped us," I said, "and he has the slipper!"

"God help him!" replied Bristol. "For by now he has that hell-pack at his heels! What a case! Heavens above, it will drive me mad!"

## CHAPTER XIX
## A RAPPING AT MIDNIGHT

Inspector Bristol finished his whisky at a gulp and stood up, a tall, massive figure, stretching himself and yawning.

"The detective of fiction would be hard at work on this case, now," he said, smiling, "but I don't even pretend to be. I am at a standstill and I don't care who knows it."'

"You have absolutely no clue to the whereabouts of Earl Dexter?"

"Not the slightest, Mr. Cavanagh. You hear a lot about the machinery of the law, but as a matter of fact, looking for a clever man hidden in London is a good deal like looking for a needle in a haystack. Then, he may have been bluffing when he told you he had the Prophet's slipper. He's already had his hand cut off through interfering with the beastly thing, and I really can't believe he would take further chances by keeping it in his possession. Nevertheless, I should like to find him."

He leaned back against the mantelpiece, scratching his head perplexedly. In this perplexity he had my sympathy. No such pursuit, I venture to say, had ever before been required of Scotland Yard as this of the slipper of the Prophet. An organization founded in 1090, which has made a science of assassination, which through the centuries has perfected the malign arts, which, lingering on in a dark spot in Syria, has suddenly migrated and established itself in London, is a proposition almost unthinkable.

It was hard to believe that even the daring American cracksman should have ventured to touch that blood-stained relic of the Prophet, that he should have snatched it away from beneath the very eyes of the fanatics who fiercely guarded it. What he hoped to gain by his possession of the slipper was not evident, but the fact remained that if he could be believed, he had it, and provided Scotland Yard's information was accurate, he still lurked in hiding somewhere in London.

Meanwhile, no clue offered to his hiding-place, and despite the ceaseless vigilance of the men acting under Bristol's orders, no trace could be found of Hassan of Aleppo nor of his fiendish associates.

"My theory is," said Bristol, lighting a cigarette, "that even Dexter's cleverness has failed to save him. He's probably a dead man by now, which accounts for our failing to find him; and Hassan of Aleppo has recovered the slipper and returned to the East, taking his gruesome company with him—God knows how! But that accounts for our failing to find *him*."

I stood up rather wearily. Although poor Deeping had appointed me legal guardian of the relic, and although I could render but a poor account of my stewardship, let me confess that I was anxious to take that comforting theory to my bosom. I would have given much to have known beyond any possibility of doubt that the accursed slipper and its blood-lustful guardian were far away from England. Had I known so much, life would again have had something to offer me besides ceaseless fear, endless watchings. I could have slept again, perhaps; without awaking, clammy, peering into every shadow, listening, nerves atwitch to each slightest sound disturbing the night; without groping beneath the pillow for my revolver.

"Then you think," I said, "that the English phase of the slipper's history is closed? You think that Dexter, minus his right hand, has eluded British law—that Hassan and Company have evaded retribution?"

"I do!" said Bristol grimly, "and although that means the biggest failure in my professional career; I am glad—damned glad!"

Shortly afterward he took his departure; and I leaned from the window, watching him pass along the court below and out under the arch into Fleet Street. He was a man whose opinions I valued, and in all sincerity I prayed now that he might be right; that the surcease of horror which we had recently experienced after the ghastly tragedies which had clustered thick about the haunted slipper, might mean what he surmised it to mean.

The heat to-night was very oppressive. A sort of steaming mist seemed to rise from the court, and no cooling breeze entered my opened windows. The clamour of the traffic in Fleet Street came to me but remotely. Big Ben began to strike midnight. So far as I could see, residents on the other stairs were all abed and a velvet shadow carpet lay unbroken across three parts of the court. The sky was tropically perfect, cloudless, and jewelled lavishly. Indeed, we were in the midst of an Indian summer; it seemed that the uncanny visitants had brought, together with an atmosphere of black Eastern deviltry, something, too, of the Eastern climate.

The last stroke of the Cathedral bell died away. Other more distant bells still were sounding dimly, but save for the ceaseless hum of the traffic, no unusual sound now disturbed the archaic peace of the court.

I returned to my table, for during the time that had passed I had badly neglected my work and now must often labour far into the night. I was just reseated when there came a very soft rapping at the outer door!

No doubt my mood was in part responsible, but I found myself thinking of Poe's weird poem, "The Raven"; and like the character therein I found myself hesitating.

I stole quietly into the passage. It was in darkness. How odd it is that in moments of doubt instinctively one shuns the dark and seeks the light. I pressed the switch lighting the hall lamp, and stood looking at the closed door.

Why should this late visitor have rapped in so uncanny a fashion in preference to ringing the bell?

I stepped back to my table and slipped a revolver into my pocket.

The muffled rapping was repeated. As I stood in the study doorway I saw the flap of the letter-box slowly raised!

Instantly I extinguished both lights. You may brand me as childishly timid, but incidents were fresh in my memory which justified all my fears.

A faintly luminous slit in the door showed me that the flap was now fully raised. It was the dim light on the stairway shining through. Then quite silently the flap was lowered. Came the soft rapping again.

"Who's there?" I cried.

No one answered.

Wondering if I were unduly alarming myself, yet, I confess, strung up tensely in anticipation that this was some device of the phantom enemy, I stood in doubt.

The silence remained unbroken for thirty seconds or more. Then yet again it was disturbed by that ghostly, muffled rapping.

I advanced a step nearer to the door.

"Who's there?" I cried loudly. "What do you want?"

The flap of the letter box began to move, and I formed a sudden determination. Making no sound in my heelless Turkish slippers I crept close up to the door and dropped upon my knees.

Thereupon the flap became fully lifted, but from where I crouched beneath it I was unable to see who or what was looking in; yet I hesitated no longer. I suddenly raised myself and thrust the revolver barrel through the opening!

"Who are you?" I cried. "Answer or I fire!"—and along the barrel I peered out on to the landing.

Still no one answered. But something impalpable—a powder—a vapour—to this hour I do not know what—enveloped me with its nauseating fumes; was puffed fully into my face! My eyes, my mouth, my nostrils became choked up, it seemed, with a deadly stifling perfume.

Wildly, feeling that everything about me was slipping away, that I was sinking into a void, for ought I knew that of dissolution, I pulled the trigger once, twice. Thrice...

"My God!"—the words choked in my throat and I reeled back into the passage—"it's not loaded!"

I threw up my arms to save myself, lurched, and fell forward into what seemed a bottomless pit.


## CHAPTER XX
### THE GOLDEN PAVILION

When I opened my eyes it was to a conviction that I dreamed. I lay upon a cushioned divan in a small apartment which I find myself at a loss adequately to describe.

It was a yellow room, then, its four walls being hung with yellow silk, its floor being entirely covered by a yellow Persian carpet. One lamp, burning in a frame of some lemon-coloured wood and having its openings filled with green glass, flooded the place with a ghastly illumination.

The lamp hung by gold chains from the ceiling, which was yellow. Several low tables of the same lemon-hued wood as the lamp-frame stood around; they were inlaid in fanciful designs with gleaming green stones. Turn my eyes where I would, clutch my aching head as I might, this dream chamber would not disperse, but remained palpable before me— yellow and green and gold.

There was a niche behind the divan upon which I lay framed about with yellow wood. In it stood a golden bowl and a tall pot of yellow porcelain; I lay amid yellow cushions having golden tassels. Some of them were figured with vivid green devices.

To contemplate my surroundings assuredly must be to court madness. No door was visible, no window; nothing but silk and luxury, yellow and green and gold.

To crown all, the air was heavy with a perfume wholly unmistakable by one acquainted with Egypt's ruling vice. It was the reek of smouldering *hashish*—a stench that seemed to take me by the throat, a vapour damnable and unclean. I saw that a little censer, golden in colour and inset with emeralds, stood upon the furthermost corner of the yellow carpet. From it rose a faint streak of vapour; and I followed the course of the sickly scented smoke upward through the still air until in oily spirals it lost itself near to the yellow ceiling. As a sick man will study the veriest trifle I studied that wisp of smoke, pencilled grayly against the silken draperies, the carven tables, against the almost terrifying persistency of the yellow and green and gold.

I strove to rise, but was overcome by vertigo and sank back again upon the yellow cushions. I closed my eyes, which throbbed and burned, and rested my head upon my hands. I ceased to conjecture if I dreamed or was awake. I knew that I felt weak and ill, that my head throbbed agonizingly, that my eyes smarted so as to render it almost impossible to keep them open, that a ceaseless humming was in my ears.

For some time I lay endeavouring to regain command of myself, to prepare to face again that scene which had something horrifying in its yellowness, touched with the green and gold.

And when finally I reopened my eyes, I sat up with a suppressed cry. For a tall figure in a yellow robe from beneath which peeped yellow slippers, a figure crowned with a green turban, stood in the centre of the apartment!

It was that of a majestic old man, white bearded, with aquiline nose, and the fierce eagle eyes of a fanatic set upon me sternly, reprovingly.

With folded arms he stood watching me, and I drew a sharp breath and rose slowly to my feet.

There amid the yellow and green and gold, amid the abominable reek of burning *hashish* I stood and faced Hassan of Aleppo!

No words came to me; I was confounded.

Hassan spoke in that gentle voice which I had heard only once before.

"Mr. Cavanagh," he said, "I have brought you here that I might warn you. Your police are seeking me night and day, and I am fully alive to my danger whilst I stay in your midst. But for close upon a thousand years the *Sheikh-al-jebal*, Lord of the *Hashishîn*, has guarded the traditions and the relics of the Prophet, *Salla—'lláhu 'aleyhi wasellem!* I, Hassan of Aleppo, am Sheikh of the Order to-day, and my sacred duty has brought me here."

The piercing gaze never left my face. I was not yet by any means my own man and still I made no reply.

"You have been wise," continued Hassan, "in that you have never touched the sacred slipper. Had you lain hands upon it, no secrecy could have availed you. The eye of the *Hashishîn* sees all. There is a shaft of light which the true Believer perceives at night as he travels toward El-Medineh. It is the light which uprises, a spiritual fire, from the tomb of the Prophet (*Salla—'lláhu 'aleyhi wasellem!*). The relics also are radiant, though in a lesser degree."

He took a step toward me, spreading out his lean brown hands, palms downward.

"A shaft of light," he said impressively, "shines upward now from London. It is the light of the holy slipper." He gazed intently at the yellow drapery at the left of the divan, but as though he were looking not at the wall but through it. His features worked convulsively; he was a man inspired. "I see it now!" he almost whispered—"that white light by which the guardians of the relic may always know its resting place!"

I managed to force words to my lips.

"If you know where the slipper is," I said, more for the sake of talking than for anything else, "why do you not recover it?"

Hassan turned his eyes upon me again.

"Because the infidel dog," he cried loudly, "who has soiled it with his unclean touch, defies us—mocks us! He has suffered the loss of the offending hand, but the evil *ginn* protect him; he is inspired by *efreets!* But God is great and Mohammed is His only Prophet! We shall triumph; but it is written, oh, daring infidel, that you again shall become the guardian of the slipper!"

He spoke like some prophet of old and I stared at him fascinated. I was loth to believe his words.

"When again," he continued, "the slipper shall be in the receptacle of which you hold the key, that key must be given to me!"

I thought I saw the drift of his words now; I thought I perceived with what object I had been trapped and borne to this mysterious abode for whose whereabouts the police vainly were seeking. By the exercise of the gift of divination it would seem that Hassan of Aleppo had forecast the future history of the accursed slipper or believed that he had done so. According to his own words I was doomed once more to become trustee of the relic. The key of the case at the Antiquarian Museum, to which he had prophesied the slipper's return, would be the price of my life! But—

"In order that these things may be fulfilled," he continued, "I must permit you to return to your house. So it is written, so it shall be. Your life is in my hands; beware when it is demanded of you that you hesitate not in yielding up the key!"

He raised his hands before him, making a sort of obeisance, I doubt not in the direction of Mecca, drew aside one of the yellow hangings behind him and disappeared, leaving me alone again in that nightmare apartment of yellow and green and gold. A moment I stood watching the swaying curtain. Utter silence reigned, and a sort of panic seized me infinitely greater than that occasioned by the presence of the weird Sheikh. I felt that I must escape from the place or that I should become raving mad.

I leapt forward to the curtain which Hassan had raised and jerked it aside; it had concealed a door. In this door and about level with my eyes was a kind of little barred window through which shone a dim green light. I bent forward, peering into the place beyond, but was unable to perceive anything save a vague greenness.

And as I peered, half believing that the whole episode was a dreadful, fevered dream, the abominable fumes of *hashish* grew, or seemed to grow, quite suddenly insupportable. Through the square opening, from the green void beyond, a cloud of oily vapour, pungent, stifling, resembling that of burning Indian hemp, poured out and enveloped me!

With a gasping cry I fell back, fighting for breath, for a breath of clean air unpolluted with *hashish*. But every inhalation drew down into my lungs the fumes that I sought to escape from. I experienced a deathly sickness; I seemed to be sinking into a sea of *hashish*, amid bubbles of yellow and green and gold, and I knew no more until, struggling again to my feet, surrounded by utter darkness—I struck my head on the corner of my writing-table... for I lay in my own study!

My revolver, unloaded, was upon the table beside me. The night was very still. I think it must have been near to dawn.

"My God!" I whispered, "did I dream it all? Did I dream it all?"

## CHAPTER XXI
## THE BLACK TUBE

There's no doubt in my mind," said Inspector Bristol, "that your experience was real enough."

The sun was shining into my room now, but could not wholly disperse the cloud of horror which lay upon it. That I had been drugged was sufficiently evident from my present condition, and that I had been taken away from my chambers Inspector Bristol had satisfactorily proved by an examination of the soles of my slippers.

"It was a clever trick," he said. "God knows what it was they puffed into your face through the letter box, but the devilish arts of ten centuries, we must remember, are at the command of Hassan of Aleppo! The repetition of the trick at the mysterious place you were taken to is particularly interesting. I should say you won't be in a hurry to peer through letter boxes and so forth in the future?"

I shook my aching head.

"That accursed yellow room," I replied, "stank with the fumes of *hashish*. It may have been some preparation of *hashish* that was used to drug me."

Bristol stood looking thoughtfully from the window.

"It was a nightmare business, Mr. Cavanagh," he said; "but it doesn't advance our inquiry a little bit. The prophecy of the old man with the white beard—whom you assure me to be none other than Hassan of Aleppo—is something we cannot very well act upon. He clearly believes it himself; for he has released you after having captured you, evidently in order that you may be at liberty to take up your duty as trustee of the slipper again. If the slipper really comes back to the Museum the fact will show Hassan to be something little short of a magician. I shan't envy you then, Mr. Cavanagh, considering that you hold the keys of the case!"

"No," I replied wearily. "Poor Professor Deeping thought that he acted in my interests and that my possession of the keys would constitute a safeguard. He was wrong. It has plunged me into the very vortex of this ghastly affair."

"It is maddening," said Bristol, "to know that Hassan and Company are snugly located somewhere under our very noses, and that all Scotland Yard can find no trace of them. Then to think that Hassan of

Aleppo, apparently by means of some mystical light, has knowledge of the whereabouts of the slipper and consequently of the whereabouts of Earl Dexter (another badly wanted man) is extremely discouraging! I feel like an amateur; I'm ashamed of myself!"

Bristol departed in a condition of irritable uncertainty.

My head in my hands, I sat for long after his departure, with the phantom characters of the ghoulish drama dancing through my brain. The distorted yellow dwarfs seemed to gibe apish before me. Severed hands clenched and unclenched themselves in my face, and gleaming knives flashed across the mental picture. Predominant over all was the stately figure of Hassan of Aleppo, that benignant, remorseless being, that terrible guardian of the holy relic who directed the murderous operations. Earl Dexter, The Stetson Man, with his tightly bandaged arm, his gaunt, clean-shaven face and daredevil smile, figured, too, in my feverish daydream; nor was that other character missing, the girl with the violet eyes whose beautiful presence I had come to dread; for like a sybil announcing destruction her appearances in the drama had almost invariably presaged fresh tragedies. I recalled my previous meetings with this woman of mystery. I recalled my many surmises regarding her real identity and association with the case. I wondered why in the not very distant past I had promised to keep silent respecting her; I wondered why up to that present moment, knowing beyond doubt that her activities were inimical to my interests, were criminal, I had observed that foolish pledge.

And now my door-bell was ringing—as intuitively I had anticipated. So certain was I of the identity of my visitor that as I walked along the passage I was endeavouring to make up my mind how I should act, how I should receive her.

I opened the door; and there, wearing European garments but a green turban... stood Hassan of Aleppo!

When I say that amazement robbed me of the power to speak, to move, almost to think, I doubt not you will credit me. Indeed, I felt that modern London was crumbling about me and that I was become involved in the fantastic mazes of one of those Oriental intrigues such as figure in the *Romance of Abû Zeyd*, or with which most European readers have been rendered familiar by the glowing pages of "The Thousand and One Nights."

"Effendim," said my visitor, "do not hesitate to act as I direct!"

In his gloved hand he carried what appeared to be an ebony cane. He raised and pointed it directly at me. I perceived that it was, in fact, a hollow tube.

"Death is in my hand," he continued; "enter slowly and I will follow you."

Still the sense of unreality held me thralled and my brain refused me service. Like an hypnotic subject I walked back to my study, followed by my terrible visitor, who reclosed the door behind him.

He sat facing me across my littered table, with the mysterious tube held loosely in his grasp.

How infinitely more terrifying are perils unknown than those known and appreciated! Had a European armed with a pistol attempted a similar act of coercion, I cannot doubt that I should have put up some sort of fight; had he sat before me now as Hassan of Aleppo sat, with a comprehensible weapon thus laid upon his knees, I should have taken my chance, should have attacked him with the lamp, with a chair, with anything that came to my hand.

But before this awful, mysterious being who was turning my life into channels unsuspected, before that black tube with its unknown potentialities, I sat in a kind of passive panic which I cannot attempt to describe, which I had never experienced before and have never known since.

"There is one about to visit you," he said, "whom you know, whom I think you expect. For it is written that she shall come and such events cast a shadow before them. I, too, shall be present at your meeting!"

His eagle eyes opened widely; they burned with fanaticism.

"Already she is here!" he resumed suddenly, and bent as one listening. "She comes under the archway; she crossed the courtyard—and is upon the stair! Admit her, effendim; I shall be close behind you!"

The door-bell rang.

With the consciousness that the black tube was directed toward the back of my head, I went and opened the door. My mind was at work again, and busy with plans to terminate this impossible situation.

On the landing stood a girl wearing a simple white frock which fitted her graceful figure perfectly. A white straw hat, of the New York tourist type, with a long veil draped from the back suited her delicate beauty very well. The red mouth drooped a little at the corners, but the big violet eyes, like lamps of the soul, seemed afire with mystic light.

"Mr. Cavanagh," she said, very calmly and deliberately, "there is only one way now to end all this trouble. I come from the man who can return the slipper to where it belongs; but he wants his price!"

Her quiet speech served completely to restore my mental balance, and I noted with admiration that her words were so chosen as to commit her in no way. She knew quite well that thus far she might appear in the matter with impunity, and she clearly was determined to say nothing that could imperil her.

"Will you please come in?" I said quietly—and stood aside to admit her.

Exhibiting wonderful composure, she entered—and there, in the badly lighted hallway, came face to face with my other visitor!

It was a situation so dramatic as to seem unreal.

Away from that tall figure retreated the girl with the violet eyes—and away—until she stood with her back to the wall. Even in the gloom I could see that her composure was deserting her; her beautiful face was pallid.

"Oh, God!" she whispered, all but inaudible—"*You!*"

Hassan, grasping the black rod in his hand, signed to her to enter the study. She stood quite near to me, with her eyes fixed upon him. I bent closer to her.

"My revolver—in left-hand table drawer," I breathed in her ear. "Get it. He is watching me!"

I could not tell if my words had been understood, for, never taking her gaze from the Sheikh of the Assassins, she sidled into the study. I followed her; and Hassan came last of all. Just within the doorway he stood, confronting us.

"You have come," he said, addressing the girl and speaking in perfect English but with a marked accent, "to open your impudent negotiations through Mr. Cavanagh for the return of the thrice holy relic to the Museum! Your companion, the man, who is inspired by the Evil One, has even dared to demand ransom for the slipper from *me!*"

Hassan was majestic in his wrath; but his eyes were black with venomous hatred.

"He has suffered the penalty which the Koran lays down; he has lost his right hand. But the lord of all evil protects him, else ere this he had lost his life! Move no closer to that table!"

I started. Either Hassan of Aleppo was omniscient or he had overheard my whispered words!

"Easily I could slay you where you stand!" he continued. "But to do so would profit me nothing. This meeting has been revealed to me. Last night I witnessed it as I slept. Also it has been revealed to me by *Erroohânee*, in the mirror of ink, that the slipper of the Prophet, *Salla—'lláhu 'aleyhi wasellem!* Shall indeed return to that place accursed, that infidel eyes may look upon it! It is the will of Allah, whose name be exalted, that I hold my hand, but it is also His will that I be here, at whatever danger to my worthless body."

He turned his blazing eyes upon me. "To-morrow, ere noon," he said, "the slipper will again be in the Museum from which the man of evil stole it. So it is written; obscure are the ways. We met last night, you and I, but at that time much was dark to me that now is light. The holy 'Alee spoke to me in a vision, saying: 'There are two keys to the case in which it will be locked. Secure one, leaving the other with him who holds it! Let him swear to be secret. This shall be the price of his life!'"

The black tube was pointed directly at my forehead.

"Effendim," concluded the speaker, "place in my hand the key of the case in the Antiquarian Museum!"

Hands convulsively clenched, the girl was looking from me to Hassan. My throat felt parched, but I forced speech to my lips.

"Your omniscience fails you," I said. "Both keys are at my bank!"

Blacker grew the fierce eyes—and blacker; I gave myself up for lost; I awaited death—death by some awful, unique means—with what courage I could muster.

From the court below came the sound of voices, the voices of passers-by who so little suspected what was happening near to them that had someone told them they certainly had refused to credit it. The noise of busy Fleet Street came drumming under the archway, too.

Then, above all, another sound became audible. To this day I find myself unable to define it; but it resembled the note of a silver bell.

Clearly it was a signal; for, hearing it, Hassan dropped the tube and glanced toward the open window.

In that instant I sprang upon him!

That I had to deal with a fanatic, a dangerous madman, I knew; that it was his life or mine, I was fully convinced. I struck out then and caught him fairly over the heart. He reeled back, and I made a wild clutch for the damnable tube, horrid, unreasoning fear of which thus far had held me inert.

I heard the girl scream affrightedly, and I knew, and felt my heart chill to know, that the tube had been wrenched from my hand! Hassan of Aleppo, old man that he appeared, had the strength of a tiger. He recovered himself and hurled me from him so that I came to the floor crashingly half under my writing-table!

Something he cried back at me, furiously—and like an enraged animal, his teeth gleaming out from his beard, he darted from the room. The front door banged loudly.

Shaken and quivering, I got upon my feet. On the threshold, in a state of pitiable hesitancy, stood the pale, beautiful accomplice of Earl Dexter. One quick glance she flashed at me, then turned and ran!

Again the door slammed. I ran to the window, looking out into the court. The girl came hurrying down the steps, and with never a backward glance ran on and was lost to view in one of the passages opening riverward.

Out under the arch, statelily passed a tall figure—and Inspector Bristol was entering! I saw the detective glance aside as the two all but met. He stood still, and looked back!

"Bristol!" I cried, and waved my arms frantically.

"'Stop him! Stop him! *It's Hassan of Aleppo!*"

Bristol was not the only one to hear my wild cry—not the only one to dash back under the arch and out into Fleet Street.

But Hassan of Aleppo was gone!


CHAPTER XXII

THE LIGHT OF EL-MEDINEH

Bristol and I walked slowly in the direction of the entrance of the British Antiquarian Museum. It was the day following upon the sensational scene in my chambers.

"There's very little doubt," said Bristol, "that Earl Dexter has the slipper and that Hassan of Aleppo knows where Dexter is in hiding. I don't know which of the two is more elusive. Hassan apparently melted into thin air yesterday; and although The Stetson Man has never within my experience employed disguises, no one has set eyes upon him since the night that he vanished from his lodgings off the Waterloo Road. It's always possible for a man to baffle the police by remaining closely within doors, but during all the time that has elapsed Dexter must have taken a little exercise occasionally, and the missing hand should have betrayed him."

"The wonder to me is," I replied, "that he has escaped death at the hands of the *Hashishîn.* He is a supremely daring man, for I should think that he must be carrying the slipper of the Prophet about with him!"

"I would rather he did it than I!" commented Bristol. "For sheer audacity commend me to The Stetson Man! His idea no doubt was to use you as intermediary in his negotiations with the Museum authorities, but that plan failing, he has written them direct, thoughtfully omitting his address, of course!"

We were, in fact, at that moment bound for the Museum to inspect this latest piece of evidence.

"The crowning example of the man's audacity and cleverness," added my companion, "is his having actually approached Hassan of Aleppo with a similar proposition! How did he get in touch with him? All Scotland Yard has failed to find any trace of that weird character!"

"Birds of a feather—" I suggested.

"But they are not birds of a feather!" cried Bristol. "On your own showing, Hassan of Aleppo is simply waiting his opportunity to balance Dexter's account forever! I always knew Dexter was a clever man; I begin to think he's the most daring genius alive!"

We mounted the steps of the Museum.

In the hallway Mostyn, the curator, awaited us. Having greeted Bristol and myself he led the way to his private office, and from a pigeon-hole in his desk took out a letter typewritten upon a sheet of quarto paper.

Bristol spread it out upon the blotting pad and we bent over it curiously.

SIR—

I believe I can supply information concerning the whereabouts of the missing slipper of Mohammed. As any inquiry of this nature must be extremely perilous to the inquirer and as the relic is a priceless one, my fee would be £10,000. The fanatics who seek to restore the slipper to the East must not know of any negotiations, therefore I omit my address, but will communicate further if you care to insert instructions in the agony column of *Times*.

Faithfully,
EARL DEXTER.

Bristol laughed grimly.

"It's a daring game," he said; "a piece of barefaced impudence quite characteristic. He's posing as a sort of private detective now, and is prepared for a trifling consideration to return the slipper which he stole himself! He must know, though, that we have his severed hand at the Yard to be used in evidence against him."

"Is the Burton Room open to the public again?" I asked Mostyn.

"It is open, yes," he replied, "and a quite unusual number of visitors come daily to gaze at the empty case which once held the slipper of the Prophet."

"Has the case been mended?"

"Yes, it is quite intact again; only the exhibit is missing."

We ascended the stairs, passed along the Assyrian Room, which seemed to be unusually crowded, and entered the lofty apartment known as the Burton Room. The sun-blinds were drawn, and a sort of dim, religious light prevailed therein. A group of visitors stood around an empty case at the farther end of the apartment.

"You see," said Mostyn, pointing, "that empty case has a greater attraction than all the other full ones!"

But I scarcely heeded his words, for I was intently watching the movements of one of the group about the empty case. I have said that the room was but dimly illuminated, and this fact, together no doubt with some effect of reflected light, enhanced by my imagination, perhaps produced the phenomenon which was occasioning me so much amazement.

Remember that my mind was filled with memories of weird things, that I often found myself thinking of that mystic light which Hassan of Aleppo had called the light of El-Medineh—that light whereby, undeterred by distance, he claimed to be able to trace the whereabouts of any of the relics of the Prophet.

Bristol and Mostyn walked on then; but I stood just within the doorway, intently, breathlessly watching an old man wearing an out-of-date Inverness coat and a soft felt hat. He had a gray beard and moustache, and long, untidy hair, walked with a stoop, and in short was no unusual type of visitor to that institution.

But it seemed to me, and the closer I watched him the more convinced I became, that this was no optical illusion, that a faint luminosity, a sort of elfin light, played eerily about his head!

As Bristol and Mostyn approached the case the old man began to walk toward me and in the direction of the door. The idea flashed through my mind that it might be Hassan of Aleppo himself, Hassan who had predicted that the stolen slipper should that day be returned to the Museum!

Then he came abreast of me, passed me, and I felt that my surmise had been wrong. I saw Bristol, from farther up the room, turn and look back. Something attracted his trained eye, I suppose, which was not perceptible to me. But he suddenly came striding along. Obviously he was pursuing the old man, who was just about to leave the apartment. Seeing that the latter had reached the-doorway, Bristol began to run.

The old man turned; and amid a chorus of exclamations from the astonished spectators, Bristol sprang upon him!

How it all came about I cannot say, cannot hope to describe; but there was a short, sharp scuffle, the crack of a well-directed blow... and Bristol was rolling on his back, the old man, hatless, was racing up the Assyrian Room, and everyone in the place seemed to be shouting at once!

Bristol, with blood streaming from his face, staggered to his feet, clutching at me for support.

"After him, Mr. Cavanagh!" he cried hoarsely. "It's your turn to-day! After him! *That's Earl Dexter!*"

Mostyn waited for no more, but went running quickly through the Assyrian Room. I may mention here that at the head of the stairs he found the caped Inverness which had served to conceal Dexter's mutilated arm, and later, behind a piece of statuary, a wig and a very ingenious false beard and moustache were discovered. But of The Stetson Man there was no trace. His brief start had enabled him to make good his escape.

As Mostyn went off, and a group of visitors flocked in our direction, Bristol, who had been badly shaken by the blow, turned to them.

"You will please all leave the Burton Room immediately," he said.

Looks of surprise greeted his words; but with his handkerchief raised to his face, he peremptorily repeated them. The official note in his voice was readily to be detected; and the wonder-stricken group departed with many a backward glance.

As the last left the Burton Room, Bristol pointed, with a rather shaky finger, at the soft felt hat which lay at his feet. It had formed part of Dexter's disguise. Close beside it lay another object which had evidently fallen from the hat—a dull red thing lying on the polished parquet flooring.

"For God's sake don't go near it!" whispered Bristol. "The room must be closed for the present. And now I'm off after that man. Step clear of it."

His words were unnecessary; I shunned it as a leprous thing.

It was the slipper of the Prophet!


## CHAPTER XXIII
## THE THREE MESSAGES

I stood in the foyer of the Astoria Hotel. About me was the pulsing stir of transatlantic life, for the tourist season was now at its height, and I counted myself fortunate in that I had been able to secure a room at this establishment, always so popular with American visitors. Chatting groups surrounded me and I became acquainted with numberless projects for visiting the Tower of London, the National Gallery, the British Museum, Windsor Castle, Kew Gardens, and the other sights dear to the heart of our visiting cousins. Loaded lifts ascended and descended. Bradshaws were in great evidence everywhere; all was hustle and glad animation.

The tall military-looking man who stood beside me glanced about him with a rather grim smile.

"You ought to be safe enough here, Mr. Cavanagh!" he said.

"I ought to be safe enough in my own chambers," I replied wearily. "How many of these pleasure-seeking folk would believe that a man can be as greatly in peril of his life in Fleet Street as in the most uncivilized spot upon the world map? Do you think if I told that prosperous New Yorker who is buying a cigar yonder, for instance, that I had been driven from my chambers by a band of Eastern assassins founded some time in the eleventh century, he would believe it?"

"I am certain he wouldn't!" replied Bristol. "I should not have credited it myself before I was put in charge of this damnable case."

My position at that hour was in truth an incredible one. The sacred slipper of Mohammed lay once more in the glass case at the Antiquarian Museum from which Earl Dexter had stolen it. Now, with apish yellow faces haunting my dreams, with ghostly menaces dogging me day and night, I was outcast from my own rooms and compelled, in self-defence, to live amid the bustle of the Astoria. So wholly nonplussed were the police authorities that they could afford me no protection. They knew that a group of scientific murderers lay hidden in or near to London; they knew that Earl Dexter, the foremost crook of his day, was also in the metropolis—and they could make no move, were helpless; indeed, as Bristol had confessed, were hopeless!

Bristol, on the previous day, had unearthed the Greek cigar merchant, Acepulos, who had replaced the slipper in its case (for a monetary consideration). He had performed a similar service when the bloodstained thing had first been put upon exhibition at the Museum, and for a considerable period had disappeared. We had feared that his religious pretensions had not saved him from the avenging scimitar of Hassan; but quite recently he had returned again to his Soho shop, and in time thus to earn a second cheque.

As Bristol and I stood glancing about the foyer of the hotel, a plainclothes officer whom I knew by sight came in and approached my companion. I could not divine the fact, of course, but I was about to hear news of the money-loving and greatly daring Græco-Moslem.

The detective whispered something to Bristol, and the latter started, and paled. He turned to me.

"They haven't overlooked him this time, Mr. Cavanagh," he said. "Acepulos has been found dead in his room, nearly decapitated!"

I shuddered involuntarily. Even there, amid the chatter and laughter of those lighthearted tourists, the shadow of Hassan of Aleppo was falling upon me.

Bristol started immediately for Soho and I parted from him in the

Strand, he proceeding west and I eastward, for I had occasion that morning to call at my bank. It was the time of the year when London is full of foreigners, and as I proceeded in the direction of Fleet Street I encountered more than one Oriental. To my excited imagination they all seemed to glance at me furtively, with menacing eyes, but in any event I knew that I had little to fear whilst I contrived to keep to the crowded thoroughfares. Solitude I dreaded and with good reason.

Then at the door of the bank I found fresh matter for reflection. The assistant manager, Mr. Colby, was escorting a lady to the door. As I stood aside, he walked with her to a handsome car which waited, and handed her in with marks of great deference. She was heavily veiled and I had no more than a glimpse of her, but she appeared to be of middle age and had gray hair and a very stately manner.

I told myself that I was unduly suspicious, suspicious of everyone and of everything; yet as I entered the bank I found myself wondering where I had seen that dignified, gray-haired figure before. I even thought of asking the manager the name of his distinguished customer, but did not do so, for in the circumstances such an inquiry must have appeared impertinent.

My business transacted, I came out again by the side entrance which opens on the little courtyard, for this branch of the London County and Provincial Bank occupies a corner site.

A ragged urchin who was apparently waiting for me handed me a note. I looked at him inquiringly.

"For me?" I said.

"Yes, sir. A dark gentleman pointed you out as you was goin' into the bank."

The note was written upon a half sheet of paper and, doubting if it was really intended for me, I unfolded it and read the following—

> Mr. Cavanagh, take the keys of the case containing the holy slipper to your hotel this evening without fail.
>
> HASSAN.

"Who gave you this, boy?" I asked sharply.

"A foreign gentleman, sir, very dark—like an Indian."

"Where is he?"

"He went off in a cab, sir, after he give me the note."

I handed the boy sixpence and slowly pursued my way. An idea was forming in my mind to trap the enemy by seeming acquiescent. I wondered if my movements were being watched at that moment. Since it was more than probable, I returned to the bank, entered, and made some trivial inquiry of a cashier, and then came out again and walked on as far as the *Report* office.

I had not been in the office more than five minutes before I received a telegram from Inspector Bristol. It had been handed in at Soho, and the message was an odd one.

> CAVANAGH, *Report*, London.
> Plot afoot to steal keys. Get them from bank and join me
> 11 o'clock at Astoria. Have planned trap.
>                                                    BRISTOL.

This was very mysterious in view of the note so recently received by me, but I concluded that Bristol had hit upon a similar plan to that which was forming in my own mind. It seemed unnecessarily hazardous, though, actually to withdraw the keys from their place of safety.

Pondering deeply upon the perplexities of this maddening case, I shortly afterward found myself again at the bank. With the manager I descended to the strong-room, and the safe was unlocked which contained the much-sought-for keys of the case at the Antiquarian Museum.

"There are the keys, quite safe!—and by the way, this is my second visit here this morning, Mr. Cavanagh," said the manager, with whom I was upon rather intimate terms. "A foreign lady who has recently become a customer of the bank deposited some valuable jewels here this morning—less than an hour ago, in fact."

"Indeed," I said, and my mind was working rapidly. "The lady who came in the large blue car, a gray-haired lady?"

"Yes," was the reply, "did you notice her, then?"

I nodded and said no more, for in truth I had no more to say. I had good reason to respect the uncanny powers of Hassan of Aleppo, but I doubted if even his omniscience could tell him (since I had actually gone down into the strong-room) whether when I emerged I had the keys, or whether my visit and seeming acceptance of his orders had been no more than a subterfuge!

That the *Hashishîn* had some means of communicating with me at the Astoria was evident from the contents of the note which I had received, and as I walked in the direction of the hotel my mind was filled with all sorts of misgivings. I was playing with fire! Had I done rightly or should I have acted otherwise? I sighed wearily. The dark future would resolve all my doubts.

When I reached the Astoria, Bristol had not arrived. I lighted a cigarette and sat down in the lounge to await his coming. Presently a boy approached, handing me a message which had been taken down from the telephone by the clerk. It was as follows—

> Tell Mr. Cavanagh, who is waiting in the hotel, to take what I am expecting to his chambers, and say that I will join him there in twenty minutes.
>
> INSPECTOR BRISTOL.

Again I doubted the wisdom of Bristol's plan. Had I not fled to the Astoria to escape from the dangerous solitude of my rooms? That he was laying some trap for the *Hashishîn* was sufficiently evident, and whilst I could not justly suspect him of making a pawn of me I was quite unable to find any other explanation of this latest move.

I was torn between conflicting doubts. I glanced at my watch. Yes! There was just time for me to revisit the bank ere joining Bristol at my chambers! I hesitated. After all, in what possible way could it jeopardize his plans for me merely to *pretend* to bring the keys?

"Hang it all!" I said, and jumped to my feet. "These maddening conjectures will turn my brain! I'll let matters stand as they are, and risk the consequences!"

I hesitated no longer, but passed out from the hotel and once more directed my steps in the direction of Fleet Street.

As I passed in under the arch through which streamed many busy workers, I told myself that to dread entering my own chambers at high noon was utterly childish. Yet I *did* dread doing so! And as I mounted the stair and came to the landing, which was always more or less dark, I paused for quite a long time before putting the key in the lock.

The affair of the accursed slipper was playing havoc with my nerves, and I laughed dryly to note that my hand was not quite steady as I turned the key, opened my door, and slipped into the dim hallway.

As I closed it behind me, something, probably a slight noise, but possibly something more subtle—an instinct—made me turn rapidly.

There facing me stood Hassan of Aleppo.

## CHAPTER XXIV
## I KEEP THE APPOINTMENT

That moment was pungent with drama. In the intense hush of the next five seconds I could fancy that the world had slipped away from me and that I was become an unsubstantial thing of dreams. I was in no sense master of myself; the effect of the presence of this white-bearded fanatic was of a kind which I am entirely unable to describe. About Hassan of Aleppo was an aroma of evil, yet of majesty, which marked him strangely different from other men—from any other that I have ever known. In his venerable presence, remembering how he was Sheikh of the Assassins, and recalling his bloody history, I was always conscious of a weakness, physical and mental. He appalled me; and now, with my back to the door, I stood watching him and watching the ominous black tube which he held in his hand. It was a weapon unknown to Europe and therefore more fearful than the most up-to-date of death-dealing instruments.

Hassan of Aleppo pointed it toward me.

"The keys, effendim," he said; "hand me the keys!"

He advanced a step; his manner was imperious. The black tube was less than a foot removed from my face. That I had my revolver in my pocket could avail me nothing, for in my pocket it must remain, since I dared to make no move to reach it under cover of that unfamiliar, terrible weapon.

The black eyes of Hassan glared insanely into mine.

"You will have placed them in your pocket-case," he said. "Take it out; hand it to me!"

I obeyed, for what else could I do? Taking the case from my pocket, I placed it in his lean brown hand.

An expression of wild exultation crossed his features; the eagle eyes seemed to be burning into my brain. A puff of hot vapour struck me in the face—something which was expelled from the mysterious black tube. And with memories crowding to my mind of similar experiences at the hands of the *Hashishîn*, I fell back, clutching at my throat, fighting for my life against the deadly, vaporous thing that like a palpable cloud surrounded me. I tried to cry out, but the words died upon my tongue. Hassan of Aleppo seemed to grow huge before my eyes like some *ginn* of Eastern lore. Then a curtain of darkness descended. I experienced a violent blow upon the forehead (I suppose I had pitched forward), and for the time resigned my part in the drama of the sacred clipper.

## CHAPTER XXV
## THE WATCHER IN BANK CHAMBERS

At about five o'clock that afternoon Inspector Bristol, who had spent several hours in Soho upon the scene of the murder of the Greek, was walking along Fleet Street, bound for the offices of the *Report*. As he passed the court, on the corner of which stands a branch of the London County and Provincial Bank, his eye was attracted by a curious phenomenon.

There are reflectors above the bank windows which face the court, and it appeared to Bristol that there was a hole in one of these, the furthermost from the corner. A tiny beam of light shone from the bank window on to the reflector, or from the reflector on to the window, which circumstance in itself was not curious. But *above* the reflector, at an acute angle, this mysterious beam was seemingly projected upward. Walking a little way up the court he saw that it shone through, and cast a disc of light upon the ceiling of an office on the first floor of Bank Chambers above.

It is every detective's business to be observant, and although many thousands of passersby must have cast their eyes in the same direction that day, there is small matter for wonder in the fact that Bristol alone took the trouble to inquire into the mystery—for his trained eye told him that there was a mystery here.

Possibly he was in that passive frame of mind when the brain is particularly receptive of trivial impressions; for after a futile search of the Soho cigar store for anything resembling a clue, he was quite resigned to the idea of failure in the case of Hassan and Company. He walked down the court and into the entrance of Bank Chambers. An inspection of the board upon the wall showed him that the first floor apparently was occupied by three firms, two of them legal, for this is the neighbourhood of the law courts, and the third a press agency. He stepped up to the first floor. Past the doors bearing the names of the solicitors and past that belonging to the press agent he proceeded to a fourth suite of offices. Here, pinned upon the door frame, appeared a card which bore the legend—

### THE CONGO FIBRE COMPANY

Evidently the Congo Fibre Company had so recently taken possession of the offices that there had been no time to inscribe their title either upon the doors or upon the board in the hall.

Inspector Bristol was much impressed, for into one of the rooms occupied by the Fibre Company shone that curious disc of light which first had drawn his attention to Bank Chambers. He rapped on the door, turned the handle, and entered. The sole furniture of the office in which he found himself apparently consisted of one desk and an office stool, which stool was occupied by an office boy. The windows opened on the court, and a door marked "Private" evidently communicated with an inner office whose windows likewise must open on the court. It was the ceiling of this inner office, unless the detective's calculation erred, which he was anxious to inspect.

"Yes, sir?" said the boy tentatively.

Bristol produced a card which bore the uncompromising legend: John Henry Smith.

"Take my card to Mr. Boulter, boy," he said tersely. The boy stared.

"Mr. Boulter, sir? There isn't any one of that name here."

"Oh!" said Bristol, looking around him in apparent surprise: "how long is he gone?"

"I don't know, sir. I've only been here three weeks, and Mr. Knowlson only took the offices a month ago."

"Oh," commented Bristol, "then take my card to Mr. Knowlson; he will probably be able to give me Mr. Boulter's present address."

The boy hesitated. The detective had that authoritative manner which awes the youthful mind.

"He's out, sir," he said, but without conviction.

"Is he?" rapped Bristol. "Well, I'll leave my card."

He turned and quitted the office, carefully closing the door behind him. Three seconds later he reopened it, and peering in, was in time to see the boy knock upon the private door. A little wicket, or movable panel, was let down, the card of John Henry Smith was passed through to someone unseen, and the wicket was reclosed!

The boy turned and met the wrathful eye of the detective. Bristol reentered, closing the door behind him.

"See here, young fellow," said he, "I don't stand for those tricks! Why didn't you tell me Mr. Knowlson was in?"

"I'm very sorry, sir!"—the boy quailed beneath his glance—"but he won't see any one who hasn't an appointment."

"Is there someone with him, then?"

"No."

"Well, what's he doing?"

"I don't know, sir; I've never been in to see!"

"What! never been in that room?"

"Never!" declared the boy solemnly. "And I don't mind telling you," he added, recovering something of his natural confidence, "that I am leaving on the 31st. This job ain't any use to me!"

"Too much work?" suggested Bristol.

"No work at all!" returned the boy indignantly. "I'm just here for a blessed buffer, that's what I'm here for, a buffer!"

"What do you mean?"

"I just have to sit here and see that nobody gets into that office. Lively, ain't it? Where's the prospects?"

Bristol surveyed him thoughtfully. "Look here, my lad," he said quietly; "is that door locked?"

"Always," replied the boy.

"Does Mr. Knowlson come to that shutter when you knock?"

"Yes."

"Then go and knock!"

The boy obeyed with alacrity. He rapped loudly on the door, not noticing or not caring that the visitor was standing directly behind him. The shutter was lowered and a grizzled, bearded face showed for a moment through the opening.

Bristol leant over the boy and pushed a card through into the hand of the man beyond. On this occasion it did not bear the legend "John Henry Smith," but the following—

CHIEF INSPECTOR BRISTOL
C.I.D.
NEW SCOTLAND YARD

"Good afternoon, Mr. Knowlson," said the detective dryly. "I want to come in!"

There followed a moment of silence, from which Bristol divined that he had blundered upon some mystery, possibly upon a big case; then a key was turned in the lock and the door thrown open.

"Come right in, Inspector," invited a strident voice. "Carter, you can go home."

Bristol entered warily, but not warily enough. For as the door was banged upon his entrance he faced around only in time to find himself looking down the barrel of a Colt automatic.

With his back to the door which contained the wicket, now reclosed, stood the man with the bearded face. The revolver was held in his *left* hand; his right arm terminated in a bandaged stump. But without that his steel-gray eyes would have betrayed him to the detective.

"Good God!" whispered Bristol. "It's Earl Dexter!"

"It is!" replied the cracksman, "and you've looked in at a real inconvenient time! My visitors mostly seem to have that knack. I'll have to ask you to stay, Inspector. Sit down in that chair yonder."

Bristol knew his man too well to think of opening any argument at that time. He sat down as directed, and ignoring the revolver which covered him all the time, began coolly to survey the room in which he found himself. In several respects it was an extraordinary apartment.

The only bright patch in the room was the shining disc upon the ceiling; and the detective noted with interest that this marked the position of an arrangement of mirrors. A white-covered table, entirely bare, stood upon the floor immediately beneath this mysterious apparatus. With the exception of one or two ordinary items of furniture and a small hand lathe, the office otherwise was unfurnished. Bristol turned his eyes again upon the daring man who so audaciously had trapped him—the man who had stolen the slipper of the Prophet and suffered the loss of his hand by the scimitar of an *Hashishîn* as a result. When he had least expected to find one, Fate had thrown a clue in Bristol's way. He reflected grimly that it was like to prove of little use to him.

"Now," said Dexter, "you can do as you please, of course, but you know me pretty well and I advise you to sit quiet."

"I am sitting quiet!" was the reply.

"I am sorry," continued Dexter, with a quick glance at his maimed arm, "that I can't tie you up, but I am expecting a friend any moment now."

He suddenly raised the wicket with a twitch of his elbow and, without removing his gaze from the watchful detective, cried sharply—

"Carter!"

But there was no reply.

"Good; he's gone!"

Dexter sat down facing Bristol.

"I have lost my hand in this game, Mr. Bristol," he said genially, "and had some narrow squeaks of losing my head; but having gone so far and lost so much I'm going through, if I don't meet a funeral! You see I'm up against two tough propositions."

Bristol nodded sympathetically.

"The first," continued Dexter, "is you and Cavanagh, and English law generally. My idea—if I can get hold of the slipper again—oh! you needn't stare; I'm out for it—is to get the Antiquarian Institution to ransom it. It's a line of commercial speculation I have worked successfully before. There's a dozen rich highbrows, cranks to a man, connected with it, and they are my likeliest buyers—sure. But to keep the tone of the market healthy there's Hassan of Aleppo, rot him! He's a dangerous customer to approach, but you'll note I've been in negotiation with him already and am still, if not booming, not much below par!"

"Quite so," said Bristol. "But you've cut off a pretty hefty chew nevertheless. They used to call you The Stetson Man, you used to dress like a fashion plate and stop at the big hotels. Those days are past, Dexter, I'm sorry to note. You're down to the skulking game now and you're nearer an advert for Clarkson than Stein-Bloch!"

"Yep," said Dexter sadly, "I plead guilty, but I think here's Carnéta!"

Bristol heard the door of the outer office open, and a moment later that upon which his gaze was set opened in turn, to admit a girl who was heavily veiled, and who started and stood still in the doorway, on perceiving the situation. Never for one unguarded moment did the American glance aside from his prisoner.

"The Inspector's dropped in, Carnéta!" he drawled in his strident way. "You're handy with a ball of twine; see if you can induce him to stay the night!"

The girl, immediately recovering her composure, took off her hat in a businesslike way and began to look around her, evidently in search of a suitable length of rope with which to fasten up Bristol.

"Might I suggest," said the detective, "that if you are shortly quitting these offices a couple of the window-cords neatly joined would serve admirably?"

"Thanks," drawled Dexter, nodding to his companion, who went into the outer office, where she might be heard lowering the windows. She was gone but a few moments ere she returned again, carrying a length of knotted rope. Under cover of Dexter's revolver, Bristol stoically submitted to having his wrists tied behind him. The end of the line was then thrown through the ventilator above the door which communicated with the outer office and Bristol was triced up in such a way that, his wrists being raised behind him to an uncomfortable degree, he was almost forced to stand upon tiptoe. The line was then secured.

"Very workmanlike!" commented the victim. "You'll find a large handkerchief in my inside breast pocket. It's a clean one, and I can recommend it as a gag!"

Very promptly it was employed for the purpose, and Inspector Bristol found himself helpless and constrained in a very painful position. Dexter laid down his revolver.

"We will now give you a free show, Inspector," he said, genially, "of our camera obscura!"

He pulled down the blinds, which Bristol noted with interest to be black, but through an opening in one of them a mysterious ray of light—the same that he had noticed from Fleet Stret—shone upon that point in the ceiling where the arrangement of mirrors was attached. Dexter made some alteration, apparently in the focus of the lens (for Bristol had divined that in some way a lens had been fixed in the reflector above the bank window below) and the disc of light became concentrated. The white-covered table was moved slightly, and in the darkness some further manipulation was performed.

"Observe," came the strident voice—"we now have upon the screen here a minute moving picture. This little device, which is not protected in any way, is of my own invention, and proved extremely useful in the Arkwright jewel case, which startled Chicago. It has proved useful now. I know almost as much concerning the arrangements below as the manager himself. In confidence, Inspector, this is my last bid for the slipper! I have plunged on it. Madame Sforza, the distinguished Italian lady who recently opened an account below, opened it for £500 cash. She has drawn a portion, but a balance remains which I am resigned to lose. Her motor-car (hired), her references (forged), the case of jewels which she deposited this morning (duds!)—all represent a considerable outlay. It's a nerve-racking line of operation, too. Any hour of the day may bring such a visitor as yourself, for example. In short, I am at the end of my tether."

Bristol, ignoring the increasing pain in his arms and wrists, turned his eyes upon the white-covered table and there saw a minute and clear-cut picture, such as one sees in a focussing screen, of the interior of the manager's office of the London County and Provincial Bank!


## CHAPTER XXVI
## THE STRONG-ROOM


I wonder how often a sense of humour has saved a man from desperation? Perhaps only the Easterns have thoroughly appreciated that divine gift. I have interpolated the adventure of Inspector Bristol in order that the sequence of my story be not broken; actually I did not learn it until later, but when, on the following day, the whole of the facts came into my possession, I laughed and was glad that I could laugh, for laughter has saved many a man from madness.

Certainly the Fates were playing with us, for at a time very nearly corresponding with that when Bristol found himself bound and helpless in

Bank Chambers I awoke to find myself tied hand and foot to my own bed!

Nothing but the haziest recollections came to me at first, nothing but dim memories of the awful being who had lured me there; for I perceived now that all the messages proceeded, not from Bristol, but from Hassan of Aleppo! I had been a fool, and I was reaping the fruits of my folly. Could I have known that almost within pistol shot of me the Inspector was trussed up as helpless as I, then indeed my situation must have become unbearable, since upon him I relied for my speedy release.

My ankles were firmly lashed to the rails at the foot of my bed; each of my wrists was tied back to a bedpost. I ached in every limb and my head burned feverishly, which latter symptom I ascribed to the powerful drug which had been expelled into my face by the uncanny weapon carried by Hassan of Aleppo. I reflected bitterly how, having transferred my quarters to the Astoria, I could not well hope for any visitor to my chambers; and even the event of such a visitor had been foreseen and provided against by the cunning lord of the *Hashishîn*. A gag, of the type which Dumas has described in "Twenty Years After," the *poire d'angoisse*, was wedged firmly into my mouth so that only by preserving the utmost composure could I breathe. I was bathed in cold perspiration. So I lay listening to the familiar sounds without and reflecting that it was quite possible so to lie, undisturbed, and to die alone, my presence there wholly unsuspected!

Once, toward dusk, my 'phone bell rang, and my state of mind became agonizing. It was maddening to think that someone, a friend, was virtually within reach of me, yet actually as far removed as if an ocean divided us! I tasted the hellish torments of Tantalus. I cursed fate, heaven, everything; I prayed; I sank into bottomless depths of despair and rose to dizzy pinnacles of hope, when a footstep sounded on the landing and a thousand wild possibilities, vague possibilities of rescue, poured into my mind.

The visitor hesitated, apparently outside my door; and a change, as sudden as lightning out of a cloud, transformed my errant fancies. A gruesome conviction seized me, as irrational as the hope which it displayed, that this was one of the *Hashishîn*—an apish yellow dwarf, a strangler, the awful Hassan himself!

The footsteps receded down the stairs. And my thoughts reverted into the old channels of dull despair.

I weighed the chances of Bristol's seeking me there; and, eager as I was to give them substance, found them but airy—ultimately was forced to admit them to be *nil*.

So I lay, whilst only a few hundred yards from me a singular scene was being enacted. Bristol, a prisoner as helpless as myself, watched the concluding business of the day being conducted in the bank beneath him; he watched the lift descend to the strong-room—the spying apparatus being slightly adjusted in some way; he saw the clerks hastening to finish their work in the outer office, and as he watched, absorbed by the novelty of the situation, he almost forgot the pain and discomfort which he suffered.

"This little peep-show of ours has been real useful," Dexter confided out of the darkness. "I got an impression of the key of the strong-room door a week ago, and Carnéta got one of the keys of the safe only this morning, when she lodged her box of jewellery with the bank! I was at work on that key when you interrupted me, and as by means of this useful apparatus I have learnt the combination, you ought to see some fun in the next few hours!"

Bristol repressed a groan, for the prospect of remaining in that position was thus brought keenly home to him.

The bank staff left the premises one by one until only a solitary clerk worked on at a back desk. His task completed, he, too, took his departure and the bank messenger commenced his nightly duty of sweeping up the offices. It was then that excitement like an anæsthetic dulled the detective's pain—indeed, he forgot his aching body and became merely a watchful intelligence.

So intent had he become upon the picture before him that he had not noticed the fact that he was alone in the office of the Congo Fibre Company. Now he realized it from the absolute silence about him, and from another circumstance.

The spying apparatus had been left focussed, and on to the screen beneath his eyes, bending low behind the desks and creeping, Indian-like, around toward the head of the stair which communicated with the strong-room and the apartment used by the messenger, came the alert figure of Earl Dexter!

It may be a surprise to some people to learn that at any time in the day the door of a bank, unguarded, should be left open, when only a solitary messenger is within the premises; yet for a few minutes at least each evening this happens at more than one City bank, where one of the duties of the resident messenger is to clean the outer steps. Dexter had taken advantage of the man's absence below in quest of scrubbing material to enter the bank through the open door.

Watching, breathless, and utterly forgetful of his own position, Bristol saw the messenger, all unconscious of danger, come up the stairs carrying a pail and broom. As his head reached the level of the railings The Stetson Man neatly sand-bagged him, rushed across to the outer door, and closed it!

Given duplicate keys and the private information which Dexter so ingeniously had obtained, there are many London banks vulnerable to similar attack. Certainly, bullion is rarely kept in a branch storeroom, but the detective was well aware that the keys of the case containing the slipper were kept in this particular safe!

He was convinced, and could entertain no shadowy doubt, that at last Dexter had triumphed. He wondered if it had ever hitherto fallen to the lot of a representative of the law thus to be made an accessory to a daring felony!

But human endurance has well-defined limits. The fading light rendered the ingenious picture dim and more dim. The pain occasioned by his position became agonizing, and uttering a stifled groan he ceased to take an interest in the robbery of the London County and Provincial Bank.

Fate is a comedian; and when later I learned how I had lain strapped to my bed, and, so near to me, Bristol had hung helpless as a butchered carcass in the office of the Congo Fibre Company, whilst, in our absence from the stage, the drama of the slipper marched feverish to its final curtain, I accorded Fate her well-earned applause. I laughed; not altogether mirthfully.


## CHAPTER XXVII
## THE SLIPPER


Someone was breaking in at the door of my chambers!

I aroused myself from a state of coma almost death-like and listened to the blows. The sun was streaming in at my windows.

A splintering crash told of a panel broken. Then a moment later I heard the grating of the lock, and a rush of footsteps along the passage.

"Try the study!" came a voice that sounded like Bristol's, save that it was strangely weak and shaky.

Almost simultaneously the Inspector himself threw open the bedroom door—and, very pale and haggard-eyed, stood there looking across at me. It was a scene unforgettable.

"Mr. Cavanagh!" he said huskily—"Mr. Cavanagh! Thank God you're alive! But"—he turned—"this way, Marden!" he cried. "Untie him quickly! I've got no strength in my arms!"

Marden, a C.I.D. man, came running, and in a minute, or less, I was sitting up gulping brandy.

"I've had the most awful experience of my life," said Bristol. "You've fared badly enough, but I've been hanging by my wrists—you know Dexter's trick!—for close upon sixteen hours! I wasn't released until Carter, an office boy, came on the scene this morning!"

Very feebly I nodded; I could not talk.

"The strong-room of your bank was rifled under my very eyes last evening!" he continued, with something of his old vigour; "and five minutes after the Antiquarian Museum was opened to the public this morning quite an unusual number of visitors appeared.

"I saw the bank manager the moment he arrived, and learned a piece of news that positively took my breath away! I was at the Museum seven minutes later and got another shock! There in the case was the red slipper!"

"Then," I whispered—"it hadn't been stolen?"

"Wrong! It *had!* This was a duplicate, as Mostyn, the curator, saw at a glance! Some of the early visitors—they were Easterns—had quite surrounded the case. They were watched, of course, but any number of Orientals come to see the thing; and, short of smashing the glass, which would immediately attract attention, the authorities were unprepared, of course, for any attempt. Anyway, they were tricked. Somebody opened the case. The real slipper of the Prophet is gone!"

"They told you at the bank—"

"*That you had withdrawn the keys!* If Dexter had known that!"

"Hassan of Aleppo took them from me last night! At last the *Hashishîn* have triumphed!"

Bristol sank into the armchair.

"Every port is watched," he said. "But—"


## CHAPTER XXVIII
### CARNÉTA

"I am entirely at your mercy; you can do as you please with me. But before you do anything I should like you to listen to what I have to say."

Her beautiful face was pale and troubled. Violet eyes looked sadly into mine.

"For nearly an hour I have been waiting for this chance—until I knew you were alone," she continued. "If you are thinking of giving me up to the police, at least remember that I came here of my own free will. Of course, I know you are quite entitled to take advantage of that; but please let me say what I came to say!"

She pleaded so hard, with that musical voice, with her evident helplessness, most of all with her wonderful eyes, that I quite abandoned any project I might have entertained to secure her arrest. I think she divined this masculine weakness, for she said, with greater confidence—

"Your friend, Professor Deeping, was murdered by the man called Hassan of Aleppo. Are you content to remain idle while his murderer escapes?"

God knows I was not. My idleness in the matter was none of my choosing. Since poor Deeping's murder I had come to handgrips with the assassins more than once, but Hassan had proved too clever for me, too clever for Scotland Yard. The sacred slipper was once more in the hands of its fanatic guardian.

One man there was who might have helped the search, Earl Dexter. But Earl Dexter was himself wanted by Scotland Yard!

From the time of the bank affair up to the moment when this beautiful visitor had come to my chambers I had thought Dexter, as well as Hassan, to have fled secretly from England. But the moment that I saw Carnéta at my door I divined that The Stetson Man must still be in London.

She sat watching me and awaiting my answer.

"I cannot avenge my friend unless I can find his murderer."

Eagerly she bent forward.

"But if *I* can find him?"

That made me think, and I hesitated before speaking again,

"Say what you came to say," I replied slowly. "You must know that I distrust you. Indeed, my plain duty is to detain you. But I will listen to anything you may care to tell me, particularly if it enables me to trap Hassan of Aleppo."

"Very well," she said, and rested her elbows upon the table before her. "I have come to you in desperation. I can help you to find the man who murdered Professor Deeping, but in return I want you to help me!"

I watched her closely. She was very plainly, almost poorly, dressed. Her face was pale and there were dark marks around her eyes. This but served to render their strange beauty more startling; yet I could see that my visitor was in real trouble. The situation was an odd one.

"You are possibly about to ask me," I suggested, "to assist Earl Dexter to escape the police?"

She shook her head. Her voice trembled as she replied

"That would not have induced me to run the risk of coming here. I came because I wanted to find a man who was brave enough to help me.

We have no friends in London, and so it became a question of terms. I can repay you by helping you to trace Hassan."

"What is it, then, that Dexter asks me to do?"

"*He* asks nothing. I, Carnéta, am asking!"

"Then you are not come from him?"

At my question, all her self-possession left her. She abruptly dropped her face into her hands and was shaken with sobs! It was more than I could bear, unmoved. I forgot the shady past, forgot that she was the associate of a daring felon, and could only realize that she was a weeping woman, who had appealed to my pity and who asked my aid.

I stood up and stared out of the window, for I experienced a not unnatural embarrassment. Without looking at her I said—

"Don't be afraid to tell me your troubles. I don't say I should go out of my way to be kind to Mr. Dexter, but I have no wish whatever to be instrumental in"—I hesitated—"in making *you* responsible for his misdeeds. If you can tell me where to find Hassan of Aleppo, I won't even ask you where Dexter is—"

"God help me! I don't know where he is!"

There was real, poignant anguish in her cry. I turned and confronted her. Her lashes were all wet with tears.

"What! has he disappeared?"

She nodded, fought with her emotion—a moment, and went on unsteadily.

"I want you to help me to find him for in finding him we shall find Hassan!"

"How so?"

Her gaze avoided me now.

"Mr. Cavanagh, he has staked everything upon securing the slipper— and the *Hashishîn* were too clever for him. His hand—those Eastern fiends cut off his hand! But he would not give in. He made another bid— and lost again. It left him almost penniless."

She spoke of Earl Dexter's felonious plans as another woman might have spoken of her husband's unwise investments! It was fantastic hearing that confession of The Stetson Man's beautiful partner, and I counted the interview one of the strangest I had ever known.

A sudden idea came to me. "When did Dexter first conceive the plan to steal the slipper?" I asked.

"In Egypt!" answered Carnéta. "Yes! You may as well know! He is thoroughly familiar with the East, and he learned of the robbery of Professor Deeping almost as soon as it became known to Hassan. I know what you are going to ask—"

"Ahmad Ahmadeen!"

"Yes! He travelled home as Ahmadeen—the only time he ever used a disguise. Oh! the thing is accursed!" she cried. "I begged him, implored him, to abandon his attempts upon it. Day and night we were watched by those ghastly yellow men! But it was all in vain. He knew, had known for a long time, where Hassan of Aleppo was in hiding!"

And I reflected that the best men at New Scotland Yard had failed to pick up the slightest clue!

"The *Hashishîn*, of whom that dreadful man is leader, are rich, or have supporters who are rich. The plan was to make them pay for the slipper."

"My God! it was playing with fire!"

She sat silent awhile. Emotion threatened to get the upper hand. Then—

"Two days ago," she almost whispered, "he set out—to... get the slipper!"

"To steal it?"

"To steal it!"

"From Hassan of Aleppo?"

I could scarcely believe that any man, single-handed, could have had the hardihood to attempt such a thing.

"From Hassan, yes!"

I faced her, amazed, incredulous.

"Dexter had suffered mutilation, he knew that the *Hashishîn* sought his life for his previous attempts upon the relic of the Prophet, and yet he dared to venture again into the very lions' den?"

"He did, Mr. Cavanagh, two days ago. And—"

"Yes?" I urged, as gently as I could, for she was shaking pitifully.

"He never came back!"

The words were spoken almost in a whisper. She clenched her hands and leapt from the chair, fighting down her grief and with such a stark horror in her beautiful eyes that from my very soul I longed to be able to help her.

"Mr. Cavanagh," (she had courage, this bewildering accomplice of a cracksman) "I know the house he went to! I cannot hope to make you understand what I have suffered—since then. A thousand times I have been on the point of going to the police, confessing all I knew, and leading them to that house! O God! if only he is alive, this shall be his last crooked deal—and mine! I dared not go to the police, for his sake! I waited, and watched, and hoped, through two such nights and days... then I ventured. I should have gone mad if I had not come here. I knew you had good cause to hate, to detest me, but I remembered that you had a great grievance against Hassan. Not as great, O heaven! not as great as mine, but yet a great one. I remembered, too, that you were the kind of man—a woman can come to...."

She sank back into the chair, and with her fingers twining and untwining, sat looking dully before her.

"In brief," I said, "what do you propose?"

"I propose that we endeavour to obtain admittance to the house of Hassan of Aleppo—secretly, of course, and all I ask of you in return for revealing the secret of its situation—"

"That I let Dexter go free?"

Almost inaudibly she whispered: "If he lives!"

Surely no stranger proposition ever had been submitted to a law-abiding citizen. I was asked to connive in the escape of a notorious criminal, and at one and the same time to embark upon an expedition patently burglarious! As though this were not enough, I was invited to beard Hassan of Aleppo, the most dreadful being I had ever encountered, East or West, in his mysterious stronghold!

I wondered what my friend, Inspector Bristol, would have thought of the project; I wondered if I should ever live to see Hassan meet his just deserts as a result of this enterprise, which I was forced to admit a foolhardy one. But a man who has selected the career of a war correspondent from amongst those which Fleet Street offers, is the victim of a certain craving for fresh experiences; I suppose, has in his character something of an adventurous turn.

For a while I stood staring from the window, then faced about and looked into the violet eyes of my visitor.

"I agree, Carnéta!" I said.


## CHAPTER XXIX
## WE MEET MR. ISAACS

Quitting the wayside station, and walking down a short lane, we came out upon Watling Street, white and dusty beneath the afternoon sun. We were less than an hour's train journey from London but found ourselves amid the Kentish hop gardens, amid a rural peace unbroken. My companion carried a camera case slung across her shoulder, but its contents were less innocent than one might have supposed. In fact, it contained a neat set of those instruments of the burglar's art with whose use she appeared to be quite familiar.

"There is an inn," she said, "about a mile ahead, where we can obtain some vital information. *He* last wrote to me from there."

Side by side we tramped along the dusty road. We both were silent, occupied with our own thoughts. Respecting the nature of my companion's I could entertain little doubt, and my own turned upon the foolhardly nature of the undertaking upon which I was embarked. No other word passed between us then, until upon rounding a bend and passing a cluster of picturesque cottages, the yard of the Vinepole came into view.

"Do they know you by sight here?" I asked abruptly.

"No, of course not; we never made strategic mistakes of that kind. If we have tea here, no doubt we can learn all we require."

I entered the little parlour of the inn, and suggested that tea should be served in the pretty garden which opened out of it upon the right.

The host, who himself laid the table, viewed the camera case critically.

"We get a lot of photographers down here," he remarked tentatively.

"No doubt," said my companion. "There is some very pretty scenery in the neighbourhood."

The landlord rested his hands upon the table.

"There was a gentleman here on Wednesday last," he said; "an old gentleman who had met with an accident, and was staying somewhere hereabouts for his health. But he'd got his camera with him, and it was wonderful the way he could use it, considering he hadn't got the use of his right hand."

"He must have been a very keen photographer," I said, glancing at the girl beside me.

"He took three or four pictures of the Vinepole," replied the landlord (which I doubted, since probably his camera was a dummy); "and he wanted to know if there were any other old houses in the neighbourhood. I told him he ought to take Cadham Hall, and he said he had heard that the Gate House, which is about a mile from here, was one of the oldest buildings about."

A girl appeared with a tea tray, and for a moment I almost feared that the landlord was about to retire; but he lingered, whilst the girl distributed the things about the table, and Carnéta asked casually, "Would there be time for me to photograph the Gate House before dark?"

"There might be time," was the reply, "but that's not the difficulty. Mr. Isaacs is the difficulty."

"Who is Mr. Isaacs?" I asked.

"He's the Jewish gentleman who bought the Gate House recently. Lots of money he's got and a big motor car. He's up and down to London almost every day in the week, but he won't let anybody take photographs of the house. I know several who've asked."

"But I thought," said Carnéta, innocently, "you said the old gentleman who was here on Wednesday went to take some?"

"He went, yes, miss; but I don't know if he succeeded."

Carnéta poured out some tea.

"Now that you speak of it," she said, "I too have heard that the Gate House is very picturesque. What objection can Mr. Isaacs have to photographers?"

"Well, you see, miss, to get a picture of the house, you have to pass right through the grounds."

"I should walk right up to the house and ask permission. Is Mr. Isaacs at home, I wonder?"

"I couldn't say. He hasn't passed this way to-day."

"We might meet him on the way," said I. "What is he like?"

"A Jewish gentleman sir, very dark, with a white beard. Wears gold glasses. Keeps himself very much to himself. I don't know anything about his household; none of them ever come here."

Carnéta inquired the direction of Cadham Hall and of the Gate House, and the landlord left us to ourselves. My companion exhibited signs of growing agitation, and it seemed to me that she had much ado to restrain herself from setting out without a moment's delay for the Gate House, which, I readily perceived, was the place to which our strange venture was leading us.

I found something very stimulating in the reflection that, rash though the expedition might be, and, viewed from whatever standpoint, undeniably perilous, it promised to bring me to that secret stronghold of deviltry where the sinister Hassan of Aleppo so successfully had concealed himself.

The work of the modern journalist had many points of contact with that of the detective; and since the murder of Professor Deeping I had succumbed to the man-hunting fever more than once. I knew that Scotland Yard had failed to locate the hiding-place of the remarkable and evil man who, like an *efreet* of Oriental lore, obeyed the talisman of the stolen slipper, striking down whomsoever laid hand upon its sacredness. It was a novel sensation to know that, aided by this beautiful accomplice of a rogue, I had succeeded where the experts had failed!

Misgivings I had and shall not deny. If our scheme succeeded it would mean that Deeping's murderer should be brought to justice. If it failed— well, frankly, upon that possibility I did not dare to reflect!

It must be needless for me to say that we two strangely met allies were ill at ease, sometimes to the point of embarrassment. We proceeded on our way in almost unbroken silence, and, save for a couple of farm hands, without meeting any wayfarer, up to the time that we reached the brow of the hill and had our first sight of the Gate House lying in a little valley beneath. It was a small Tudor mansion, very compact in plan and its roof glowed redly in the rays of the now setting sun.

From the directions given by the host of the Vinepole it was impossible to mistake the way or to mistake the house. Amid well-wooded grounds it stood, a place quite isolated, but so typically English that, as I stood looking down upon it, I found myself unable to believe that any other than a substantial country gentleman could be its proprietor.

I glanced at Carnéta. Her violet eyes were burning feverishly, but her lips twitched in a bravely pitiful way.

Clearly now my adventure lay before me; that red-roofed homestead seemed to have rendered it all substantial which hitherto had been shadowy; and I stood there studying the Gate House gravely, for it might yet swallow me up, as apparently it had swallowed Earl Dexter.

There, amid that peaceful Kentish landscape, fantasy danced and horrors unknown lurked in waiting.

The eminence upon which we were commanded an extensive prospect, and eastward showed a tower and flagstaff which marked the site of Cadham Hall. There were homeward-bound labourers to be seen in the lanes now, and where like a white ribbon the Watling Street lay across the verdant carpet moved an insect shape, speedily.

It was a car, and I watched it with vague interest. At a point where a dense coppice spread down to the roadway and a lane crossed west to east, the car became invisible. Then I saw it again, nearer to us and nearer to the Gate House. Finally it disappeared among the trees.

I turned to Carnéta. She, too, had been watching. Now her gaze met mine.

"Mr. Isaacs!" she said; and her voice was less musical than usual. "His chauffeur, who learned his business in Cairo, is probably the only one of his servants who remains in England."

"What!" I began—and said no more.

Where the road upon which we stood wound down into the valley and lost itself amid the trees surrounding the Gate House, the car suddenly appeared again, and began to mount the slope toward us!

"Heavens!" whispered Carnéta. "He may have seen us—with glasses! Quick! Let us walk back until the hill-top conceals us; then we must hide somewhere!"

I shared her excitement. Without a moment's hesitation we both turned and retraced our steps. Twenty paces brought us to a spot where a stack of mangel wurzels stood at the roadside.

"This will do!" I said.

We ran around into the field, and crouched where we could peer out on the road without ourselves being seen. Nor had we taken up this position a moment too soon.

Topping the slope came a light-weight electric, driven by a man who, in his spruce uniform, might have passed at a glance for a very dusky European. The car had a limousine back, and as the chauffeur slowed down, out from the open windows right and left peered the solitary occupant.

He had the cast of countenance which is associated with the best type of Jew, with clear-cut aquiline features wholly destitute of grossness. His white beard was patriarchal and he wore gold-rimmed pince-nez and a glossy silk hat. Such figures may often be met with in the great money-markets of the world, and Mr. Isaacs would have passed for a successful financier in even more discerning communities than that of Cadham.

But I scarcely breathed until the car was past; and, beside me, my companion, crouching to the ground, was trembling wildly. Fifty yards toward the village Mr. Isaacs evidently directed the man to return.

The car was put about, and flashed past us at high speed down into the valley. When the sound of the humming motor had died to something no louder than the buzz of a sleepy wasp, I held out my hand to Carnéta and she rose, pale, but with blazing eyes, and picked up her camera case.

"If he had detected us, everything would have been lost!" she whispered.

"Not everything!" I replied grimly—and showed her the revolver which I had held in my hand whilst those eagle eyes had been seeking us, "If he had made a sign to show that he had seen us, in fact, if he had once offered a safe mark by leaning from the car, I should have shot him dead without hesitation!"

"We must not show ourselves again, but wait for dusk. He must have seen us, then, on the hilltop, but I hope without recognizing us. He has the sight and instincts of a vulture!"

I nodded, slipping the revolver into my pocket, but I wondered if I should not have been better advised to have risked a shot at the moment that I had recognized "Mr. Isaacs" for Hassan of Aleppo.

# CHAPTER XXX
## AT THE GATE HOUSE

From sunset to dusk I lurked about the neighbourhood of the Gate House with my beautiful accomplice—watching and waiting: a man bound upon stranger business, I dare swear, than any other in the county of Kent that night.

Our endeavour now was to avoid observation by any one, and in this, I think, we succeeded. At the same time, Carnéta, upon whose experience I relied implicitly, regarded it as most important that we should observe (from a safe distance) any one who entered or quitted the gates.

But none entered, and none came out. When, finally, we made along the narrow footpath skirting the west of the grounds, the night was silent—most strangely still.

The trees met overhead, but no rustle disturbed their leaves and of animal life no indication showed itself. There was no moon. A full appreciation of my mad folly came to me, and with it a sense of heavy depression. This stillness that ruled all about the house which sheltered the awful Sheikh of the Assassins was ominous, I thought. In short, my nerves were playing me tricks.

"We have little to fear," said my companion, speaking in a hushed and quivering voice. "The whole of the party left England some days ago."

"Are you sure?"

"Certain! We learned that before Earl made his attempt. Hassan remains, for some reason; Hassan and one other—the one who drives the car."

"But the slipper?"

"If Hassan remains, so does the slipper!"

From the knapsack, which, as you will have divined, did not contain a camera, she took out an electric pocket lamp, and directed its beam upon the hedge above us.

"There is a gap somewhere here!" she said. "See if you can find it. I dare not show the light too long."

Darkness followed. I clambered up the bank and sought for the opening of which Carnéta had spoken.

"The light here a moment," I whispered. "I think I have it!"

Out shone the white beam, and momentarily fell upon a black hole in the thickset hedge. The light disappeared, and as I extended my hand to Carnéta she grasped it and climbed up beside me.

"Put on your rubber shoes," she directed. "Leave the others here."

There in the darkness I did as she directed, for I was provided with a pair of tennis shoes. Carnéta already was suitably shod.

"I will go first," I said. "What is the ground like beyond?"

"Just unkempt bushes and weeds."

Upon hands and knees I crawled through, saw dimly that there was a short descent, corresponding with the ascent from the lane, and turned, whispering to my fellow conspirator, to follow.

The grounds proved even more extensive than I had anticipated. We pressed on, dodging low-sweeping branches and keeping our arms up to guard our faces from outshoots of thorn bushes. Our progress necessarily was slow, but even so quite a long time seemed to have elapsed ere we came in sight of the house.

This was my first expedition of the kind; and now that my goal was actually in sight I became conscious of a sort of exultation hard to describe. My companion, on the contrary, seemed to have become icily cool. When next she spoke, her voice had a businesslike ring, which revealed the fact that she was no amateur at this class of work.

"Wait here," she directed. "I am going to pass all around the house, and I will rejoin you."

I could see her but dimly, and she moved off as silent as an Indian deer-stalker, leaving me alone there crouching at the extreme edge of the thicket. I looked out over a small wilderness of unkempt flower-beds; so much it was just possible to perceive. The plants in many instances had spread on to the pathways and contested survival with the flourishing weeds. All was wild—deserted—eerie.

A sense of dampness assailed me, and I raised my eyes to the low-lying building wherein no light showed, no sign of life was evident. The nearer wing presented a verandah apparently overgrown by some climbing plant, the nature of which it was impossible to determine in the darkness.

The zest for the nocturnal operation which temporarily had thrilled me succumbed now to loneliness. With keen anxiety I awaited the return of my more experienced accomplice. The situation was grotesque, utterly bizarre; but even my sense of humour could not save me from the growing dread which this seemingly deserted place poured into my heart.

When upon the right I heard a faint rustling I started, and grasped the revolver in my pocket.

"Not a sound!" came in Carnéta's voice. "Keep just inside the bushes and come this way. There is something I want to show you."

The various profuse growths rendered concealment simple enough— if indeed any other concealment were necessary than that which the strangely black night afforded. Just within the evil-smelling thicket we made a half circuit of the building, and stopped.

"Look!" whispered Carnéta.

The word was unnecessary, for I was staring fixedly in the direction of that which evidently had occasioned her uneasiness.

It was a small square window, so low-set that I assumed it to be that of a cellar, and heavily cross-barred.

From it, out upon a tangled patch of vegetation, shone a dull red light!

"There's no other light in the place," my companion whispered. "For God's sake, what can it be?"

My mind supplied no explanation. The idea that it might be a dark room no doubt was suggested by the assumed role of Carnéta; but I knew that idea to be absurd. The red light meant something else.

Evidently the commencing of operations before all lights were out was irregular, for Carnéta said slowly—

"We must wait and watch the light. There was formerly a moat around the Gate House; that must be the window of a dungeon."

I little relished the prospect of waiting in that swamp-like spot, but since no alternative presented itself I accepted the inevitable. For close upon an hour we stood watching the red window. No sound of bird, beast, or man disturbed our vigil; in fact, it would appear that the very insects shunned the neighbourhood of Hassan of Aleppo. But the red light still shone out.

"We must risk it!" said Carnéta steadily. "There are French windows opening on to that verandah. Ten yards farther around the bushes come right up to the wall of the house. We'll go that way and around by the other wing on to the verandah."

Any action was preferable to this nerve-sapping delay, and with a determination to shoot, and shoot to kill, any one who opposed our entrance, I passed through the bushes and, with Carnéta, rounded the southern border of that silent house and slipped quietly on to the verandah.

Kneeling, Carnéta opened the knapsack. My eyes were growing accustomed to the darkness, and I was just able to see her deft hands at work upon the fastenings. She made no noise, and I watched her with an ever-growing wonder. A female burglar is a personage difficult to imagine. Certainly, no one ever could have suspected this girl with the violet eyes of being an expert crackswoman; but of her efficiency there could be no question. I think I had never witnessed a more amazing spectacle than that of this cultured girl manipulating the tools of the house breaker with her slim white fingers.

Suddenly she turned and clutched my arm.

"The windows are not fastened!" she whispered.

A strange courage came to me—perhaps that of desperation. For, ignoring the ominous circumstance, I pushed open the nearest window and stepped into the room beyond! A hissing breath from Carnéta acknowledged my performance, and she entered close behind me, silent in her rubber-soled shoes.

For one thrilling moment we stood listening. Then came the white beam from the electric lamp to cut through the surrounding blackness.

The room was totally unfurnished!


CHAPTER XXXI
THE POOL OF DEATH

Not a sound broke the stillness of the Gate House. It was the most eerily silent place in which I had ever found myself. Out into the corridor we went, noiselessly. It was stripped, uncarpeted.

Three doors we passed, two upon the left and one upon the right. We tried them all. All were unfastened, and the rooms into which they opened bare and deserted. Then we came upon a short, descending stair, at its foot a massive oaken door.

Carnéta glided down, noiseless as a ghost, and to one of the blackened panels applied an ingenious little instrument which she carried in her knapsack. It was not unlike a stethoscope; and as I watched her listening, by means of this arrangement, for any sound beyond the oaken door, I reflected how almost every advance made by science places a new tool in the hands of the criminal.

No word had been spoken since we had discovered this door; none had been necessary. For we both knew that the place beyond was that from which proceeded the mysterious red light.

I directed the ray of the electric torch upon Carnéta, as she stood there listening, and against that sombre oaken background her face and profile stood out with startling beauty. She seemed half perplexed and half fearful. Then she abruptly removed the apparatus, and, stooping to the knapsack, replaced it and took out a bunch of wire keys, signing to me to hand her the lamp.

As I crept down the steps I saw her pause, glancing back over her shoulder toward the door. The expression upon her face induced me to direct the light in the same direction.

Why neither of us had observed the fact before I cannot conjecture; but a key was in the lock!

Perhaps the traffic of the night afforded no more dramatic moment than this. The house which we were come prepared burglariously to enter was thrown open, it would seem, to us, inviting our inspection!

Looking back upon that moment, it seems almost incredible that the sight of a key in a lock should have so thrilled me. But at the time I perceived something sinister in this failure of the Lord of the *Hashishîn* to close his doors to intruders. That Carnéta shared my doubts and fears was to be read in her face; but her training had been peculiar, I learned, and such as establishes a surprising resoluteness of character.

Quite noiselessly she turned the key, and holding a dainty pocket revolver in her hand, pushed the door open slowly!

An odour, sickly sweet and vaguely familiar, was borne to my nostrils. Carnéta became outlined in dim, reddish light. Bending forward slightly, she entered the room, and I, with muscles tensed nervously, advanced and stood beside her.

I perceived that this was a cellar; indeed, I doubt not that in some past age it had served as a dungeon. From the stone roof hung the first evidence of Eastern occupation which the Gate House had yielded; in the form of an Oriental lantern, or *fánoos*, of rose-coloured waxed paper upon a copper frame. Its vague light revealed the interior of the hideous place upon whose threshold we stood.

Straight before us, deep set in the stone wall, was the tiny square window, iron-barred without, and glazed with red glass, the light from which had so deeply mystified us. Within a niche in the wall, a little to the left of the window, rested an object which, at that moment, claimed our undivided attention the sight of which so wrought upon us that temporarily all else was forgotten.

*It was the red slipper of the Prophet!*

"My God!" whispered Carnéta—"my God!"—and clutched at me, swaying dizzily.

A few inches from our feet the floor became depressed, how deeply I could not determine, for it was filled with water, water filthy and slimy! The strange, nauseating odour had grown all but unsupportable; it seemingly proceeded from this fetid pool which, occupying the floor of the dungeon, offered a barrier, since its depth was unknown, of fully twelve feet between ourselves and the farther wall.

There was a faint, dripping sound: a whispering, echoing *drip-drip* of falling water. I could not tell from whence it proceeded.

Almost supporting my companion, whose courage seemed suddenly to have failed her, I stared fascinatedly at that blood-stained relic. Something then induced me to look behind; I suppose a warning instinct of that sort which is unexplainable. I only know that upholding Carnêta with my left arm, and nervously grasping my revolver in my right, I turned and glanced over my shoulder.

Very slowly, but with a constant, regular motion, the massive door was closing!

I snatched away my arm; in my left hand I held the electric torch, and springing sharply about I directed the searching ray into the black gap of the stairway. A yellow face, a malignant Oriental face, came suddenly, fully, into view! Instantly I recognized it for that of the man who had driven Hassan's car!

Acting upon the determination with which I had entered the Gate House, I raised my revolver and fired straight between the evil eyes! To the fact that I dropped my left hand in the act of pulling the trigger with my right, and thus lost my mark, the servant of Hassan of Aleppo owed his escape. I missed him. He uttered a shrill cry of fear and went racing up the wooden stair. I followed him with the light and fired twice at the retreating figure. I heard him stumble and a second time cry out. But, though I doubt not he was hit, he recovered himself, for I heard his tread in the corridor above.

Propping wide the door with my foot, I turned to Carnêta. Her face was drawn and haggard; but her mouth set in a sort of grim determination.

"Earl is dead!" she said, in a queer, toneless voice. "He died trying to get—that thing! *I* will get it, and destroy it!"

Before I could detain her, even had I sought to do so, she stepped into the filthy water, struggled to recover her foothold, and sank above her waist into its sliminess. Without hesitation she began to advance toward the niche which contained the slipper. In the middle of the pool she stopped.

What memory it was which supplied the clue to the identity of that nauseating smell, heaven alone knows; but as the girl stopped and drew herself up rigidly—then turned and leapt wildly back toward the door—I knew what occasioned that sickly odour!

She screamed once, dreadfully—shrilly—a scream of agonizing fear that I can never forget. Then, roughly I grasped her, for the need was urgent—and dragged her out on to the floor beside me. With her wet garments clinging to her limbs, she fell prostrate on the stones.

A yard from the brink the slimy water parted, and the yellow snout of a huge crocodile was raised above the surface! The saurian eyes, hungrily malevolent, rose next to view!

The extremity of our danger found me suddenly cool. As the thing drew its slimy body up out of the pool I waited. The jaws were extended toward the prostrate body, were but inches removed from it, dripped their saliva upon the soddened skirt—when I bent forward, and at a range of some ten inches emptied the remaining three loaded chambers of my revolver into the creature's left eye!...

Upchurned in bloody foam became the water of that dreadful place.... As one recalls the incidents of a fevered dream, I recall dragging Carnéta away from the contorted body of the death-stricken reptile. A nightmare chaos of horrid, revolting sights and sounds forms my only recollection of quitting the dungeon of the slipper.

I succeeded in carrying her up the stairs and out through the empty rooms on to the verandah; but there, from sheer exhaustion, I laid her down. I had no means of reviving her and I lacked the strength to carry her farther. Having recharged my revolver, I stood watching her where she lay, wanly beautiful in the dim light.

There was no doubt in my mind respecting the fate of Earl Dexter, nor could I doubt that the slipper in the dungeon below was a duplicate of the real one. It was a death-trap into which he had lured Dexter and which he had left baited for whomsoever might trace the cracksman to the Gate House. Why Hassan should have remained behind, unless from fanatic lust of killing, I could not imagine.

When at last the fresher night air had its effect, and Carnéta opened her eyes, I led her to the gates, nor did she offer the slightest resistance, but looked dully before her, muttering over and over again, "Earl, Earl!"

The gates were open; we passed out on to the open road. No man pursued us, and the night was gravely still.


## CHAPTER XXXII
## SIX GRAY PATCHES


When the invitation came from my old friend Hilton to spend a week "roughing it" with him in Warwickshire I accepted with alacrity. If ever a man needed a holiday I was that man. Nervous breakdown threatened me at any moment; the ghastly experience at the Gate House together with Carnéta's grief-stricken face when I had parted from her were obsessing memories which I sought in vain to shake off.

A brief wire had contained the welcome invitation, and up to the time when I had received it I had been unaware that Hilton was back in England. Moreover, beyond the fact that his house, "Uplands," was near H—, for which I was instructed to change at New Street Station, Birmingham, I had little idea of its location. But he added "Wire train and will meet at H—"; so that I had no uneasiness on that score.

I had contemplated catching the 2:45 from Euston, but by the time I had got my work into something like order, I decided that the 6:55 would be more suitable and decided to dine on the train.

Altogether, there was something of a rush and hustle attendant upon getting away, and when at last I found myself in the cab, bound for Euston, I sat back with a long-drawn sigh. The quest of the Prophet's slipper was ended; in all probability that blood-stained relic was already Eastward bound. Hassan of Aleppo, its awful guardian, had triumphed and had escaped retribution. Earl Dexter was dead. I could not doubt that; for the memory of his beautiful accomplice, Carnéta, as I last had seen her, broken-hearted, with her great violet eyes dulled in tearless agony—have I not said that it lived with me?

Even as the picture of her lovely, pale face presented itself to my mind, the cab was held up by a temporary block in the traffic—and my imagination played me a strange trick.

Another taxi ran close alongside, almost at the moment that the press of vehicles moved on again. Certainly, I had no more than a passing glimpse of the occupants; but I could have sworn that violet eyes looked suddenly into mine, and with equal conviction I could have sworn to the gaunt face of the man who sat beside the violet-eyed girl for that of Earl Dexter!

The travellers, however, were immediately lost to sight in the rear, and I was left to conjecture whether this had been a not uncommon form of optical delusion or whether I had seen a ghost.

At any rate, as I passed in between the big pillars, "The gateway of the North," I scrutinized, and closely, the numerous hurrying figures about me. None of them, by any stretch of the imagination, could have been set down for that of Dexter, The Stetson Man. No doubt, I concluded, I had been tricked by a chance resemblance.

Having dispatched my telegram, I boarded the 6:55. I thought I should have the compartment to myself, and so deep in reverie was I that the train was actually clear of the platforms ere I learned that I had a companion. He must have joined me at the moment that the train started. Certainly, I had not seen him enter. But, suddenly looking up, I met the eyes of this man who occupied the corner seat facing me.

This person was olive-skinned, clean-shaven, fine featured, and perfectly groomed. His age might have been anything from twenty-five to forty-five, but his hair and brows were jet black. His eyes, too, were nearer to real black than any human eyes I had ever seen before—excepting the awful eyes of Hassan of Aleppo.

Hassan of Aleppo! It was, to that hour, a mystery how his group of trained assassins—the *Hashishîn*—had quitted England. Since none of them were known to the police, it was no insoluble mystery, I admit; but nevertheless it was singular that the careful watching of the ports had yielded no result. Could it be that some of them had not yet left the country? Could it be—

I looked intently into the black eyes. They were caressing, smiling eyes, and looked boldly into mine. I picked up a magazine, pretending to read. But I supported it with my left hand; my right was in my coat pocket—and it rested upon my Smith and Wesson!

So much had the slipper of Mohammed done for me: I went in hourly dread of murderous attack!

My travelling companion watched me; of that I was certain. I could feel his gaze. But he made no move and no word passed between us. This was the situation when the train slowed into Northampton. At Northampton, to my indescribable relief (frankly, I was as nervous in those days as a woman), the Oriental traveller stepped out on to the platform.

Having reclosed the door, he turned and leaned in through the open window.

"Evidently you are not concerned, Mr. Cavanagh," he said. "Be warned. Do not interfere with those that are!"

The night swallowed him up.

My fears had been justified; the man was one of the *Hashishîn*—a spy of Hassan of Aleppo! What did it mean?

I craned from the window, searching the platform right and left. But there was no sign of him.

When the train left Northampton I found myself alone, and I should only weary you were I to attempt to recount the troubled conjectures that bore me company to Birmingham.

The train reached New Street at nine, with the result that having gulped a badly needed brandy and soda in the buffet, I grabbed my bag, raced across—and just missed the connection! More than an hour later I found myself standing at ten minutes to eleven upon the H—platform, watching the red taillight of the "local" disappear into the night. Then I realized to the full that with four miles of lonely England before me there hung above my head a mysterious threat—a vague menace. The solitary official, who but waited my departure to lock up the station, was the last representative of civilization I could hope to encounter until the gates of "Uplands" should be opened to me!

*What* was the matter with which I was warned not to interfere? Might I not, by my mere presence in that place, unwittingly be interfering now?

With the station-master's directions humming like a refrain in my ears, I passed through the sleeping village and out on to the road. The moon was exceptionally bright and unobscured, although a dense bank of cloud crept slowly from the west, and before me the path stretched as an unbroken thread of silvery white twining a sinuous way up the bracken-covered slope, to where, sharply defined against the moonlight sky, a coppice in grotesque silhouette marked the summit.

The month had been dry and tropically hot, and my footsteps rang crisply upon the hard ground. There is nothing more deceptive than a straight road up a hill; and half an hour's steady tramping but saw me approaching the trees.

I had so far resolutely endeavoured to keep my mind away from the idea of surveillance. Now, as I paused to light my pipe—a never-failing friend in loneliness—I perceived something move in the shadows of a neighbouring bush.

This object was not unlike a bladder, and the very incongruity of its appearance served to revive all my apprehensions. Taking up my grip, as though I had noticed nothing of an alarming nature, I pursued my way up the slope, leaving a trail of tobacco smoke in my wake; and having my revolver secreted up my right coat-sleeve.

Successfully resisting a temptation to glance behind, I entered the cover of the coppice, and, now invisible to any one who might be dogging me, stood and looked back upon the moon-bright road.

There was no living thing in sight, the road was empty as far as the eye could see. The coppice now remained to be negotiated, and then, if the station-master's directions were not at fault, "Uplands" should be visible beyond. Taking, therefore, what I had designed to be a final glance back down the hillside, I was preparing to resume my way when I saw something—something that arrested me.

It was a long way behind—so far that, had the moon been less bright, I could never have discerned it. What it was I could not even conjecture; but it had the appearance of a vague gray patch, moving—not along the road, but through the undergrowth—in my direction.

For a second my eye rested upon it. Then I saw a second patch—a third—a fourth!

Six!

There were six gray patches creeping up the slope toward me!

The sight was unnerving. What were these things that approached, silently, stealthily—like snakes in the grass?

A fear, unlike anything I had known before the quest of the Prophet's slipper had brought fantastic horror into my life, came upon me. Revolver in hand I ran—ran for my life toward the gap in the trees that marked the coppice end. And as I went something hummed through the darkness beside my head—some projectile, some venomous thing that missed its mark by a bare inch!

Painfully conversant with the uncanny weapons employed by the *Hashishîn*, I knew now, beyond any possibility of doubt, that death was behind me.

A pattering like naked feet sounded on the road, and, without pausing in my headlong career, I sent a random shot into the blackness.

The crack of the Smith and Wesson reassured me. I pulled up short, turned, and looked back toward the trees.

Nothing—no one!

Breathing heavily, I crammed my extinguished briar into my pocket—re-charged the empty chamber of the revolver—and started to run again toward a light that showed over the treetops to my left.

That, if the man's directions were right, was "Uplands"—if his directions were wrong—then....

A shrill whistle—minor, eerie, in rising cadence—sounded on the dead silence with piercing clearness! Six whistles—seemingly from all around me—replied!

Some object came humming through the air, and I ducked wildly.

On and on I ran—flying from an unknown, but, as a warning instinct told me, deadly peril—ran as a man runs pursued by devils.

The road bent sharply to the left then forked. Overhanging trees concealed the house, and the light, though high up under the eaves, was no longer visible. Trusting to Providence to guide me, I plunged down the lane that turned to the left, and, almost exhausted, saw the gates before me—saw the sweep of the drive, and the moonlight, gleaming on the windows!

None of the windows were illuminated.

Straight up to the iron gates I raced.

They were locked!

Without a moment's hesitation I hurled my grip over the top and clambered up the bars! As I got astride, from the blackness of the lane came the ominous hum, and my hat went spinning away across the lawn!—the black cloud veiled the moon and complete darkness fell.

Then I dropped and ran for the house—shouting, though all but winded—"Hilton! Hilton! Open the door!"

Sinking exhausted on the steps, I looked toward the gates—but they showed only dimly in the dense shadows of the trees.

*Bzzz! Bzzz!*

I dropped flat in the portico as something struck the metal knob of the door and rebounded over me. A shower of gravel told of another mis-directed projectile.

Crack! Crack! Crack! The revolver, spoke its short reply into the mysterious darkness; but the night gave up no sound to tell of a shot gone home.

"Hilton! Hilton!" I cried, banging on the panels with the butt of the weapon. "Open the door! Open the door!"

And now I heard the coming footsteps along the hall within; heavy bolts were withdrawn—the door swung open—and Hilton, pale-faced, appeared. His hand shot out, grabbed my coat collar; and weak, exhausted, I found myself snatched into safety, and the door re-bolted.

"Thank God!" I whispered. "Thank God! Hilton, look to all your bolts and fastenings. Hell is outside!"


## CHAPTER XXXIII
## HOW WE WERE REINFORCED


Hilton, I learned, was living the simple life at "Uplands." The place was not yet decorated and was only partly furnished. But with his man, Soar, he had been in solitary occupation for a week.

"Feel better now?" he asked anxiously.

I reached for my tumbler and blew a cloud of smoke into the air. I could hear Soar's footsteps as he made the round of bolts and bars, testing each anxiously.

"Thanks, Hilton," I said. "I'm quite all right. You are naturally wondering what the devil it all means? Well, then, I wired you from Euston that I was coming by the 6:55—"

"H—Post Office shuts at 7. I shall get your wire in the morning!"

"That explains your failing to meet me. Now for my explanation!

"Surrounding this house at the present moment," I continued, "are members of an Eastern organization—the *Hashishîn*, founded in Khorassan in the eleventh century and flourishing to-day!"

"Do you mean it, Cavanagh?"

"I do! One Hassan of Aleppo is the present Sheikh of the order, and he has come to England, bringing a fiendish company in his train, in pursuit of the sacred slipper of Mohammed, which was stolen by the late Professor Deeping—"

"Surely I have read something about this?"

"Probably. Deeping was murdered by Hassan! The slipper was placed in the Antiquarian Museum—"

"From which it was stolen again!"

"Correct—by Earl Dexter, America's foremost crook! But the real facts have never got into print. I am the only pressman who knows them, and I have good reason for keeping my knowledge to myself! Dexter is dead (I believe I saw his ghost to-day). But although, to the best of my knowledge, the accursed slipper is in the hands of Hassan and Company, I have been watched since I left Euston, and on my way to 'Uplands' my life was attempted!"

"For God's sake, why?"

"I cannot surmise, Hilton. Deeping, for certain reasons that are irrelevant at the moment, left the keys of the case at the Museum in my perpetual keeping—but the case was rifled a second time—"

"I read of it!"

"And the keys were stolen from me. I am utterly at a loss to understand why the *Hashishîn*—for it is members of that awful organization who, without a doubt, surround this house at the present moment—should seek my life. Hilton, I have brought trouble with me!"

"It's almost incredible!" said Hilton, staring at me. "Why do these people pursue *you?*"

Ere I had time to reply Soar entered, arrayed, as was Hilton, in his night attire. Soar was an ex-dragoon and a model man.

"Everything fast, sir," he reported; "but from the window of the bedroom over here—the room I got ready for Mr. Cavanagh—I thought I saw someone in the orchard."

"Eh?" jerked Hilton—"in the orchard? Come on up, Cavanagh!"

We all ran upstairs. The moonlight was streaming into the room.

"Keep back!" I warned.

Well within the shadow, I crept up to the window and looked out. The night was hot and still. No breeze stirred the leaves, but the edge of the frowning thunder cloud which I had noted before spread a heavy carpet of ebony black upon the ground. Beyond, I could dimly discern the hills. The others stood behind me, constrained by the fear of this mysterious danger which I had brought to "Uplands."

There was someone moving among the trees!

Closer came the figure, and closer, until suddenly a shaft of moonlight found passage and spilled a momentary pool of light amid the shadows, I could see the watcher very clearly. A moment he stood there, motionless, and looking up at the window; then as he glided again into the shade of the trees the darkness became complete. But I watched, crouching there nervously, for long after he was gone.

"For God's sake, who is it?" whispered Hilton, with a sort of awe in his voice.

"It's Hassan of Aleppo!" I replied.

Virtually, the house, with the capital of the Midlands so near upon the one hand, the feverish activity of the Black Country reddening the night upon the other, was invested by fanatic Easterns!

We descended again to the extemporized study. Soar entered with us and Hilton invited him to sit down.

"We must stick together to-night!" he said. "Now, Cavanagh, let us see if we can find any explanation of this amazing business. I can understand that at one period of the slipper's history you were an object of interest to those who sought to recover it; but if, as you say, the *Hashishîn* have the slipper now, what do they want with you? If you have never touched it, they cannot be prompted by desire for vengeance."

"I have never touched it," I replied grimly; "nor even any receptacle containing it."

As I ceased speaking came a distant muffled rumbling.

"That's the thunder," said Hilton. "There's a tremendous storm brewing."

He poured out three glasses of whisky, and was about to speak when Soar held up a warning finger.

"Listen!" he said.

At his words, with tropical suddenness down came the rain.

Hilton, his pipe in his hand, stood listening intently.

"What?" he asked.

"I don't know, sir; the sound of the rain has drowned it."

Indeed, the rain was descending in a perfect deluge, its continuous roar drowning all other sounds; but as we three listened tensely we detected a noise which hitherto had seemed like the overflowing of some spout.

But louder and clearer it grew, until at last I knew it for what it was.

"It's a motor-car!" I cried.

"And coming here!" added Soar. "Listen! it's in the lane!"

"It certainly isn't a taxicab," declared Hilton. "None of the men will come beyond the village."

"That's the gate!" said Soar, in an awed voice, and stood up, looking at Hilton.

"Come on," said the latter abruptly, making for the door.

"Be careful, Hilton!" I cried; "it may be a trick!"

Soar unbolted the front door, threw it open, and looked out. In the darkness of the storm it was almost impossible to see anything in the lane outside. But at that moment a great sheet of lightning split the gloom, and we saw a taxicab standing close up to the gateway!

"Help! Open the gate!" came a high-pitched voice; "open the gate!"

Out into the rain we ran and down the gravel path. Soar had the gate open in a twinkling, and a woman carrying a brown leather grip, but who was so closely veiled that I had no glimpse of her features, leapt through on to the drive.

"Lend a hand, two of you!" cried a vaguely familiar voice—"this way!"

Hilton and Soar stepped out into the road. The driver of the cab was lying forward across the wheel, apparently insensible, but as Hilton seized his arm he moved and spoke feebly.

"For God's sake be quick, sir!" he said. "They're after us! They're on the other side of the lane, there!"

With that he dropped limply into Hilton's arms!

He was dragged in on to the drive—and something whizzed over our heads and went sputtering into the gravel away up toward the house. The last to enter was the man who had come in the cab. As he barred the gate behind him he suddenly reached out through the bars and I saw a pistol in his hand.

Once—twice—thrice—he fired into the blackness of the lane.

"Take that, you swine!" he shouted. "Take that!"

As quickly as we could, bearing the insensible man, we hurried back to the door. On the step the woman was waiting for us, with her veil raised. A blinding flash of lightning came as we mounted the step—and I looked into the violet eyes of Carnéta! I turned and stared at the man behind me.

*It was Earl Dexter.*

Three of the mysterious missiles fell amongst us, but miraculously no one was struck. Amid the mighty booming of the thunder we re-entered the house and got the door barred. In the hall we laid down the unconscious man and stood, a strangely met company, peering at one another in the dim lamplight.

"We've got to bury the hatchet, Mr. Cavanagh!" said Dexter. "It's a case of the common enemy. I've brought you your bag!" and he pointed to the brown grip upon the floor.

"*My* bag!" I cried. "My bag is upstairs in my room!"

"Wrong, sir!" snapped The Stetson Man. "They are like as two peas in a pod, I'll grant you, but the bag you snatched off the platform at New Street was mine! That's what I'm after; I ought to be on the way to Liverpool. That's what Hassan's after!"

"The bag!"

"You don't need to ask what's *in* the bag?" suggested Dexter.

"What *is* in the bag?" asked Hilton hoarsely.

"The slipper of the Prophet, sir!" was the reply.


## CHAPTER XXXIV
## MY LAST MEETING WITH HASSAN OF ALEPPO


I felt dazed, as a man must feel who has just heard the death sentence pronounced upon him. Hilton seemed to have become incapable of speech or action; and in silence we stood watching Carnéta tending the unconscious man. She forced brandy from a flask between his teeth, kneeling there beside him with her face very pale and dark rings around her eyes. Presently she looked up.

"Will you please get me a bowl of water and a sponge?" she said quietly.

Soar departed without a word, and no one spoke until he returned, bringing the sponge and the water, when the girl set to work in a businesslike way to cleanse a wound which, showed upon the man's head.

"She's a good nurse is Carnéta," said Dexter coolly. "She was the only doctor I had through this"—indicating his maimed wrist. "If you will fetch my bag down, there's some lint in it."

I hesitated.

"You needn't worry," said Dexter; "as well be hung for a sheep as a lamb. You've handled the bag, and I'm not asking you to do any more."

I went up to my room and lifted the grip from the chair upon which I had put it. Even now I found it difficult to perceive any difference between this and mine. Both were of identical appearance and both new. In fact, I had bought mine only that morning, my old one being past use, and being in a hurry, I had not left it to be initialled.

As I picked up the bag the lightning flashed again, and from the window I could see the orchard as clearly as by sunlight. At the farther end near the wall someone was standing watching the house.

I went downstairs carrying the fatal bag, and rejoined the group in the hall.

"He will have to be got to bed," said Carnéta, referring to the wounded man; "he will probably remain unconscious for a long time."

Accordingly, we took the patient into one of the few furnished bedrooms, and having put him to bed left him in care of the beautiful nurse. When we four men met again downstairs, amazement had rendered the whole scene unreal to me. Soar stood just within the open door, not knowing whether to go or to remain; but Hilton motioned to him to stay. Earl Dexter bit off the end of a cigar and stood with his left elbow resting on the mantelpiece.

His gaunt face looked gaunter than ever, but the daredevil gray eyes still nursed that humorous light in their depths.

"Mr. Cavanagh," he said, "we're brothers! And if you'll consider a minute, you'll see that I'm not lying when I say I'm on the straight, now and for always!"

I made no reply: I could think of none.

"I'm a crook," he resumed, "or I was up to a while ago. There's a warrant out for me—the first that ever bore my name. I've sailed near the wind often enough, but it was desperation that got me into hot water about *that!*"

He jerked his cigar in the direction of his grip, which lay now on the rug at his feet.

"I lost a useful right hand," he went on—"and I lost every cent I had. It was a dead rotten speculation—for I lost my good name! I mean it! Believe me, I've handled some shady propositions in the past, but I did it right in the sunlight! Up to the time I went out for that damned slipper I could have had lunch with any detective from Broadway to the Strand! I didn't need any false whiskers and the Ritz was good enough for The Stetson Man. What now? I'm 'wanted!' Enough said."

He tossed the cigar—he had smoked scarce an inch of it—into the empty grate.

"I'm an Aunt Sally for any man to shy at," he resumed bitterly. "My place henceforth is in the dark. Right! I've finished; the book's closed. From the time I quit England—if I *can* quit—I'm on the straight! I've promised—Carnéta, and—I mean to keep my word. See here—"

Dexter turned to me.

"You'll want to know how I escaped from the cursed death-trap at Hassan's house in Kent? I'll tell you. I was never in it! I was hiding and waiting my chance. You know what was left to guard the slipper while the Sheikh—rot him—was away looking after arrangements for getting his mob out of the country?"

I nodded.

"*You* fell into the trap—you and Carnéta. By God! I didn't know till it was all over! But two minutes later I was inside that place—and three minutes later I was away with the slipper! Oh, it wasn't a duplicate; it was the goods! What then? Carnéta had had a sickening of the business and she just invited me to say Yes or No. I said Yes; and I'm a straight man onward."

"Then what were you doing on the train with the slipper?" asked Hilton sharply.

"I was going to Liverpool, sir!" snapped The Stetson Man, turning on him. "I was going to try to get aboard the *Mauretania* and then make terms for my life! What happened? I slipped out at Birmingham for a drink—grip in hand! I put it down beside me, and Mr. Cavanagh here, all in a hustle, must have rushed in behind me, snatched a whisky and snatched my grip and started for H—!"

A vivid flash of lightning flickered about the room. Then came the deafening boom of the thunder, right over the house it seemed.

"I knew from the weight of the grip it wasn't mine," said Dexter, "and I was the most surprised guy in Great Britain and Ireland when I found whose it was! I opened it, of course! And right on top was a waistcoat and right in the first pocket was a telegram. Here it is!"

He passed it to me. It was that which I had received from Hilton. I had packed the suit which I had been wearing that morning and must previously have thrust the telegram into the waistcoat pocket.

"Providence!" Dexter assured me. "Because I got on the station in time to see Hassan of Aleppo join the train for H—! I was too late, though. But I chartered a taxi out on Corporation Street and invited the man to race the local! He couldn't do it, but we got here in time for the fireworks! Mr. Cavanagh, there are anything from six to ten *Hashishîn* watching this house!"

"I know it!"

"They're bareheaded; and in the dark their shaven skulls look like nothing human. They're armed with those damned tubes, too. I'd give a thousand dollars—if I had it!—to know their mechanism. Well, gentlemen, deeds speak. What am I here for, when I might be on the way to Liverpool, and safety?"

"You're here to try to make up for the past a bit!" said a soft, musical voice. "Mr. Cavanagh's life is in danger."

Carnéta entered the room.

The light played in that wonderful hair of hers; and pale though she was, I thought I had never seen a more beautiful woman.

"Tell them," she said quietly, "what must be done."

Soar glanced at me out of the corner of his eyes and shifted uneasily. Hilton stared as if fascinated.

"Now," rapped Dexter, in his strident voice, "putting aside all questions of justice and right (we're not policemen), what do we want—you and I, Mr. Cavanagh?"

"I can't think clearly about anything," I said dully. "Explain yourself."

"Very well. Inspector Bristol, C.I.D., would want me and Hassan arrested. I don't want that! What I want is *peace*; I want to be able to sleep in comfort; I want to know I'm not likely to be murdered on the next corner! Same with you?"

"Yes—yes."

"How can we manage it? One way would be to kill Hassan of Aleppo; but he wants a lot of killing—I've tried! Moreover, directly we'd done it, another *Sheikh-al-jebal* would be nominated and he'd carry on the bloody work. We'd be worse off than ever. Right! we've got to connive at letting the bloodstained fanatic escape, and we've got to give up the slipper!"

"I'll do that with all my heart!"

"Sure! But you and I have both got little scores up against Hassan, which it's not in human nature to forget. But I've got it worked out that there's only one way. It may nearly choke us to have to do it, I'll allow. I'm working on the Moslem character. Mr. Hilton, make up a fire in the grate here!"

Hilton stared, not comprehending.

"Do as he asks," I said. "Personally, I am resigned to mutilation, since I have touched the bag containing the slipper, but if Dexter has a plan—"

"Excuse me, sir," Soar interrupted. "I believe there's some coal in the coal-box, but I shall have to break up a packing-case for firewood—or go out into the yard!"

"Let it be the packing-case," replied Hilton hastily.

Accordingly a fire was kindled, whilst we all stood about the room in a sort of fearful uncertainty; and before long a big blaze was roaring up the chimney. Dexter turned to me.

"Mr. Cavanagh," said he, "I want you to go right upstairs, open a first-floor window—I would suggest that of your bedroom—and invite Hassan of Aleppo to come and discuss terms!"

Silence followed his words; we were all amazed. Then—

"Why do you ask me to do this?" I inquired.

"Because," replied Dexter, "I happen to know that Hassan has some queer kind of respect for you—I don't know why."

"Which is probably the reason why he tried to kill me to-night!"

"That's beside the question, Mr. Cavanagh. He will believe *you*—which is the important, point.

"Very well. I have no idea what you have in mind but I am prepared to adopt any plan since I have none of my own. What shall say?"

"Say that we are prepared to return the slipper—on conditions."

"He will probably try to shoot me as stand at the window."

Dexter shrugged his shoulders.

"Got to risk it," he drawled.

"And what are the conditions?"

"He must come right in here and discuss them! Guarantee him safe conduct and I don't think he'll hesitate. Anyway, if he does, just tell him that the slipper will be destroyed immediately!"

Without a word I turned on my heel and ascended the stairs.

I entered my room, crossed to the window; and threw it widely open. Hovering over the distant hills I could see the ominous thunder cloud, but the storm seemed to have passed from "Uplands," and only a distant muttering with the faint dripping of water from the pipes broke the silence of the night. A great darkness reigned, however, and I was entirely unable to see if any one was in the orchard.

Like some *mueddin* of fantastic fable I stood there.

"Hassan!" I cried—"Hassan of Aleppo!"

The name rang out strangely upon the stillness—the name which for me had a dreadful significance; but the whole episode seemed unreal, the voice that had cried unlike my voice.

Instantly as any magician summoning an *efreet* I was answered.

Out from the trees strode a tall figure, a figure I could not mistake. It was that of Hassan of Aleppo!

"I hear, effendim, and obey," he said. "I am ready. Open the door!"

"We are prepared to discuss terms. You may come and go safely"— still my voice sounded unfamiliar in my ears.

"I know, effendim; it is so written. Open the door."

I closed the window and mechanically descended the stairs.

"Mind it isn't a trap!" cried Hilton, who, with the others, had overheard every word of this strange interview. "They may try to rush the door directly we open it."

"I'll stand the chest behind it," said Soar; "between the door and the wall, so that only one can enter at a time."

This was done, and the door opened.

Alone, majestic, entered Hassan of Aleppo.

He was dressed in European clothes but wore the green turban of a *Sherif*. With his snowy beard and coal-black eyes he seemed like a vision of the Prophet, of the Prophet in whose name he had committed such ghastly atrocities.

Deigning no glance to Soar nor to Hilton, he paced into the room, passing me and ignoring Carnéta, where Earl Dexter awaited him. I shall never forget the scene as Hassan entered, to stand looking with blazing eyes at The Stetson Man, who sat beside the fire with the slipper of Mohammed in his hand!

"Hassan," said Dexter quietly, "Mr. Cavanagh has had to promise you safe conduct, or as sure as God made me, I'd put a bullet in you!"

The Sheikh of the *Hashishîn* glared fixedly at him.

"Companion of the evil one," he said, "it is not written that I shall die by your hand—or by the hand of any here. But it has been revealed to me that to-night the gates of Paradise may be closed in my face."

"I shouldn't be at all surprised," drawled Dexter. "But it's up to you. You've got to swear by Mohammed—"

"*Salla—'lláhu 'aleyhi wasellem!*"

"That you won't lay a hand upon any living soul, or allow any of your followers to do so, who has touched the slipper or had, anything to do with it, but that you will go in peace."

"You are doomed to die!"

"You don't agree, then?"

"Those who have offended must suffer the penalty!"

"Right!" said Dexter—and prepared to toss the slipper into the heart of the fire!

"*Stop!* Infidel! *Stop!*"

There was real agony in Hassan's voice. To my inexpressible surprise he dropped upon his knee, extending his lean brown hands toward the slipper.

Dexter hesitated. "You agree, then?"

Hassan raised his eyes to the ceiling.

"I agree," he said. "Dark are the ways. It is the will of God...."

Dimly the booming of the thunder came echoing back to us from the hills. Above its roll sounded a barbaric chanting to which the drums of angry heaven formed a fitting accompaniment.

I heard Soar shooting the bolts again upon the going of our strange visitor.

Faint and more faint grew the chanting, until it merged into the remote muttering of the storm—and was lost. The quest of the sacred slipper was ended.

THE END

# Sax Rohmer Bibliography
## (1983-1959)

Pause! (1910) [essays, monologues & dramatic sketches, published anonymously]

Little Tich (1911) [autobiography of the Music Hall entertainer ghost-written by Ward]

The Sins of Severac Bablon (1914)

The Romance of Sorcery (1914; nonfiction study of the occult)

The Exploits of Captain O'Hagan (1916; stories)

Brood of the Witch Queen (1918)

Tales of Secret Egypt (1918; stories)

The Orchard of Tears (1918)

The Quest of the Sacred Slipper (1919)

The Dream Detective (1920; Moris Klaw stories)

The Green Eyes of Bast (1920)

The Haunting of Low Fennel (1920; stories)

Tales of Chinatown (1922; stories)

Grey Face (1924)

Moon of Madness (1927)

She Who Sleeps (1928)

The Emperor of America (1929)

Yu'an Hee See Laughs (1932)

Tales of East and West (1932; stories)

The Bat Flies Low (1935)

White Velvet (1936)

Salute to Bazarada (1939)

Egyptian Nights (1944; US Title: Bimbashi-Baruk of Egypt; stories)

Hangover House (1949)

Wulfheim (1950; originally credited to Michael Furey, later printings listed as by Sax Rohmer)

The Moon is Red (1954)

The Secret of Holm Peel and Other Strange Stories (1970)

The Green Spider and Other Forgotten Tales of Mystery & Suspense (2011)

The Leopard Couch and Other Stories of the Fantastic & Supernatural (2012)

The Complete Cases of the Crime Magnet (2012; stories)

**Fu Manchu series**

The Mystery of Dr. Fu-Manchu (1913; US Title: The Insidious Dr. Fu-Manchu)

The Devil Doctor (1916: US Title: The Return of Dr. Fu-Manchu)

The Si-Fan Mysteries (1917; US Title: The Hand of Fu Manchu)

The Daughter of Fu Manchu (1931)

The Mask of Fu Manchu (1932)

The Bride of Fu Manchu (1933; original US Title: Fu Manchu's Bride)

The Trail of Fu Manchu (1934)

President Fu Manchu (1936)

The Drums of Fu Manchu
(1939)
The Island of Fu Manchu (1941)
The Shadow of Fu Manchu
(1948)
Re-enter: Fu Manchu (1957; UK
Title: Re-Enter: Dr. Fu
Manchu)
Emperor Fu Manchu (1959)
The Wrath of Fu Manchu and
Other Stories (UK: 1973; US:
1976; 12 stories including four
previously uncollected Fu
Manchu stories)
Gaston Max series
The Yellow Claw (1915)
The Golden Scorpion (1919)
The Day the World Ended (1930)
Myself and Gaston Max (a series
of six BBC radio plays, 1942)
Seven Sins (1943)

**"Red" Kerry series**
Dope (1919)
Yellow Shadows (1925)

**Paul Harley series**
Bat-Wing (1921)
Fire Tongue (1921)
The Voice of Kali: The Early Paul
Harley Mysteries (2013)

**Sumuru series**
The Sins of Sumuru (1950; US
Title: Nude in Mink)
The Slaves of Sumuru (1951; US
Title: Sumuru)
Virgin in Flames (1952; US Title:
The Fire Goddess)
Sand and Satin (1954; US Title:
Return of Sumuru)
Sinister Madonna (1956)

**Related Works:**
Bianca in Black by Elizabeth Sax
Rohmer (1958; Rohmer's wife)
Master of Villainy: A Biography
of Sax Rohmer by Cay Van
Ash and Elizabeth Sax Rohmer,
edited by Robert E. Briney
(1972)
Ten Years Beyond Baker Street:
Sherlock Holmes Matches Wits
with the Diabolical Dr. Fu
Manchu by Cay Van Ash
(1984)
The Fires of Fu Manchu by Cay
Van Ash (1987)
The Terror of Fu Manchu by
William Patrick Maynard
(2009)
The Destiny of Fu Manchu by
William Patrick Maynard
(2012)
The Triumph of Fu Manchu by
William Patrick Maynard
(2015)

# Classic Fiction from ALGERNON BLACKWOOD

**The Empty House & Other Ghost Stories / The Listener & Other Stories**
978-1-933586-45-8  $19.95
Blackwood's first two story collections, which include such classics as "The Haunted Island," "The Insanity of Jones," "The Dance of Death" and his best-known tale, "The Willows." Includes a new introduction by fantasy author, Storm Constantine.

**Ten Minute Stories / Day and Night Stories**
978-1-933586-62-5  $19.95
Two more superlative story collections of ghost stories, strange nature tales, weird events and dark fantasy from one of the greatest writers of supernatural fiction in the 20th century. Includes a new introduction by Mike Ashley, and a bonus short story.

**Jimbo / The Education of Uncle Paul**
978-1-933586-13-7  $19.95
Two mystical adventures set in the world of children. "I have rarely read a book that has given me such unqualified delight." Sidney Dark, *Daily Express*. New introduction by Mike Ashley, author of *The Starlight Man*.

**Pan's Garden / Incredible Adventures**
978-1-933586-15-1  $23.95
Classic stories that defy categorization—introductions by Mike Ashley and Tim

Lebbon. "[Blackwood's imagination has] no rival at all for strength, sincerity, and poetic vision." *The Standard*.

**The Lost Valley / The Wolves of God**
978-1-933586-04-5  $23.95
Two classic short story collections in one volume, including the "The Wendigo." Introduction by Simon Clark.

**Julius LeVallon / The Bright Messenger**
978-0-9749438-7-9  $23.95
"The culmination of a lifetime's experience... you will encounter nothing like them anywhere else in the whole of fantastic literature." Mike Ashley, from his introduction.

**The Face of the Earth**
978-1-93358670-0  $19.95
"Blackwood biographer Mike Ashley has created a new collection of stories and essays by the master supernaturalist, most of which have never been in book format before. Also included is a definitive bibliography of Blackwood's writings as well as a new introduction by Ashley. A publishing event for classic horror fans!

**The Human Chord / The Centaur**
978-1-944520-01-4  $19.95
"The masterpiece of the new romantic movement... It is quite the best thing that Mr. Blackwood has given us."
*The Bookman*.

**Stark House Press**
1315 H Street, Eureka, CA 95501
707-498-3135
www.StarkHousePress.com